I0663934

Rise of the Giants

Rise of the Giants Series: Book 1

Theo Mann

The Invisible Publishing Company

Rise of the Giants Series

Contents

Chapter 1

A young boy stepped into a clearing between two high cliff walls surrounded by dense jungle.

The boy stopped there and raised a stone axe in front of him to protect himself, but there was nothing to see.

He ignored the sound of a feral warthog thrashing and bellowing in a tangle of thick ropes behind the boy's back.

The creature thrashed, roared, and let out an occasional squeal of protest, but it couldn't break free. The ropes wrapped around the creature's body to hold it in place against the rocks.

Not even the razor quills along its sides could sever the ropes. They had been positioned right up against the warthog's skin where the quills wouldn't damage them.

The boy took a position in front of the warthog and kept his back to it. The creature's squeals and bellows echoed through the jungle.

The area throbbed with damp heat and the chirp of hundreds of birds and insects. He strained every nerve looking and listening for something coming toward him through the thick trees.

He paced a dozen feet to his left and stopped again to listen before he came pacing back the other way.

He completely ignored the warthog's roars, even when the creature pawed at the ground and tossed its spiked tusks at the boy from behind.

The warthog stood as tall as the boy's shoulders. The creature could gore the boy easily if it broke even one of those ropes.

The boy came back and planted himself right in front of the creature, but he still didn't turn around. He flexed his legs into a crouch and tightened his grip on his axe handle with both hands.

That was the moment when the distant thump of heavy footsteps shook the ground coming closer. The boy tensed every muscle and raised his weapon higher.

The warthog heard the footsteps, too. The creature flew into a panic pawing the ground, squealing in terror, and hurling itself against the ropes with all its might.

The boy shut out all awareness of the creature and concentrated all his attention on those footsteps coming closer.

They thumped the ground hard enough to rustle the surrounding foliage. Even the cliffs vibrated from the impact.

The boy froze when the trees in front of him shook. The curtain of undergrowth parted and a massive, towering monster burst through into the clearing in front of the rocks.

The warthog flew into a hysterical burst of frenzy and threw itself against the ropes hard enough to knock itself completely off its feet.

It hit the ground, scrambled to stand up, and did the same thing again and again trying to flee from the monster.

The creature towered as high as the jungle's tallest canopy—as high as the surrounding cliffs. The boy didn't even come up to the monster's knee.

Armored, razor feathers covered its forelimbs and angled backward in the shape of wings, but this creature was too big to fly.

Giant black claws studded the three toes of its scaly feet. Rough fur covered its body as far as the curve of its leathery neck where it rose to support a fierce, beaked head.

The creature looked down at the warthog. The monster's eyes went hard when it saw the boy standing there blocking its way.

The creature opened its beak and screeched at the boy. He took a step back and almost ran straight into the warthog's tusks.

The warthog lunged against the ropes again and again. The monster cocked its head from side to side to look back and forth between the boy and the warthog—its favorite prey.

These enormous monsters were too smart not to recognize the tiny human standing between it and its next meal.

The boy stiffened under that look, raised his axe, and swung it behind him. He didn't have to look to see what he was doing when he chopped through the ropes holding the warthog in place.

The ropes fell away and the warthog charged off into the undergrowth. It scooted out of sight so fast that the monster didn't react in time to catch it.

The monster dove its long neck down and snapped its beak trying to grab the warthog, but not fast enough.

The boy reacted in a split second, swung his axe down, and struck the creature a wicked blow across the side of the head.

His axe blade glanced off the creature's bony skull and the monster spun back the other way screeching in rage.

The creature dove for the boy next. He somersaulted away to his left and got himself into another position farther down the wall from where the warthog had been tied.

The monster understood this standoff only too well. The creature stomped around to confront the boy. He raised his axe to strike, but the creature knew better than to come within range a second time.

It advanced on him snapping its beak, but it never brought its head near his axe again. He swung time after time, but he never landed another blow.

The creature screeched again, reared to its full height, and beat its wings while the boy crouched in front of it.

The boy coiled himself for another strike, but it took him completely off guard when it did come.

The creature swiped its wing at him. He swung, but his blade went straight through the creature's feathers.

They brushed around the weapon and the rest of the wing clubbed him off his feet. The feathers' sharp edges slashed his face before the creature swiped its wing back the other way and cut him a second time.

The blow sent him flying across the clearing, slammed him into the cliff wall, and he hit the ground. His axe fell next to him. He didn't move to rise or pick it up.

A dozen men watched the fight from a protected ledge on the clifftops above him.

"Get up, Jono!" Hangman whispered. "Come on! Get up!"

"Be quiet!" his father Shadow hissed a few places down the row from him. "Don't attract the Gorlock's attention or you could disqualify the test."

"The Gorlock can't hear us," Shadow's nephew Alien murmured. "The test is still valid."

"Come on, boy," Hangman's other cousin Chaos growled. "Come on. Get up."

"He's unconscious," Shadow's brother Butcher muttered. "It's all over. He lost."

Silence fell over the group as the Gorlock moved in on Jono's lifeless body. The boy didn't move. Hangman couldn't tell from up here if his younger brother was even still breathing.

Hangman could see just enough of the boy's face to see blood seeping from the slash marks left by the Gorlock's feathers. If Jono survived this battle, he would be scared for life.

Hangman's hand automatically drifted to the scars on his own face. They disfigured him and left him ugly. He wouldn't want anyone to suffer the same fate, especially not his younger brother.

The scars always itched. He had developed a habit of rubbing them whenever he went into his own thought about something.

The rite of initiation had to play out until its natural end. If Jono didn't regain consciousness pretty soon, he wouldn't survive long enough to worry about his appearance.

The Gorlock strutted over to him. He didn't revive even when the creature screeched down at him in open challenge.

It tilted its head this way and that to study him. When he still didn't respond, it pecked at him.

Alien turned away first. "I can't watch this. I'm going home."

Butcher grabbed his nephew's arm. "You have to stay. We all have to bear witness or the test won't be valid."

Alien yanked his muscular arm out of his uncle's grip. "It's already over. There is no test. I don't have to stand here and watch him die."

"Wait a minute," Hangman interrupted. "He's still conscious. He's coming around."

Alien turned back. Silence fell over the watching men as the Gorlock pecked at Jono two more times.

It clamped its jaws around him each time, picked him up, dropped him on the ground, and then nudged him with its beak.

When it still didn't get the response it wanted, it reared back and squawked at him. Still nothing.

"He's gone," Hangman's cousin Viking murmured. "He can't win now."

Hangman didn't answer. He wasn't even sure how he knew it, but he no longer doubted that Jono would win.

He would complete the rite of initiation into manhood in their Clan. He would take his place with his father, brother, uncles, and cousins as a man of this family.

The Gorlock dove its head toward Jono's still body. The creature opened its mouth one more time—but not to just pick him up and toy with him. It really planned to eat him now.

The boy reacted so fast that a few of the men on the cliff actually yelled out in surprise that he could move at all.

He snatched his axe handle. It lay right next to his hand. Hangman couldn't even see until now how Jono even knew where the axe was.

He must have. He grabbed it and swung hard enough to chop the creature's head away.

The weapon cracked across the Gorlock's cheekbone. Its head whipped sideways and the Gorlock shrieked out loud before it recovered enough to come at him again.

That one moment gave Jono just a fraction of an instant to drag himself off the ground and back against the cliff behind him.

Blood saturated his face and dripped down his neck to cover his chest. More slash marks marked his torso and abdomen, but he didn't notice his own injuries.

That one blow infuriated the Gorlock beyond all restraint. It dove for him again and again, but he defended himself better each time.

The Gorlock probably could have killed him instantly if it only thought to use its wings, but it didn't. Its injured pride drove it wild.

It stayed low in close quarters trying again and again to snap him in its beak. The Gorlock's own actions saved Jono's life.

His axe connected with the creature's head three more times. He pulled himself up a little more each time he smacked it away, but anyone could see he was seriously injured.

He got onto one knee the second time. He could barely use one of his legs. His axe started to sink the minute he swung it. Holding it up caused him pain.

He worked himself to his feet after the third blow, but he couldn't go on.

The Gorlock reared back, extended its head high above him, screeched again, and dove for the killing blow.

It bobbed its head from side to side to avoid his axe, knocked it aside before it touched any part of the creature's body, and then lunged for him before he recovered from his swing.

Jono must have seen the same thing. He, his brothers, and their Clan and band had fought Gorlocks too many times not to recognize their behavior when they wanted to kill something.

He raised his axe with a heroic effort. The Gorlock's head plunged down from on high, but he didn't swing.

He hurled himself between the Gorlock's legs, tucked and rolled, and landed a brutal stroke on the tendon behind the creature's left foot.

The creature shrieked at the top of its lunges, thrashed in pain, and spun around to confront Jono, but the creature could only balance on one foot now.

It tried to put its weight down, stumbled, and landed hard on its chest before it struggled upright again.

It kept bellowing in pain and fury. Jono limped backward to get clear of the thing, but it couldn't come after him—not very fast.

"Come on, Jono!" Hangman whispered. "Come on! Hit it again! You can kill it!"

"Come on, boy!" Shadow muttered under his breath. "Come on!"

All the men on the cliff crowded to the edge to watch, now that Jono was back on his feet. He disabled the Gorlock. One more hit like that and he would turn the tables in his favor.

Hangman's pulse started pounding when he saw the Gorlock hobbling one painful step closer. Jono backed away again to give it more space.

The Gorlock's injury made it even more irrationally dangerous and murderously enraged. It might have lived if it just walked away right then and there.

It couldn't. It needed revenge.

The Gorlock kept advancing. It took full advantage of its long neck, now that it couldn't maneuver on its feet anymore.

It dove for him a dozen times and measured each movement to avoid his axe.

The Gorlock didn't stop until it backed him up against another wall. Jono's injuries stopped him from attacking the way he might have if he had been healthy.

He stopped there and flattened his back against the unforgiving rock. He looked absolutely awful with blood all over himself.

His dark eyes shone out of a film of blood. Gore saturated his long black hair. He didn't look human. He didn't even seem to recognize where he was or what he was doing here.

The blows he delivered to the Gorlock's head started to bleed, too. They made the creature even more monstrous and revolting.

Blood even got into the creature's eyes and drove it ballistic. It lunged for him again and he pulled the same maneuver.

He threw himself under the creature's body, rolled behind it, and swung his axe a second time at the creature's right foot.

This time, he flipped his axe backward and used the heavy, blunt back edge of the weapon to smash the Gorlock's foot bones.

The creature screamed in agony, tried to lift both its feet at the same time, and went down hard just as Jono rolled clear behind the creature.

He rolled to his feet and wheeled around fast, all trace of his pain and injury gone. He raised his axe again and turned to brandish the sharp edge at the Gorlock, but he didn't strike. He actually backed away.

The creature thrashed on the ground howling and bellowing in rage. It kept trying to stand up, missed its footing, and crashed back down on the ground.

The head and neck still posed just as much of a danger as before. The creature finally worked itself over onto its chest and stomach where it could dart its head at him and snap its beak. He couldn't get close to it like this.

The two stood off at a safe distance and eyed each other. Hangman really couldn't tell from here just how injured Jono was.

He didn't flinch or wince or protect his side. He stood up straight as if he never had been injured.

The cuts across his face made him look insane and ferocious. All trace vanished of the young boy who left camp this morning. He wasn't a boy anymore. He was a man in every way that counted.

The Gorlock couldn't advance anymore. It couldn't move at all. It couldn't touch him as long as he stayed outside the length of its neck.

He inched a few steps closer and stopped within inches of the snapping beak. The Gorlock tried time and again, but it couldn't get any closer to him.

"Finish it, boy," Shadow murmured. "End it now."

"Come on, Jono," Hangman breathed. "You can do it."

Jono took a step back and raised his axe. He did everything with excruciating slowness now. He knew he had won. No one could ever take this victory away from him.

He flexed every muscle in his body. The Gorlock shrieked at him again and lunged to snap.

He struck without mercy, clubbed the creature hard across the face, and charged.

The blow slapped the Gorlock's head out of the way just long enough for him to dart behind the head. He stopped next to the creature's neck.

The creature saw him instantly and swung around to attack again. It curved its neck to swallow him, now that he stood within its range.

It would have won, but its own movements played into his hands. The neck arched toward him and he grabbed it right behind the head.

He hung on tight and the Gorlock thrashed and whipped its neck back and forth trying to shake him off.

The force of its struggles inched him up the neck closer to the head. That must be where he wanted to go.

He waited until the creature's thrashing movements bumped him against its skull. It tried its hardest to unseat him, but nothing worked.

He strapped his legs and one arm behind its skull and raised his axe in the other hand, but he still didn't strike.

The Gorlock tried a different technique and squirmed its neck from side to side trying to loosen his hold.

He took advantage of that and pushed himself up a little further without letting go. The Gorlock saw the axe hovering in its peripheral vision and tried to screw its head all the way backward to bite at him.

It had to stop thrashing to do that, and as soon as it kept still for two seconds, he reared upright, gripped with his legs, seized the axe handle in both hands, and brought it down in a crushing blow on the creature's head.

A dull crack echoed through the clearing. The rock walls amplified the sound and made it louder than it was.

A collective sigh of relief went through the men on the ledge when the Gorlock's head crashed down onto the ground with Jono still clinging to its neck.

The head bounced and jostled him in his seat, but he didn't fall—not until he brought his axe down again in a brutal, crushing blow that completely demolished the creature's skull.

Cheers broke out amongst the men on the cliff. Hangman's cousins grabbed him and they all laughed.

Hangman rushed the ledge, raised his fist in triumph, and whooped down at his brother, but Jono didn't hear anything.

He wrenched his axe out of the Gorlock's head—and then all the fight drained out of him.

He stared at the blood drenching his axe blade. He didn't even seem to think about getting off the fallen Gorlock before he toppled sideways and sprawled in the dirt, utterly unconscious.

Chapter 2

Hangman vaulted over the ledge, landed on another rock below him, and sprang from ledge to ledge until he landed on the ground.

He only glanced at the Gorlock long enough to make sure it was really dead. It was.

He squatted down next to his brother and turned the boy over. Jono was fourteen, the age of initiation in the Godless Clan.

He looked a lot younger and a lot smaller than only four years younger than Hangman. He didn't remember ever being that young or that small.

Hangman scooped up the boy in his arms. Jono's blood made him slippery, but that didn't matter.

Hangman walked out of the clearing just as his father, cousins, and uncles entered it. They surrounded the Gorlock and started hacking it to pieces to take the meant back to their camp.

Hangman didn't wait around to help. He carried Jono through the jungle, down a mile of winding pathways, and back to the place where the men camped the night before.

Hangman kicked the party's woven reed sleeping mats into place by the fire, laid Jono on the mats, and rolled some of the party's baggage into a knot to make a pillow.

Jono didn't come around during the whole trip back to the camp.

Hangman had the place to himself until the men returned. No women came with them on this trip. Women weren't allowed to attend a boy's initiation rite.

Women weren't even allowed to come on the journey or even to know where the men took the boy for initiation. This rite belonged only to the men.

Memories of Hangman's initiation flooded back to him while he soaked a piece of soft fur in a bowl of water and used it to wash the blood off Jono's face.

The sequence always followed the same pattern. The boy to be initiated had to go through the whole camp of women on his way to leave with the men who would initiate him.

It usually started with the boy's mother sobbing over him, hugging him, and talking to him a mile a minute about all the different ways he had to be careful so he didn't hurt himself or get himself killed.

Then all the boy's other female relatives wound up doing the same thing one after the other. His sisters, cousins, aunts, and more distant relatives all had to come and cry over him when they realized he might not come back that day.

Hangman remembered his mother doing the same thing to him—not to mention all his aunts and female cousins.

At least he didn't have any sisters to cry over him. He was the oldest of four boys. Now Jono initiated, too—the first after Hangman.

Hangman found himself studying his little brother more closely. These wounds would scar over. They would mark this young man in ways no one could see from the outside.

The same thing happened to Hangman. The scars on the outside didn't hold a candle to the change that happened on the inside when he went through his initiation.

The men came back, butchered the Gorlock, put a hunk of meat on the fire to cook, and sliced up the rest to dry it out for traveling rations.

Hangman paid no attention to them and went on tending Jono's wounds. No one knew better than Hangman the life Jono could look forward to after this.

Hangman mopped down all the blood on Jono's chest, but those wounds were only scratches. They didn't go any deeper than the surface.

The slashes on Jono's face were the worst. Hangman left, found the leaves of a certain plant in the jungle, brought it back, and ground it into a paste in one of the bowls the party used to eat out of.

He smeared the paste on the wounds. The sensation woke Jono up.

He jolted back to consciousness and tried to fight Hangman off before Jono recognized who it was.

"Lie down, little brother," Hangman told him. "You're safe. You're in the camp. You did it. You're initiated."

"Is it dead, Hangman?" Jono husked. "Is it really dead?"

"You killed it. Do you see the meat on the fire over there? You'll be eating that Gorlock for dinner tonight. You're a man now. You can lie down and rest. You don't have to fight anymore—not today at least."

Jono didn't relax right away. His head jerked the other way.

Hangman followed his brother's gaze. Their father, Shadow, sat across the camp talking to his brothers, Butcher and Fang.

Butcher was Kral of their band—the leader of this family group of the Godless Clan. Hangman, Jono, and their two younger brothers were the youngest of the cousins—the sons of Butcher, Fang, and their now-deceased oldest brother Midnight.

Midnight's sons were the oldest cousins. Now Alien, Feather, and Banjo served Butcher as their Kral.

If anything happened to Butcher, his sons Boxer and Magnet would serve Shadow as the next Kral until no men of that family's generation remained. Then the position of Kral would pass to the oldest son of whoever happened to be Kral at the time.

The cousins sat together or worked on the other side of the camp. Fang's sons, Viking, Chaos, and Vulture worked to construct a frame over the fire to dry the Gorlock meat for travel.

"You see?" Hangman murmured. "Father and the others are probably over there deciding on a name for you." Hangman pushed on his brother's shoulder. "Lie down. You don't have to do anything else right now. You can rest."

"Did you see, Hangman?" Jono husked. "Did you all see?"

"We all saw. The test was perfectly valid. You were too dazed to hear us cheering for you, but we all saw."

Jono looked away. "I don't remember. I don't remember much of anything."

"You went down hard and fell unconscious. We all thought you would die, but you got up and you defeated it. You did very well. I'm proud of you and I'm sure Father is very proud of you. Just imagine the weeping and crying when Mother sees you."

Jono didn't take the joke. His dark eyes darted back to Hangman. "How bad is it, Hangman? Tell me the truth."

Hangman looked up from his task of grinding some more of the leaf paste. He couldn't look away from his brother's eyes.

No one understood that question as well as Hangman did. He saw it in the eyes of everyone who looked at him every day of his life.

He even saw his own reflection in his brother's eyes right now. The glassy surface of other people's eyes was the one place where Hangman saw his own reflection.

In those moments, he saw himself as other people saw him. He saw himself as a grotesque, hideous, deformed creature as disgusting to them as all the blood-thirsty monsters roaming this country.

Hangman would have liked to look away from that reflection—and from everything it meant to his life.

He had trained himself ever since his initiation never to look away—from any-thing—especially not that. He always faced it head on. He had to. He couldn't run from his own face.

"It isn't as bad as mine," he murmured. "You will be scarred, but only slightly—like Viking over there."

Hangman waved his grinding stone over his shoulder toward his big cousin.

Viking was easily one of the tallest, burliest men of their family band. All the men of the Godless Clan wore a combination of cured skins tied into loincloths around their waists.

That was their only clothing apart from footwear and knee-high leggings also sewn from the skins of creatures they hunted. The jungle was too hot to wear anything else.

The men let their straight black hair grow long. Some tied it into bunches with strips of hide or twisted cordage from the jungle. Others wove it into plaits or any other arrangement to keep it neat and out of the way for hunting trips.

Viking was one of those who used vines and hand-twisted cordage to bind his hair into thin, rope-like strands. He kept his hair bound up away from his forehead all the way back across his whole scalp.

It gave him a much harsher look than most Godless men, but he had one of the softest, kindest personalities in the whole band. Everyone loved him, especially women and children.

A long, whitish scar cut down one side of Viking's face. The scar started just below the left eye and ran straight down to the jawline.

Most people thought Viking's scar made him look powerful, masculine, and distin-guished—which it did. No one thought Viking's scar made him ugly.

Jono sank back on the mat, but he didn't relax and he didn't look away. "You wouldn't lie to me about it, would you, Hangman?"

"Never. I can bring you a basin of water so you can see your reflection if you want. The cuts look worse now than they will after they scar. They won't make you look different—not like mine make me look different."

That finally satisfied Jono. He settled down and turned his face away to watch the activity of the camp. "I can't believe it's over. I looked forward to this day for so long. Now I feel nothing."

"It comes later," Hangman told him. "The mark grows over time. It grows with you. You don't become a man at initiation. This is just the bridge that takes you across the river to the road to manhood on the other side."

"You make it look so easy," Jono breathed.

Hangman snorted. "You only think that because I'm your older brother. I would think the same thing about you if our positions were reversed."

"No," Jono murmured. "It isn't that. It's you."

Hangman didn't answer. No one had to explain to him how everyone treated him differently—in ways that had nothing to do with his looks.

Everyone in Butcher's band treated Hangman like he was much older than he really was. They all treated him as though he had much more authority than he did—more than a man his age should have.

Everyone treated him as though he was actually more like Butcher's brother instead of his nephew—one of his youngest nephews.

Hangman didn't realize until now that his status had been affecting his younger brothers, but it must have been.

Jono, Landus, and Jarun must have grown up seeing everyone treat Hangman differently—and not because of his looks.

Hangman didn't try to come up with a sensible objection to this because there wasn't one. It was just one of the undeniable facts of his reality—just like his scars.

Chapter 3

Hangman was still grinding the leaf paste when his father, Butcher, and Fang came over to where Jono lay on the mats.

Hangman didn't think anything of their approach until his father glared down at him in a deep scowl. "Leave the man alone and stop treating him like a baby." He turned to Jono. "Stand up and be a man. Your initiation is over. You aren't so hurt that you can't stand up and face the world on your own two feet."

Jono gulped and heaved himself off the mat. He winced a lot, but he tried to hide it.

Hangman didn't find any visible injury to Jono's leg earlier. He might have torn or strained something.

He tried to put his weight on it, limped again, and then pulled himself up straight in front of his father and uncles.

Shadow surveyed the boy up and down, pursed his lips at the sight of the cuts on Jono's face, and nodded.

"That's good. You did well against the Gorlock. I'm proud of you. You're a man of the Godless Clan now. After today, you'll be called Cross after those scars on your face. You'll come with us on our missions from now on."

Cross burst into a huge smile. "Thank you, Father!" He turned to Butcher. "Thank you, Uncle!"

"You have nothing to thank us for," Butcher told him. "You earned that one all by yourself. You earned your place."

Cross practically burst out laughing in joy and relief, but the three older men only turned away and waved behind them. "You two come with us," Butcher told them. "We need to discuss our next move."

The three older men crossed the camp to Butcher's shelter. It was a shake hut made of thick, flexible saplings bent into a frame.

A covering of leafy vines formed the roof and walls on three sides. The front stood open to the air.

The Godless always built shelters like this no matter where they went. They built their shelters with four walls for privacy reasons, but only in camps where men and women lived together.

No one had to protect themselves from the weather in this jungle. The shake roof barely blocked rain from entering. Other than that, the temperature always stayed oppressively hot and steamy.

Hangman's cousins stood off on their side of the camp listening to Shadow change Cross's name. No one would ever use his old name again. He was Cross now.

The women and children would call him that, too, as soon as the men returned to the rest of the band. His old name belonged to his boyhood and that time was over. The name no longer applied to him.

The cousins followed the three older men back to Butcher's shelter. He sat down in the very rear with Shadow on one side and Fang on the other.

The cousins gathered around the three men. Some of the cousins squatted. Others sat on the ground.

Cross limped in the rear. Hangman slowed his pace to stay near his brother. Shadow could afford to act harshly toward his son and insist that no on treat him like a baby.

Hangman kept an eye on Cross to make sure he pulled through this all right, but he just looked sore. He would recover.

His swollen face looked worse than it was. The leaf paste exaggerated the swelling, too. All of that would subside in time.

There wasn't enough room inside the shelter for everyone by the time Cross and Hangman got there.

Hangman didn't want Cross to go through the ordeal of sitting down and then having to stand back up again, so the two brothers remained standing in the back.

Butcher pulled forward one of half a dozen leather bags he wore slung across his chest. All the Godless men carried their personal goods in bags like this.

Butcher wore the two frontmost locks of his hair in two plaits down the side of his face. They hung in front of his ears. He wore the rest of it loose.

He, Shadow, and Fang presented a picture in contrasts even though they were brothers.

Butcher had a young, almost baby-like face with too much extra padding around his jaw and neckline. It made him look like the youngest of the three even though he was the oldest.

He was also the biggest, the strongest, and the tallest. He wasn't as big as Viking or Alien, but Butcher cut an imposing figure—on the outside at least.

He lacked Shadow's sharper, more astute strategic thinking abilities, though. Butcher wouldn't have been able to lead the band at all without Shadow's constant guidance and suggestions.

Fang was the youngest, but he looked like the oldest. He looked older than Hangman imagined Midnight would have looked if he had been alive.

Fang aged long before his time. He had been lanky, wizened, and distant for as long as Hangman could remember.

Fang didn't participate much in any strategic decision-making that Hangman could see. From what Hangman could tell, Fang just sat there and followed Butcher around to show everyone that Fang supported Butcher's leadership—which was better than nothing.

Shadow was a completely different story. He wasn't as big as Butcher. Shadow was nowhere near as big as the bulkier nephews.

He made up for it by being the brains behind the operation. He had a way of dropping information and suggestions into Butcher's ear to make it seem like Butcher thought of all these details himself.

Shadow had an expertly subtle way of steering his older brother into making the decisions Shadow wanted him to make. Shadow held the power that kept Butcher in position no matter what.

It always puzzled Hangman that Shadow never challenged his brother for the position of Kral. Shadow might not have been as big or as strong, but he was big and strong enough to defeat his bigger, slower, less agile, and less alert brother.

Shadow could have marshaled the support of every man in their band. He could probably even have marshaled the support of Butcher's own sons.

Shadow never stepped out of line. He never once showed by even a hint of facial expression that he ever questioned Butcher's leadership.

Butcher never questioned Butcher's leadership, either, thanks to Shadow's diplomacy. It never crossed Butcher's mind that he wasn't the one in charge of this band or that he might not be the most qualified to be in charge.

He rummaged in his bag and pulled out a handful of ancient sheets of some material the Godless had never seen anywhere else.

Whatever material it was didn't come from any known source in the jungle.

The sheets resembled the glossy leaves of some jungle trees, but the sheets didn't have veins nor did they take the same shape of leaves.

Each sheet showed a different picture. The images didn't come from the jungle, either.

Hangman had seen these sheets for the first time the night of his initiation—the same way Cross was seeing them for the first time right now.

The sheets puzzled Hangman as much now as they did every time he'd seen them since. They puzzled everyone in Butcher's band. No one could figure out what the pictures were or where they came from.

Butcher spread them out on the ground in front of him. There were nine sheets, each with a different picture on it.

Most of them showed giant mountain ranges in the background with blue skies and some kind of symbols printed across the top.

In the foreground, the pictures showed banks of some kind of iron tubes all facing in the same direction.

Each tube attached to some kind of box or, in some cases, a lump of some kind of stone as far as Hangman could tell.

Other pictures showed one or two individual, much larger tubes pointing up at the sky.

Butcher pointed at the mountains in three of the pictures' backgrounds. "We know these three are the same mountain shown from different angles. We also know that this mountain doesn't belong to the Jagged Points to the west of our territory. Wherever this mountain is, it must be somewhere else."

"We might be able to see it if we got on top of one of the Jagged Points," Boxer pointed out.

The group should have taken his suggestion as almost as important as Butcher's own opinion. Boxer was Butcher's oldest son. He would probably become Kral one day.

No one treated Boxer's opinion as anything important. Alien actually sneered at him. "We can't get on top of the Jagged Points. That's ridiculous. The Jagged Points are inside the Renegade Clan's territory. We would lose our lives going in there."

"We don't have enough men to attack the Renegades outright," Butcher decided. "We need to find another way to see what lies beyond those mountains."

"What other way is there?" Viking asked. "The Renegades patrol their territory, especially where it adjoins Godless territory. The Renegades are already encroaching. There is no way to get past them."

"These weapons could change everything," Butcher replied. "We could turn the tables on the Renegades, drive them back over the mountains, and reclaim the territory they took from us."

"Then the question is how do we get across," Butcher's younger son Magnet added. "Without the Renegades finding out that we're there."

"We don't even know if that mountain is beyond the Jagged Points—or if the weapons are beyond the Jagged Points," Feather pointed out. "We would risk our lives for nothing."

"It wouldn't be for nothing," Shadow replied. "We would be doing it to find out if the mountain is over there. Once we know where the mountain is, anyone who comes back from this raid will have a better idea of whether we need to push further inside the Renegades' territory or not."

Feather raised his eyebrows. "Raid? We're going on a raid—on the Renegades?"

"We don't have to drive back their entire invasion effort," Butcher replied. "We only have to strike hard enough to get behind their front line. Once we do that, we can penetrate to the top of the Jagged Points. From there, we'll see if the mountain is anywhere in sight. Then we'll retreat and regroup before we make a play for the weapons."

The cousins exchanged glances. Hangman caught Vulture, Chaos, and Banjo all looking at him.

Banjo even brought his eyebrows together in the center. The three cousins wanted Hangman to say something about this.

He didn't say anything. He was only eighteen. He didn't make decisions on behalf of the band. Feather, Alien, and Viking were all so much older. They could get away with objecting to Butcher's decisions right to his face.

Hangman never did that—or almost never. He watched his father and the other men negotiate. Hangman learned from what worked for them and what didn't.

"Which peak do you want to go for?" Vulture asked.

Butcher pointed toward the west. None of the men could see the Jagged Points from here. The men didn't have to see. Every man of their band could visualize the Points as clearly in his mind's eye as if he was seeing them in real life.

"We'll go for the Grey Ghost," Butcher decided. "It's the closet and the least rugged. We'll be able to get to it the fastest and climb it the fastest both going up and going down."

"How do we ambush the Renegades?" Chaos asked. He always thought everything through in his calm, level-headed, insightful way. He inherited Fang's reserve but none of his dullness.

"We'll scout the Renegades in the area first," Butcher ordered. "We'll see how many of them are blocking our way to the Grey Ghost."

Hangman spoke up for the first time. "And if they discover us while we're scouting? It could turn into a fight—in which case, we might as well fight our way through then and there. If we pull back, we'll only alert them that we're in the area and trying to get through."

Butcher nodded. "I was just about to say that. If it comes to a fight, break through if you can. Get to the peak and see what's on the other side. One person bringing back news whether the mountain is there or not will be a big help.'

Vulture caught Hangman's eye and made a face. Hangman didn't return it.

Vulture seemed to take it as a personal insult that Butcher claimed other people's ideas as his own to make himself look smarter.

Vulture often made faces behind Butcher's back to express how displeased Vulture was with Butcher's leadership.

Some men of the band openly supported Shadow for Kral—or at least people like Vulture supported Shadow behind Butcher's back.

It would never work for someone like Vulture to challenge Butcher on Shadow's behalf. Then Vulture would wind up fighting Butcher.

Vulture couldn't challenge Butcher unless Shadow actually wanted to become Kral in his brother's place. Shadow obviously didn't want that. He was practically Kral already. He didn't need to betray his own brother to do it.

Hangman didn't understand his father's need to support Butcher by giving him these ideas and letting him take credit for them.

Hangman decided early on to follow his father's example, make suggestions, and then accept them when Butcher gave these orders as if he came up with them himself.

Vulture saw Hangman doing it—which meant all the other men of their band saw Hangman doing it, too.

They saw him following his father's example. They saw Hangman's and Shadow's words coming out of Butcher's mouth.

He nodded as if the whole thing was already settled. "We'll move out tomorrow and see how far we get. You all better get some sleep."

The party broke up. Cross and Hangman returned to their mats by the fire.

The cousins worked around it hanging up the Gorlock meat to smoke overnight. Chaos squatted next to the haunch cooking over the flames.

He cut it up and passed the to everyone, including Cross and Hangman.

"Is it like this every night?" Cross whispered.

"Like what?" Hangman asked. "Camp life is the same no matter where you go. Nothing ever changes."

"I'm talking about all of that between Father and Butcher," Cross hissed. "I'm talking about Butcher saying he was just about to say what you just said."

Now it was Hangman's turn to make a face. "You know it is. You must have heard enough in our camps to know what it's like."

"I didn't know it was like *that!*"

"Well, it is, so you better get used to it. Butcher is Kral. What he decides is what we do. If you want things done a certain way, you have to convince him to go along with your idea."

"*Convince* him to go along with it," Cross corrected. "Not tell everyone that he was just about to say that. That's outrageous! And Father just puts up with it."

Hangman turned around, leveled his brother with a piercing stare, and lowered his voice to a barely audible murmur. "You're a man now and in the company of men. I don't know or care what you've heard in the company of women. If you honor Father so much, then do as he does. Use your brain and keep your mouth shut around those who are bigger, stronger, smarter, and more powerful than you. You can call it convincing them. You can call it suggesting things to them. You can call it whatever you want." He pointed in his brother's face. "Just remember what will happen if a Kral of the Godless hears you speaking against his rule and accuses you as a traitor. There are some things worse than someone taking your idea and saying he was just about to say that."

Cross shut his mouth, but he didn't stop fuming about it. Hangman didn't say anything else.

Butcher was Kral of this band. He could order any of these men to their deaths if Butcher thought someone was arguing too much, questioning or challenging his leadership, or stepping out of line in any other way.

Cross better learn that real quick if he was going to survive out here.

Chapter 4

Hangman jolted wide awake when someone shook him by the shoulder. He grabbed for his kukri blade before he realized it was Viking standing over him.

"Time to get up, little brother," Viking husked. "It's your turn to stand watch."

Hangman wilted in relief. "Make more noise when you come up on me. I could have taken your arm off."

Viking grinned at him. "I would have fought back."

Hangman looked away to stop himself from glaring at his big cousin. Viking didn't notice. He was too good-natured to notice anyone acting annoyed with him.

He walked off to his shelter and left Hangman sitting there rubbing the sleep out of his eyes.

He shifted his kukri to his left hand and pulled his second one out of his waistband. He always fought with two, one in each hand.

He was the one who hand-chipped their inward-curving blades out of black volcanic glass. They didn't need sharpening unless they got damaged in battle. Then he had to chip out the broken place to repair them.

He was the only man in his band who fought with this kind of weapon. He had never even seen them in all the band's dealings with other Godless. Plenty of men fought with kukris of various sizes, but they made their weapons out of bone or other kinds of stone.

He glanced over at Cross sleeping next to him. Hangman would have left his younger brother asleep if this had been any other night.

The whole initiation came back into Hangman's mind in a flash. Cross wasn't a boy anymore. He was a man of their band.

That came with responsibilities as well as privileges. Cross knew this as well as anyone.

Hangman laid his hand on Cross's shoulder. "Time to wake up, little brother. It's time to stand the watch."

Cross floundered out of a sound sleep and looked around. "Huh? Where are we?"

"We're in the camp. It's our turn to stand watch. Get up and bring your axe. We're already late."

Hangman left Cross there and joined up with Fang and Alien. The four of them were supposed to stand watch over the camp until morning.

Fang sloped around as listlessly as ever. He barely looked at the surroundings.

Alien gave Fang a sharp look on the side and then scowled when he made eye contact with Hangman. Fang might be useful to have around tonight. Then again, he might not be.

Cross limped over to join them. Alien gave him a sharp look, too, and then made another moment of eye contact with Hangman.

Hangman shared that fleeting instant of silent communication with his much bigger, much stronger, much older cousin.

Alien was hands down the biggest man in their band. He was even bigger than Viking, which is how Alien got his name. He really didn't look human—or rather, he looked like another species of human because he was so big.

He also didn't wear his hair down the way every other man in their Clan wore it. He twisted his hair into dozens of knobs that stuck out of his skull in points. He never took his hair down except when it grew so long that he needed to retie the knobs.

Alien had already been an adult by the time Hangman got old enough to remember him. Alien kept his hair tied up like that all day every day in all that time. He went off alone where no one could see him when he needed to take his hair down and retie it.

His hairstyle made him look even more bizarre, but he had a straightforward, take-no-prisoners, get-out-of-my-way style of doing everything.

If someone wanted something done, they only had to turn Alien loose on the project. He wouldn't stop until he accomplished whatever it was, no matter how outlandish it might be.

He had always taken a big-brotherly attitude toward Hangman—or, to be more accurate, Alien had taken a big-brotherly attitude toward Hangman since Hangman initiated as a man of their band. Alien didn't pay Hangman the slightest attention before that. None of the men did.

Alien pointed behind Hangman's back. "You go over there, little brother. I'll stand watch over here. Cross, you go over there. Uncle, you take that side. We'll start at the four points of the camp and revolve around it. If anyone sees anything or engages with anything, the others will join him to combine our efforts."

Hangman nodded. "Sounds good."

The four men separated. Hangman retreated to the place Alien indicated. Fang and Cross did the same thing.

Fang obeyed Alien to the letter. Fang didn't seem to realize or care that his nephew was ordering him around.

Hangman had never been too sure about this, either. Midnight had been much older than Butcher and Shadow. Midnight's sons were all much older than their younger cousins. Alien might even have been older than Fang, but Hangman couldn't be sure.

He turned outward to train his ears into the jungle. He couldn't see much in the dark. The canopy blocked out moonlight and starlight. The firelight from the center of the camp didn't penetrate the jungle.

He could hear much more than he could see. He heard and identified countless night insects, most of them dangerous ones.

He had stood on watch practically every night since his initiation. He grew up in this jungle. He knew the sounds of every creature moving around out there.

Long years of practice trained his ears to pick up if they were moving toward him, away from him, or from one side to the other. None of them were coming toward the camp right now.

He kept one of his kukris in his hand. He carried the other stuck in his waistband where he could get it easily if he needed it.

He also carried a hunting knife in a horizontal carry sheath across his back. It always paid to come armed whenever someone went anywhere in the jungle.

Movement caught his eye. Alien, Fang, and Cross drifted to their right to circle the camp.

Hangman turned aside to do the same thing. He didn't hear anything threatening out there—or at least nothing threatening to the camp.

Everything in the jungle threatened in one way or the other. Humans were by far the least threatening creatures out here.

The four men drifted five feet to the right. Hangman stopped again and listened.

He heard a lot of dangerous creatures moving around out there. He even heard some of them pouncing, attacking, and killing each other. He followed their movements with his ears.

The hunters caught their prey and faded into the jungle. Other creatures emerged to take their places.

Alien, Fang, and Cross moved again. Hangman turned away to do the same thing, but he stopped in his tracks when he heard a rapid series of clicks one after the other.

They blended together into a stream of noise. It rose and fell getting louder, softer, and then louder again.

He grabbed his second kukri without turning around. Every nerve stretched to the breaking point.

He snapped his tongue in his mouth extra loudly. The sound echoed across the camp and got the other three men's attention instantly without him saying a word.

Alien stormed over to Hangman's side. Alien didn't even have to ask. He heard the noise, too.

Cross skip-hopped across the camp and pulled up on Hangman's other side. Cross didn't let his injuries slow him down at all.

Fang ambled slowly. He didn't hurry. He also didn't hurry about pulling his twin axes from his belt. At least he was getting ready to fight.

The four men held their breath to listen to that stream of clicks coming straight for them.

Hangman snapped his tongue a second time. He already heard his cousins stirring behind him.

The second snap woke up everyone else. Chaos and Vulture showed up next followed by Boxer, Magnet, and Banjo.

Hangman didn't pay attention to anything anyone else did. He tightened his grip on his weapons just as a giant whipping snake body uncoiled from the darkness right in front of him.

The Krakelow didn't fly at the men head on. That would have been way too easy.

The creature unwound its enormous body from the surrounding tree branches. The Krakelow moved at lightning speed and controlled its movements with pinpoint accuracy.

It coiled sideways to cover that whole side of the camp and hurled itself side on to collide with all the men at the same time.

The Krakelow flexed the scales on its outer hide as it came. The scales fired out from the skin. Tiny whizzing darts slashed and pierced the defender's skin—and then the creature's body hit the men full force.

Hangman stood his ground as multiple darts sliced his face and arms. Some embedded in his chest and stomach, but he couldn't let himself flinch or even feel the pain right now.

He raised his kukris and concentrated everything on the creature coming at him.

It whipped and contorted its body in a thousand directions at once. The thing could coil and tangle itself in any direction at mind-numbing speed.

Its contortions made it impossible to judge where the first blow would land. Hangman just had to wait for the thing to hit him before he struck back.

The creature lengthened its long sinuous coils to an unbelievable size, slammed into the men, and whipped and looped itself in every possible configuration to wrap the men in knots.

Hangman struck out with his blades, stabbed through the hide, and hacked the coils lashing around him.

The Krakelow's powerful muscles clamped around his ribs and one of the coils caught his arm. The creature's weight and power dragged his arm down. He couldn't raise it to strike out at the thing.

He spun around and hacked the coil again and again at the same spot. He chopped a bloody fissure in the muscular flesh until he hit the spinal column.

His kukri stuck in the bone, but he yanked it loose. Pain, fury, and terror for his life gave him superhuman strength. He had to free his other arm before the Krakelow bound him completely.

Chapter 5

Hangman vented all his power on the Krakelow's spinal column, shattered one of the vertebrae, and his next strike severed the column, but the creature didn't weaken at all.

The men around him fought just as hard. Viking fought with two huge axes. He chopped the creature's body into pieces in multiple spots, but each piece kept lashing just as much and trying to grab and restrain the men.

The spinal column gave way. Hangman hacked through the rest of the body easily after that and pulled his arm free, but not without a dozen dart scales embedded in his flesh.

He couldn't pay attention to that. Yells and bellows echoed through the camp with all the men fighting this one creature. The noise attracted others. Their night sounds pulsed louder beyond the trees.

They would wait until the Krakalow brought down one or more of the men. Then all the other creatures would move in and fight over the spoils.

The rest of the Krakalow's body functioned just as well as ever even after Hangman cut it in half. It stretched out, elongated itself, and the remaining section tried again to lash itself around him.

He spun to his right and heard Cross yelling in the distance. Cross's higher voice drifted over his uncles' and cousins' deeper bellows.

Hangman took a second to locate his brother in the confusion. The process took even longer because the Krakalow's coils almost completely enveloped Cross.

Only his head, his right shoulder, and his right arm remained visible above a solid pillar of coils wrapped around him in a crushing grip.

Cross didn't stop fighting even then. He raised his axe a dozen times and brought it down again and again on the coils binding him. His own efforts stopped the Krakelow from killing him.

Hangman wheeled in that direction to help his brother. Hangman didn't even get a chance to move before the severed end of the body he just hacked in half elongated again, whip-cracked sideways, and knocked him flat onto his face.

He flinched as more darts stuck into his back. The fall dazed him for a second. That was the moment when he felt the coils creeping up his legs. The Krakelow was trying to bind him again.

He pushed himself up on his arms to turn around and free himself before it was too late.

He pried himself off the ground—and stiffened when he heard a different noise. It approached the camp from out in the darkness on the opposite side of the circle from where the Krakalow attacked.

All the men fought the Krakelow on this side of the camp. They all had their backs to the new threat.

They all yelled and roared in fury fighting the creature. None of them even realized the danger they were in. Hangman was the only man here who could do anything to stop it.

He forced himself to freeze and lie still even as the Krakelow's coils inched higher up his legs. The coils surrounded his waist, but he still didn't move.

He stayed where he was facing the other side of the camp. His mind blocked out all his cousins' yells and even Cross's cries for help.

Hangman's hearing zeroed in on that sound and nothing else. He tracked it getting closer.....and closer......

The coils surrounded his ribs, but he didn't care. At that moment, a colossal force shattered the trees on the opposite side of the camp.

A massive creature taller than the canopy broke through into the camp and looked down on all the helpless men fighting the Krakalow. None of the men could break free to defend themselves against this new attacker.

Thick black fur covered the monster below the neck and left its black, scaly head bald. The creature's tiny forelimbs barely stuck out of its massive chest.

The fur stopped at the hip joint. Powerful, scaly muscular, backward-jointed legs ended at clawed feet digging into the ground.

The creature cracked open enormous jaws studded with fangs. Hangman counted down the seconds before the Crusher actually entered the camp itself.

The creature kept tilting its head from one side to the other. Its black eyes glittered in the firelight when it spotted its helpless prey.

Hangman waited until the Crusher took one more step into the ring of firelight. He could see every detail of the creature now.

He summoned all his strength, but he didn't try to loosen the Krakelow coils. He pushed himself up on his knees, arched back, and hurled his kukri at the Crusher.

The weapon embedded itself in the creature's neck right next to the windpipe. The Crusher bellowed in fury, raised one of its giant legs, and clawed at the weapon.

The Crusher sealed its own fate by knocking the kukri out of position. The kukri fell onto the ground and blood poured from the wound.

The Crusher didn't notice. It took one more fateful step closer to the men still locked in battle against the Krakelow.

Chaos, Shadow, and Boxer noticed the Crusher first, but they couldn't turn around to confront it. Only Viking managed to work himself far enough out of the battle to face the monster.

The Crusher didn't understand where its injury came from. It didn't pay any attention to Hangman.

The Krakelow's coils wrapped the rest of the way up his chest. He had to strike a blow against the Crusher before the Krakelow restricted his arm movements.

He reared back and threw his second kukri. It was his only remaining weapon. If this didn't work, he was done.

The weapon tumbled end over end through the air. He timed his throw for one of the Crusher's head movements. It turned aside at exactly that moment and the kukri buried its point in the soft place at the corner of the creature's jaw where it met the skull.

The Crusher reared on its legs, gave one bellow of hopeless protest, and toppled with a ground-shaking crash. It lay there twitching and shivering. It didn't get up again.

Hangman watched just long enough to make sure he brought the thing down. None of that helped his cousins, uncles, and brother against the Krakalow.

Hangman flipped himself onto his back. He had to work fast before the coils took his arms, too.

He didn't get a chance to do anything before Alien stormed over to him. Alien fought with two kukris, too, but his were three times the size of Hangman's.

Alien roared in fury and hacked his weapon down full force onto Hangman's legs.

The blade severed the coils, split Hangman's legs apart, and the stone blade embedded in the soft soil underneath him.

The coils fell away. Hangman didn't wait around to thank his big cousin. He wrenched off the rest of the coils and scrambled to his feet before they could capture him again.

Alien tossed Hangman one of his huge kukris. The weapon took all the strength in both of Hangman's arms just to raise the thing.

Alien dove back into the battle. Hangman charged over to Cross.

The coils had brought him down completely and wrapped him up to his neck. They surrounded his right arm. He couldn't fight at all anymore.

Hangman swung Alien's giant kukri and hacked down onto the coils with all his might. They cleaved under the blow and started to fall away.

He had to keep hacking and hacking without stopping to free Cross. Countless dart wounds soaked him in blood, but the rest of the men suffered the same injuries, too.

Hangman turned back to face the battle, but it was already swinging in the men's favor. The men cut the Krakelow into so many pieces that the pieces couldn't bind anyone anymore.

They whipped, snaked, and danced on the ground trying to find something to latch onto. The men backed away and pulled each other to a safe distance so no one got caught again.

"We have to retreat," Shadow panted. "The blood will attract every nightcrawler in the area—and that's not counting the ants."

"Pack up," Butcher ordered. "Get ready to move."

The men were all too out of breath and injured to argue. Hangman could barely lift his arms when he handed Alien his kukri back.

Hangman retrieved his own weapons from the Crusher. No one wanted to waste all that good meat, but his father was right. The blood would bring out every dangerous monster living in the jungle.

The men only took a few minutes to hang their bags across their shoulders and wipe as much of the blood off their weapons as they could before they filed out of camp.

Hangman made sure to bring the leaf paste he made for Cross. He and his companions would need that tonight.

Chapter 6

Hangman and his cousins searched the surrounding jungle for any sign of danger, but danger lurked all around them.

The sun rose above the high canopy and gave the travelers a clear view of the jungle around them.

The creatures Hangman could see all belonged to dangerous species, but that was nothing compared to what the men could hear.

His ears traced the movements of dozens of different creatures of many kinds. Some came toward the party drawn by the smell of blood.

Sweat stung all the cuts and scratches covering every inch of Hangman's skin. He didn't wipe the blood away. It protected him from his own sweat.

Butcher led the way through miles of dense jungle until the men got to a steep ravine with a stream running through the bottom.

The party divided into three groups and took turns washing the blood off in the water while their relatives stood guard.

Hangman handed around the leaf paste. He didn't get a chance to use it while he was standing guard.

His group went to the stream last. He gritted his teeth to stop himself from flinching when he wiped the blood off. Then he had to pull out the darts buried in his arms and legs.

Chaos came over to him. "Stand still, little brother. Let me do it."

Hangman shut his eyes and sent his mind somewhere else while Chaos pulled the darts out of Hangman's back. Chaos splashed water on the wounds and then smeared leaf paste on them.

Hangman pretended not to notice Chaos spreading the paste on all of Hangman's other wounds. Hangman could have done that himself, but he let his cousin do it for him.

Godless men didn't show affection very often. They didn't have time and now wasn't the time.

None of Hangman's relatives mentioned him killing that Crusher. He could accept this little show of care as a token of his cousins' appreciation for saving all their lives.

Hangman had been getting used to this kind of thing ever since he initiated as a man of the Godless Clan. He would have to be blind not to notice how rarely any of the men did anything like this for each other.

They only did it when they wanted to acknowledge some favor or exceptional act one of them performed for the others.

They did it to Hangman often, but only because he seemed to always be in the right place at the right time to bail them out of situations like this.

Chaos swiveled in front of him and grinned when he wiped the last of the paste on Hangman's face. "At least you won't get any uglier," Chaos told him.

Hangman snorted. "Maybe I should. Then I could scare the monsters to death just by looking at them. I wouldn't have to fight them."

Chaos laughed. He was only a few years older than Hangman. They had grown up together, fought together, and shared hardship and danger together.

Chaos's laughter disturbed Butcher. "We can move out if you're done playing around," he snapped. "We need to put some distance between us and this blood."

The two cousins didn't argue. They fell in line together and the group started climbing out of the ravine.

They moved a lot faster now and covered the miles to get as far away as possible from their previous camp.

The party camped at sundown the next day in a different clearing many miles from where they started.

Boxer, Banjo, and Chaos unpacked the dried Gorlock meat they brought with them. The men shared it between them and sat around the fire to eat it.

Butcher pulled out his picture sheets again. Hangman didn't look at them. He had already studied them as closely as he needed to. He remembered every detail of the strange weapons and the unknown mountain range in the background.

Alien broke the silence. "We can't go any further west without running into Renegade patrols."

"We'll carry out our raid in the morning," Butcher decided. "We'll forge as deeply into their territory as we can and try to get to the top of the Jagged Points. Then we'll see what we need to do."

No one answered. Hangman could think of a lot of reasons to go after these weapons. He could think of just as many reasons not to, but no one asked his opinion.

Cross stayed close to him for most of the day and sat near him that night. Hangman didn't comment on it.

Cross's injured leg didn't slow him down on the journey here, so it must not have been severe.

The swelling in his face seemed to be getting worse, though. Hangman gathered more leaves, made more paste, and put it on the cuts that night before the men went to sleep.

"Put some of the paste on your own face," Boxer called across the fire. "See it helps anything."

"No amount of paste will make you smarter," Hangman returned. "Unless you put the paste on your mouth and it seals up. That would heal what's really wrong with you."

Dead silence answered him. Not many people had the nerve to tease Hangman about his appearance anymore. He didn't take it lightly and he retaliated in spades if anyone dared.

Boxer was a big guy, but he had a blundering, sloppy way of doing everything. He had no iron in him the way Viking did.

Boxer wore his hair tied back into a bunch behind his head. Hangman couldn't explain why, but this style made Boxer look even more bumbling, idiotic, and ineffectual than he otherwise would have.

Boxer stumbled through life by virtue of being Butcher's oldest son. That was about the best thing Hangman could think to say about the guy.

Butcher assigned the men to another three shifts to stand watch that night. He put Hangman on the first watch with Boxer, Banjo, and Shadow.

Boxer didn't make any more comments about Hangman's face. Boxer was the only man stupid enough to try it anymore.

He was too stupid even to get the message to keep his mouth shut, but that was fine with Hangman.

He caught Boxer giving him side glances before immediately looking away. Boxer wouldn't have been able to take down that Crusher—not from that distance.

Hangman could think of a lot of things he did since his initiation that Boxer wouldn't have been able to do.

That could be the reason Boxer kept trying to needle Hangman. Hangman had noticed a correlation between his own actions to protect his relatives and Boxer's insulting comments.

Boxer obviously didn't like that the other men thought so highly of Hangman even though he was so much younger than everyone else.

Hangman put the subject out of his mind, but he already knew Boxer would do it again the next time Hangman did something, especially something that saved Boxer.

Shadow took charge of the first watch and assigned the three younger men to different sides of the camp as usual.

It wasn't usual for him to post Hangman on the west side of the camp—the side the Renegade Clan would attack from if they did attack the Godless camp.

It would have been unheard of for anyone to post such a young man in the most dangerous position, but no one questioned Shadow's decision.

Hangman no longer considered this anything unusual anymore. Shadow and Butcher did things like this to him all the time nowadays. It had become normal for them to treat him the same way they would have treated a man decades older than he was now.

Shadow was too smart and knew his son too well to post Boxer anywhere other than on the farthest opposite eastern side of the camp—as far away from Hangman as it was possible to put him.

Hangman caught Banjo giving them all side looks, too, but he stayed out of it. Banjo followed his brother Chaos's example by keeping quiet most of the time.

If anything, Banjo became even more silently watchful than either Fang or Chaos, but no one could accuse Banjo of bumbling, dullness, or lacking in iron.

He and Chaos were cut from the same cloth as their oldest brother Alien. Hangman really couldn't comprehend how the three of them descended from such a sloping, brainless father.

The four men patrolled the camp, but nothing happened until the watch changed. Viking woke up Cross, Butcher, and Feather.

Hangman stretched out in Cross's place by the fire, shut his eyes, and fell into an exhausted sleep. The pain and fatigue of the past two days caught up with him.

He didn't wake up until daylight broke through the canopy.

Chapter 7

Hangman, Chaos, Viking, and Alien crept through the undergrowth extra slowly so they wouldn't make any noise.

Hangman chose every footstep with exaggerated care and eased branches out of his way. He paused every few steps to listen and search the surrounding jungle, but he didn't see anything.

Renegades patrolled the area even though he couldn't see them. The tracks of their footprints got thicker the deeper the Godless penetrated into Renegade territory.

The Godless also found offal, bones, and skins lying around to indicate where the Renegades made their kills.

The Renegades even left a few of their own dead comrades lying in plain view. The Renegades didn't bother to carry their dead deeper inside their territory for burial.

Hangman could have understood that if the Renegades had been waging war against someone. They weren't. They captured this territory from the Godless long ago. No Godless had come back since then to challenge the Renegades for it.

The bodies were too recent to have fallen in those early skirmishes. Hangman didn't stop to check if these people fell to other human combatants or creatures attacking from the jungle. It could have been either.

Hangman motioned for his cousins to widen their formation so they wouldn't advance so closely together. He didn't want the Renegades to ambush the party.

The cousins advanced another fifty yards before Hangman heard voices ahead. He didn't recognize them.

He and his cousins slowed even more, stopped under a dense overhang of foliage, and peered through the leaves at a party of Renegade men standing around their makeshift camp.

The Renegades cut their hair short. No one in the Godless Clan wore short hair. Cutting someone's hair would have been something like torture to the Godless.

The Renegades' short hair gave them a ferocious look. Long hair had a way of softening and humanizing the Godless. It made them look more relatable—more like real people instead of enemies.

The Renegades wore full suits of clothing that covered their bodies. The Renegades wore a kind of sewn trousers over their legs and sleeveless vests that covered their chests.

Hangman never understood how the Renegades could stand to wear so many clothes in the jungle heat, but they all dressed the same way.

Hangman couldn't count the number of Renegades he'd killed in just the few years since he initiated as a man of the Godless Clan.

The Godless always had to fight the Renegades for something. The Renegades would have taken every square inch of Godless territory if the Godless didn't stop them.

Hangman and his cousins huddled in the shadows watching the Renegades move through their camp. They built much more elaborate, more permanent structures even though these men were only patrolling the area.

The Renegades built strong huts of straight tree branches lashed together into sturdy walls. The Renegades thatched their roofs with bundled grasses.

The construction of even one of these huts must have taken hours or maybe even days. Hangman only counted fifteen men down there with fifteen huts between them. Such a small patrol didn't justify that much work.

A Godless patrol this small might not even build shelters or fires to camp each night. The men usually just squatted in the trees and slept there.

Hangman waited until he saw Shadow, Cross, Feather, and Banjo advancing from the right. Butcher, Viking, and Vulture closed from the other side.

The Godless flanked the patrol on three sides. The Grey Ghost raised its foggy heights against the sky beyond this patrol's camp.

The Godless only had to take out this patrol. Then Hangman and his party would break through to the mountain with nothing and no one to stand in their way.

Hangman glanced left and right. Butcher nodded from the party on the left. Shadow nodded back from the right.

Hangman sprang out of his hiding place with his cousins right with him. The four men roared in fury, burst through the undergrowth making as much noise as possible, and charged down the hill raising their weapons to attack.

Their appearance gave the Renegades all the time they needed to grab their weapons and rush out to meet the attack.

Hangman didn't charge right into the Renegade camp. He could have run faster and gotten to the Renegade camp sooner, but he slowed down and let them come out to meet him. He didn't want to get caught between all those huts.

His cousins stayed with him. None of them broke away to run farther forward and no one fell behind.

The four cousins pretended to falter at the sight of so many Renegades responding to their assault. Hangman and his cousins drew to a halt outside the ring of huts.

The Renegades slowed, too. They advanced with their weapons draw. The Renegades used metal weapons—not that it made any difference.

Hangman tensed for the battle to close. He and his three cousins didn't stand a chance against fifteen Renegades. Everyone here knew it.

The Renegades grinned when they saw the odds in their favor. It made them overconfident.

They rushed in to attack. Hangman found himself surrounded by four Renegades all stabbing, hacking, and slashing at him.

He spun in all directions trying to deflect their strikes fast enough. He didn't have to defeat the Renegades. He just had to distract them and hold them here.

The minutes dragged by. Every second felt like an eternity.

Those four Renegades struck at him again and again. One of them sliced him across the side while his back was turned. If his father and Butcher didn't bring in the two flanks soon......

The Renegades fought silently. They clamped their mouths shut and narrowed their eyes in grim determination.

Hangman and his cousins yelled extra loudly to cover up their comrades' approach. Hangman got so focused on defending himself that he didn't see his relatives until it was already too late.

Shadow's group and Butcher's group timed their maneuver to close at the same moment. They flanked the Renegades from behind and from both sides at once.

The Renegades all spun around to face the new attack. That gave Hangman and his three cousins the chance they needed to strike back.

Hangman lashed out and cut down a heavy-set man on his left. The others tried to turn around and confront him a second time only for Shadow, Butcher, and their men to move in.

The situation disintegrated into a bloodbath with the Renegades trapped in the middle.

Vulture and Alien flanked the Renegade who injured Hangman. He rushed up behind the guy, chopped his kukri into the guy's skull, and took him down.

The Godless worked their way through the patrol with meticulous precision. Only eight Renegades remained.

They closed together into a huddle on the camp side of the battle. The Renegades backed together toward their huts.

The Godless advanced. Hangman opened his mouth to suggest that he and his cousins circle the enemy from the sides and behind to stop the Renegades from escaping.

They could have broken through the camp and run for it back to their own territory.

They could have alerted more Renegades farther to the rear that the Godless were trying to break through and penetrate Renegade territory.

He didn't get a chance to say anything before another squad of Renegades swept in from behind the camp. Hangman didn't see where these Renegades came from. They may have been out in the jungle doing something else until right this moment.

Their silence unnerved him, but not as much as their numbers. Forty of them rushed between the huts and overwhelmed the Godless in an instant.

Hangman couldn't decide who to fight first. So many Renegades rushed all around him. They attacked everyone, but they fought more chaotically than the first group.

Renegades attacked him only to run off as soon as he started fighting back. Renegades ran from Godless to Godless trying to fight everyone at once.

He retreated toward the trees where he and his cousins scouted this camp. He overtook Alien, Chaos, Vulture, and finally Shadow, Viking, and Banjo.

The Godless men closed together to defend themselves. Hangman searched everywhere for the rest of his relatives. He heard the sounds of combat in the distance, but he couldn't see Butcher, Cross, Fang, Boxer, or Magnet.

Two dozen Renegades followed the men out of the village to hunt the party down. None of Hangman's group could get back in there to find out what happened to the others.

Vulture tried to take a step forward to meet the enemy, but Shadow grabbed his arm and pulled him away.

"Fall back!" Shadow ordered. "Meet back up under the overhang! Go!"

Hangman turned away. He couldn't do anything here—not now.

His cousins backed off a few more feet, put some distance between themselves and the Renegades, and then broke and ran for it.

Chapter 8

Hangman pulled up short somewhere deep in the jungle. He couldn't even be sure where he was. He didn't know this territory.

This used to be Godless country before Hangman was born—before the Renegades crossed the Jagged Points and drove the Godless out.

He glanced around him and up at the trees just to make sure no creatures came after him, his father, and his cousins. Then Hangman finally let himself double over, prop his hands on his knees, and catch his breath.

Alien collapsed against a tree and slumped on the ground. "We have to go back," he husked. "We have to save them from the Renegades."

"Of course we have to go back," Shadow stifled a cough. "We have to rescue the others and we also have to get through the Grey Ghost."

"Is that wise?" Viking asked. "Butcher isn't here. You're Kral now."

"Butcher is still alive," Chaos pointed out. "No one else can be Kral as long as he's still alive."

"I'm flattered that you think of me that way," Shadow replied. "If I was Kral, I would make the same decision. We have to get through to at least one of the Jagged Points. We have to find out if these strange mountains are beyond them to the west. We won't know for certain unless we check. The Grey Ghost is the closest."

"We just have to get past the Renegades," Hangman panted. "What's so difficult about that?"

"Did you not see how many of them there are?" Banjo countered. "They overwhelmed us."

"Feather is over there," Alien snapped. "We're going back for him. I don't care if I have to go alone."

"We all have someone over there," Shadow murmured. "We won't leave any of them behind."

"They overwhelmed us because we didn't see them coming," Hangman pointed out. "We can overcome their numbers by changing our strategy. We can wipe them out to the last man. Then none of them will stop us from going up to the Grey Ghost and none of them will tell any other Renegades that we were here."

"How?" Viking asked. Then he glanced at Shadow. "I'm sorry, Uncle. I should have asked you."

"Go on and tell us your idea," Shadow told Hangman. "You seem to have already thought about this."

"Of course he has," Alien muttered. "He always does."

"The Renegades won't have gone far—not with prisoners," Hangman replied. "The Renegades will either stay in the same camp to find out why the Godless are in the area or else the Renegades will retreat to another camp to do the same thing. Six prisoners will slow them down no matter what they do. We can catch up with them and ambush them on the way—but not the way we did it just now."

"What other way is there?"

"We pick them off one at a time," Hangman replied. "We either wait for them to separate from the main group or else make noises in the jungle to lure the Renegades out of their camp. They won't all come. They'll leave men behind to guard the prisoners. We won't have to fight them more than two or three at a time."

"That's cowardice," Vulture pointed out. "Hitting a man from behind or without warning is the coward's way."

"I didn't say we would hit them from behind or without warning," Hangman replied. "I said we would lure them into the jungle one or two or three at a time. We can at least reduce their numbers. Then we won't have to face so many of them when it comes time to free the prisoners."

"It's a good plan," Alien interjected. "I like it."

"You always like Hangman's ideas," Banjo pointed out.

"That's because they're always good ideas," Alien countered. "He has a brain in his head—which is more than I can say for some people."

"That's enough discussion," Shadow cut in. "Let's go. We'll split up into three the way we did before. We'll flank the Renegade camp from three sides. If we see anyone isolated, we'll fight them and eliminate them. If not, we can make noise to alert them where we are. They'll go and check. We'll reduce their numbers until we can free the prisoners."

No one argued. Shadow was acting as Kral now.

Hangman would have gone with Chaos, but Alien collared Hangman instead. "You come with me, little brother."

"You always have a favorite, Alien," Banjo grumbled.

"You can come with us," Hangman pointed out. "There are seven of us. One group will have three."

"No," Alien snapped. "Let Vulture come with us instead."

Hangman glanced around the group. He half-expected his father to object, but Shadow was already walking away with Vulture.

Banjo shot Alien a glare and left with Viking instead. That left Chaos to come with Hangman and Alien.

Chaos was too easygoing to care who he went with. He bounced with a spring in his step when he followed Hangman and Alien back along the route they took to get here.

Hangman led the way to the same spot where he and his party attacked the Renegade camp the first time.

Alien had a hard time hiding his big body behind the curtain of foliage, but it didn't matter in the end.

The Renegades had tied up Butcher, Boxer, Magnet, Cross, Fang, and Feather. Renegades stood guard over the prisoners.

One big man kept kicking the prisoners one after the other and yelling at them. He kept demanding to know what the Godless were doing this far west in someone else's territory.

The other Renegades in the camp crowded around to watch. Some leaned against their huts. Others squatted nearby or just stood out in the open.

Hangman stiffened when the big Renegade kicked Cross. Cross winced from the blow, but he didn't cry out.

He huddled close to his bigger relatives, especially Feather and Magnet, but Cross didn't say a word. He was proving himself today even more than he did during his initiation.

Butcher glared at the Renegades in outright hatred. Fang stared off in the other direction. Did he even realize he was a prisoner?

Magnet and Feather roared at the Renegades every time that one man tried to confront them. Both Feather and Magnet struggled to break the ropes binding them.

The only prisoner in any danger of spilling the Godless' secret was Boxer. Even his younger brother Magnet turned out to be braver than Boxer.

The big Renegade worked his way through the group again. If he was half as smart as he was strong, he would quickly realize who was the weakest link.

The Renegades could have gotten more information out of Boxer if they only isolated him from his relatives.

The Renegades didn't think of that—or maybe they had orders from someone else not to separate the prisoners.

Everything Hangman suggested turned out to be true. Clusters of Renegades kept splitting away from the interrogation to patrol the camp.

Some of these patrollers went out into the jungle to make sure no dangerous creatures attacked while the Renegades were busy with their prisoners.

Hangman signaled his cousins. They crept through the undergrowth to the right to intercept one of the patrols.

The three cousins communicated using hand signals to separate and put distance between them.

The Godless didn't bushwhack their enemies. The Godless frowned on that as cowardly. The men had to do everything head-on.

It worked out for the best in the end. A Renegade patrol circled their camp and moved into the jungle to follow the sounds of warthogs rooting through the undergrowth.

Hangman, Alien, and Chaos cut across the Renegades' path. The Renegades fell right into the Godless' trap by staying close together.

The Renegades were too busy looking for stray warthogs. It took the Renegades way too long even to realize they were facing Godless invaders instead.

Hangman took out his kukri while he watched them come. He stood on Alien's left with Chaos on Alien's other side.

The Renegades almost blundered straight into the three men. The Renegades reared back in surprise. Then they had to scramble to draw their weapons and bring them up.

The Renegades' surprise played to the Godless' advantage. The three Renegades separated and came at the Godless one on one.

The biggest Renegade went after Alien, of course. The guy was big, but not as big as Alien.

The second biggest went after Chaos. The Renegade stood six inches taller and much bigger in the shoulders.

He misjudged Chaos, though. Chaos always stayed affable and laid back as in ordinary life with his relatives, but he could switch it off and became as bloodthirsty and ruthless as any man Hangman had ever met.

Chaos would have been one of the most dangerous men in the whole Clan if he had been any less outgoing. He also proved to be a much more agile and intelligent fighter than his adversary anticipated.

The guy rushed Chaos. The Renegade fought with two long, rectangular metal blades. He relied on his strength to overpower Chaos, but it backfired.

Chaos saw at first glance that he couldn't overcome the guy by brute force. That was never Chaos's game anyway.

He danced around the guy in blinding circles, forced the enemy to constantly whirl from one direction to another, and Chaos slashed and sliced his opponent again and again in all the most strategic places.

Blood drenched the guy within a few minutes. He staggered and missed his strikes more often and by a wider margin.

Hangman didn't see how that fight ended. The last Renegade was a smallish guy not much bigger than Hangman himself.

The guy was small enough to be quick and sharp. Hangman wouldn't be able to use speed, agility, or superior strategy against this man.

Hangman made up his mind and stepped forward to engage the guy. The Renegade sprang to his left and dove in to stab at Hangman's leg to cripple him.

Hangman didn't really care what the Renegade's first move was going to be. He waited for the man to act.

The guy never got a chance to recover from his first stroke before Hangman sprang forward, but he didn't engage his enemy.

Hangman leapt to a spot behind and to the guy's right, swung around, and chopped his kukri into the back of the guy's neck.

Chapter 9

Hangman's enemy Renegade hit the ground just as Alien overpowered his opponent. He brought his massive stone weapons down in a shattering blow that splintered his adversary's metal blades.

The blades crackled all the way down to their fancy hilts. Alien left the guy standing there holding nothing but the two handgrips.

The guy looked down at his handgrips and then up at Alien just as Alien stormed forward a second time.

Alien brought his kukris together in a punishing chop on either side of the big Renegade's head. The man went down hard.

Alien shot a scowl in Hangman's direction. Then both of them turned around to see Chaos finish his fight.

That was the moment when Hangman noticed movement from his left. He glanced that way for a split second and spotted four more Renegades coming closer.

The noise of fighting told these men exactly what was going on.

Hangman didn't wait for them to come. If the noise attracted these Renegades, it would attract others, too.

He raced between the trees and engaged with the Renegades right away. Alien followed him. Chaos showed up a second later. He must have just been toying with his adversary.

Now the three Godless men faced off against four Renegades instead of three.

The one good thing in all of this was that the Renegades fought silently. They didn't yell out in fury or alarm. They never made a sound all through the fight.

Hangman, Alien, and Chaos only had to keep quiet, too. No other Renegades would find out what was going on.

Hangman closed with the two Renegades on this end of the line. They tried to split apart to send two of their men after Alien. Alien's size fooled them. They never thought the smaller, younger men would be more dangerous.

Alien's sheer size, strength, and skill overwhelmed the Renegades soon enough. He didn't have to rely on his strength. He could fight just as well without it.

The other two went after Hangman and Chaos, but the fight against Alien distracted both of them.

Hangman's adversary tried to break away to go support his friends. A few seconds later, Chaos's opponent did exactly the same thing.

Hangman didn't go after his enemy—not yet. He stayed where he was and let the guy break off the skirmish. The guy rushed over to attack Alien—and Hangman struck without mercy.

He cut down his own adversary and then took out one of Alien's opponents. That left one for Alien and one for Chaos.

Hangman didn't wait around to help them. He already spotted another patrol coming—a bigger patrol.

The Renegades must have heard the noise from their camp. They sent out ten men this time—too many for Hangman and his cousins to handle on their own.

Hangman didn't know where the other Godless were in the jungle. Hangman wouldn't have called out to them for help even if he knew.

He, Alien, and Chaos had to handle this side of the camp. The three cousins had to make sure every Renegade who came over here met their end and never returned.

He rushed the ten Renegades, faked, and pretended to change his mind. He darted away into the trees, but the Renegades turned out to be faster and smarter than the jungle creatures Hangman usually fought.

The Renegades chased him down. He wove between trees, hurdled fallen obstacles, and would have run all the way back into the camp.

He dodged sideways, darted deeper into the jungle, and doubled back to meet up with his cousins.

His strategy worked. The Renegades ran after him trying to stop him from getting away. Then they widened their formation to cover more territory.

He kept veering this way and that until the Renegades separated enough. He spun around to confront those nearest them. That was the last thing they expected.

He charged two of them who hounded him right on his tail. He hacked one of them across the front of the neck. The other one pulled up short and Hangman cleaved the guy's skull down to the eyebrows.

Both bodies dropped and left the way clear for him to charge the other Renegades following in a messy line.

He met up with a single Renegade and chopped the guy's head clean off in one stroke.

The other Renegades realized their mistake and closed their formation to encircle him. He couldn't let that happen.

At that moment, he heard the sound of scratching in the jungle. He knew that sound.

He waited just long enough for the Renegades to gather into a tighter cluster. They all chased him from behind.

He headed straight for the sound. He even slowed down to make sure the Renegades caught up with him. He didn't want them to fall behind or leave him alone.

They closed the gap exactly the way he hoped they would. They actually sped up thinking they were about to catch him.

He dashed for the scratching sound, dove through another curtain of leafy vines, and burst out into a small clearing.

There was only room in the clearing for one creature. The Gurlg was an enormous bird-thing with long feathers on its wings, dirty brown downy fluff on its chest, and not much else.

It stood twice as tall as Hangman with thick, muscular legs and scratched its long claws in the dirt at the base of a tree. The creature uncovered grubs and worms, pecked them up, and spun around with a ferocious shriek when Hangman blundered into its clearing.

He was running too fast to stop. The Gurlg snapped its beak at him as he ran right into its face.

He took a running leap, grabbed the creature by the neck right behind its head, and the creature tossed its head in annoyance trying to get rid of him.

It flung its head back carrying him with it. He let go at the top of the arc, sailed clear, and flew off into a dense patch of canopy directly above the Gurlg and the Renegades.

He scrambled to turn over just as his pursuers blundered into the Gurlg's hunting grounds. The creature couldn't see anything else to attack, so of course it attacked the Renegades instead.

Hangman couldn't get comfortable here in the trees. He barely straightened himself out on the branches before he spotted a Krakelow coming for him. The commotion in the canopy must have attracted it.

This one came in just as fast.

He got a good look at this one in the light of day. He'd seen their gaping mouths, dripping fangs, and beady eyes every other day for as long as he could remember.

He couldn't fight this creature—not in the treetops. He wouldn't have been able to fight it on his own at all.

He jumped out of the canopy, grabbed another branch, and swung from branch to branch on his way to the ground. He let gravity take him, but the Krakelow picked up speed to match him.

He barely stayed ahead of it until he landed in another dense thicket thirty yards away from the Gurlg.

The noise of combat drifted out of the Gurlg's clearing. The Renegades must be fighting the creature.

Branches snapped above his head as the Krakelow smashed down through the trees falling from branch to branch.

He hit the ground and took off running, but it still wasn't enough. The Krakelow landed right behind him and sprang after him.

Its scratchy, dart-infested skin made a whipping noise when the creature coiled itself in rapid contortions, bounced off tree trunks, and used its scales to propel itself forward.

Hangman didn't have to turn around. His ears told him exactly how close the creature was to capturing him and taking him down.

He took off running back toward the Renegade camp. His only thought was to lead the Krakelow back to the camp and turn the creature loose on his enemies.

Then he remembered. There were Renegades running around out here in the jungle right this minute.

He swerved to his right and led the Krakelow straight into the Gurlg. Five Renegades fought the creature, but they were already starting to disengage and back away. They would escape any second now.

Hangman veered farther left, came up behind them, and the Gurlg looked up at him. The creature would attack him the minute he came within its range.

At that moment, he heard a different sound behind him. It wasn't the scratching of the Krakelow's scales against tree bark.

This sounded more like the whistle of fast-moving wind. The Krakelow was making its move.

The Renegades all saw and heard him coming. They turned around to face him.

He flung himself full length onto the ground and sprawled on his face right in front of them. The Krakelow sailed clear over his head and collided with the Renegades instead.

The Gurlg shrieked in fright, took wing, and launched into the canopy to get away from the Krakelow.

Hangman didn't wait around. He sprang to his feet and took off running back in the other direction toward the Renegade camp.

Chapter 10

Hangman forced himself to cower in the bushes and stifle his breathing while he peered out through the undergrowth toward the Renegade camp.

He had no idea what his father and cousins were doing out in the jungle, but Hangman's plan worked.

That big man who questioned the captive Godless must be the Renegade's leader—or at least the man in charge of this patrol.

He strode back and forth through the camp giving orders to everyone. He paced with his back to the prisoners.

He kept pointing to different areas of the jungle and sending out different groups of Renegades in different directions. Did he even realize this was exactly what the Godless wanted him to do?

How many Renegades could this man call on to come after the Godless? Hangman couldn't tell from here and he really didn't care.

The camp emptied out—at least as far as Hangman could tell. The big man kept five Renegades behind to guard the prisoners. He sent everyone else out to find Shadow's party.

The big man knew that more Godless were in the area. He wouldn't rest until he hunted them all down. That would be his fatal error—but not before Hangman rescued his people.

Cross sat between Feather and Magnet and stared at the ground in stoic silence. Hangman couldn't have felt prouder of his younger brother. Cross really belonged in the company of men after this ordeal.

Hangman couldn't wait for his pulse to slow down or his lungs to stop burning. He saw his opening—and he was alone. He didn't have to consult with anyone about what he was going to do.

He skirted the camp and made sure to avoid any other skirmishes between Godless and Renegades. He had more important things to do.

The noise in the jungle told him all he needed to know. His father and cousins were still locked in mortal combat against the Renegades out there. Hangman wouldn't find a more perfect time than now to free the prisoners.

He worked his way all the way around to the south side of the camp, darted out of the trees, and hid behind one of the huts.

That was one disadvantage of these huts. They were too solid. They did more than block fresh air from blowing through the interior. They stopped anyone from seeing a person sneaking up on the patrol.

He peeked out from behind the wall, made sure the Renegades were all facing the other way, and sprinted to another hut.

He didn't head straight for the captive Godless. That would have been too obvious.

He circled the group to the western side—the opposite side from where the Godless first approached this camp.

He hid behind another hut and then crept forward three more huts to position himself behind the prisoners. They didn't see him and neither did the Renegades.

Cross sat right in front of Hangman. Cross didn't look up when Hangman peeked out a second and third time. Hangman had to get his brother's attention somehow.

Hangman crouched in his hiding place and had to hide when one of the Renegades happened to cross the camp going in another direction.

Hangman slid one of his kukris back into his waistband and pulled out the knife from the horizontal sheath across his back. He didn't like parting with any weapon, but he would get it back as soon as he freed his relatives.

He waited for the Renegades to leave for the other side of the camp. The noise of combat escalated out there. Practically the whole surviving Renegade force must be out there now.

He hunkered down behind the same wall, put his knife on the ground, and slid it out across the ground so it came to rest right next to Cross's thigh.

He stared at it—and his eyes snapped up to meet Hangman's. Hangman showed himself just enough to let Cross know what was going on.

Cross's eyes went hard, but right then, a different Renegade came back. He would have seen the knife, but Cross moved his legs just enough to cover the weapon with his thigh.

His movements attracted Magnet's attention. He was a sturdy, methodical, intelligent man who somehow missed his older brother Boxer's sloppy tendencies.

Magnet wore his hair long, straight, loose, and simple. He always did his work reliably and well.

He never distinguished himself by any great feats of heroism or leadership. He didn't have to because he always did what was necessary for his Clan, his band, his Kral, and his family.

Hangman had to continually remind himself practically every day that he had no reason to hold it against Magnet that he was Butcher's son and Boxer's brother. None of that reflected badly on Magnet, but Hangman still had to stop himself from thinking that way.

Magnet's head snapped around. He scowled at Cross for squirming around.

Cross looked up, caught Magnet's eye, and moved his leg just enough to show Magnet the knife.

Magnet froze—and then his eyes snapped up to meet Cross's. Cross sliced his eyes toward the hut where Hangman was hiding. Magnet pretended to go back to facing front—and he saw Hangman, too.

Hangman showed himself just enough to motion Magnet toward himself. Magnet acknowledged the message by looking away. His face closed up in a scowl of determination. He didn't pay any attention when Cross started squirming around again.

He maneuvered his legs in a different direction, adjusted his weight on his seat, and used his new position to push the knife behind him.

He had to keep hitching himself up on one side or the other until he worked the knife all the way back behind himself and into his own bound hands.

Butcher barked at Cross to keep still. Cross stopped squirming. He didn't need to anymore. He had the knife.

Hangman's nerves threatened to snap while he waited for Cross to cut the ropes. Hangman had no idea how this was going to work with the Renegades standing guard.

In the worst scenario, Hangman could give Magnet or Feather one of his kukris—at least until he rearmed the rest of the captive Godless.

The party could attack the Renegades and fight them right here in the middle of the camp. The numbers would match up. It would have been a fair fight if the Godless had been armed.

Cross could use Hangman's knife—but it didn't work out that way in the end.

Cross's shoulders strained from the effort of cutting the ropes while he still had his hands bound behind him. Hangman didn't see what Cross did.

It all made sense when Magnet sat up and pulled his arms free. Cross must have been sitting in a position where he could cut Magnet's bonds before his own.

Magnet glanced up at the Renegades, but right then, another five Renegades came back into the camp from the east—where the Godless were out there killing everyone.

These five gathered around their leader and held a quick conference. The other Renegades who should have been guarding the prisoners also gathered around to listen.

The five patrollers pointed behind them up the hill toward the jungle.

The noise up there sounded like a lot more than combat. It sounded like a bunch of men locked in battle against a Krakelow—or maybe more than one Krakelow.

Hangman could only hope the Krakelows were fighting Renegades instead of Godless.

He knew what he had to do either way. The big Renegade leader directed another five of his men to stay behind and guard the prisoners he still thought were bound and helpless.

Then the leader and all the rest of his men went up there to check out the situation.

Hangman saw his chance, skirted the hut, and came out on its other side. The five men standing guard barely looked at the prisoners.

The Renegades all faced eastward and stared up the hill listening. They followed the battle with their ears.

Hangman didn't hear any men yelling out there—which they would have been if Godless warriors had been fighting Krakelows.

He heard a lot of crashing around, but he didn't hear any voices. The Renegades must be up there.

Shadow and the others should stay out of it and let the Krakelows do their work for them if they were smart.

Hangman didn't wait for a better opportunity. He charged out from behind the hut and rushed the Renegades from that side.

They turned to face him just fast enough for him to attack without completely losing his honor as a warrior.

The first man raised his weapon, but not fast enough. Hangman struck his kukri across the guy's face, shattered his skull, and engaged the second man before any of the others realized what was happening.

Magnet launched to his feet in a split second. He was still unarmed, but he must have connected the dots while he was sitting there with his arms tied behind his back.

He shot upright so fast that he distracted the other Renegades who had been about to overwhelm Hangman.

Hangman raised his kukris to block the second attacker's blade. Magnet charged, collided with two of the remaining Renegades, and barreled them into their third companion.

The whole cluster went down in a ball of tangled limbs. Hangman was too busy fighting that one guy to help Magnet or anyone else.

Hangman caught a glimpse out of his peripheral vision of Cross pivoting onto his knees, turning around, and working fast to cut his fellow prisoners free.

He knew exactly which order to free them. He started with Feather, then Boxer, and then Butcher. Cross freed Fang last.

Magnet rolled onto his feet holding one of the Renegade's weapons. He spun around to attack his enemies, but there were too many of them. They overwhelmed him in seconds.

They would have cut him down, but Feather showed up first and snatched the weapon from the fallen Renegade that Hangman first killed.

Feather charged over to Magnet and chopped one of the Renegades down while the man still grappled with Magnet.

That left three. Hangman used one of his kukris to hold his enemy's weapon overhead, pulled back, and stabbed his other kukri under the guy's ribs.

His enemy folded and the rest of the Godless overcame the final two Renegades easily.

"This way!" Hangman waved his people toward the south—back in the direction he came to get here.

The others raced after him and the party dove into the trees where any returning Renegades couldn't see them.

"Stay here!" Hangman whispered. "The Renegades will expect you to head back toward the east to rejoin the others."

"We should rejoin them," Butcher pointed out. "We should help them annihilate these Renegades the way we said we would."

"There's a better way," Hangman breathed. "The Renegades won't rejoin before they return to the camp. They won't combine into one fighting force. We can hit them as they return—but we have to be stealthy."

"What about the others?" Boxer asked. "Your father is out there. Would you abandon him to the Renegades?"

"I'm not abandoning anyone. Father and the others won't be able to kill all the Renegades. Any that survive will retreat to the camp. Then we can finish the job."

"Tell us what to do," Magnet replied. "We need more weapons."

"We can go out there, take the dead Renegades' remaining weapons, and take positions behind the huts the way I did." Hangman turned to Butcher. "If you agree, of course, Uncle."

Butcher nodded. He learned a long time ago to let others do his thinking for him. "It's a good plan."

Cross held out the knife. "Here. Take this."

"The Renegades put our weapons in that hut over there." Feather pointed across the camp to one of the huts on the far western edge.

"Good," Butcher decided. "We'll take those first and then find our positions. Let's go."

Hangman stood back and let his uncle take charge. The others followed his instructions to the letter, retrieved their weapons from that hut, and spread through the camp to take sheltered hiding places behind the huts.

They barely got into place before fifteen Renegades came running back with all the other Godless in pursuit.

It took Hangman and his party a minute to realize what was happening. The Renegades all fled westward. Pieces of Krakelows still clung to the Renegades' limbs.

Hangman sprang out of hiding and planted himself in the Renegades' path. Butcher and the others joined him a minute later.

They closed the Renegades between themselves and pursuers. The Renegades tried to flee to either side, but the Godless turned the tables and slaughtered all the remaining Renegades in a few minutes.

Chapter 11

"Spread out and head up to the Grey Ghost," Butcher ordered. "We need to survey the west country and retreat into our own territory before any more Renegades come over here and find out what's happening."

"Wait a minute, Uncle," Viking panted. "Vulture is injured. He won't be able to climb all that way."

"I'll stay with him," Hangman offered. "I'll take him out to the jungle and wait for you to return."

Butcher nodded, pulled the pictures out of his bag, and spread them on the ground. "Look for these peaks while you're up there. Look for anything that might resemble these lines of mountains—and look for any sign of the weapons. These flat sections of stone should be visible from a distance."

He pointed out huge perfectly flat expanses of hardened stone underneath the strange weapons. Hangman didn't see how any stone could be that big and flat.

Butcher was right, though. The area covered a massive valley between the mountains. If the area was anywhere beyond the western mountains, the Godless would have been able to see it easily from the top of the Jagged Points.

Then again, the area and the mountains in question might not be in the west country at all.

The party split up. Butcher put his pictures away, gave orders to the other men, and they left the Renegade camp on their way west.

Hangman turned his attention to Vulture. He looked like he might have gotten into a fight against another Gurlg. The wound in his leg didn't look clean enough to have been made by a blade, especially not one of the Renegade's metal blades.

Hangman didn't ask. He tore off some of the dead Renegades' clothes, bound the skins tightly around the wound, got under his bigger cousin's arm, and helped Vulture hobble up the hill into the trees.

Vulture winced a lot, but he kept his mouth shut and didn't complain. He gasped in pain when Hangman lowered him to the ground under a tree where no one from the Renegade camp would be able to see them.

"Stay here," Hangman murmured. "I'll get you some water and some leaves to make the paste."

Vulture only nodded. He wouldn't be able to leave even if he wanted to.

Hangman returned to the camp—or he tried to. A small stream ran behind the camp on the west side. That was the closest water source. The Renegades must have chosen this spot for that reason.

He made it as far as the fringe of trees and almost walked out into the open before he saw movement at the edge of the camp.

He crouched in the shadows and watched four Renegades hiding in a clump of bushes on the north side of the camp. The Godless didn't see these last remaining Renegades from the camp, but Hangman saw them from the hilltop.

They hid close enough to see and hear every word Butcher just said to his men. The Renegades pointed up the western mountains where the Godless just passed out of sight.

Hangman's brain went into a tailspin. Those Renegades knew about the Godless now.

Those men knew the Godless attacked this camp. They knew the Godless were scouting the west country for some kind of weapons.

The Renegades also knew which mountains and features the Godless were looking for.

Hangman realized the truth in a heartbeat. He had to eliminate these Renegades at all costs. He couldn't let them make it back to their own people with this information.

The Godless hoped to use these weapons against the Renegades. It would be catastrophic if the Renegades found the weapons first.

The Renegades had all the advantage on their side. They controlled all the country to the west.

The weapons could be right there inside Renegade territory—right where the Renegades would be able to use these weapons against the Godless instead of the other way around.

Hangman couldn't let that happen. He considered going back to Vulture and explaining the problem to him, but Hangman didn't have time for that.

The Renegades pulled back from their position and headed west to follow the Godless. They would overtake his relatives and probably spring a surprise attack on the Godless from behind.

That would never happen because Hangman would get to the Renegades first. He would pull the same maneuver, isolate them in the jungle, and cut them down before his relatives even knew the Renegades were there.

He set off through the undergrowth to catch up with them. He had to move fast, but he also had to make sure not to give himself away.

He came to a rough patch of ground, scaled a tree, and traveled much faster through the canopy. He balanced along branches and used their springy bounce to jump to new branches.

The canopy got so thick that it gave him plenty of branches to hold onto with his hands. He could get closer to the Renegades like this without them detecting that he was following them.

They made it easier for him by creeping along more slowly. They didn't want to alert the Godless to their presence.

He came in sight of them and measured how to attack them. He was still following them when he noticed a pack of Abnormits on a nearby tree.

Each of these large insects was as big as he was. The Abnormits scuttled along the ground on six jointed legs attached to a horizontal, cylindrical body.

Their heads blended in with the rest of their bodies except for long feelers waving and undulating from their heads.

He had to climb out of the branches to avoid them, but it was too late. They picked up his scent and started dropping to the ground all around him.

Their armored bodies thumped into the dirt, the Abnormits flailed their jointed limbs to turn themselves over, and they all scurried after him trying to catch him.

He made a snap decision, took off running for the Renegades, and drew his weapons before he came insight of them. They wouldn't be able to go near the Godless with a bunch of Abnormits trying to get them.

The Abnormits could run faster than Hangman could. They closed the gap and would have devoured him if not for the Renegades.

They heard him coming and turned around to confront him. They might even have heard the Abnormits' feet rushing through the leaf litter.

He raised his kukris above his head, bellowed at the top of his lungs, and charged attack with his weapons.

The Renegades saw him first, closed ranks to meet him—and then they saw the Abnormits. The Renegades all pivoted away from Hangman to confront the creatures. It was too late to run.

He took advantage of the Renegades' surprise, hacked one of them through the neck, and kept on running.

The oncoming Abnormits swarmed the Renegades. Two of them actually did scream as the creatures pulled the men to the ground.

Hangman sprang back into the branches of a low-growing tree and scrambled back into the canopy.

It was all over except for the munching and crunching sounds drifting up from below. He watched for a minute, but there was nothing left of the Renegades.

The Abnormits devoured everything, including bones, clothing, and hair. The insects eventually crawled away into the jungle leaving only the Renegades' weapons lying on the ground.

Chapter 12

Hangman squatted down next to Vulture, dropped four metal blades on the ground, and handed Vulture a gourd carved into a water flask. "Drink some. I'll use the rest on your leg."

Vulture raised his eyebrows at the weapons. "Where have you been? I heard screaming."

Hangman looked away. "I told you. I got the water and I gathered leaves for the paste."

Vulture snorted and tipped up the gourd. "You're a terrible liar, brother."

Hangman rummaged in his bag and pulled out a wooden bowl he used for eating. "As soon as we treat your leg, we should withdraw to Godless territory. It will take you extra time to travel. We shouldn't wait for the others to return."

"You said you would meet up with them," Vulture pointed out.

"We will meet up with them. We just won't do it here." Hangman nodded at the gourd. "Are you done? I can get more if you need it. There's a stream just there beyond the Renegade camp."

Vulture handed the gourd back. "I'll only slow you down. I shouldn't have gotten hurt."

"Everyone gets hurt. It's no one's fault." Hangman untied the wrap around Vulture's leg. "This looks ragged. How did you get it? It couldn't have been made by a Renegade weapon."

"It wasn't the Renegades," Vulture grumbled. "One of them came at me with part of a Krakelow wrapped around his face. I couldn't even see the fool's face behind the fragment. He came straight at me and I stumbled back to get away from him. I tripped over a fallen branch and slashed my leg on a crack in the wood."

Hangman looked up and then snorted with laughter. "Don't tell anyone else how it happened."

"I wasn't planning to."

Hangman couldn't stop laughing. He shouldn't laugh at his cousin's misfortune. Hangman just wished he had been there to see it.

"Go on and laugh," Vulture snapped. "Enjoy yourself while you can."

Hangman chuckled. "At least the women will still like you for your looks. You have nothing to complain about."

Vulture humphed under his breath. "A lot of good that will do me."

Hangman let it go and got to work grinding the leaf paste. He smeared a thick covering on the wound and rewrapped it much tighter this time. "That will hold it closed so it seals."

"Thank you, brother," Vulture muttered. "You didn't have to stay behind."

"Someone had to. We couldn't leave you to the ants, could we?"

Vulture looked away. "Someone else could have stayed. You should have gone with them. Butcher needs you more than he needs Boxer or Fang."

Hangman didn't answer. He wouldn't have seen those Renegades sneaking around if he went with Butcher to the Grey Ghost.

Hangman packed up his goods. He hung the four Renegade weapons from the strap of one of his bags.

He couldn't explain to himself why he wanted the weapons. He wouldn't be able to use them while he was carrying his kukris.

He didn't even want to use them. He preferred his kukris. He just didn't want to discard these weapons—not yet.

"Get up," he told Vulture. "Let's get going before the sun goes down."

He got under his cousin's arm again. Vulture did his best to keep up the pace, but he couldn't walk fast.

They covered only a few miles before Vulture's one good leg started to give out. He trembled in Hangman's arms.

Hangman lowered him to the ground again. Vulture collapsed shaking and sweating against another tree trunk. He didn't open his eyes.

Hangman knew the signs only too well. He laid his hand on Vulture's thigh above the wound. The skin already felt hot. Redness spread outward from the wound. It was getting infected.

Hangman surveyed the surrounding jungle and canopy. Predators would come for Vulture. Hangman had to do something, but he didn't trust leaving Vulture on the ground.

Vulture brought Hangman back from his thoughts. "You should go on," Vulture husked. "Leave me here."

"I don't think so. Come on. I'll carry you."

Hangman stood up and took hold of Vulture's wrist. Vulture groaned in agony for the first time when Hangman hauled his cousin back onto his one good leg.

Vulture could barely hold himself up. He wouldn't last ten minutes out here alone.

Hangman didn't explain what he was going to do. He slung Vulture over his shoulder and climbed into the branches again.

Hangman couldn't move fast with all this extra weight, but that didn't matter. Vulture was too good a warrior and too smart to sacrifice him over a stupid, careless wound like this.

Hangman climbed all the way up into the canopy, but he wouldn't be able to leave Vulture unattended for long. Night was coming. Predators could find him in the trees as well as they could find him on the ground.

Hangman propped Vulture into the crotch of three trees growing too closely together. Their limbs made a cradle that supported Vulture's body even when he couldn't sit upright on his own.

Hangman left Vulture there and balanced out into the canopy. Hangman had to work fast, but at least he could move freely now.

He found a different tree, stripped the leaves off, carried them back to Vulture, and Hangman stuffed the leaves into his own mouth.

They tasted absolutely putrid when he chewed them up. He fought down nausea until he spat the rancid mass back into his hand. It smelled as bad as it looked. He spat into his hand again and again, but the taste didn't go away.

He got busy rubbing the stinking mass of chewed leaves all over Vulture's face, back, chest, arms, and down his legs.

Hangman took extra pains to rub the stuff over the bandage wrapped around Vulture's injured leg.

The leaf smell wouldn't hide Vulture completely, but the smell would repel enough creatures at a distance to buy Vulture a little extra time—just long enough for Hangman to hopefully save his life.

Hangman scraped the last of the leaf goo off his hands and even dragged his tongue over the tree bark to try to get the taste out of his mouth. It didn't work very well, but it was better than nothing.

He finally gave it up, left Vulture there, and went back out into the canopy.

He had to search a lot longer and a lot harder this time before he found what he wanted. The gathering darkness didn't help, but he already knew what he was looking for.

He spotted another pack of Abnormits scuttling up and down a certain tree. Hangman squatted in the branches and watched them before he decided how to get rid of them.

He waited until another Gurlg landed nearby. Hangman climbed through the branches and came out in a different tree above the Gurlg's head.

The creature saw him, which was exactly what Hangman wanted. He descended close enough for the creature to screech at him and dive to try to bite him.

Hangman took one of the Renegade weapons from his bag strap. This one had a longer, thinner blade than his kukri.

The Gurlg dove for him again and again. He jabbed the weapon into its face to antagonize it. It screeched louder and pumped its wings as its temper rose.

He poked it under the chin and then in the cheek to infuriate it. The Gurlg eventually lost its composure entirely, lunged to snap him off the branch, and Hangman struck out with his weapon.

He chopped the Gurlg across the neck straight through the large blood vessels on the right side.

The blade stuck into the creature's spinal column and reared away bellowing and shrieking. Blood spurted from the wound. Hangman didn't even try to keep his hold on the weapon.

He let it go down with the Gurlg. The body landed on the ground with a deep thump.

The vibrations attracted the Abnormits. They scurried to the ground, discovered the Gurlg, and started feasting.

That left the tree bare. Hangman climbed up it and used his knife to scrap off a bunch of dried sap that oozed from the bark.

He carefully folded a large portion of the sap into a piece of cured hide from his bag. Then he took the sap back to Vulture.

He was still out cold in the branches. Hangman didn't see or hear any dangerous creatures around, so Vulture was as safe now as he was likely to get.

Hangman couldn't say the same thing about himself. He descended to the ground, built a fire, and put some rocks in the coals to heat them. He needed to boil water to make medicine for Vulture.

The process took a long time. Hangman had to constantly fight his patience under control. The longer this took, the less likely Vulture would be to recover.

That didn't matter because this was the only way to save Vulture's life. Hangman had to go through every step of the process carefully and exactly. The medicine wouldn't work otherwise.

He carved out a much larger bowl while he waited for the rocks to heat. He filled the bowl with water, sprinkled his sap dust into it, and then added the rocks to bring the water to a boil.

Then he had to wait for the mixture to cool enough before he gave it to Vulture. Hangman was still sitting there when Butcher, Shadow, and the others returned.

Butcher frowned at Hangman. "What is going on? We heard screaming. We thought you were in danger."

"I'm fine, Uncle. I was just making Gooji juice for Vulture."

"Where is he?" Viking asked. "Is he dead?"

"I wouldn't be making Gooji juice for him if he was." Hangman pointed up at the sky. "He's in the trees covered in monk's leaf juice. He's perfectly safe—apart from the infection in his leg." He stuck his finger into the Gooji juice. "This is ready. I'll go get him."

Hangman tried not to notice his relatives exchanging glances when he climbed into the trees and vanished into the dark.

He found his way by smell to Vulture's tree, pried his cousin out of the branches, and carried him down to the fire.

Vulture groaned louder this time when Hangman tried to sit him up. Vulture's eyes glazed over. He didn't respond and his limbs flopped everywhere Hangman tried to move him.

"Chaos—help me sit him up," Hangman called over his shoulder.

Chaos got on Vulture's other side. He and Hangman held Vulture in a sitting position. Viking came over, grabbed a fistful of Vulture's long braids, and pried Vulture's head up so Hangman could pour the Gooji juice down Vulture's throat.

He choked on it and almost spat it out before Viking clamped his hand over Vulture's mouth to hold his lips shut.

"Swallow it, boy!" Viking snapped. "Swallow all of it. Don't waste it."

Vulture gasped out and started howling in agony when Viking took his hand away.

Viking didn't let up. He grabbed Vulture by the jaw and pried his mouth open so Hangman could dump in the next dose. Then Viking held Vulture's mouth shut a second time.

They repeated the process five times before they let him sink back against a bank and rest. He whimpered in his sleep and immediately passed out again.

The other men settled down after the procedure. Chaos shared his food with Hangman.

"What did you find up on the mountain?" Hangman asked. "What did you see?"

"Nothing," Chaos replied. "There's nothing over there but hundreds of miles of jungle. We didn't even see any mountains."

"We haven't searched to the south," Hangman pointed out. "That's the one place we haven't searched."

"We can't search to the south," Shadow replied. "There are too many other Clans down there. We would have to trespass on their territory and potentially start a war we can't win."

Hangman didn't answer. He already knew that. He just hated to give up on a weapon that could stop the Renegade Clan from encroaching any further into Godless territory.

He pushed that thought away. The Godless wouldn't be able to use those weapons against anyone even if the band found them. The Godless didn't know how to use the weapons at all.

Chapter 13

Hangman bent over a stream, washed the monk's leaf juice off his hands, rinsed out his mouth, and washed his face, neck, and chest.

He was still squatting there enjoying the rare sensation of cool on his skin when Viking came down the bank toward him.

Viking squatted down next to Hangman and cupped some water into his mouth. "Vulture just woke up. The heat is down in his leg. Thank you for saving my brother."

"Of course," Hangman exclaimed. "I wouldn't let him die. He's too good a man to lose."

Viking cocked his eyebrow and studied Hangman on the side. "You'll be Kral one day. You're too smart and skilled not to be."

Hangman looked away. "I will never be Kral. Boxer will become Kral after Butcher. Even Magnet has a better chance of becoming Kral than I do."

"Boxer will never become Kral," Viking snarled. "The men wouldn't take him."

"It doesn't matter because too many people are in line before me. I'm the youngest man here apart from Cross. The men wouldn't take me, either."

"You're wrong, brother," Viking returned. "The men would more likely take you than Boxer, Magnet, or maybe even Shadow. Everyone respects you."

"If they respect me, that's the best I can hope for as a warrior of our Clan." Hangman looked up. "What is Butcher's plan, now that we know the weapons aren't in the west country?"

"Butcher doesn't make plans. He waits to hear what you and Shadow say."

Hangman tried not to grin. "Then what is Shadow's plan?"

Viking pierced him with an unwavering stare. "What is *your* plan, little brother?"

"I don't have plans. I follow my Kral's orders."

Viking snorted. "Please. Don't insult me. All right. If that's the way you want it, what would your plan be if you were Kral in place of Butcher and Shadow?"

Hangman looked down at his hands. He shouldn't let his cousin's flattery tempt him into voicing his opinion, not even between themselves.

He found it impossible not to dwell on the weapons. His mind wandered in quiet moments and came up with strategies to get the weapons the Godless needed to use against the Renegades.

He lowered his voice before he spoke. He didn't want anyone else to hear him contradict his father's and uncle's decisions.

"We've searched the west and the east country. That leaves the south and the north."

"We already know these mountains don't exist in the north," Viking pointed out.

"I know," Hangman murmured. "That leaves the south and Uncle already decided against that."

"Would you go to the south if you were Kral?" Viking asked.

Hangman shrugged. "I don't know because I'm not Kral. I might decide it was worth the risk if I was responsible for all the lives the Renegades would cost if they invaded. They might yet invade and then it might be necessary to go south anyway." He shook that off. "I don't know what I would do because I'm not Kral and I'm not responsible for all those people. There is no point in talking about it."

Viking frowned down at the water. "You may have a point. At any rate, we'll be going south soon anyway."

"Not far enough. We would have to go farther south than we've ever been. We would already know about these mountains if they were anywhere to the south we've already been."

Viking clasped Hangman's shoulder and stood up. "Come back to the camp and see Vulture, little brother. He wants to thank you himself."

Viking climbed the bank on his way back to the camp. Hangman stayed where he was. He didn't want Vulture thanking him—or Fang thanking him—or Chaos thanking him—or any of the others thanking him for saving Vulture—as if Hangman would have done anything else.

He splashed some more water on his face. Butcher wouldn't decide anything today apart from returning to Godless territory so the party could meet up with the rest of their band.

The party accomplished their objectives for this trip. Cross had completed his initiation and the men had climbed the Jagged Points to scout the west country.

The Godless didn't need to stay here anymore. It was too close to Renegade territory. There were no more benefits that could possibly justify the risks.

He didn't feel like going back yet. Life felt so much less complicated when he went out into the jungle by himself.

He didn't have to worry about consulting anyone or letting them make decisions for him. He could trust his own judgment about what risks to take, what was important enough for him to do, and how to do it.

He lingered by the stream and used the time to listen to the jungle noises. Everything sounded peaceful—as peaceful as it could be as long as he considered the sounds of hunting, capturing, and eating normal.

None of the dangerous species came after him. He could take his time and catch up with his relatives later.

They knew him well enough not to wait for him. He went off by himself often enough.

No one expected him to act like the other men of his band. He seemed to be on a completely different path than every other man he'd ever known.

Everyone he knew seemed to accept the same thing about him. The scars on his face only confirmed in everyone's minds that he was different. The rules didn't apply to him unless he applied them to himself.

He eventually got to his feet, but he still didn't feel like going back—not yet. He didn't want Fang and his sons to make a fuss about Hangman saving Vulture.

Hangman hung his bags across his chest and climbed into the canopy, but he didn't go in the direction of his relatives' camp. He went the opposite way—back toward the west.

He shouldn't have. He didn't really think about where he was going. He just wanted to wander by himself until he absolutely had to go back.

He would have liked to skip all the weeping and crying his mother, aunts, and female cousins would do when Cross went home.

Then there would be the days of sitting around the camp with nothing to do until Butcher decided on the band's next move.

Hangman stopped in another fork between trees. He settled himself in the crotch and took some of the dried Gorlock meat out of his bag. He didn't mind sitting around with nothing to do as long as he did it out in the jungle by himself.

He sometimes wondered in these peaceful moments if it wouldn't be better if he didn't belong to a Clan at all. His life would be simpler if he did everything by himself without relying on others to make decisions for him.

He didn't agree with very many decisions his father and Butcher made. They had to consider a thousand other factors besides whether a certain decision was actually the best one.

Hangman found it impossible not to second-guess almost every decision they made simply because he wasn't the one making it.

He always made sure to do his second-guessing silently. He never raised any outright objections. That would constitute betrayal of his Kral—not to mention a grave insult to his father.

No one could survive in this jungle without a Clan. Hangman would have died the night of the Krakelow attack if Viking hadn't chopped those coils off him. Things like that happened all the time.

It just happened by coincidence that Hangman was the one to save Vulture last night. It could just as easily have gone the other way. Then Hangman would be the one thanking whoever saved him.

He eventually sighed and stood up to leave the area. He would always belong to a Clan. There was no other way around it.

Besides, his Clan needed him. He wouldn't leave his mother, younger brothers, female relatives, and all the children unprotected.

The Clan needed every able-bodied man to work together to defend the band. That was Hangman's only real consideration at this point.

He turned away and grabbed the nearest branch to travel back toward the east to meet up with the others.

That was the moment when he heard voices in the distance. They were coming from farther west.

No one should have been over there. The Godless definitely weren't over there. Only one group of people could be coming from the west—the Renegade Clan.

Chapter 14

Hangman crept through the branches and crouched unseen where he could observe a different party of Renegades.

Ten of them stood around a clearing while they talked and pointed at the ground. Did they find traces of Hangman, Vulture, or any other Godless? He couldn't hear the Renegades' conversation from here to find out.

He could have slipped away unseen, but this new party gave him an idea.

The Godless would have to search Renegade territory for years to find out if the weapons were there, but they didn't have to. The Renegades knew more about their own territory than the Godless could ever learn in their lifetimes.

He decided to play a trick on them and retraced his steps along the same route through the trees. He returned to the spot where he and the others camped last night. His cousins, uncles, father, and brother were all long gone.

Hangman stashed his kukris and his knife in the hollow of a rotten tree. He took the three remaining Renegade weapons with him and hung them from his waistband as if he carried them that way all the time.

He headed back the way he came toward where he would find the Renegade party. He kept going until he heard their voices.

He swerved sideways, let his vision slip out of focus, and staggered from right to left in a drunken stupor. He even collided with tree trunks, tripped over things, and crashed into piles of leaves and dry branches.

He made as much noise as possible, blundered to his feet, and stumbled on. He barged through the undergrowth, snapped twigs, and startled birds and insects in the jungle.

His behavior alerted the Renegades long before he got near them. He kept weaving, stumbling, and changing his course.

He didn't let himself focus his eyes even to see how close he was getting to them. He fell over again and scrambled to get up.

The Renegades overtook him before he got off his hands and knees. One of them kicked him over onto his back. He tumbled sideways and sprawled before they pounced on him and pinned him down again.

He looked around in bleary confusion. "Cosmos....?" he husked. "Breaker.....? Are you there?"

"Who's Cosmos?" one of the Renegades snapped. "What are you doing here?"

Hangman looked off in the other direction. "Nothos? Where's Nothos?"

"He's out of his mind," another Renegade snarled.

"Hey! I'm talking to you!" The nearest man jammed his foot down on Hangman's chest and flattened him. "What are you doing out here? Do you belong to that party of Godless that came through here last night?"

Hangman looked up at the guy, but Hangman kept his vision blurry. "The flats.....the flat place of stone.....between the mountains......"

"He's delirious," the second Renegade went on. "Leave him alone. He's probably dying."

"He can tell us what the Godless are doing." The first man bent over, grabbed Hangman by his shoulders, and shook him. "Hey!! Who are you? Where did you come from?"

"Gotta find it....." Hangman croaked. "Gotta find....the flat....stone....place...... between the mountains......"

"What flat stone place?" the fourth man asked. "The mountains could be anywhere."

"Valley.....of stone......"

The first man threw Hangman down on the ground and smacked his lips in annoyance. "He can't tell us anything."

Hangman pretended to look around. "Cosmos? Nothos? I can't see you! Where are you?"

"What do we do with him?" a different man asked.

"We don't do anything with him," the first one decided. "He's useless to us."

"So we just have to leave him here?" the second one asked. "We should take him back to Akon. This deadbeat might revive. Then Akon could interrogate him."

"I'm not dragging some semi-conscious Godless freak halfway across the countryside for nothing." The first man bent over and shook Hangman harder. "Hey! Where did you come from?"

Hangman dragged his eyes up and went through a torturous effort to focus his eyes. "Take me there....." he croaked. "Take me.......to the flat stone......between the mountains......with the ancient relics......"

"What in the name of all that's holy is he talking about?" the third man muttered. "What flat stone place? There is no flat stone place—not anything as big as a valley."

Hangman didn't need to hear anything else. He sank back on the ground and let his head loll.

"Hey—Godless!" The first man kicked Hangman hard in the ribs and then jabbed him with something sharp. "Pay attention and tell me which band you belong to! What are your people doing this far out of your territory?"

The pain of the stab made Hangman startle even though he didn't mean to. He planned to pretend to be completely unconscious.

He spun around and roared at his attacker louder than he should have. The Renegade stood over him holding one of their metal weapons.

He stabbed Hangman in the leg. The same man was in the act of raising his weapon again to stab Hangman either in the chest or the stomach.

Hangman overreacted, but he couldn't let these Renegades injure him more than he already was. He swung out and smacked the weapon away before the guy could strike.

Hangman realized his mistake and collapsed back on the ground, but he couldn't stay here any longer. He already knew what he came here to find out.

The Renegades didn't know about the valley of the flat stone. They definitely would have known about that if it was anywhere in their territory.

The first guy corrected and brought his weapon around, but he didn't raise it to strike again. Hangman rolled onto his knees, blundered to his feet, and took off staggering farther west.

He was going in the opposite direction from where he wanted to go, but his ploy worked. The Renegades didn't know about the valley of flat stone or the weapons.

The Renegades followed him. "Where do you think he's going?" the third one asked.

"He's heading for Renegade territory," the fourth one remarked.

"That proves he's out of his mind," the first one added. "He doesn't know where he is or where he's going. That's why he keeps calling out for those other people. They must be other Godless."

"Then we have to question him," the second one insisted. "Or we have to let Akon question him. If one Godless is venturing into our territory, others might be doing the same thing."

"Look at him!" the first man countered. "Does he look like he's with anyone or planning anything? He's lost and insane. He probably just stumbled here......"

"It's too far away from everything," the second man pointed out. "One of the creatures would have munched him long ago if he was just stumbling around and falling all over the place."

The first man stopped and stared at Hangman's back. The four Renegades halted there to consider the situation.

"You're right," the first man muttered. "It's suspicious."

"Come on," the second one murmured. "Let's restrain him and see if we can find out what he knows. He must know something."

He heard them coming up behind him. He couldn't let them restrain him or interrogate him. He reacted again without thinking.

He spun around at the last second and grabbed the first man as the Renegade extended his hands to take hold of Hangman.

Hangman wheeled too fast for the others to see him coming. He snapped the guy's neck and let the body fall right there on the ground. That left three.

They weren't prepared for him to suddenly come out of his stupor so fast. His trick worked better than he expected.

None of them had a chance to draw their weapons. Neither did he, so he used the next best thing.

The other three Renegades hesitated when they saw their friend fall. Hangman took advantage of that moment, seized the second man by the shirt, and shoved his head into the opening of a different hollow tree.

Larval Abnormits squirmed around in there. Each one was as big as Hangman's thumb.

He squashed the guy's face down into the nest of larvae. They started gnawing at him and he screamed out. He reared away and pulled his head free, but not before a dozen larvae stuck to his face.

They started chewing into his eyes and cheeks. He clawed trying to get them off, but they squirmed out of his way and burrowed right into his flesh.

His screams snapped the last two Renegades out of their trance. They rushed Hangman, now that they saw him fully alert and standing up straight in front of them.

One of them hacked his blade at Hangman's head. He dodged out of the way and the blade thunked into the trunk behind him.

The wood cracked and thousands of larval Abnormits poured from the fissure. They covered the ground in a sea of white.

Hangman tried to spring away, but they washed around his legs, crawled up him, and chewed their way into his thighs.

The larvae surrounded the last remaining Renegades. They forgot about him completely and started scraping their blades across their legs trying to get the larvae off.

The Renegades' efforts only exposed them to more larvae squirming and crawling all over the ground around their ankles. The two men completely forgot to try to get away.

Hangman couldn't make the same mistake. The pain in his legs drove him into a panic. He had to get off the ground fast.

He jumped straight up, grabbed a low-hanging branch, and swung himself up into the canopy with dozens of the larvae still gnawing and chewing at him. They crawled higher toward his pelvis.

He didn't stop running through the branches until he heard screaming in the distance behind him. He stopped there and blocked out his own pain to listen. He heard three different voices. The Renegades were going down.

He ran for another ten minutes before he collapsed in the crook of a different tree. He sank back against the trunk, shut his eyes, and swallowed down the sting of bile before he dared to look at how bad his wounds were.

He had to use his knife to dig the larvae out of his legs and thighs. They had eaten their way into his calves and thighs. One latched onto his hip, but they couldn't chew through bone.

He threw them over the side onto the jungle floor far below. They couldn't crawl back up here, but he had bigger things to worry about.

He pried off the last one and collapsed shaking and shivering against the trunk. He had to seal these wounds before they got any worse.

His hands shook so badly that he almost dropped his bowl of leaf paste when he took it out of his bag. He concentrated on smearing the paste to the worst wounds on his legs, including the blade cut the Renegades gave him.

He couldn't travel now. He didn't trust himself in the canopy and he couldn't travel on the ground at night.

He dragged his bleary eyes open. He was as dazed and insensible now as he pretended to be in front of the Renegades.

He forced himself to concentrate just long enough to find another tangled nook between multiple tree trunks. He curled up inside it and fell into a black sleep.

Chapter 15

Hangman swam back to his senses and felt the pain of a dozen wounds in his legs. The memory came back to him of yesterday's fight against the Renegades. At least he didn't have to worry about them anymore.

He pried himself out of the tree branches and winced when he straightened his legs. They hurt—a lot—but at least they weren't infected.

He started to make his way through the canopy, but his injured legs interfered with his balance. He lowered himself painfully to the ground and set off at a slow walk through the jungle.

He would have run to catch up with his uncle's hunting party. He really hoped Cross and Shadow weren't worried about why Hangman disappeared for so long.

If they weren't worried now, they would be when he came back injured. It wouldn't be the first time.

He didn't try to rush it. He returned to the spot where he left his kukris, retrieved all his weapons, and continued on his journey.

He had to climb into the branches more than once to avoid dangerous creatures. He couldn't fight them—not now.

He overtook his uncle's hunting part after dark that day. Hangman wouldn't have been able to overtake them at all if they hadn't stopped for the night.

Shadow and Cross shot to their feet when Hangman limped into their camp. "Where have you been?!" Shadow's eyes darted down to Hangman's body. "What happened?!"

Hangman wilted next to the fire. "You'll all be happy to know that the weapons aren't in the west country. The Renegades don't know where they are."

Butcher's head snapped around up. "How do you know?"

"They told me." Hangman held out his hand to Vulture. "Give me some food, will you please? I'm all out."

Vulture handed over a fistful of the dried Gorlock strips. Hangman sank back on his elbow and flinched again when he straightened his legs. They were starting to stiffen after the effort of walking here.

"You're hurt, Hangman," Cross murmured.

"It's nothing, little brother." Hangman waved his dried meat at his father and brother. "Sit down. When are you going to learn not to worry about me?"

They wouldn't stop staring at him. Viking had gotten to his feet and grabbed his weapon when he heard someone coming.

He, Shadow, and Cross took a long time before they resumed their seats, but they didn't relax.

Butcher broke the uncomfortable silence. "What do you mean—the Renegades told you about the weapons? You better not have told them we were looking for those weapons."

"Don't worry, Uncle," Hangman replied. "All of the Renegades I questioned are dead now."

"You questioned them?!" Alien snapped. "How did you question them?"

"They tried to question me about why the Godless are in this area so far west. I pretended to be delirious and I kept babbling that I had to find the valley of stone between the mountains. They had no idea what I was talking about. They've never even seen it."

Butcher scratched his chin. "That's interesting. I wonder what it means."

"I just told you. It means the weapons aren't in Renegade territory. They would have seen a valley of stone that wide. If you're right that the west country doesn't have any mountains beyond the Jagged Points, then the valley of stone can't be there."

"You're right," Viking murmured. "Excellent thinking."

"It was just something to do to pass the time." Hangman put another piece of dried meat in his mouth and looked around. "What's been happening here while I've been gone? How is your leg, Vulture?"

Vulture nodded. "It's coming along. It isn't infected anymore."

"That's good. I'm tired. I might go to sleep." Hangman stretched out on his back and shut his eyes while he chewed his Gorlock meat.

His pain exhausted him more than anything else—and he really didn't want to talk about his escapade anymore—to anyone. He didn't want to see the way they were all looking at him.

His personal brand of entertainment didn't quite mesh with anyone else's. He'd never met anyone who enjoyed his particular taste in adventure.

He didn't think what he did with those Renegades was an adventure—at least, he didn't think so when he started it or while he was in it.

He did things like that all the time. His family and relatives always treated his exploits as unusual, heroic, or dangerous. He didn't see them as any of those things. He just did them without thinking much about them first, during, or afterward.

He wanted to find out what those Renegades knew about the weapons, so he did it. What more was there to say?

He really didn't understand why all the men of the Godless Clan didn't do it this way. He knew on a rational level that he was different from the others. He just didn't understand why.

The others had been talking when he showed up. It took them a long time to restart their conversation.

Butcher went back to talking to Shadow about traveling south, but not before meeting up with the rest of their band for at least a few days' rest.

"The whole party doesn't need to come," Butcher decided. "We can leave behind some of our men and the women more distantly related to the family."

"We'll need to leave behind a defensible party," Shadow pointed out. "They'll need to be able to repel incursions if they happen."

Butcher nodded. "Yes, of course. We can decide all of that when we return to our long camp."

Hangman didn't open his eyes or participate in the discussion. He stayed where he was even after the others started dropping off to sleep.

Butcher set Viking, Cross, Vulture, and Magnet on the first watch. "You'll stand the second watch, Hangman," Butcher told him. "Get your sleep in now because you'll be on your feet again in a few hours."

"Of course, Uncle," Hangman replied. "I'll be ready."

He dragged himself up on his elbow, now that he couldn't pretend he'd been asleep all this time. He squinted in the firelight and spotted a water gourd sitting by the rocks surrounding the fire.

He held out his hand. "Hand me the water, will you please?"

Cross handed it over and then squatted down next to Hangman. "How bad is it, Hangman? I can bring you some Gooji sap if you need it."

"I'll be fine, little one. Go on watch with the others. I'll see you in a few hours."

Cross dragged himself away, but not without looking back over his shoulder.

Hangman didn't move. His legs hurt. He didn't want to get up to go back on watch, especially not if something came to attack their party during the night.

He hauled himself into a sitting position, chugged down some water, and flopped back on the ground.

He crashed hard, only to wake up a few hours later when Cross shook him by the shoulder. "It's time to go on watch, Hangman. It's your turn."

"Thank you, little brother." Hangman had to brace himself and take a few deep breaths before he summoned the will to bend his legs, much less put any weight on them.

Cross held out his hand to help him. Hangman grabbed it, and right at that moment, Magnet called from the other side of the camp. "Ants!! Ants coming!!"

Those words woke up everyone else in a heartbeat. Viking and Vulture had both been about to lie down to go to sleep.

They launched to their feet in a flash. "Everybody out!" Butcher ordered. "Everybody—up into the trees! NOW!!"

All of Hangman's pain evaporated. He took off running into the jungle. He only slowed down long enough to make sure Cross kept up.

The other men bolted in all directions. Most of them raced away from where Magnet raised the alarm. He ran across the camp heading away from where he'd just been standing guard.

The men plunged into the trees, scrambled into the branches, and kept climbing to get as high as possible.

Hangman didn't feel the pain in his legs until he sat down on a sturdy branch next to Cross. Shadow, Alien, and Chaos perched nearby. Hangman couldn't see anyone else, but they must be here.

This position gave all the men a perfect vantage point to see the camp they just vacated. The fire still flickered and glowed in the center.

Butcher, Shadow, and Fang had all built shelters for themselves. Three of the cousins had woven reed mats to sleep on. The cousins left their mats behind when they fled from the ants.

Hangman didn't see anything at first, but he heard them coming through the darkness. A steady hum of scuttling, scratching. rustling, and chewing sounds spread through the trees in a wall of unbroken noise.

The ants took a long time to get to the camp—at least it seemed like a long time. It couldn't have been more than a few seconds because the ants traveled fast.

They flooded out of the darkness and invaded the camp by the thousands. Each ant stood as high as a man's knee. Their pinchers could snap bone. A swarm this size could devour a full-grown Crusher in seconds.

The ants marched in a carpet of black bodies that covered the camp chewing up everything in their path. All three shelters disintegrated under all those marching feet and snapping jaws.

The ants even crawled across the fire. It didn't damage their exoskeletons. Their feet scattered the embers and put the fire out.

The coals gave enough light for the men to watch the ants flow out of the jungle, cross the camp, and keep going into the undergrowth on the other side.

Each ant bumped into tree trunks, started to climb up them, and corrected to stay with the swarm. None of them crawled more than a few feet off the ground.

They kept coming without end, but the swarm eventually passed. The last ants crossed the camp and vanished. They left nothing behind them, not even the woven mats or any trace of the shelters.

Chapter 16

Hangman lowered himself to the ground and put his weight on his legs. Sleeping in the trees for the second night didn't do them any favors, but he didn't complain. Complaining was the coward's way.

He switched the incident on its head in his mind. He told himself he was happy about these injuries. He did his band a huge favor by finding out that information.

His legs would heal. He could still run and fight when he had to. He could afford to limp along and do the bare minimum for as long as it lasted. It was worth it to find out what the Renegades didn't know.

The party set off heading farther east. Walking worked out the stiffness in his legs and helped ease the pain even if walking didn't take it away completely.

That didn't matter. He would have to walk either way, so he did.

He kept just as close a watch on the surroundings. He didn't leave that to his cousins.

Cross stayed close to him all day. Cross's concern touched Hangman, but Hangman refused to accept anyone's help or attention. He continually deflected it if anyone mentioned it.

They camped one more time before they left that part of the jungle and entered a steep valley between two different mountain ranges.

Jungle clung to towering granite cliffs on both sides. The jungle covered the valley floor and then opened out into a wide plateau stretching to flatlands farther east.

Hangman couldn't even be happy about the sight of his home country—not knowing what he would face there.

The party entered the cliff valley and met up on second morning with a group of women from their own band. The men found the women camping next to a larger stream with a few sturdier shelters constructed along the banks.

The women all got to their feet when they saw the men coming. No one said anything for a minute until Cross stepped out from behind the other men.

His mother rushed him, threw her arms around him, and burst into tears exactly the way mothers of newly initiated men always did.

Hangman stood back and watched. His mother, Katha, did the same thing to him when he came home scarred beyond recognition.

When he left for his initiation, when he came back, when Cross left for his initiation, and when Cross came back were the only times Hangman had ever seen his mother cry. She was the toughest woman he'd ever met. She was as tough as any Godless woman could be.

She pushed her son back, held him at arm's length, gripped him by both shoulders, and cried when she saw his face.

Cross looked a lot better now than he did after it happened. The swelling was already going down.

The slash marks looked wicked and ferocious. They didn't disfigure Cross's good looks at all.

Shadow shoved between them and pushed her away. "Don't baby him. He's a man now." Shadow raised his voice and called to all the women within earshot. "He's a man now and his name is Cross. He'll go out with us from now on—so treat him as a man."

That was the last word on the subject. Katha dragged her wrist across her face, but she kept crying for a long time afterward.

She went down to the stream to wash her face. Cross entered the camp with the other men. His female relatives hugged him, congratulated him, and made a big deal about his face.

"Be grateful it's only the two cuts," Alien's sister Neia remarked. "You still look as handsome as ever."

"It's true, Cross," Boxer's wife Zyria added. "You don't look as bad as Hangman does."

Cross shot a glance at Hangman, but Cross was the only one who did. The others treated Hangman's looks as normal now. No one remarked on his scars much at all anymore.

The party sat down together. The men shared out the Gorlock meat from Cross's kill.

All the women asked about his initiation fight, but he couldn't tell them much. The rest of the men had to fill in the details that he didn't remember.

Hangman stayed out of it. The other men offered enough detail. He didn't need to get involved or correct anything.

He remembered every single second of his own initiation. He would never forget that fight. It was the day that changed his life—for the better.

If he had known going into it that he would be left hideously ugly and irrevocably changed on the inside, too, he would have done everything exactly the same. His initiation fight was the best thing that ever happened to him. It made him the man he was now.

Everyone in their band respected him because of what he became that day. He wouldn't give that up for anything.

The women all exclaimed over Cross's exploits. Then the men chimed in with tales from their own initiations. No one asked Hangman to add his own story to the mix. Everyone already knew it.

He could afford to stay silent and let others take the recognition for a change. He didn't want to talk about his initiation or how it affected him. That was only for him to know and cherish in his heart as his finest hour.

The party camped there that night. The women disassembled their shelters the next morning and scattered all the materials back into the jungle where they came from.

The women fell in line with the men. The women wore exactly the same combination of clothing except that they also wore short, sleeveless tops around their chests to cover them up. That was their only garment besides the loincloth, shoes, and leggings laced up to his knees.

The women carried multiple shoulder bags each just like the men as well as plenty of weapons. No one went anywhere in this jungle without fighting.

The women wore their hair long like the men, too. The women used the same combination of braids, ties, knots, or any other arrangement they felt like according to their tastes.

Hangman caught Katha watching him limp, but she knew better than to ask what happened or if he was okay.

The group turned south and continued farther east before they entered the flatlands. The mood relaxed as the party approached their home territory, but Hangman didn't. He was actually starting to dread it.

He paused at the head of the gorge and looked out over the flat country. Butcher's band kept their long camp over there—their permanent camping place they used as their central location and ventured out from.

Hangman really didn't want to go back there. He didn't want to face what he knew was waiting for him out there, but he had to.

In that moment when he stopped at the head of the gorge, he spotted movement in the jungle above him. He looked up.

He recognized all the movements of creatures in the canopy. He recognized this movement, too, but it didn't come from any creature.

Alien came up behind him. "What is it, little brother?"

"There's someone up there." Hangman turned away heading back up the gorge. "There are people up there."

"Hey!" Alien called after him and then squinted up the cliffs.

Katha's eyes widened when Hangman limped past her. "What's the matter?"

"Someone is up on the ridge. Come on. We have to find out who it is."

Everyone looked up and saw exactly the same movement. The whole party turned back.

It didn't take them long to overtake Hangman. "Did you see them?" Butcher asked.

"I only saw the trees moving."

Hangman couldn't climb uphill as well as he could walk downhill. Every step hurt, but he pushed through it.

The group traveled much faster now. They scaled back to the top of the gorge and clambered onto the cliffs.

Shadow and Butcher led the way down the ridge. The party slowed as they drew nearer to the place where Hangman saw the trees moving.

He pulled his kukris as they got nearer. He wasn't even surprised when he spotted another fifteen Renegades.

They stood at the very edge of the cliff looking over the side. It couldn't be more obvious that they'd been watching the Godless approach their own territory.

Hangman would normally have waited for some signal from Butcher or at least Shadow before striking. Hangman didn't wait for any signal.

He also didn't wait for the Renegades to turn around and see the Godless approaching.

He deliberately missed his step, snapped a twig underfoot to alert them, and then charged them.

They glanced behind them and saw him running straight at them with his kukris raised. His actions triggered the rest of the Godless to attack just as fast.

The Renegades started to turn around. Hangman had to act now.

He bellowed out loud, but instead of striking with his kukris the way the Renegades probably expected him to, he changed his strategy at the last second.

He threw both his arms out to the sides, concentrated his attack on the five Renegades standing at the center of their group, and collided with them.

They raised their weapons to cut him down. They didn't expect it when he threw all his weight against them and made them stagger backward.

They tumbled off the edge of the cliff and fell screaming to their deaths on the rocky valley floor far below.

His one act cut their numbers by a third. That left ten against a greater number of Godless.

Another three saw him and came at him from his left. They rushed him to hack him to pieces with their blades, but he only dodged them.

Two missed their footing and went wheeling off into open space. That left one.

The guy checked himself when he saw his friends vanish completely off the map. Hangman struck out with his kukri and hit the guy across the side of the head, but Hangman didn't hit him hard enough to kill him.

The man staggered, lost his footing, and he went down, too.

The other Godless didn't think about using the cliff to their advantage. They fought the Renegades in the old-fashioned way—weapon against weapon. The women fought alongside the men.

Hangman went through the group one after the other, yanked the Renegades away from his relatives, and threw each man off the cliff. They cartwheeled into oblivion and vanished.

Viking and Magnet ran over to Butcher to help him against the last remaining Renegade. The man backed away from the three Godless warriors—and wound up backing straight into Hangman's clutches. He pulled the man away and shoved him over the side.

Butcher frowned first at Hangman and then at the cliff edge. None of the Renegades remained. "That isn't the Godless way, little brother," he growled.

"I'm injured and they're just as dead, aren't they? We should go check the long camp. There may be other Renegades in the area. They may already be scouting the long camp while we've been away."

He walked off into the jungle. No one could accuse Hangman of cowardice. Not even Butcher would dare.

The group fell in line again on their way back down the gorge. The party stopped when they found the Renegades' bodies squashed and bloody on the rocks below the cliff.

"Rifle their pockets for anything we can use," Butcher ordered.

Hangman helped his relatives roll the dead Renegades, go through their pockets, and check their weapons. The Renegades didn't have anything useful except more weapons.

Butcher ordered the party to take the weapons with them. He wouldn't have done that if the party hadn't been this close to their long camp.

The rest of the trip passed without incident. Hangman got increasingly tense and silent as he and his relatives approached their destination.

Butcher's hunting party entered a cluster of shelters with a bunch of women and children working in and out of the structures.

Most of the shelters followed the same loose design as the makeshift shelters the warriors used on their journey.

The shelters in the long camp had been built larger and with a slightly sturdier construction, fewer gaps between the branches that made up the walls, and with a fourth wall across the front to give each family more privacy.

The women came forward to greet their husbands and male relatives. Couples split off to their homes.

Cross went off with his younger brothers to tell them how his initiation went. Shadow and Katha returned to their own shelter. Hangman didn't go with them.

He hung back during all the greetings. As soon as everyone split up to go their own way, he went off alone into the jungle.

He didn't come back until the next morning.

Chapter 17

Hangman squatted in the middle of the long camp waiting for his relatives to get ready to leave again. The hunting party only returned for one night. Now they were leaving again.

The same warriors left this time, but they took their wives with them. Estia, Butcher's wife, came with them along with Boxer's wife, Zyria, Magnet's wife, Kealra, and Viking's wife, Nagana.

Midnight's daughter, Neia, and Chaos's wife, Rila, came, too.

The party assembled in the middle of the camp and exchanged farewells with everyone else in Butcher's band.

A few people tried to wish Hangman the best of luck. He let them wish him goodbye, but he didn't answer them. He wouldn't have the best of luck. He left on this trip like he was going to his own death.

At least he only had to do this once in his life. As soon as it ended, he would come home and everyone would forget it ever happened.

The party moved out and headed due south. The band knew this territory well and didn't deviate along the way.

The band remained quiet until midafternoon when the travelers entered another narrow ravine that opened into the next valley system farther south.

The travelers turned a corner in their path and walked in on another Godless band sitting under the trees resting—or at least the women sat under the trees resting.

Five armed men stood by the path to block the way. They must have heard the travelers coming.

They relaxed when they saw who it was. "We thought you were Renegades," one of the biggest warriors gasped. "They're everywhere these days."

Butcher furrowed his brow at the guy. "Wish? My God! You're huge!"

Wish burst out laughing. "Everyone says that when they see me after a long while."

Butcher glanced around. "Where's your father? He should be here."

The man on their right spoke up. "The Renegades killed Bantam in a raid last year. Wish is our Kral now."

Shadow stepped forward and held out his hand. "Congratulations. You'll be a great Kral to your band."

Wish's cheeks colored. "Thank you, Uncle."

"Who are you taking to the gathering?" Butcher asked. "Your daughter Arda can't be eighteen already. That isn't possible."

A tall, slender young woman stood up from the place where she'd been squatting with the other women. She burst into a beautiful, glowing smile. "Hello again, Uncle."

Butcher gasped and his hand shot to his forehead. "It isn't possible! The last time I saw you, you could barely hold a bundle of sticks!"

Arda laughed. "I wasn't that small, Uncle. It was only four years ago."

"Are you taking anyone else?" Shadow asked.

"She's the only one. What about you?"

Shadow waved at Hangman. "Hangman is going. He's the only man of our band who is of age."

Wish's eyes darted to Hangman and he immediately looked away. Arda did the same thing and sat down. She sat sideways so she wouldn't see him. She never looked at him again.

Wish recovered by waving behind him. "Join us. We're all going to the gathering. We can travel together. It will be safer and we can catch up on the news on the way."

The two parties merged. Hangman knew almost everyone here.

Wish's band wasn't technically related by blood to Butcher's band—not that Hangman knew about. The Godless of Wish's band only called him, "Uncle" out of respect for his age and position.

The two groups sat down together, but only for a few minutes. Then everyone set off on their way south.

"I remember when I went to the gathering." Butcher laughed. "That seems so long ago."

"You got yourself a good wife, it seems," Wish remarked. "She must be strong and healthy if she's still going after all these years—and your sons are strong and married. We should all be as lucky as you."

"Yes, I've done well—but I would have come away from that gathering with a wife either way. There were more than twenty young women there waiting to pair up with only four men. We got to take our pick."

Shadow snorted. "I'm sure it won't be like that this time."

"Of course not," Butcher replied. "It almost never happens that the women outnumber the men. All those young women came back the next year and they were the only women available for over thirty young men. The women got to take their pick and all the other men left alone. It's a shame so many men go unmarried, but it's the way of things, isn't it?"

Hangman didn't interject. He stayed near the back of the group and hoped no one noticed him, especially not Arda.

She avoided him and made sure to walk as far away from him as possible.

He could distinguish himself as a warrior on raids and hunting parties. He could earn the respect of his Clan.

No force under the sun would make a young woman choose him as her husband. That was never going to happen.

He had been dreading this gathering for over a year, but he already made up his mind to just get through it and put it behind him.

Plenty of young men left the gathering without wives. He wouldn't be unique in that. He would probably be one of many the way Butcher said.

Unpaired young men left the gathering every year. If they didn't get a wife that year, they stayed single for life. That was the rule.

There were already too few women to go around. Unpaired young women went with the next year's young men. The unpaired young men from the previous year never got another chance to marry.

No one had to spell it out for Hangman. He had to go through this gathering, but it would only happen once in his life. Then he could dedicate the rest of his days to defending the Clan. He never had to think about women ever again.

The rest of his band—and Wish's band—they all understood this, too. No one said the words out loud.

Arda must have been dreading what would happen if no one else chose her and she had to go with Hangman after all.

He would almost rather spend his life alone than marry someone like her—someone who couldn't stand the sight of him.

He would only marry someone exactly like her because no one would go with him willingly. A young woman would only become his wife if she had no other options and she had absolutely no choice but to leave with him.

The band had to bring him to the gathering. That was never up for debate. All the surrounding Clans brought their young people to the gathering in their eighteenth year.

This was the only way all the Clans could ensure that their young people married partners from different families. No one married into the same family.

Hangman's relatives laughed and talked about their own experiences at the gathering. Then some of the wives related funny or interesting incidents that happened when they left with their husbands' bands and tried to integrate into a new family group.

Hangman barely listened. None of this applied to him because he wouldn't find a wife at the gathering. He wasn't sure of much else, but he was certain of that.

The party camped together that night. The conversation drifted to other subjects, especially the Renegade Clan's incursions into Godless territory.

Somehow, the conversation always came back to the gathering itself. Everyone else in the party stayed in high spirits. The subject made them happy.

Hangman sat with his family for a while. No one asked him about the gathering or even looked in his direction.

After a while, he walked off into the dark and stayed away until morning. He wouldn't have returned at all unless he absolutely had to.

The party was just packing up to leave when one of Wish's warriors pointed up the nearest hill. "It looks like Wizard's band is coming in, too."

The party stopped what they were doing. The third group of Godless saw the travelers and diverted to join them.

Hangman hovered on the fringes while everyone hugged, exchanged the news, and then the conversation inevitably turned to the gathering.

"Who are you bringing?" Wizard asked Wish.

Wish waved at Arda. "My daughter Arda is the only one we have of age. Butcher is bringing his nephew, Hangman. What about you?"

Wizard gestured to the group behind him. "We have Bullseye, Dodge, and Distra."

Three young people stepped out of Wizard's group. Dodge and Bullseye were both strong, well-formed young warriors. Distra was another beautiful young woman with a much rounder, cheerier face than Arda.

The four young people came together talking and smiling at each other. Distra couldn't marry anyone from her own band, but Dodge and Bullseye both took an interest in Arda.

Hangman kept out of their conversation. It never once crossed his mind to approach Distra.

It always happened like this. If bands of the same Clan came together on their way to the gathering, their young people could decide to stay together.

They couldn't officially marry until they actually went to the gathering and showed themselves, but they could choose each other based on attraction and mutual interest.

The older adults spent a long time talking and catching up on all their family news. Wizard finally suggested that everyone keep moving south.

The four young people stayed in a group, but when the combined party made camp that night, Arda sat much closer to Bullseye than she should have.

Dodge didn't seem to have a problem with this. Arda leaned against Bullseye with his arms around her while all four of them talked about their home bands, their territories, and every detail of their lives.

Hangman stayed on the opposite side of the camp so no one got the wrong idea about him expressing an interest in either of the two young women.

He stayed near Cross, Chaos, Magnet, and their wives. No one could suspect Hangman of getting any ideas as long as he stayed here.

The evening wore on. Everyone from all three bands eventually got tired of talking about the gathering and went back to talking about political maneuverings, hunting practices, and clashes with hostile Clans.

Hangman did his best not to see what Arda and Bullseye were doing. Hangman avoided even looking at them until it was time to go to sleep.

Cross stretched out on his side. Chaos and Rila curled up in each other's arms. She rested her head on his chest and he wrapped his arms around her.

Magnet and Kealra both lay on their sides facing the same direction. He wrapped his arms around her from behind and she snuggled into him before they both went to sleep.

Hangman didn't want to see that, so he turned onto his other side. Almost everyone else in the combined party was already lying down—except Arda and Bullseye.

They sat in the same place across the camp. He leaned his back against a tree while she reclined against him with his arms around her.

They kissed passionately with all their lips and tongues involved. Their hands were already starting to migrate all over each other's bodies.

They couldn't go all the way until they officially left the gathering as husband and wife, but they could lay the groundwork now.

It sure looked like that's what they were doing. Hangman shut his eyes so he wouldn't see anything else.

Chapter 18

The Godless band moved out of their camp the next day and continued on their way to the gathering. Arda and Bullseye walked with their arms around each other.

Dodge and Distra walked with them and all four of them chatted together for the whole day.

Hangman kept his distance again. No one encouraged him to do anything else.

One more night. He just had to get through tonight. The party would arrive at the gathering tonight. The selection process and any negotiation would conclude in an hour—two hours at the absolute maximum. Then he could leave.

Arda and Bullseye would go with Wizard's band. Distra would depart with whoever she married. If Dodge took a wife, she would go with Wizard's band.

Hangman would go home with his own people. He never had to come back to the gathering—not as an eligible young man.

He would return to support his younger brothers. That was all.

The party crossed an open grassland and battled a few different creature attacks, but such a large group of travelers had no problem defeating anything that came along.

The group passed alongside more cliffs, climbed down some hills into a plane, and approached the crumbling wreckage of an ancient city in the distance.

"We should look for supplies while we're in there," Butcher suggested.

"Uncle....." Hangman got his uncle's attention and pointed to the west.

Four enormous Crushers strode across the landscape toward the city. The creatures passed some tall metal towers with clusters of knobs on top. Wires hung from these knobs and trailed down to the ground.

The Crushers stepped on the wires and occasionally tangled the wires around their toes. One of the Crushers pulled the tower sideways when the creature tried to yank its foot out of the knots.

"They're heading for the city," Magnet pointed out. "They're probably going in there to hunt for scavengers."

Wizard pointed to the eastern side of all the wrecked buildings. "We'll go around the city on the east side. The Crushers won't bother us there."

No one argued. The party started forward again, but everyone kept an eye on the Crushers.

Magnet turned out to be right. The Crushers entered the city streets and eyed the ground looking for anyone moving around in there.

People always went into the cities, especially anyone not attached to a particular Clan. Living in the jungle was hard enough even with entire family bands working, hunting together, and protecting each other.

The cities tempted isolated scavengers with dreams of forgotten food stashes and abandoned objects. The scavengers' presence attracted opportunistic predators like the Crushers.

The cities were no safer than the jungle and sometimes far more dangerous.

The party circled the city and entered another dense patch of jungle in the afternoon. The gathering grounds occupied a plateau on the other side of this ridge. Just a few more hours and Hangman's ordeal would be over.

He wasn't thinking about anything in particular when a fast-moving object dropped from the high canopy. No one heard or saw a thing before a massive creature plummeted through the treetops and landed right on top of Arda and Bullseye.

The impact knocked the couple apart. Bullseye toppled flat on his back and the creature pinned Arda under its weight.

Hangman saw the creature clearly in that moment and the world stopped. It was a large Demonex, a species of enormous cat with horn spikes surrounding its head in a mane of dagger points.

Most Demonex stood as tall at the shoulder as a man's sternum, but this one was even bigger. He was a male in his prime.

More of the same armored quills covered the creature's body flowing backward to a whipping tail with a ball of spikes on the end.

The creature curled its lips back from its long, recurved fangs. Poison dripped from those fangs. The Demonex eyed Arda from inches away.

She screamed when it flattened her under its weight. She couldn't get out from under it. Hangman didn't see if she was armed.

Bullseye struggled to get up in time to save her life, but it was already too late. The Demonex was too close to her for any man to get to her in time.

Hangman reacted without thinking, ripped out his kukri, and hurled it at the creature. The blade tumbled end over end, but not fast enough.

The Demonex lunged for Arda's face to deliver the killing bite. Hangman had been aiming for the soft spot behind the creature's ear. That was the only place to hit it to take it down instantly.

The creature's movements made the kukri miss. The blade sank into the creature's neck.

The Demonex spun around with a frightful roar. The creature didn't see where the attack came from. The Demonex roared at everyone in the whole party, but at least he wasn't looking at Arda anymore.

Hangman didn't think. He charged across the gap, tackled the creature off of her, yanked his kukri out of the Demonex's spiked hide, and the two of them rolled away grappling and struggling.

Hangman knew how to position his weight against the creature's side so its spikes didn't impale him. He could have killed himself if he held the Demonex any other way.

The Demonex tried to raise its hind legs to kick out its claws at Hangman. He used the creature's movements to plunge his kukri deep into the Demonex's abdomen and ripped the weapon up.

The creature bellowed in agony and its legs fell away, but only for a split second before it recovered enough to try again.

That one instant gave Hangman the time he needed to raise his bloody weapon on high and drive it under the creature's ribs. Hangman twisted and the Demonex collapsed groaning.

It still wasn't dead yet. It tried to slash its poison fangs at him. He ripped the blade out and finally sank it into the soft place behind the creature's ear.

The Demonex wilted onto the ground. Hangman toppled off onto his back dripping with blood and shaking from the effort. He didn't even have the strength left to pull his kukri out of the creature's skull.

Viking and Alien both came over to him and bent over him. "Are you hurt, little brother?" Alien asked.

"Just.....just....just a minute....." Hangman panted. "Just....give me.....a minute......"

Alien waved at some of Wish's people. "Give him some water, will you?"

The surrounding people stepped forward and handed Alien one of their water gourds. "Sit up and drink some water, brother," Alien told him.

Hangman opened his eyes. He didn't want to sit up—not yet.

In that moment when he opened his eyes, he spotted five more Demonex perched in the high canopy.

They crouched in the branches observing the Godless on the ground.

"Alien.....look......." Hangman pointed up at the creatures. "Get everyone....moving out......"

Viking and Alien looked up. Then they stood up. "Everybody move out!" Alien bellowed. "There are more Demonex stalking us right now. Uncle—take everyone farther down the path. We need to get out onto the plateau before dark."

The surrounding people turned away and left Hangman lying there on his back. He tried to shut his eyes, but not before he spotted Bullseye putting his arms around Arda and leading her away.

Saving her from the Demonex didn't change anything. Hangman didn't expect it to. He didn't save her because he expected her to change her mind about him. Nothing would.

She and Bullseye left with the others. Viking and Alien waited for a minute, helped Hangman to sit up, and waited for him to drink some water before they pulled him to his feet.

He had to break the Demonex's skull to get his kukri out. He wiped it on some leaves and kept following his relatives. Viking and Alien stayed with him until they caught up.

"It was well done, little brother," Alien murmured. "You saved that girl."

"I'm sure anyone else would have done it," Hangman mumbled.

"Anyone else *would* have done it," Viking added. "Not many other people *could* have done it. I bet you anything her young husband couldn't have done it."

"It doesn't matter," Hangman replied. "As soon as we leave here, they can all forget about me and that's for the best."

His cousins didn't argue. They stopped at a stream where he washed the blood off his arms and body. At least he could show up at the gathering without looking like more of a monster than he already did.

Bullseye kept his arms around Arda the whole way to the plateau. She huddled close against him and stayed by his side when the party stopped for breaks.

"Anyone watching her would think *he* was the one who saved her from the Demonex," Alien snarled.

Hangman didn't answer. He didn't resent any of these young people for shunning him.

He actually started to feel relieved that he would leave the gathering without a wife. He didn't want to deal with one. His life made more sense when he walked alone.

Arda and Bullseye had to separate when the party got to the plateau. Dozens of different bands already assembled there from multiple different Clans.

All the bands stayed separate. They had to for the sake of propriety. Wish's band, Wizard's band, and Butcher's band separated, too.

Arda retreated with Wish's band to the other side of the plateau. Bullseye, Dodge, and Distra went with Wizard's band.

The young people weren't allowed to mix until the gathering started. They weren't allowed to mix even after the gathering started. The gathering didn't work that way.

Hangman sensed his relatives closing around him in a protective huddle. They all knew what was about to happen.

He couldn't stop himself from glancing around at all the young women in every band. They all looked as nervous as he was—and they all looked beautiful—too beautiful for him.

A few people sat down on the ground. Then everyone else did the same thing. The different family groups pretended to relax until the gathering started. They lit fires, cooked food, and conversation drifted on the night air as the sun went down.

Everyone all over the plateau glanced around at everyone else. Everyone evaluated everyone else for their looks, size, shape, and facial expressions.

Hangman spotted plenty of people looking in his direction. They all looked away just as quickly and went straight back to what they were doing.

Without warning, someone clamped a muscular hand on Hangman's shoulder in a tight, comforting grip. It was Viking.

That touch meant a lot. Whatever happened tonight, Hangman would go home with his family. He would go home with the people who knew him and valued him for what he was. He didn't need to impress anyone else. He already knew where he belonged.

He actually pitied the young women who had to leave their families to join other bands and, in some cases, completely different Clans. He couldn't have tolerated that. He would rather have lived alone than leave his family.

Chapter 19

A young girl squatted on the ground, set a basket in front of her, and pulled off the top.

She lifted a juvenile warthog out of the basket and held it between her knees while she slipped a piece of knotted rope around the creature's neck.

The little creature grunted softly to itself and started snuffling around in the dry leaves at her feet.

An old man came over to her and watched her set the basket aside.

"You always find the best ones, Mora," he told her.

She smiled up at him. "This one is the perfect size—not too big and not too small. Is everything else ready?"

"It's all ready when you are. Everyone is in position."

Mora stood up straight still holding the rope in one hand. The young warthog walked in circles around her ankles. She had to pass the rope from hand to hand around and around herself to stop it from tangling her body.

The old man picked up the basket. "Agro and Erus are scouting the perimeter to make sure no other creatures come while we're hiding."

"I suppose that's the best we can do," Mora replied. "This shouldn't take long."

The pair crossed the clearing and stopped next to another tree. Mora tied her rope around the trunk and left the young warthog there.

"You should get up to the ridge, Papi," she told the old man.

He laughed at her. "You can't blame me for wanting to watch my favorite grandchild work her magic. It's a pleasure to see what pains you take with this project."

Mora made a face at her grandfather, but she couldn't stop her cheeks from coloring. "You tell all your grandchildren they're your favorite. Mother even said you told her and her siblings the same thing when they were growing up. You can't fool me."

He only laughed. "Finish torturing the little thing and let's go."

Mora bit back a smirk, took a second rope from the pocket of her long dress, and looped that around the young warthog's neck, too. The little creature was too busy exploring the jungle floor to notice.

Mora and her grandfather Rono circled the clearing. Mora let out more and more lengths of the second rope and stopped next to another tree opposite the one where she tied the warthog.

She wrapped the second rope around the second trunk, made a knot, and pulled it as tight as it would go.

The two ropes stretched taut and trapped the young warthog between them. The ropes held the little creature in one place so it couldn't move.

The warthog immediately started to struggle. It kicked its hooves against the hard-packed dirt and squealed loudly while it fought to get out of the double noose.

Mora worked fast to secure the knot in that position. Her grandfather kept looking back and forth between her and the warthog. Its screams escalated to shrieks.

She tied off the knot extra tightly, spun away, and she and her grandfather ran for it. The warthog's screams followed them all the way through the undergrowth and up the nearest hill.

Mora clambered through the trees and flopped down on her stomach between her mother Alura and her two sisters, Yena and Grea.

A long line of their other relatives lay in the same position on the ridge overlooking the jungle below.

A clear place between the trees gave a view of the little warthog struggling and thrashing between the two ropes.

Its tiny hooves dug deeper into the dirt when it tried to run away. "It will break the sheet if it doesn't stop," Grea remarked.

"Here it comes," Yena murmured.

Everyone looked up and turned to the east. The treetops trembled and then the canopy broke.

The scaly beaked head of a Gorlock broke the canopy for a second before the creature plunged back under the foliage.

The disturbance came fast and straight toward the warthog. Its screams attracted the Gorlock faster than anything.

The Gorlock's head broke the canopy one more time before it vanished again and reappeared right there in the clearing.

The little warthog panicked and shrieked even louder. Its screams echoed through the jungle again and again. The noise set Mora's hair on end.

The Gorlock eyed the warthog from high above. The Gorlock strutted toward the little creature. The warthog couldn't even get to its feet anymore. It lay in the dirt struggling to rise, but its legs trembled too badly.

"Just a few more steps....." Rono murmured.

The Gorlock took two more steps. The minute it put its weight on that leg, the ground beneath it collapsed. A structure of thin saplings, woven grass mats, and a thin film of dirt covered a vast pit dug out of the ground.

The Gorlock shrieked and spread its wings, but the monster was too big to fly. It plunged downward into the pit and impaled itself on dozens of sharpened spikes buried in the ground.

The Gorlock thrashed in its death throes, but the spikes were too thick and too well anchored. The creature eventually stopped twitching and lay there bleeding from all those puncture wounds.

Rono stood up chucking. "Mora strikes again."

Her father Dagu stood up and yelled down the line. "Everyone get down there and start butchering the creature. We need to retreat to safe camp before dark! Don't leave anything behind!"

The rest of their family band got to their feet and headed down the hill at a leisurely pace. Mora went with them. The family would eat well tonight with plenty left over for the days ahead.

Her family band consisted of four sets of grandparents, two sets of great-grandparents, dozens of uncles and aunts, and at least thirty children.

They flooded into the clearing. The children got to work pulling away the saplings and mats from the edge of the pit. Mora untied the young warthog and put it back in her basket for next time.

Then she helped the other children stack the poles and mats in the nearby undergrowth. Their band didn't go to all the effort of digging this pit just for one kill.

The party pulled hand-tied ladders out of the nearby bushes, lowered them to the bottom of the pit, and Mora's uncles climbed down there to butcher the Gorlock.

They had to balance on the ladders to stand level with the creature's body. The uncles used long, sharpened metal machetes to hack the creature apart at the joints.

The uncles handed the pieces up to the aunts who laid the joints on clean skins and blankets on the ground. The aunts boned the meat, sectioned it into smaller portions, wrapped everything in cured hides, and tied the bundles for transport.

Everyone helped. As soon as the children finished putting the sapling poles and mats away, they came back to the pit and ran errands for the aunts.

Mora went back and forth between all her aunts and older relatives. No one stopped working until the uncles handed the last piece of the Gorlock up and the aunts wrapped it up.

The children had to carry water in handmade pots from the nearby stream. The aunts went to great pains to wash all the blood off their hands, clothes, and the bundles so no dangerous predators would smell the blood and come after the party.

Mora's brothers Agro and Erus came back during the process. Both were married now with their own children on the way.

"Ah, excellent work as always, Mora," Erus remarked. "No harm done."

She smiled at him. "Thank you for patrolling."

"We wouldn't want any other creatures to interfere or come upon our trap from another direction." He had to stop talking when his wife Sinda handed him one of the meat bundles. "It looks like we're moving out."

Everyone in their band picked up a bundle of meat. Some people had to carry two. Everyone fell into a single file line on their way out of the area.

All the relatives kept a sharp eye on the surroundings. If the party saw any dangerous creatures on the way, everyone would have to hide.

The Followers Clan didn't fight creatures. The Followers didn't fight anyone. They avoided violence whenever possible.

Their members stayed alive much longer than anyone from other Clans. Followers usually lived to great ages. Some survived long enough to see their great-grandchildren become grandparents. A few people lived longer than that.

The Followers valued their old people for their knowledge and experience. Old people were too valuable to risk anything happening to them.

The Followers valued all human life too much to risk it in any kind of violent endeavor. There were better ways to hunt and avoid conflict with other Clans.

None of the Followers even carried weapons. The men only carried their machetes for building things and butchering animals. No Follower would ever consider raising a weapon against anyone or anything. That would have been horrible.

Mora kept a sharp eye on the surroundings. Everything in the jungle hunted humans as prey. She knew the dangers. She and her family just had to avoid them.

Chapter 20

Mora's arms started to get tired from carrying such a large bundle of meat, but the band arrived at their safe camp in a little while.

It occupied a cliff ledge high above the jungle floor. A tiny path winding between jagged rocks offered the only pathway onto the ledge.

An overhang protected the ledge from bird and creature attacks from the air. The overhang arched over the ledge in a roof with one narrow slit facing the steep valley beyond. It was the perfect hiding place.

The family settled down for the evening. The uncles went back and forth to the jungle, brought back sticks, and built a fire in the established central fire circle.

The aunts opened their bundles, put several haunches of meat on spits to cook, and brought out a trestle of boughs to smoke the rest over the fire.

Mora took her little warthog out of its basket and tied it in a corner. "He won't stay little forever," Rono remarked.

"I'll have to find a female for him and mate them together. They can have little warthogs. We can use them as bait for the pit trap. Then I won't have to keep catching them in the jungle every time we want fresh meat."

Her grandfather looked up at her and his eyes softened. "You won't do any of that, my dear girl. You'll go to the gathering in a few weeks. You'll leave us and go to some other band."

Mora looked away. "Then someone else can find a female for him and raise the little ones."

He rested his hand on top of hers. "I'll miss you, my sweet child."

His voice sounded so broken that she couldn't look at him. She had known for a long time that this day would come.

She had to go to the gathering—which meant she would leave her family to marry some young man of another band. Too few young women went to the gathering already. She wouldn't leave the gathering unmarried.

Even if too few young men came this year, she would certainly marry into another band next year. She would never see her family again.

Eighteen years seemed so short all of a sudden. The days seemed to last forever when she was younger. Now they flew past so fast. She just wanted to slow everything down and stay here forever, but she couldn't.

She pulled some nuts out of the pocket of her dress. Followers wore long clothing down to the wrists and ankles and buttoned up to the chin. The Followers valued modesty, especially among women.

The women wore long dresses with big pockets in the front. The long bell sleeves came together in a tight cuff around the wrists.

The women also wore long pantaloons under their dresses just in case circumstances happened to blow a woman's dress aside. No one would be able to see anything even if a woman had to climb a tree or scramble into rocks to hide from danger.

Mora got used to wearing these clothes after long years of wearing them. They felt comfortable and protective. She'd never worn any other clothing and didn't want to.

She might get lucky, marry a Follower man, and come back to the south country. Then she would see her family regularly. She wouldn't have to learn a completely different way of life.

She used a rock to crack the nuts and fed them to the little warthog. Then she helped her mother and aunts cut up the meat for smoking.

The uncles gathered enough firewood for tonight and most of tomorrow. Then they rolled a huge rock across the entrance pathway. No creatures could get onto the ledge while the family slept.

The atmosphere relaxed after that. Everyone talked and laughed and exchanged stories. Mora eventually sat down with some of her younger cousins. They took books out of their luggage, crowded closer to Mora, and they all fell silent while she read to them.

The little ones interrupted her with questions and comments. As soon as she finished that book, they brought out a second one and wanted her to read that one.

"You should be learning to read this yourselves," she told them. "Bring your pencils and I'll give you a lesson. Come on. You won't learn by listening to me read it."

They complained a lot, but they eventually retreated. Each child came back with a stick charred black at the end.

She got one of her own, stuck it into the coals to burn it some more, and used it to write letters on the walls. She wrote out letters for the youngest children, words for the middle age group, and whole sentences for the oldest children.

She strode up and down through the group instructing, correcting, and using a piece of hide to erase their mistakes.

They used their blackened sticks to write what she told them to write. Then she told them to read it back.

She was in the middle of the lesson when her mother called her. "It's dinnertime, children. Put your pencils away and come eat. You can read some more after dinner."

The children meticulously erased all their writing from the walls, circled the fire, and the aunts handed out food to everyone.

The Followers only ate a small amount of meat with each meal. The rest of their diet included of grains, vegetables, nuts, and seeds gathered from the jungle.

Hunting was too dangerous to be a regular source of food. This one Gorlock would keep the band going for a month. The band would gather as much other food as they could find. That was the best way to avoid the dangers.

Mora was still eating when one of her aunts took over teaching the children to read and write. She brought out a book, gave it to one of the middle cousins, and had the girl read it in front of the group.

The girl stumbled over words and the aunt corrected her. Every evening passed this way.

Mora didn't think anything when her father went to get himself a drink of water from the cistern in the corner. He didn't return to the same place. He sat down next to Mora.

"We'll leave for the gathering in the morning, my child."

Mora stared down into her bowl. "Yes, Father."

He didn't look at her. He stared into the flames. "I know you'll make a man an excellent wife. I know you'll make our Clan proud."

"Yes, Father," she mumbled. "I'll do my best for my husband and my Clan, whoever it happens to be."

"I'm proud of what you've become." His voice cracked the same way Rono's did. "You're a credit to our Clan. I hope you go with other Followers. You should stay in the

Clan and pass your skills and knowledge to those who come after you. You're too valuable for us to lose."

She didn't answer. Neither they nor anyone else could decide ahead of time who she would marry. He already knew that.

For some reason, her mind simply refused to accept that she would leave her family. Nothing about the gathering seemed real.

She had been there before. She attended twice when her brothers married. Agro married a Follower girl from a nearby band.

Erus married a girl from the Chosen Clan farther south. The Chosen didn't have the same customs as the Followers, but the girl had no problem becoming one of their family.

Mora simply couldn't comprehend any other life. She would leave here tomorrow and travel to the plateau to attend the gathering, but she didn't go to find a husband.

She felt like she was attending the gathering for someone else. She would watch from a distance while some other Follower girl joined her husband's band.

Then Mora would come back here and everything would go on as before. She didn't see how it could be otherwise. Life just didn't make sense if it played out any other way.

The night wore on. The jungle beyond the slit fell into darkness.

The aunts put their books away and pulled thick, stuffed mattresses from an alcove in the wall.

The rest of the family helped set up the mattresses on the floor, covered them with hides and blankets, and everyone settled down to sleep.

The mothers tucked in their children. Mora and her two sisters occupied one mattress together the way they always did since their earliest memories.

The mattress crinkled and crunched under their weight. The mattress had been constructed of beaten reed mats and stuffed with dry grass.

The blankets and hides made the mattresses comfortable and Mora fell asleep.

She woke up to the sounds of her mother and aunts preparing breakfast. Mora sat up and looked around. Her father, grandfathers, and uncles stood off to one side loading more bundles for the journey north to the gathering.

Mora stared at them across the room. This was just another journey like so many others. It didn't mean anything.

She helped her aunts package up the dried Gorlock meat. The family would eat more meat on the journey than they were used to eating. Eating this dried meat would be quicker and easier than taking the time to gather from the countryside.

No one talked much. The children were too sleepy. Some of them complained about having to leave at all.

Mora sat apart from it all. None of this concerned her. She wasn't going to the gathering. Some other Follower girl was going. Then Mora would come home.

She had to snap out of it when the time came to put the bedding away. Force of habit kept her moving after that. She helped her family pack up and clean the safe camp before they left.

She took the young warthog by its lead rope when the family filed out through the same narrow pathway, through the jungle, and out onto the planes.

The family found a wide, paved road heading straight north through one of the many ruined cities that dotted the landscape.

The warthog trotted at her heels the whole way. Some of the children wanted to lead the warthog for a while, so she let them.

She kept an eye on the little creature and fed it nuts at certain times of the day to keep it happy.

She didn't let herself believe she would part from her pet, either. No one else in her band ever thought to tame one of these creatures to bait their traps.

The idea of mating a female warthog and raising young warthogs instead of capturing them—the idea was beginning to grow on her. Why not? Why waste the effort and take the risk of capturing them?

Rono and the older men surveyed the fallen city from a distant hilltop. "I don't see any predators," Rono remarked. "We should go in, take a look around, and move on. We shouldn't spend too much time there."

The party entered the city in the afternoon. Rono and the others stopped at certain places to read street signs and billboards.

"There's a bookstore over there," Mora pointed out. "We should stop and get some more reading material."

"Not now," Rono decided. "We don't want to carry it all that way. We can stop on the way back."

"What about supplies?" Dagu asked. "We could use some more blades and sharpening stones."

"We can look around," Rono decided. "If any creatures come, we'll have to run for it. Just make sure you run north instead of any other direction."

"We'll stay together," Mora's other grandfather Civis added. "Then it won't be a question of anyone running in the wrong direction."

That settled it. The party entered the city. The older men followed more signs until they located a supply store.

The aunts stayed outside with the children. Mora went in with the other adults.

She spotted some books on the shelf and went over to read the titles. Her mind still tricked her into thinking she would come back this way and pick out some new reading material for herself and the rest of the band.

The men found what they were looking for, but they didn't exit the store. They got into a conversation back there. She didn't hear what they were talking about.

She looked over to see where they were. That was the moment when she spotted some plastic-coated maps scattered on the floor.

She squatted down and pushed them apart so she could read them. They covered this part of the valley—and the valley in which her family band kept its safe camp. These maps would have been useful to read the terrain.

She was still studying them when her father and the other men walked past her. "It's time to go, Mora," he told her.

"Father....look," she exclaimed. "These maps—they could be useful to us. We could find out more about our territory and the territory around us."

"We know enough about our territory. We don't need maps. Now come on. We have to keep going."

She didn't want to leave the maps behind, but she had to accept her father's decision. She cast one last backward glance at the maps and followed her male relatives out of the store.

The band met back up on the sidewalk. Rono was just giving orders to everyone to move out when everyone heard the telltale thump of heavy footsteps vibrating through the ground.

"Crushers!" Dagu gasped. "Run—this way!"

He pulled his wife and daughters around the nearest corner. All the men and women herded the children into a tight bunch.

The band dodged behind a different building. Dagu peeked out to make sure no Crushers could see the travelers.

He waved everyone across the street. The relatives sprinted for the cover of the next building and hid there just as an enormous Crusher stomped into the city.

The creature entered the streets a few miles farther south. It didn't see the family.

Dagu and the other men steered the family eastward—away from where the Crushers were coming from. The travelers dove, ducked, and hid behind one building after another before they raced out into the countryside.

The party didn't dare to return to the road—not for a long time. Rono and the other old men led the party through miles of dense jungle before the men decided it was safe to travel out in the open again.

Chapter 21

F our men of the Chosen Clan built a fire in the center of the plateau. They built it into a raging blaze and added large logs to create a cone of fire that lit up the whole area.

"Oh, look at that!" Viking sneered. "The Followers are here."

The others burst out in laughter when they saw the women wearing long dresses with their sleeves cinched around their wrists.

"How can they survive in this heat when they wear such restrictive clothing?" Zyria sneered.

"I heard they even wear undergarments under their dresses," Rila added. "Their undergarments cover the legs down to the ankles.

"You can see them from here," Estia chimed in. "Watch what happens when the women sit down."

All eyes turned to the Follower band across the plateau. The women had a distinctive way of flipping their dresses when they sat down.

They all sat with their legs bent sideways. Each women arranged her dress to cover as much of her legs as possible. No one could see any part of a woman's legs because her dress hid them.

It gave the women a strange appearance of not having legs at all. Everything below the waist looked like one large blob of colored stone.

Each time a woman arranged her skirts, she gave the observer a fleeting glimpse of her white undergarments. They really did cover the legs from the waist down to tight cinched clusters of fabric around the ankles.

Hangman couldn't imagine any attire more ill-suited to life in the jungle. The Followers must have sweltered under so many layers.

The Follower women wore their long hair twisted up in elaborate curled knots on top of their heads. These knots didn't look like Alien's small, dotted knots.

The sweeps of hair covered the whole head. The Followers' long clothing and their strange hairstyles made them look as weak, effeminate, and useless as their reputation suggested.

The Followers were famous—and not in a good way. They didn't hunt. They didn't defend themselves. They never confronted anyone who treated them hostilely.

The Followers made a point of always retreating, hiding, or negotiating with anyone or anything that threatened them. They couldn't be more opposite from the Godless.

The Godless made a few more biting remarks about the Followers.

"Heaven help the man who marries one of their women," Boxer added. "Can you imagine trying to travel with a woman who doesn't even know which end of a weapon to hold?"

"They don't even defend their own children from danger," Katha went on. "And look at all those old people. What good are they? They would only slow the band down."

"I wonder how long it took them to get here," Chaos agreed. "They would have had to stop and hide every few seconds every time they see a dangerous creature. I'm surprised they made it to the gathering at all."

"Maybe they headed north last year at the end of last year's gathering," Shadow suggested. "Maybe they never left. Maybe they've been hiding at the base of the plateau all this time. Then they would only have to climb up here and make it look like they traveled here from farther south."

The others laughed. The Godless' laughter got so brazen that the other bands noticed and looked over. The Followers looked over, too. Some of them wrinkled their noses at the Godless.

"I heard they don't eat meat," Magnet remarked. "Most of their diet is taken from plants."

"Ew!" Zyria grimaced. "Disgusting!"

"It's no wonder they're so weak if they don't eat meat," Katha replied. "They must be spindly under their clothes."

Boxer shoved Hangman against the shoulder. "You might get a Follower wife. Then you would find out and you could tell us what they're like."

More laughter broke out. Hangman didn't respond even to tell his cousin to shut up. Just a few more hours and this would all be over.

The reality was starting to set in. The Followers wouldn't be here at all if they didn't have a young person coming of age who needed to marry.

Hangman crossed his fingers that the young Follower would be a man.

Hangman cast a critical eye over the rest of the assembled bands. He couldn't tell by looking at them which young people were coming for marriage. Some might be too old or too young.

He couldn't tell which of the Followers was here for marriage, either. He really, really started to hope more young men showed up than women. Then the other young men could take all the women and he would leave alone.

Hours passed. No one made a move to start the gathering.

At some unseen signal, Dodge stood up from the cluster in Wizard's band. A few different men stood up from different bands all over the plateau. Then Arda stood up and Bullseye stood up on opposite sides of the fire.

Young people stood up one after another. Hangman finally had no choice but to stand up, too.

He did a quick head count. The number of men and women standing up was exactly equal. Everyone would pair up tonight.

His stomach dropped when a young woman stood up from the Follower group. She wore exactly the same long dress and hairstyle as all her female relatives.

Arda and Bullseye immediately stepped out of line, met up in the center of the ring, joined hands, and he led her back to Wizard's group. She sat down with Bullseye and he put his arm around her. So that was over.

The other couples took longer to pair off. One other young man crossed the circle, approached a young woman he liked, asked her a few questions in an undertone, and led her back to his family.

They sat down. That was all they had to do. Now they were married.

No one moved for a long time. Wizard finally got to his feet, murmured something to Dodge, and crossed the fire to one of the other bands. It was a band of the Whisperers Clan, another hunting Clan that lived farther east of Godless territory.

Another older man advanced out of that band and met Wizard in the center near the fire. The men talked for a few minutes.

They still stood there talking when a few other men broke away from their bands, met up in the middle, and negotiated about their unpaired young people.

"Who do you like, Hangman?" Boxer asked and laughed again.

No one answered him. Hangman pretended not to hear. He could already see where this was going.

Wizard accompanied the other father to the Whisperers group and came back with a young woman for Dodge. Then Wizard got into a lengthy negotiation with another Whisperer father about finding a husband for Distra.

Hangman's heart sank as more and more of the unpaired young people crossed the plateau and sat down. No one approached the Followers. That young woman would be the last one left. Then Hangman would have no choice but to take her.

Chapter 22

C old sweat broke out on Mora's palms when she glanced across the plateau to the last young man standing on the other side of the fire.

He was tall with long, midnight-black hair hanging loose to his shoulders. A mass of twisted, hideous scars covered his face. They distorted his mouth into the wrong shape and made his nose a grotesque caricature of what it should have been.

The rest of him looked normal. He was strong, lean, and muscular, but his face looked like something out of her worst nightmares.

The fact that she could see so much of his body turned her stomach. The Godless wore hardly any clothes at all. How could anyone stand to act so indecently?

The Godless had a reputation for being brutal, reckless, violent hunters. They ate only meat—and they hated the Followers with a passion.

The Godless couldn't read. They didn't value any kind of education like that. They turned up their noses at everything the Followers held sacred.

The Godless even sent out their old people to fight dangerous creatures in the jungle. The Godless didn't value human life at all.

All eyes turned to the last two young people standing. Mora's stomach turned when the young man's dark eyes locked on her.

His scars didn't interfere with his eyes at all. They stared out of his ruined face with a kind of haunted ferocity. He hated her. She saw that written all over his disgusting face.

Her father got to his feet and stepped forward. Another, older Godless man stood up from the crowd around the young man.

Mora lunged for her father, grabbed his arm, and pulled him back. "No! Don't go out there, Father—please! You can't make me go with him! Send me anywhere—just not with the Godless! They're wild animals! They're barbaric! You can't do this to me!"

Dagu lowered his voice to a harsh growl. Everyone could hear her outburst, but he made sure no one heard him. "You have to go with him. You're the last two left. If you didn't go with him, we would never be able to bring anyone else to the gatherings. The other Clans would shun us. You would ruin your sisters' chances of finding husbands and bring shame on all the Followers. The other Clans already look down on us. Don't make it any worse."

He tore his arm out of her grasp much more harshly than he'd ever treated her before. He even grabbed her by the wrist and forced her to lower her arm to her side.

Then he turned his back on her and walked out there to meet up with the young man's father.

The older Godless man made it to the center of the plateau before Dagu got there. The other father stood there waiting until Dagu joined him.

Mora trembled in her shoes while the two men talked to each other in an undertone. She didn't want to think about what they were saying to each other—but she already knew.

This wasn't happening. She couldn't marry any Godless—much less a man as grotesque as that one.

He glared at her across the plateau in such undisguised hatred that she wanted to look away. The power of his gaze forced her to keep staring into those black pits of eyes. He didn't look human. He *wasn't* human.

He radiated all the violence and blood-thirsty madness the Godless Clan was known for. He looked like the kind of man who could kill without a moment's hesitation. He looked like he even wanted to kill her.

She tore her eyes away and cast helpless, desperate glance around the plateau, but that only made her feel worse. All the other young people were already sitting down. Some of them sat with their arms around each other.

Everyone else on the plateau stared at her. They all watched and waited for the outcome of the negotiation between the two fathers.

It went on for a long time—much longer than any of the other negotiations. What were they talking about? Was Dagu getting the other father's assurance that the Godless wouldn't roast Mora on a spit the minute they took her away from her family?

That wouldn't happen. The Godless were a lot of things. The other Clans talked endlessly about their exploits in battle and in hunting, but no one ever accused the Godless of being cannibals.

Mora started shaking when she looked over the other people in the young man's family group. They wore hardly any clothing.

Parts of their bodies showed underneath what little clothing they wore. Mora had never seen anything so indecent—and the Godless didn't even notice that they were showing anything. They probably wouldn't have cared if they did notice.

Dagu and the other father concluded their negotiation. Both men returned to their own bands. This would have been the time when the young man would normally approach the young woman, exchange a few words with her, and convince her to cross the plateau to join his band.

The scarred young man didn't do that. He didn't move at all. He stayed exactly where he was and glared at Mora in outright challenge.

If they married at all, she had to be the one who crossed the plateau. He wouldn't do it. She saw that in his eyes.

He would just dig in and never budge. Nothing on God's green Earth would make him budge—on anything.

Her father came back over to her and stood right in front of her to block her from seeing the young man. Dagu got right in her face.

"You have to go with him, my child. It isn't a question. The young man's father assures me that they'll protect you and see that you're taken care of."

Mora couldn't stop her voice from shaking. "Don't make me do this, Father. I'm begging you. I just want to go home....."

"You can't go home, my child. If you don't go with him right now, you might as well stay here and go out into the jungle alone. You have to go with him. You don't have a choice. If you don't go right now—if you don't show that you're going willingly, I'll have to carry you over there and hand you over to them. Don't you dare shame our family like this. Don't bring any shame on the Followers. I didn't raise you for that."

She cast a glance past his shoulder at the young man across the plateau. She immediately looked away.

She had to summon all her resolve to go over there. She untied the little warthog's rope and handed it to her sister Yena.

Her mother Alura stood up, hugged Mora once, and kissed her on the cheek. "Make us proud, my dear. I know you'll do your best for your new Clan."

Mora went through the whole hasty goodbye in a numb trance. This wasn't happening.

The other Godless sitting around the young man's ankles were already turning away and collecting their few possessions to leave. It was all over.

Dagu pushed Mora away. "Go on—and God's speed."

She turned her back on her family. She would never see any of them again.

She blundered across the plateau too dazed to think straight. The Godless got to their feet as she drew nearer. She couldn't even see the young man anymore.

They all turned away. Everyone else on the plateau stood up. Conversation broke out as everyone milled around and drifted off into the night.

People surrounded Mora. She didn't give herself the option to focus on them well enough to see who they were, what they were doing, or any other incriminating body parts that might peek out from under their clothes when they moved their arms or legs.

She heard some of them laughing—and then the group migrated away from the fire to leave the gathering and everything Mora knew and loved behind.

Chapter 23

S omeone grabbed Mora by the arm and pulled her down onto the ground. She tried to struggle, but when she turned around to confront the person, she found herself facing a woman.

The woman wasn't young, but she was strong and fierce looking. She wore her long, black hair tied into a thick mass of tightly braided strands on the back of her head.

She wore as little clothing as the other Godless women. Her bare arms, legs, and stomach showed how muscular she was despite her age.

She carried two matching stone axes stuck into the waistband of her loincloth. Her axes weren't as big as the Godless men's weapons, but hers were still impressive.

Those weapons made Mora shudder. It was bad enough that she was surrounded by Godless. Now this murderous woman was grabbing Mora and yanking her around.

The woman glared at her when Mora shook off the woman's hand. Then the woman sneered and burst into a sickening grin.

"Settle down, little one," the woman told her. "My name is Katha and I'm Hangman's mother—so I'm your mother-in-law. Sit down. We're camping here for the night."

Mora looked around in confusion. The scarred young man she was supposed to be married to squatted on the opposite side of the group. He didn't come near her.

Other members of the Godless band gathered sticks and started a fire on the bare ground. They used a strange method for starting the blaze.

One broad-shouldered man with a smooth, round face took a single stick, pressed it between his palms, and spun it back and forth.

Its tip bored into another piece of wood. Smoke billowed from the end until it formed an ember.

He used the ember to ignite a ball of dried grass. He used that to light the bigger fire. The whole process took only a minute or two.

The Followers never did it that way. They carried live embers with them in wooden containers to keep them alive while the family band traveled from place to place. The Followers didn't waste anything, not even fire. They didn't have to create it every time they pitched a new camp.

The other Godless sat and sprawled on the ground. They chose a deep cave to camp in for the night. Mora didn't notice that until now.

The firelight flickered off the walls and gave all the light Mora needed to see what everyone else in the party was doing.

Men and women lounged together with their arms around each other. They even kissed and touched each other's unclothed bodies in full view of everyone.

She averted her eyes as much as possible, but she couldn't stop herself from seeing. She also couldn't stop herself from seeing too much every time one of the Godless squatted down.

Their loincloths failed to hide everything. Some of them sat facing her with their legs far enough apart for her to see straight up between their legs.

A man and a woman lay reclining together against a nearby rock. The woman smiled at Mora and the man laughed out loud.

"She's a scared little rabbit!" the guy brayed. "She's scared of the big, bad Godless!"

"She should be scared," another woman sneered. "Look at her. She looks like she would be scared of a strong breeze." The woman raised her voice and called over to Mora. "Don't think you're going to travel with us dressed like that. You look like an Abnormit grub."

Loud laughter broke out all over the cave. The scarred young man kept his body turned sideways so he didn't see her nor did he get involved in the conversation even to make fun of her.

"What's your name, Rabbit?" the younger woman asked from the man's arms. "I'm Zyria and this is Boxer."

"Mora," Mora mumbled under her breath. "My name is Mora."

A few more people laugh. "She doesn't talk much," a much larger, dangerous-looking man remarked. He had a whole bunch of tiny knots of hair dotting his scalp. "At least she won't talk us to death while we're trying to hunt."

Katha put out her hand and tried to grab the collar of Mora's dress. "Take this off, Rabbit. You can't wear this....."

Mora lashed out and knocked the woman's hands away. "Don't you touch me!"

Katha glared at her and finally turned away. More people laughed at the scene, but that moment changed something. Everyone else in the group scooted over to the fire, took dried meat out of their shoulder bags, and started eating.

"We should take more time on the way back to the long camp," Hangman's father remarked. "We should look out for more Renegades invading."

"We should try to capture one of them and question them about how many people they have in the area," another enormous man added. He had a scar running down one side of his face.

"It's a good idea," the guy with the knotted hair agreed. "We could eliminate them before they have a chance to strike or carry word back to their own people."

Their discussion went on. Mora didn't understand much of it. They talked a lot about attacking people, killing them, and getting into fights against other groups.

The conversation made her sick, but she forced herself to listen. She started to pick up their names.

The big guy with the knotted hair was Alien. The man with the long scar on his face was Viking. The young boy with two crossed scars was called Cross, of course.

The scarred young man Mora was supposed to consider her husband was Hangman. The others talked about him as though he was some mighty warrior who carried out heroic feats no one else could accomplish.

He didn't look like much—not compared to his much bigger relatives.

He ignored the entire discussion. He faced the other way and ate his food in silence as though he was completely alone in this cave.

No one offered Mora anything to eat. She didn't want to eat. She didn't want to get into the habit of eating only meat, but she would have to. The Godless didn't eat any other food.

She would rather go hungry, at least for tonight. She could feel sorry for herself just a little longer.

Why did this have to happen? She couldn't think of a worse Clan to marry into than the Godless. They were everything the Followers were not.

She couldn't think of a worse man to marry than Hangman. He obviously didn't want her. He hated her more than the other Godless did. He hated her too much to make fun of her or insult her or even look at her.

If he didn't take her, the Godless would only hand her off to another of their unmarried men—probably someone who hadn't gotten a wife at a previous gathering.

Anyone would be better than Hangman. Maybe the next one would at least be somewhat good-looking and maybe even want to talk to her.

Katha got her attention by bumping her elbow. "Take this and eat it." Katha handed Mora a piece of dried meat. "We have a long way to travel and you'll need your strength. We don't want you to fall over on the way. No one is going to carry you, so you better eat it."

Mora didn't want to, but her parents' words came back to her. She wouldn't bring shame on the Followers. She owed it to them to do her best for the Godless.

Heaven only knew how she could do that when she didn't understand their ways. She didn't want to learn, either.

One thought changed her mind. Word would spread to the other Clans if she integrated into the Godless or not. All the other Clans would find out if she became a good wife or not. The other Clans already despised the Followers enough.

Her reputation would cast shame or credit on her Clan even after she left it. News of her behavior would follow her for the rest of her life.

If word got out that she didn't become a good wife, the other Clans would shun the Followers even more. Other Clans would become even more reluctant to marry their young people to the Followers. That would be disastrous.

She kept her eyes down when she brought the dried meat to her mouth, bit off a piece, and started chewing. It was utterly tasteless. The Godless didn't add seasonings or flavors to make it more palatable. It was just plain meat and nothing else.

Katha waited a few minutes and then handed Mora a gourd full of water. "Drink something."

Mora drank some water and put the gourd on the floor. Katha didn't try to talk to her again. No one did.

The discussion around the fire drifted to other subjects including locations the band planned to visit and their other objectives in each location.

Mora didn't understand much of that, either, and in a little while, the Godless started to lie down to go to sleep.

They stretched out on the bare stone floor with nothing underneath them, nothing covering them, and no cushion to soften the surface.

The couples groped each other deeper and in more intimate ways. Mora found herself gaping at them and trying with all her might to look away.

No one among the Followers did anything like this in view of others. People kept their mating activities hidden. Married couples waited until everyone else went to sleep and then hid under their blankets.

Katha pushed Mora from behind. "Go over there with Hangman," Katha ordered. "You're married now."

Mora stumbled to her feet. Zyria and Boxer kissed, stuck their tongues in each other's mouths, and their hands ranged all over each other right in front of Mora.

She found it difficult even to walk past them. Her every instinct told her to look away, but she couldn't.

She stumbled across the cave. All the other Godless were rolling over, curling up, stretching out, and shutting their eyes. The bubble of voices died down.

She made it halfway across the cave before Hangman turned his back on her, lay down on his side, and rolled over so he faced away from the room. He couldn't make it more obvious that he wasn't interested in her.

She couldn't go over there. She couldn't go near him, especially not for that.

Everyone else in the room ignored her. No one noticed or cared when she sat down against one of the cave walls. She was nowhere near Hangman.

At least she didn't have to see his face from this position. She would definitely have nightmares about him tonight.

She did her best to curl up on the floor to go to sleep, but the hard stone kept her awake. Her hips, back, and shoulders ached.

She wound up sitting back up and leaning against the wall behind her. This gave her a full view of two couples going at it on the other side of the room.

One of the couples was Zyria and Boxer. The other couple was the round-faced man who started the fire. Mora thought she heard someone call him Chaos.

He didn't look chaotic at all. He actually looked kind of smart in a strange way.

The woman with him must have been his wife. She was the one who said Mora looked like an Abnormit grub. Her name was Rila.

Chaos and Rila rolled in each other's arms for a minute before he twisted on top of her. He pulled both of their loincloths off and arched his hips between her spread legs while she clawed at his back and buttocks to pull him into her.

She bared her teeth, snarled up at him, and her eyes kept drifting half-shut every time he drove into her.

Mora found herself watching in fascinated horror. No one in the Followers Clan ever talked about how children were conceived. Everyone just expected the young people to figure it out when the time came.

Mora had never seen any naked human body except her own and some of the younger children and babies she helped to take care of as she got older.

She certainly had never seen adults doing it with each other like this—not right out in the open.

Once or twice in her life, she had woken up in the middle of the night and seen couples moving around under their blankets. Strange, muffled noises came from under the blankets, but she never saw more than that.

Chaos, Rila, Boxer, and Zyria didn't even try to hide what they were doing. Rila kept making pained noises, grimacing, and clamping her lips shut to stifle the noise.

Boxer and Zyria kept kissing deeper, harder, and with ever-increasing passion. Both of them clawed at each other all over.

In a minute, Boxer rolled onto his back and pulled Zyria on top of him. She straddled him, gyrated her hips on him, and he eventually pulled her loincloth off.

He manhandled her buttocks and slipped his hands between her legs until she sat up on top of him.

Mora didn't understand the look passing between them. He pulled his loincloth off and they both maneuvered themselves a few times before she settled down straddling him and looking down at him from above.

No one else in the cave noticed a thing. Neither of the two couples noticed each other.

Mora couldn't watch anymore. She turned her back to the room, but she still didn't lie down. She shut her eyes so she wouldn't see anything, but she still heard the two couples behind her. She heard the men now, too.

Their noises kept her awake. She probably wouldn't have been able to sleep that night anyway, but this made it impossible.

This was just the latest insult to everything to everything she held dear. These people were savages—and now the rest of the world expected her to become one of them.

She shuddered when she thought about Hangman trying to do something like that to her. She couldn't let that happen, but she wouldn't be able to stop him if he did.

That would be terrible, but it was bound to happen sooner or later. It was the inevitable endpoint of them getting married in the first place.

Chapter 24

Hangman opened his eyes and stared at the stone wall in front of him while he relived the nightmare of the gathering. It was over—exactly the way he looked forward to it being over.

He never had to go back to the gathering as a candidate for marriage, but his nightmare was just beginning.

He sat up and his blood started to boil when he saw the young Follower girl sitting against the wall. She had fallen asleep sitting up—probably because the stone floor was too hard for her delicate body.

He hated her. He couldn't imagine getting stuck with a worse wife. Now he was saddled with her for life. He couldn't get rid of her.

He slipped out of the cave. He was just about to go off alone to hide from reality when he spotted Chaos and Magnet nearby. They squatted near the trees outside the cave. Everyone else was asleep.

The two cousins looked up when Hangman approached them. "Is your bride still asleep?" Magnet asked.

"Yes, and let's hope she stays that way forever."

Magnet laughed. "Come hunting with us, little brother. It will take your mind off your troubles."

Hangman doubted anything would take his mind off his troubles, but he only nodded. "All right. Let's go."

The three men filed into the jungle and Hangman started looking around for something to come out and attack him. People walking through the jungle were the best bait for hunting.

Everything was always coming out to attack. Then he could kill it and take it home to share with the band.

The men travel for an hour without seeing anything. The band would wake up and travel on without them until the Hangman and his cousins caught up. He didn't have to worry about slowing them down.

The cousins stopped to consult with each other after another half an hour. "One of us should climb up to the treetops," Chaos suggested. "You're the best climber, Hangman. You can go."

Hangman snorted at him. "Thank you very much for volunteering me."

"You know you love it," Magnet interjected. "We aren't finding anything down here."

Hangman heard a noise in the distance just then. He looked up and spotted a bird soaring through the clouds overhead.

The bird was too high for him to see it clearly. He didn't need to see it clearly. He could tell what it was from the black outline of its wings.

"Look," he murmured. "It's a Ridgebeak! She must have a nest nearby."

"All the more reason for you to climb up into the canopy," Magnet added.

Hangman barely heard him. The Ridgebeak circled on thermal updrafts billowing out of the jungle. The bird was nowhere near the ground.

His cousins stood off to one side and watched him pace back and forth on the jungle floor. This was too good an opportunity to pass up.

He widened his search in concentric rings. He had to remind himself to take his eyes off the treetops and look where he was going so he didn't run face first into tree trunks.

His cousins followed him in silence. Ridgebeaks were his expertise. Magnet and Chaos wouldn't interfere. They would just stand by to help him if he needed it.

He finally spotted a denser clump of tree branches overhead and returned to his cousins. He glanced up one more time before he handed his kukris to Chaos.

"Stand over there where the canopy is thinner," Hangman told them. "Let her see you near her nest."

"So she can attack us?" Magnet countered. "I think not."

"She won't attack you because she'll see me in the nest. You making yourselves visible will lure her closer to the ground. That's all."

Magnet made a face, but he didn't argue.

Hangman located some nearby vines, cut them with his knife, and twisted then into a quick length of rope.

"Are you sure you don't want us to come with you?" Chaos added. "She looks like a big one. You may need another man if she turns out to be too big for you."

"She is a big one, but only one man can fit in the nest. Stay here. You can help me by butchering her when I finish with her."

Chaos gave him a look. Hangman smirked. Hunting and fighting a Ridgebeak definitely took his mind off his problems.

He was in his element. Ridgebeaks posed a unique hunting challenge. They were actually dangerous enough to get him nervous and excited about facing one of them.

He coiled up the rope, held it in his teeth, and took his kukris back from Magnet.

He scaled into the canopy and balanced along the branches until he came to the tangled knot of foliage he saw from the ground.

It looked like nothing but leaves from all sides and from below. He had to climb an even taller tree to see down inside the nest. The leaves hid it from all sides except for directly above.

He peered down at a dozen juvenile Ridgebeaks all crouching in the nest. Each one was already as tall as his knee and covered with hard, thorny feathers. They scraped and rustled with a dull scratching sound whenever one of the chicks adjusted its position.

Lines of sharp points ran backward from the ridge of their beaks. A blunt strike from one of those beaks could tear flesh from bone as easily as the beak itself.

The Ridgebeak's talons posed another challenge. The juveniles' talons were already as broad as Hangman's hand with long, recurved claws and powerful gripping muscles. The Ridgebeak could kill by impaling its prey with its talons long before the first bite of its beak.

He cast one last look down at the ground and up at the sky. Chaos and Magnet paced around in the open place where the mother Ridgebeak would be able to see them through the canopy.

Hangman couldn't tell what the two men were doing, but the lure sure worked.

The mother Ridgebeak descended from the sky in the time it took Hangman to braid his rope and climb up here. She dropped down to check out an easy kill or a threat to her chicks.

Hangman tucked his rope into his waistband and climbed onto the tree branches underneath the nest. He didn't want to get inside it—not yet.

He crawled up the side, found some tangled branches right at the edge of the nest, and wrapped his legs around the trunks to hold himself in position. He crouched behind the thick leaves where the chicks couldn't see him.

Lightning quick, he lunged upward, threw his arm over the side of the nest, grabbed the nearest chick by the leg, whipped it out of the nest, and swung its head hard against another nearby branch.

He hit it hard enough to stun it, chopped its head off with a swift stroke of his kukri, and threw the chick down to the ground. It landed thirty feet away from Chaos and Magnet.

Nothing happened at first. Hangman didn't hear any commotion inside the nest. The other chicks must not realize that one of their number suddenly disappeared without warning.

Hangman dove upward, grabbed another chick, and dispatched it the same way.

He definitely heard a squawk this time. When he tried to grab his third chick, all the others had gathered on this side of the nest.

They brought themselves right into his reach. They tried to attack his hand and arm, but they didn't react fast enough.

He grabbed the nearest chick, yanked it out, and it shrieked again before he chopped its head off. There were three more chicks in the nest.

That was the moment when he heard a deafening shriek from directly overhead. The mother was coming back—fast.

Hangman grabbed one more chick. This one struggled a lot more, but he clasped his hand around both its legs to stop it from sinking its talons into him.

He had to work quickly. He clipped that one across the neck, threw it over the side, and scrambled the rest of the way into the nest.

The two remaining chicks came at him in a heartbeat. One of them flew at him and hit him in the chest before he grabbed it, pinned its wings down, and then clamped his fist around its legs.

The second one attacked his leg and tried to bite him, but his leggings protected him.

Nothing would protect him from the mother bird. She kept screeching again and again getting louder as she plunged down on top of the intruder inside her nest.

He did his best to ignore the second chick, swung the first one down onto the branches that made up the nest's structure, and held it there while he raised his kukri to strike.

The creature struggled, flapped its wings, and reared up trying to bite his wrist and hand.

He waited until it fell back to try again. The creature stretched backward into exactly the right position.

He hacked his kukri into its neck, threw the carcass over the side, and grabbed the last chick. He barely had a chance to restrain the thing, kill it, and throw it over before the mother bird plummeted into the nest right in front of him.

She towered over him screeching and beating her wings. She knocked him over, but that actually worked in his favor.

He pulled the coil of rope from his waistband, rolled onto his back, and threw the noose over one of her giant clawed toes. It cinched tight.

She couldn't attack him when he was right underneath her. She flexed her wings, rose a few feet out of the nest, and hopped around to confront him.

That moment when she lifted off gave him the chance to throw a few more loops of rope around both her legs.

She angled her position to drop right on top of him with her talons extended. She could have killed him instantly, but he reacted too fast.

He rolled away just in time and pulled the rope tight to bind her legs together. She couldn't balance nor could she use her talons.

She felt back on her other two weapons—her wings and her beak.

She shrieked in fury, took wing, and dove for him cracking her beak open.

He played his strategy to the letter, rolled back underneath her, and impaled his kukri upward through the underside of her jaw to split her skull in half.

She collapsed right on top of him, buried him under her weight, and trapped him there under all her scratchy feathers.

Chapter 25

Hangman coughed and struggled to breathe under the mother Ridgebeak's weight. At least she was dead now. He could take his time figuring out how to get out from under her.

He had killed enough Ridgebeaks in his time. He wedged himself through the creature's feathers and scratched himself up really good working closer to the creature's head.

Her neck and head were the lightest part of her body. He shoved upward with his back, forced her neck to bend, and crawled the rest of the way out from under her head.

He straightened up and breathed a sigh of relief when he saw Chaos and Magnet watching him from the ground. They grinned and waved at him. He waved back.

They had collected all the dead chicks, tied their legs together into two bundles, and Chaos carried the joining rope over one shoulder so the chicks hung in front of and behind him.

Now the cousins just had to worry about taking the mother back to the band.

Hangman turned to the mother bird and squatted down to pull her feathers off. They weighed a lot and served no useful purpose—not to a band on a journey like this.

If he had been closer to the long camp, he would have taken the feathers home for the women to fashion into tools. He couldn't do that now.

He pulled all the feathers off on one side of the body, cut the head and talons off, and rolled the body over to pluck the other side before he threw the carcass down to the ground. His cousins could do the hard work of butchering the creature.

He would have liked to make them carry the meat back to the band, but the bird was too big for that. He would have to help them.

He finished plucking and put his kukris back into his waistband where they would be out of his way.

He squatted down, wedged his arms under the body—and froze when he saw something a few miles away in the jungle. He wouldn't have seen it at all if he hadn't been in the Ridgebeak's nest at the time.

He recognized instantly that he was seeing Renegade warriors moving through the jungle. They didn't travel toward him and his cousins. They head north on a parallel track to the route Butcher's band took to the gathering.

Hangman held his breath even though the Renegades were too far away to see him. He couldn't let this pass.

Viking's suggestion rang in Hangman's ears. He and his cousins could capture these Renegades and question them about what other Renegade patrols were encroaching on this area.

A thousand ideas raced through his mind. The Renegades didn't know he and his cousins were here. He abandoned the dead Ridgebeak. She would still be here when Hangman came back for her.

He swung down the branches to the ground. "Did she win your heart at last?" Chaos teased.

"Be quiet!" Hangman hissed. "There's a Renegade patrol straight west of us. They're heading north! They don't know we're here. We can ambush them, capture them, and question them the way Viking said. Come on! Hurry."

Chaos dropped the chicks on the ground. The ants or Abnormits might get the chicks by the time the cousins came back for them, but Hangman didn't care.

He did some quick mental calculations while he and his cousins took off running west. The Renegades had been directly west of him or maybe even slightly farther north when he saw them from the nest.

They would move even farther north by the time he and his cousins found them.

He ran for a long way, signaled his cousins to follow him, and circled south before the three of them heading north again.

Hangman, Chaos, and Magnet spread out and pulled their weapons. Hangman didn't know how far he would have to go before he came upon the Renegades.

He found them sooner than he expected and the three cousins struck without mercy. Hangman killed two of them. Magnet went after three of them and got himself surrounded before Hangman came to help him.

Chaos also got himself surrounded, but he counterattacked so ferociously that he took down three of them before the others overwhelmed him.

Hangman ran over to Magnet, chopped one of the Renegades across the back of the skull, and Magnet killed the other two.

Magnet and Hangman both ganged up on Chaos's three remaining opponents. Hangman stabbed one of them under the ribs and the guy went down.

Chaos and Magnet took down their opponents without killing them. Magnet pounced on his enemy, pinned the guy's arms under his knees, and jammed his axe handle into the man's neck.

Chaos hit his opponent across the thigh and crippled him. The guy tried to limp away, but Chaos tackled him from behind and hit him a second time across the small of his back.

The guy screamed and flipped over, but he couldn't use his legs. Hangman rode his enemy to the ground, held him down, and twisted the kukri deeper into the guy's flesh.

"Where are the Renegades coming from?!" he demanded. "Do you have a base inside Godless territory?! Answer me! Do you have a central base where you're launching all these strikes?!"

The guy screamed in pain and rolled his eyes in agony. He didn't answer until Hangman twisted the blade again.

"We can keep doing this until you talk!" Hangman snapped. "You won't die until I pull this out. Now tell me the truth! How are the Renegades getting all these patrols inside our territory?!"

The guy screamed again. "We don't have a base! There is no base!"

"Don't tell me you're all traveling over the mountains from the west." Hangman twisted the blade one more time. "Is that true?! Are all of you coming over on foot?!"

"YES!!" the guy shrieked. "It's the truth! You can ask them!"

Hangman gave the blade one last sadistic twist and ripped it out. The guy collapsed bleeding on the ground.

Hangman left him there and stalked over to Chaos's victim. The guy sat on the ground, leaned back on his arms, and tried to drag his useless legs farther and farther away from the three Godless.

Hangman didn't see where the guy could go without falling to some creature out here.

The guy panted, wheezed in terror, and kept grimacing in pain every time he moved. He didn't seem to grasp just how much trouble he was in.

Hangman kicked him down flat on his back and Hangman jammed his foot into the guy's neck.

The Renegade stared up at him with huge eyes. "Don't kill me!" the guy panted. "I have a family! Please don't kill me!"

"You're already dead, little brother. The Abnormits will come for you in a few minutes as soon as we leave. If you tell me what I want to know, I'll kill you now so you don't have to go through that."

The guy gasped a few more times and his eyes darted around before he came back to staring up at Hangman.

"You heard what your friend said," Hangman went on. "Is there a Renegade base inside Godless territory—somewhere the Renegade Clan is launching all these patrols? I'm warning you. I'll know if you're lying. If you lie to me, I'll leave you alive and the creatures can take you."

The guy hesitated, looked around, and made eye contact with Magnet's captive. Hangman's victim was already too out of it to raise his eyelids more than halfway.

"There is a base......there are several.....beyond the hills.....against the mountains...." the guy gasped. "They aren't in Godless territory."

"You mean they're in the territory the Renegade Clan stole from the Godless," Hangman snapped. "Is that what you mean?"

The guy nodded, averted his eyes, and didn't return his gaze to meet Hangman's.

Hangman exchanged glances with Chaos. Hangman stepped away. Chaos moved in, flipped the guy onto his stomach, and hacked his axe into the guy's neck from behind.

The body lay still. That was two Renegades down.

Chaos and Hangman gathered around the third man. He was uninjured as far as Hangman could see.

"Don't leave me....." the guy whimpered. "Don't leave me for the creatures......"

"We can't let you live," Hangman replied. "We can't let you run back to your people and tell us that we know about these bases."

"Kill me!" the guy panted. "Please! Just kill me quickly!"

"I shouldn't. I should skin you slowly...."

"NO!!" the guy whined. "Please no!"

Hangman curled his lip at the guy. "You Renegades are cowards. You attack women and children. You can't even stand a little pain. You deserve to get eaten by ants."

"No!" the guy broke down in sobs. "No, please, no!"

Magnet struck without waiting to hear anything more. He crammed his axe handle harder into the guy's neck, shattered the man's windpipe, and left him choking and strangling for air.

Magnet climbed off the stricken Renegade. The three men stood around and watched until he finished thrashing and twitching in his death throes. None of the Renegades moved anymore.

"We better get back to Father and the others," Magnet murmured. "We still have a lot of work to do to cut up the Ridgebeak. It will be late by the time we get back."

Chapter 26

Mora opened her eyes and immediately shut them when she saw all the Godless crowded inside the cave.

She would have liked to believe that last night was just a bad dream. Now she woke up to the glaring reality that it wasn't.

The sight of them didn't revolt her as much as the smell. The smell of human bodies stung her nostrils. She'd never smelled anything so disgusting.

None of the Godless seemed to notice it. They didn't notice their relatives sitting up, coughing, and some of the men blowing snot out of their noses right onto the cave floor where they had just been lying a few minutes before.

The Godless scratched themselves in obscene places and then used the same hand to eat or stick their fingers in their mouths to get scraps of meat out from between their teeth.

Mora would have liked to keep her eyes closed for the rest of eternity, but someone came over to her and kicked her in the leg.

"Get up, girl," a woman snapped. "You've slept long enough. It's time to get up and start the day."

Mora dragged her eyes open. She didn't sleep well last night.

She looked up and realized the woman standing over her was her new mother-in-law, Katha. The woman looked every bit as fierce as she did yesterday. A night sleeping on solid rock didn't bother her at all.

She didn't wait for Mora to respond. Katha took hold of Mora's elbow, pulled her to her feet, and this time, Katha didn't let go when Mora struggled to break the woman's iron grip.

Katha dragged Mora into the middle of the cave right where everyone could see her, shook her to make her stand still, and took hold of Mora's collar.

"It's time for you to take this off," Katha snapped. "You're Godless now. You aren't a Follower anymore."

"Get your hands off me!" Mora grabbed the woman's wrists and tried to pull Katha's hands away.

Katha retaliated much more harshly than Mora expected. Katha slapped Mora's hands down hard enough to make Mora cry out in pain.

"If you don't cooperate and change your clothes, I'll rip this dress off and march you back to Godless territory stark naked," Katha snapped. "Is that what you want? You're Godless now. You're a threat to all of us walking around like that. You're announcing to all our enemies that you're helpless and can't defend yourself. Now take it off before I take it off for you."

Mora hesitated one split second too long. Katha raised her hands a second time, compressed her lips in annoyance, and started to unbutton Mora's collar.

Mora cringed in shame as Katha unbuttoned all the buttons down the front of the dress, unbuttoned Mora's sleeve cuffs, and pulled the dress off her shoulders.

It fell to the floor to reveal a tight fabric binding around Mora's chest that fixed her breasts in position so they didn't show through her dress.

Katha snorted when she saw the binding and Mora's white undergarments bunched around her waist and ankles.

Katha didn't ask for permission. She walked behind Mora, sliced a knife through the binding, and it fell away.

Mora's hands flew to her breasts to cover herself up. All the Godless sat around watching Katha cut off Mora's undergarments, too. Katha left her standing in the middle of the cave completely naked.

Even the oldest men watched. One of them was Shadow, Hangman's father.

Mora covered her breasts with one hand and her crotch with the other, but the Godless could already see everything.

Mora didn't want to look around, but she wound up doing it anyway. That was the moment when she realized. Hangman wasn't here.

At least he wasn't seeing this, but he wouldn't have cared if he did see it. He wouldn't have helped her.

Katha walked away and came back with two small fragments of skins. "Put these on and cover yourself," she snapped. "You'll be able to move around better in the jungle while you learn to hunt and defend yourself.

She threw the skins at Mora. They didn't look like garments at all.

She had to take her hands down to unfold them to see how to put them on. Even then, she couldn't figure it out. They just looked like pieces of skins tied in thin tubes.

Katha lost her patience again. "Here, you stupid girl. Watch me and do it yourself from now on. You know less than a baby."

Katha yanked the garments out of Mora's hands, threw one of them on the floor, and yanked the other over Mora's head.

Katha handled her roughly, shoved one of Mora's arms through the tube followed by the other, and positioned the tube around Mora's breasts to hide them.

Then Katha lifted two other hide straps and tied the laces over Mora's shoulders so the garment hung from her shoulders.

Mora still found herself raising her arms to cover herself. Dressing like this would have been considered scandalously immodest among the Followers.

The lower curve of her breasts peeked out from under the main tube around her chest—or at least it felt like it.

She'd been seeing this from the other women every time they bent over or leaned sideways. Their tops didn't hide their breasts completely, but the Godless didn't notice or even care.

Then came the loincloth. This consisted of two inverted triangles of hide connected at the narrowest place of the two points.

Katha passed the garment between Mora's legs and made her stand with her feet apart while Katha tied the laces at each of her hips. The loincloth left Mora's legs completely bare from the hips down to her feet.

"Now sit down and put your leggings on," Katha ordered.

"What about....?" Mora's eyes darted to the discarded dress and torn binding and undergarments.

"We'll save them for bandages." Katha picked them up and tossed Mora another bundle of some kind of hides.

Mora could only stare in stunned horror as Katha started ripping the dress, binding cloth, and undergarments into strips. That was the end of Mora's clothes—the only other clothes she had ever worn.

That moment really brought the truth hit home. She would never go back to the Followers. She could never go home to her family—not after a humiliation like this.

She was trapped with these barbaric people—and not just trapped with them. She was the lowest, most despised person here.

Everyone here considered her worse than their weakest, most despicable member. Any Godless, no matter how bad, would be more welcome than she was.

She saw enough of the other Godless putting on their leggings to figure out how to do it herself.

She had to take her own shoes off first. The Followers wore sturdy leather walking shoes they scavenged from the cities. The shoes protected her feet and lasted a long time.

The Godless' leggings consisted of two foot-shaped pieces of hide sewn together into something like a sock. This part fitted over the foot itself.

One long strip of hide connected to the top of this footpiece. The strip wrapped around the shin with lengths of hide wound and crisscrossed up the calf to the knee.

That was the whole legging apart from one small tie at the front. It attached the top of the foot piece to the front of the strip to close the gap.

Standing up in these leggings felt like walking around barefoot. Mora could feel every pebble, twig, and bump in the floor beneath her feet.

She was still getting used to the sensation when Katha got hold of her again, towed her into the middle of the floor, and parked her there were everyone could see.

The men rapidly lost interest. Some left the cave on some business or other. The few who remained didn't pay attention to Mora anymore.

Katha rummaged around in Mora's hair until she found the pins holding Mora's hair in its usual knot. Katha pulled the pins and all of Mora's hair fell down in a long black cascade.

Mora stood still and didn't try to fight back while Katha plaited certain sections of Mora's hair, especially at the front. Katha left the rest hanging loose.

"You can leave it like that until you decide how to wear it." Katha gave her a hard look. "Don't even think about putting it back up like that. If you do, I'll cut it all off and you can go around bald until you learn to wear it properly."

Mora didn't dare to argue. A mixture of hatred and heartbreaking grief took hold every time Mora even looked at her mother-in-law.

Mora would almost rather have dealt with Hangman himself, but he didn't come back. He didn't have anything to do with Mora even though they were supposed to be married now.

Maybe it would always be like this. Maybe he would avoid her for the rest of their lives. At least she wouldn't have to get physical with him.

That would never happen, either. The whole point of marriage was for them to have children. They would have to do it eventually even if he avoided her the rest of the time.

Katha walked around in front of Mora again, leveled her with another hard glare, and pulled one of the axes from her waistband. "Now you need to learn how to fight. Take this and hold it out in front of you."

Mora took the axe. It turned out to be a lot heavier than she realized even though it was a fraction of the size of the men's weapons.

Her arm sank under the weight. She had to use both hands just to hold it up.

Zyria laughed from across the room. "Look at her! She can't even hold a weapon!"

A few other women stopped what they were doing to laugh at Mora, too.

Katha retreated and came back with a long pole as thick as her thumb. "Just remember I hold two of these—one in each hand. You shouldn't be this weak. Now defend yourself as if your life depended on it."

Katha stood back and jabbed her pole at Mora's head and body. Mora tried to swing the axe to knock the pole away.

She had to rally all her strength in both her arms just to lift the weapon. Even then, she had to make wild swings that almost knocked her over.

Katha could move around much faster. She parried Mora's strokes and doubled back twice as fast. She smacked the pole against Mora's shoulders, poked her in the chest and stomach, and even hit Mora across the side of the head.

Katha didn't hit Mora hard enough to injure her. The blows flustered her and eventually enraged her.

Her arms tired way too fast. She wasn't used to holding up that weight. She made one more hefty swing and Katha smacked her in the thigh.

Mora bellowed at her mother-in-law, wielded the axe one more time trying to hack Katha with it, and Katha struck her hard.

The blow landed on the axe handle, knocked it out of Mora's hands, and sent it skidding across the floor. All the surrounding women burst out in laughter.

Mora glared at her mother-in-law. Katha pretended not to notice.

She walked over to pick up her axe and came back sticking it into the other side of her waistband.

"That was pathetic," she snarled. "You won't last ten seconds out here doing it that way."

Mora bit back the urge to insult the woman in return. Mora could only think to insult things about the Godless that the Followers looked down on.

Everything Mora could think to insult would have been considered compliments to the Godless. They were brutal, violent, murderous savages with no sense of decency. They were stupid, reckless, and filthy.

Katha went around the cave and collected up all the empty water gourds. "Go outside and gather some firewood for tonight. Bring it back here and don't stop until I tell you to. Once you finish that, you can take all these water gourds down to the stream and refill them. You aren't good for anything else, so you'll just have to work for your keep. Go on. Don't make me have to punish you."

Chapter 27

Mora stalked out of the cave fuming with rage. She hated all of these people, especially Katha.

A few of the men looked up when she walked out into the light of day. Some of the men even smirked at her.

She turned her back on them and entered the trees to look for firewood. At least she knew how to do that.

The jungle throbbed with heat. She never felt it before even though she always wore such thick, tight clothing.

This skimpy outfit somehow made it so much worse. She started sweating right away, but she couldn't do anything about it.

She gathered an armload of sticks and twigs. She found a few fallen branches, but they were too big and too long for her to carry them.

She also saw quite a few dangerous creatures. She couldn't see anywhere nearby to hide from them, so she took her sticks back to the cave and unloaded them next to the center fire circle.

She thought the Godless would continue to travel north, but they seemed to be staying here for a while.

"Is that all you got?" Rila sneered. "Aren't your arms strong enough to carry more than that? We'll all freeze tonight at the rate you're going."

Mora opened her mouth to point out that the party wouldn't freeze because the jungle was too hot for that.

She didn't get a chance to say a word before Katha came over and scowled at the sticks. "We don't need twigs. I didn't send you out to gather twigs. Bring back some real wood next time or you can sleep out in the jungle with the creatures tonight. Go on and don't be so lazy next time."

Mora bolted. She couldn't get a reputation in this Clan for being lazy or worthless. That was the worst thing anyone could call a person.

She returned to the place where she found the fallen branches. Each was thicker than her arm. Some were thicker than her leg.

She had to find a way to break them into pieces she could carry. She didn't care about anything else right now except stopping the other women from insulting her—and stopping Katha from punishing her for something she didn't do.

Mora hunted around until she found a sharp, pointed rock. She found weak spots on each branch and used the rock to chop the branches into pieces, but she still couldn't carry many of the logs at one time.

The thicker ones were too long and thick for her to carry more than one. She selected the middle-sized pieces and carried five of them back to the cave.

Katha snorted when she put them down. "The wood is better, but your arms are not. You're weak. You've never done anything strenuous in your life, have you?"

"Yes, I have," Mora replied. "I've worked hard all my life."

Katha humphed at her. The other women burst out laughing. "Hold your arm up," Rila demanded.

Mora held her arm out in front of her. Rila approached her and held her arm out next to Mora's. "Do you see a difference? I do."

The other women exploded in laughter. Everyone laughed, including Katha.

Mora looked down at the two arms side by side. Her arm was thin, white, and smooth. Not a single muscle showed through the skin. She suddenly realized with a jolt that she didn't really have any muscles.

Rila's arms were thicker, more muscular, and more chiseled even than Katha's. All the Godless women had shapely, muscular arms, legs, stomachs, and everything else.

They were also much more darkly tanned over their whole bodies. Their dark skin made them look feral and inhuman, but it also made them look much stronger and more deadly when it came to facing dangers in the jungle.

Rila put her arm down and walked away to rejoin the other women. They all smirked at her and clapped her on the shoulder to congratulate her for humiliating Mora again.

"Should we have a contest to see which of us can carry the most firewood?" Rila asked over her shoulder.

Mora lowered her eyes, but that only made her look down at her body. Her legs looked as thin and wasted as the rest of her. She really did look like an Abnormit grub like this—much more than she looked like one in her dress.

She was pure white, fleshless, and soft.

Katha took hold of Mora's elbow again. "Come with me, Rabbit. We need to straighten you out before we go any further."

Mora knew better than to fight back her mother-in-law. The men all stopped what they were doing to watch when Katha marched Mora outside.

Hangman still wasn't here. At least he didn't gloat over his mother mistreating Mora like this.

Katha stopped Mora in front of one of the trees, pulled out her small axe, and chopped a long branch from the nearest foliage.

Katha hacked off the side twigs and leaves with a few strokes, made a short rod a few feet long, and then cut another identical rod just like it.

She shoved Mora out of the way. "Now watch me. You need to practice and build up your strength. You're weak and weakness doesn't mix with Godless."

She turned to the tree in front of her and raised the two rods she'd just prepared. She held one in each hand.

"You're going to strike this tree as if you were hitting an enemy or a creature that's attacking you. Strike down and across with your right hand—then down and across with your left hand—then up and across with your right hand—then up and across with your left hand—then directly across from side to side with your right hand—then directly across from side to side with your left hand. Do you understand?"

Mora watched her. Katha went through every movement extra slowly. She cut her right hand down and across to her lower left. Then she did the same thing with her left hand cutting down and across so the rod wound up on her lower right.

She created an X pattern in front the trunk and then cut side to side in both directions before bringing her rods back to their original position.

Katha looked over at Mora. "Do you understand?"

Mora nodded. "I understand."

"As soon as you get the rhythm down, you can pick up the speed—like this."

Katha stepped a little nearer to the tree and flew into a rapid, almost blurred flurry of strikes. She hit the tree again and again so fast that her rods made a purring, drumming sound.

Her arms whirled in wide, whirling circles hitting and slashing in every direction. Mora stared at the woman in stunned amazement.

Katha stopped, straightened up, and pushed the rods into Mora's hands. "Now you do it."

Mora took a step toward the tree and raised her rods. She followed the same pattern Katha used only much more slowly.

Mora crossed each stroke down and across, up and across, and across from side to side. She didn't do it quickly. She couldn't.

Katha dipped her chin once. "That's right. Now you practice that for a while." She walked off and left Mora alone.

Mora stared down at the sticks in her hands. Wielding them like this felt awkward and ungainly, but anything was better than getting laughed at, insulted, and stared at by people who obviously hated her as much as she hated them.

She raised her arms and started following the pattern. She did it slowly. Katha said to learn the pattern first before speeding up.

Mora's arms gave out after only a few minutes. She put the rods down to rest her arms for a minute, but right then, she heard the men laughing behind her. Were they laughing at her—at how weak and useless she was?

Her family band considered her one of the strongest of their party. Her relatives always praised her for being so hardworking and being able to do things no one else could do.

She had never been insulted so much in her life—and no one in her family band ever, ever called her lazy. She wasn't lazy. No way would she let the Godless call her that.

She raised the rods and started practicing again, but her arms got more and more sore and exhausted the longer this went on.

She pushed through for as long as she could. Eventually the pain in her shoulders became overwhelming.

Her hands fell to her sides. She couldn't go on and she'd only been doing this for a few minutes.

She didn't dare to go back into the cave. She didn't dare even to turn around to see the men either glaring at her or grinning over her misfortune.

Chapter 28

M ora clamped her lips shut struggling to hold back tears. Any idea she might have had about what it would be like to get married and leave her family band—none of those ideas ever came close to how bad this was turning out to be.

Her so-called husband wouldn't have anything to do with her. Her mother-in-law and all the other women hated her. The men looked down on her and considered her a misfortune to them.

She threw the rods aside. She hated them, too. She was just about to run off into the jungle where she could cry in peace.

Maybe she would get eaten or killed by one of the dangerous creatures out here. Then she wouldn't have to worry about any of this. Hangman and Katha and all the Godless could stop worrying about her.

Hangman would live the rest of his life alone. Good riddance. No woman deserved this.

She took a step closer to the trees when Zyria came up to her from the side. "That was really good!" Zyria smiled extra broadly in Mora's face, put her arm around Mora's shoulders, and squeezed. "You'll get the hang of it if you keep practicing like that."

Mora looked down at the ground and mumbled under her breath. "It wasn't really good. The women are right. I'm weak."

"You'll get stronger, now that you're with us. Don't be so upset about it! Come with me. Don't be such a rabbit. We'll gather some firewood. That will put Katha in a better mood."

Mora didn't respond right away. Why was Zyria acting so friendly all of a sudden? She had been laughing at Mora in the cave just now.

Mora had a flashback of last night—the sight of Zyria straddling Boxer on the floor.....

Mora was too grateful for Zyria's kindness to care about that. Mora stumbled after the young woman and they reentered the trees.

Zyria forged her way deeper into the jungle. She didn't even seem to look around for any creatures that might attack her.

Zyria came armed. She carried two straight, square blades chipped out of grey stone flecked with different black, brown, grey, and yellow dots.

"It's natural that you would take some time to get used to a new Clan," Zyria mused over her shoulder. "I'm originally from another Clan, too."

"Really?" Mora exclaimed. "Which Clan is it?"

"I came from the Whisperers. It isn't that different from the Godless, but it is a different Clan. I grew up learning to hunt and fight with my relatives, but I had to learn all new ways when I married Boxer."

Mora lowered her voice. "That sounds hard."

"It will be hard for you, too, but in the end, you'll be like me." Zyria turned around and grinned at her. "You'll look, act, and think like all the other Godless. No one will ever be able to tell you were ever a Follower."

Mora looked away. She didn't want to look, act, and think like all the other Godless. She didn't want to be Godless at all. She wanted to be a Follower.

Zyria kept walking. "Don't worry so much. It will work out for you in the end—as long as Hangman doesn't get you first."

Mora stopped in her tracks and her head shot up. "What do you mean?"

"You know!" Zyria exclaimed. "He's dangerous. You can see what he's like. He might be the most dangerous man in the whole Clan. Everyone knows it. Butcher is Kral of this band and even he's afraid of Hangman. Butcher has a right to be afraid of him. Hangman could challenge any man in the band and maybe even in the whole Clan. He would win, too, even though he's so much younger than they are."

Mora gulped. She couldn't stop staring at Zyria. Zyria said these thing so casually, but they confirmed Mora's worst fears.

She saw something like this in Hangman's eyes the minute she realized he was the last man left at the gathering.

She took her a minute to get her voice back. "What do you.....what do you mean....by dangerous?"

Zyria didn't notice anything out of the ordinary. She didn't turn around nor did she stop walking. She kept talking over her shoulder and pretended not to see Mora falter.

"He can fight better than anyone," Zyria went on. "On the way here, he killed a Demonex with one throw of his kukris and took the creature down in seconds. He does things like that all the time."

"Wow," Mora breathed. "That doesn't sound possible."

"He climbs into Ridgebeaks' nests and kills them for sport. He slaughters whole parties of Renegade warriors with his bare hands. He can kill anything. He enjoys it. He's never happy unless he's out there killing something. You can see how dissatisfied he is every time he comes into camp. It takes an effort for him to even talk to people. He can't wait to leave. Who knows what he would be like with a woman? I'm just glad I'm old enough that I didn't wind up married to him."

Zyria kept walking. Mora would have liked to run back to the safety of the cave. She didn't want to be out here anymore, but she couldn't even see the cave from here—or any of the other Godless.

She just had to keep going and hope to High Heaven that Zyria found her way back there.

So that was the kind of man Mora had the misfortune to marry—a bloodthirsty heathen who killed for fun and whose own people considered him dangerous.

He looked dangerous, too. He looked brutal and heartless.

She trembled at the thought of getting caught anywhere alone with him. He could force himself on her by right—so why didn't he do it already?

He could have done it right there in front of his whole family if he really wanted to humiliate her. None of the Godless would have stopped him.

Zyria halted somewhere deep in the jungle and squatted down between some huge ferns. Mora didn't realize until she got there that Zyria was squatting next to some broken-off sections of logs.

Zyria didn't pick them up right away. She pried them out of the dirt and rolled them over to scrap the mud off before she lifted them.

Mora squatted down next to her. "Thank you for telling me.....about Hangman.....and about your story. I really appreciate your encouragement."

Zyria smiled broadly again. "Sure! Don't worry. You're going to be fine. Just keep an eye on Hangman. Who knows? Maybe he'll avoid you from now on. He can't stand weakness. He may dislike you enough not to do anything."

Mora stared at the ground. "I hope so."

"What about you?" Zyria breezed. "What was your life like in the south?"

Mora looked up. "You don't know what the Followers are like? Don't you already know?"

"I was wondering about you—if your experience was any different from what we've all heard and seen."

Mora lowered her eyes again. "It wasn't different. My family band is a typical Followers band. We don't hunt or kill or fight anything. We trap and gather food from trees and plants in the jungle. We avoid violence whenever possible."

Zyria studied her until she finished speaking. "Did you see anything unusual in the south—any unusual structures or objects from ancient times?"

Mora frowned back at the woman. "I don't know what you mean. We scavenge supplies from the cities all the time. They're full of ancient things."

"I mean anything outside the cities....anything unusual....."

Mora furrowed her brow. "I don't understand. What else would there be outside the cities?"

Zyria shrugged and turned back to scraping the mud off the logs. "I don't know. I just asked. None of the Godless have traveled that far south before. The Followers are known for traveling around a lot. I thought you might have seen something."

"Something like what? You must have seen all the ancient ruins."

"Of course. I meant something else."

Mora didn't understand what the woman was asking. As far as Mora knew, jungle covered the rest of the world outside the ancient cities.

The jungle crawled closer and encroached on the cities more and more each year. Plants forced themselves through paved roads and turned them into jungle. The jungle would take the cities completely one of these years.

Mora pushed the thought out of her mind. She didn't know of any ancient things outside the cities, so she couldn't answer Zyria's question—whatever it was.

Mora got ready for the ordeal of carrying these logs back to the cave. Her arms and shoulders already ached. She might tear a muscle if she tried to carry even one of these logs.

Zyria startled her alert again. "Did Hangman say anything to you about what the men are looking for?"

Mora's head shot up a second time. "Huh? What are they looking for?"

"I don't know. That's why I asked."

"I didn't even know they were looking for something." Mora frowned at her. "What *are* they looking for?"

Zyria laughed. "I wouldn't have to ask if I knew that. He didn't say anything to you about it?"

"He never said anything to me at all. You saw that. He wouldn't even look at me. He left the cave before I woke up this morning. He's been gone ever since. I haven't seen him since last night."

Zyria nodded and went back to what she was doing. "I just wondered if he mentioned it to you."

Mora frowned at the side of Zyria's head. The Godless were looking for something? What was it?

Mora would probably never know. If Zyria didn't know, Mora didn't have a prayer of finding out.

She didn't foresee Hangman ever saying a word to her and she didn't want him to. She wanted him as far away from her as possible.

He was probably out there killing things right now. Better for him to kill creatures and enemy warriors in the jungle than for him to come around here and get any ideas about doing the same thing to her.

Zyria got to her feet, picked up a medium-sized log, and settled it in her hands. "We better get back. Let's go."

Mora copied her and picked up another log the same size. If one of these logs was enough for Zyria, it would be enough for Mora.

"What cities have you seen in the south?" Zyria asked over her shoulder.

"The nearest one is Seattle," Mora replied. "Portland is farther south. My family band's range is between them. Portland is as far south as I've been. In fact, I don't think anyone in my band has been farther south than Portland. I don't think even my great-grandparents have traveled farther south than that."

"How do you know what they're called? Did the Followers name them that?"

"No, we read the signs when we enter a city—that and reading maps of the area."

Zyria stopped, turned around, and frowned at her. "What does 'reading' mean?"

Mora opened her mouth and stopped herself. She had been about to scoff at this woman for not knowing what reading was.

Mora shut her mouth and didn't say that. The Godless weren't the only Clan that didn't read. They shunned all forms of written communication and everything else from ancient times.

Mora chose her words with care. "It means learning the symbols the ancients used to mark out words on a sheet. The symbols mean things. They transmit information from ancient times so we can understand how they did things and what they thought about things."

Zyria frowned at her again. "Do you know how to read?"

"Of course. The Followers teach the little children to read. Everyone reads, even the old people."

Zyria studied Mora for a second. Mora couldn't detect Zyria's reaction to this news. Zyria might have reacted in any of a dozen ways. She kept her reaction hidden.

She didn't outright turn up her nose at the idea of reading and teaching the young to read.

That might be because Zyria came from the Whisperers—although the Whisperers didn't believe in education, either. They were as backward and ignorant as the Godless.

Zyria eventually turned around and set off walking again. Mora followed her.

Maybe a few people among the Godless would start to realize the value in learning the knowledge of the ancients. Maybe the Godless would realize that Mora had skills and knowledge the Godless might actually be able to use.

She could only hope. Right now she had to struggle to hold up the log so it didn't slip out of her exhausted arms.

Zyria had no problem finding her way back to the cave. She stopped inside the fringe of trees and put her log down. Mora did the same thing.

Zyria peeked through the undergrowth at the men standing around. "Leave your log here and go back to your practice. You don't want Katha to see you shirking."

"Shouldn't I take the log into the cave? Isn't that what she wants?"

"She told you to practice, so you should practice. Don't stop until she tells you to." Mora nodded. "Okay."

Zyria squeezed her arm. "It's going to be fine! Just be careful around Hangman. He has a terrible temper, so it's probably better if you don't talk to him at all."

"Thank you," Mora murmured. "I won't."

Chapter 29

H angman leaned against a tree and cast his eye into the canopy for any sign of danger. He hardly listened at all while Butcher gave orders for the scouting party to split up.

"Shadow—take Alien, Vulture, Magnet, and Cross to the southwest and search as much of the area as you can. Concentrate on spotting the mountains behind the valley of stone. If the mountain isn't there, the weapons won't be there, either."

"What if the ancients moved the weapons away from the valley of stone?" Magnet asked.

"Then we would never find the weapons because they would be too buried in jungle," Butcher turned back to the rest of the group. "Fang—you take Chaos, Feather, and Bandit to the southeast. Boxer, Viking, and Hangman—come with me. We'll head due south and see if we can see anything there."

Hangman pushed himself off the tree. He didn't think much of traveling with Butcher and Boxer, but at least Viking would be with them. This expedition wouldn't be a total loss.

The three groups separated and the men set off single file through the jungle. Hangman could have covered the country much quicker by himself. He could have run miles to the south and seen if the mountains were there.

That would have been easier than walking over hill and dale with three other men. It would have accomplished exactly the same thing in the end.

If he had been Kral, he would have sent out each man alone. He would have sent his fastest runners to cover as many miles as possible.

They didn't need to be good fighters because they were only going there to look and see. Hangman, Magnet, Chaos, Cross, Feather, Bandit, and Vulture could have covered more territory in a few hours than these three parties could cover in days of walking.

Hangman wasn't Kral, so the whole question wasn't worth the mental effort to think about it.

He plodded along at the very end of the line. Boxer followed his father like the bigshot Boxer thought he was. They talked about the weapons, the territory the band had already searched, and what other options they had to find them.

Viking remained silent. He was too smart to open his mouth. He was also too smart to question Butcher to his face.

The party hiked for three hours before Butcher called a halt. He squatted down by a stream to drink some water.

Hangman wouldn't have stopped after such a short journey. He wouldn't have stopped at all, but no one asked him.

He didn't go down to the stream. He squatted on top of a rise where he could keep an eye on the surrounding jungle.

He sat with his back turned to the other three. He didn't have to worry about any creatures coming from that direction. His three relatives already watched in that direction.

He rotated his head from side to side so he could hear all the different sounds. He heard a mating pair of Ridgebeaks, but he didn't try to locate them. The band had enough food for now after he brought back the meat from the last bird.

He also heard a rutting Stalkion bellowing somewhere a few miles away. Muffled crashes and booms resounded across the countryside when the creature smashed its armored head into tree trunks and rock outcroppings.

The Stalkion was too far away to threaten Hangman's party, but he still kept his ears tuned. Listening like this had become so habituated that he did it without even thinking.

Listening gave him a broader, clearer picture than if he could have seen all of that territory with his eyes.

Ridgebeaks must be able to see like this from the air. They could get a snapshot of the whole countryside, which species were killing which other species, which individuals were moving in which direction, and every other detail of every other living thing on the ground.

He stiffened when he heard a different sound. Boxer made way too much noise coming up the hill to where Hangman sat.

Sometimes Hangman wondered if Boxer could hear anything at all. If he did, he would have realized how his movements gave him away at the worst possible times.

He was too bumbling and blundering even to be capable of stealth. He would never be a threat to anyone or anything, especially not to Hangman.

Hangman didn't turn around when Boxer squatted down next to him. Boxer couldn't be here for any good purpose.

He proved Hangman right with his first words. "When are you going to break in your new wife?"

"Maybe I won't," Hangman replied without turning around. "Maybe I have better, more important things to do."

"More important things to do like sleeping at night?"

"That's right," Hangman replied.

Boxer laughed and slapped Hangman on the shoulder way too hard. Hangman still refused to turn around to face his cousin.

"You're such a monk, aren't you? You should talk to her. Maybe she can tell you where the weapons are."

Hangman froze to the spot, but he didn't give it away. So this was Boxer's angle.

"You could get information out of her about what might be happening in the cities to the south," Boxer went on. "She might know something—or she might have seen those mountains."

The Godless men lived by a code. They never shared information with the women about what the men did while they were out in the jungle. It was one of their most sacred rules.

Of course the women had to find out about things like initiations. The women always knew when their sons left for initiation or when the men came back with kills.

No one was supposed to know the Godless were looking for those weapons. Not even the Godless women were supposed to know.

Boxer knew this as well as anyone. So why did he even suggest that Hangman question Mora about it?

Something strange was going on. Hangman didn't know what it was, but he had to find out, especially if it had anything to do with Mora.

He didn't like her. He might even hate her, but she was his wife now. That made her his responsibility.

If Boxer suggested that, the idea might have come from Butcher. Butcher might be planning to question Mora about the country to the south.

Hangman would have to stay on watch for that. He didn't know what he would do if Butcher did try to question Mora. Hangman would have to decide what to do about it.

It would be up to him to decide whether to let her do it—either for her own good or for the good of the band.

Hangman absolutely would not let Butcher treat her like a captive from a hostile Clan. Hell no. She was supposed to be Godless now. She might be the worst possible candidate for that, but she was still Godless even if everyone despised her.

Hangman despised her most of all, but it was his job as her husband to make sure no one harmed her.

He didn't respond to Boxer's comments. Hangman didn't care if his silence made Boxer uncomfortable, but at that moment, the Stalkion's bellows changed.

They got deeper, louder, and the booming crashes got louder. Then Hangman heard a scream in the distance. It came from the same direction as the Stalkion's bellows.

Hangman shot off the ground without giving Boxer any explanation. He wouldn't have heard the Stalkion anyway.

Hangman swung up into the branches, scaled to the highest canopy, and strained his ears for any sound in the distance. He heard more crashes, more enraged roaring from the Stalkion, and then another scream.

He pinpointed the disturbance in the jungle—and saw more Renegades fighting the creature.

Thick bristles covered the Stalkion's bulky body. The bristles hung down in sheets that looked like fur until something came along to threaten the creature.

Then the Stalkion could flex its skin to make the bristles stand up and out from its body. Each bristle came to a sharp point at the end. Its thickest point could grow to the width of a man's wrist.

The other smaller end sat in a socket embedded in the creature's tough hide. The Stalkion could flare its bristles out to surround itself in an impenetrable ball of spikes or it could throw the bristles at an attacker from the muscular skin along its back ridge.

The bristles had a nasty way of sticking into any attacker who made contact with the creature. The bristles came away from their sockets and had to be carved out of the attacker's flesh with a knife.

The rest of the Stalkion consisted of a thick body standing three feet taller than a man's head. The body hung down to the creature's knees.

Tree-trunk legs supported the creature's weight with wide, cylindrical feet resting flat on the ground. The creature's head came to a short snout below its mouth with giant curved tusks arching out from its cheeks.

The tusks also came to sharp points with barbed hooks running the length of three ridges for eight inches down the tusk shaft.

The Renegades came to grief with the creature in no time. This Stalkion was a giant bull in the prime of his size and strength. He was also raging mad from all the rutting hormones coursing through his veins.

He roared with ground-shaking bellows when the Renegades tried to defend themselves against him.

They must have stumbled upon him unawares, which meant they were stupid or incompetent or maybe both. Anyone with ears could hear the creature from fifty miles away.

Two Renegades already lay dead, dismembered, and eviscerated on the ground at the creature's giant feet. Another four brandished their weapons at the Stalkion from all sides.

Hangman couldn't see from here why the Renegades didn't just cut their losses and run for it while they had the chance.

The creature kept swiping his tusks at them and arching his back ridge, but he didn't shoot his spikes at them. He probably could have leveled all four Renegades in a few seconds if he did.

Hangman didn't wait around to tell Butcher and the others that the Renegades were in the area again. Butcher would probably do something equally stupid like order the men to retreat in the opposite direction.

Boxer would never know why Hangman climbed into the branches. Boxer was too thick to figure out something like that. He would just assume Hangman went off by himself again.

Chapter 30

Hangman took off through the canopy and left his three relatives behind. They could keep on plodding south as long as they wanted to.

Hangman covered the distance in a few minutes and took a position directly over the fight between the Stalkion and the Renegades.

Now he saw why the Renegades didn't run. They had bound the creature to a tree for some idiotic reason.

Thick ropes surrounded its two hind legs and anchored the creature to the tree trunk. The Renegades tried again and again to poke their weapons at the creature, but they never actually stabbed it.

The Stalkion turned right and left trying to fight all four of them. He occasionally turned his back on one to go after the others.

The Renegades could have used these openings to kill the creature, but the Renegades stood back and did nothing each time.

Hangman couldn't figure out why the Renegades wanted this Stalkion—and why they were going to such lengths to antagonize the creature—even at the cost of two of their comrades' lives.

Hangman watched the fight for a minute. He had to make sure these Renegades didn't leave the area alive. If the Stalkion didn't kill them, he would have to do it.

They shouldn't have ventured this far south. A Renegade patrol this far south was unheard of. What were they doing here?

He cast his eye around the area while he waited for the battle to turn. The minute he looked up, he spotted the gathering plateau in the distance. The Godless were already miles away from it, but he could never mistake the plateau for anything else.

Did the Renegades travel this far south to lay in ambush for young females coming to the gatherings? The Renegade Clan was one of the few that made a habit of raiding, capturing, and enslaving the women of other Clans.

Almost all the other Clans in this part of the country used civilized means of peacefully pairing their young people with Clans who shared their values.

These Clans didn't ravage women—either their own or anyone else's. They married and included the young women in the husband's Clan.

Hangman couldn't think of any other reason why the Renegade Clan would send patrols to this part of the country. It made sense, now that he saw the two in such close proximity to each other.

That was also the moment when he spotted the Whisperers band that came to the gathering last night—the band that Wizard negotiation with to take a wife for Dodge.

The Whisperers had traveled west from the gathering for some reason. Hangman didn't know enough about the Whisperers, their territory, or their habits to understand why they would come this way.

They seemed to have set up a camp here the way the Godless set up a camp in that cave. The Whisperers weren't traveling anywhere at the moment.

Their camp happened to be directly south of the spot where the Renegades tethered that Stalkion.

Were the Renegades trying to enrage the Stalkion to lure him into attacking the Whisperers? Surely the Renegades must have some better way of attacking the Whisperers—one not so dangerous to their own lives and limbs.

Apparently not. They kept darting in, hitting the Stalkion without injuring him, and springing out of the way in time to avoid swipes of his tusks.

The problem was that none of the Renegades could get near enough to the creature to cut it loose. The Stalkion blocked them all from going anywhere near the ropes. They couldn't free him, now that they actually succeeded in catching him.

This might go on all night. Hangman couldn't wait that long.

He balanced through the branches to the tree directly above the Stalkion—the tree to which the Renegades tethered him. He was too busy threatening them to even look around at the surroundings.

Hangman measured his position, dropped out of the branches, and landed right behind the tree. The Stalkion didn't see him. The Renegades did, but they couldn't get near him, either.

He lunged forward, hacked his kukri at the ropes binding the Stalkion's legs, and cut them both.

The Stalkion charged with a ground-shaking bellow, impaled the two Renegades directly in front of him on both tusks, and barreled across the clearing with such force that he embedded his tusks in two other trunks on the other side.

Hangman sprang into the branches without waiting to see the outcome. He scrambled back to his former height and looked down on the scene of bloodshed and chaos.

The Stalkion wrenched his big head sideways. He couldn't get his tusks unstuck from the trees, so he ripped them sideways and cracked the trunks in half with the strength of his own neck.

The collision didn't dislodge the two dead Renegades. They dangled from his tusks like some kind of warning to would-be attackers.

The creature turned around to confront the last two Renegades. Their fallen comrades' bodies flopped in front of their faces and made both men fall back.

They stood on opposite sides of the clearing with the Stalkion between them. The creature couldn't face both of them at the same time.

He kept wheeled from one side to the other, bellowed at them, and slashed his tusks and the dead Renegades at the two men.

One of them got the brilliant idea to kill the creature when it turned back to the other guy. That one man rushed in and raised his weapon to impale the creature. He misjudged his angle of attack and ran into the Stalkion's flared spines.

Three of them jabbed him in the torso and came away when he staggered clear. His weapon hung limp from his arm. He didn't think to use it.

The Stalkion and the other Renegade both turned around to look at the guy. None of the spines stuck more than a couple of inches into the guy's flesh.

One of them must have punctured a lung. He staggered, drooped, and looked down at the spines in dazed confusion. He collapsed much sooner than he would have if the spines didn't hit something vital.

The Stalkion turned his back on the guy and trained all his attention to the one remaining Renegade. The Stalkion didn't even look when the man behind him buckled onto his knees and toppled face first into the dirt.

The last man standing stared back at the Stalkion as the harsh reality sank in. The enraged creature was free now with nothing but one flimsy weapon between him and his tormentor.

The Stalkion rumbled low in its chest and snarled in venomous, murderous fury. The sound brought goosebumps up on Hangman's arms. It was the sound of death, plain and simple.

The Renegade wasn't so moronic not to see the situation for what it was. He turned on his heel and ran for it. The Stalkion charged, but the guy got a head start.

Hangman saw the guy about to make his escape. He headed west—back toward Renegade territory. He probably wanted to meet back up with another patrol or return to his own country, now that he'd failed in his mission to attack the Whisperers.

Hangman couldn't let the guy get away. Hangman sprang through the branches, overtook the man by a dozen yards, and dropped down in front of him opposite the Stalkion thundering in from behind.

Hangman drew his weapons, but he didn't plan to use them. The Stalkion would kill the guy as soon as the creature caught up with him.

Hangman's ploy worked. The Renegade slowed when he saw a Godless warrior confronting him. That moment was all the time the Stalkion needed to close the gap.

He didn't even waste his breath bellowing. He lowered his head, collided with the guy full force, and the Stalkion smashed his forehead into the guy's back.

The creature's tusks swept the guy's legs out from under him. The Stalkion was coming too fast to stop. Hangman dove sideways and rolled out of the way.

The man screamed out once as the Stalkion thundered past Hangman and the creature smashed his forehead into a tree trunk. The Renegade got trapped between the trunk and the Stalkion's bony forehead.

The impact pulverized the guy's torso to a pulp. The ground and the tree shuddered from the concussion. The vibration traveled all the way to Hangman's position twenty feet away.

The Stalkion growled to himself, stepped away, and the body flopped at his feet.

He pawed his foot at it as if to tell the man to stand up and fight. A large blood splotch stained the creature's forehead and the tree trunk. The man didn't respond at all.

The Stalkion turned around and narrowed his small eyes at Hangman. Hangman felt absolutely no desire to face this creature in combat.

Hangman vaulted into the branches before the Stalkion could do anything. Hangman grabbed the lowest branches and pulled himself out of the creature's range.

The Stalkion growled and then roared again before he ambled off into the jungle on his own business.

Chapter 31

H angman dropped to the ground in front of Butcher, Boxer, and Viking.

"Where were you, little brother?" Viking asked.

Hangman jerked his thumb over his shoulder toward the west. "There was a Renegade patrol over there, Uncle. It looked like they were staking out the gathering grounds to raid departing bands for females."

Butcher frowned. "Is that so?"

Hangman nodded. "The patrol was preparing to attack the Whisperers—the ones who negotiated with Wizard. They're camping south of here."

Butcher stood up. "We should help defend the Whisperers, then. We can't leave a Renegade patrol active in the area."

"They aren't active anymore, Uncle," Hangman told him. "They're all dead now."

"Did you kill them all again?" Viking snapped. "Didn't you leave any of them for us?"

Hangman only shrugged. "Anyway, they're all dead—but there may be others in the area. One of them tried to flee to the west. I don't suppose he planned to run all the way back to Renegade country."

Butcher rubbed his chin. "No. I suppose not. We should return to the cave. The Renegades may have sent another patrol to attack our women."

Hangman expected this intelligence to have an effect on his uncle. Butcher and the others set off through the jungle on their way back to the cave camp.

Hangman caught Viking giving him strange looks along the way. Viking's eyes kept dipping to Hangman's arms, body, and weapons, but Hangman didn't have a speck of blood on him—unlike the way he did after most of his other solo expeditions.

They returned to the cave camp in time to see Mora surrounded by the other women in the center of the cave.

Katha, Rila, Nagana, and Neia bombarded Mora with questions, demands, insults, and reprimands.

"How do you think you're going to become Godless if you always act like a scared, pathetic little rabbit?" Rila demanded.

"I gave you one task," Katha snapped. "One task and you couldn't even do that. It wasn't even a dangerous task. All you had to do was stand there and follow my instructions. What am I supposed to think?"

Mora flinched every time one of them yelled at her. She kept cringing, cowering, and whimpering before their assault.

Hangman and the others entered the cave. Zyria and Kealra sat to one side laughing themselves silly, especially when Mora started crying for real.

Tears streaked down her cheeks, her lips trembled, and her whole body shook with sobs.

"Look at you!" Estia blared. "You can't even stand up for yourself. What do we look like? Does it look like we're attacking you? None of us is even holding a weapon. What are you going to do when a Demonex comes after you? Are you going to cry and hope he just walks away?"

Mora moaned out, "No......"

"Then what are you going to do about it?" Nagana asked. "All you had to do was practice the movements Katha told you to practice. You couldn't even do that."

"I think you're a lazy, disobedient, rebellious little rabbit," Katha sneered. "I think you decided to go off into the jungle alone and feel sorry for yourself. You blatantly disobeyed my commands......"

"No....." Mora whimpered. "I didn't......."

"I saw you, so don't lie about it!" Katha raged. "I told you to stay there and practice those strikes. I turned my back for ten seconds, and when I looked, you were gone. How do you explain that?"

Mora's eyes darted around the circle. Then they darted to Zyria sitting to one side. Zyria only laughed.

Katha must have had enough. She grabbed Mora by the elbow and yanked the girl down hard to sit on the floor in the same place as last night.

"Sit down, Rabbit," Katha snapped. "Don't move until I tell you to—and don't try anything or you'll go hungry tonight."

Zyria and Kealra laughed some more. Some of the men joined in, including Boxer.

Zyria crossed the cave to him and they kissed before they sank into each other's arms.

Viking squatted down by the fire circle and started to relight it. The other two hunting parties hadn't yet returned from their journey.

From what Hangman could see, only one person here was shirking their responsibilities. That was Butcher.

Mora looked around the cave again, saw Hangman, and looked away. He moved off to the other side of the room, untied one of the sections of Ridgebeak meat he and his cousins brought back, and handed it to Viking to spit over the fire to cook it for the night.

Hangman drank some water from one of the band's gourds, went out to refill it, and came back to a much more peaceable scene.

Mora sat sniffing in the same place and running her hand across her nose and mouth. She made sure to cry silently, so maybe she wasn't irretrievably stupid after all.

The others ignored her. Hangman settled down on the opposite side of the cave where he slept last night. He had no plans to go near her or even talk to her if he could avoid it.

His conversation with Boxer made Hangman much more attuned to what the others did with her. He couldn't put her completely out of his mind.

Butcher should have at least investigated the presence of Renegades in the area. If he didn't do that bare minimum, he should have at least continued south to determine if the strange mountains were there.

That was the party's whole objective. The band wouldn't likely travel this far south until next year. Butcher let the whole band down when he failed to at least check.

The two other hunting parties could have missed the strange mountains while Butcher's party spotted them. Now the entire day's travel might have been wasted because of his negligence.

Hangman couldn't come up with one plausible reason why Butcher would do that—apart from pure laziness.

The only other alternative was that Butcher planned to question Mora about the terrain to the south. Why should he travel all over the countryside if he could find out the information he wanted from someone who was already a member of his band?

The whole thing stank to Hangman. Butcher was the one who determined that the men shouldn't tell their wives or any other women about this search.

Now Butcher was breaking his own rule—if he did in fact plan to question her.

The conversation with Boxer set off Hangman's alarm bells. Why would Boxer bring up Mora to Hangman? She shouldn't have meant anything to Boxer.

Butcher couldn't have put Boxer up to it. That made no sense. Butcher could just as easily have ordered Hangman to make Mora available for questioning.

Hangman spent the evening deciding how he would handle it if Butcher did order him to make her available—or if Butcher tried to circumvent Hangman by simply doing it without permission.

Hangman worked on his kukris while he thought it over. He had to fleck one spot on his blade where it got chipped in the Ridgebeak's nest.

He decided to stand his ground and assert his rights as Mora's husband. He wouldn't hand her over for questioning. He had to take the moral high ground on this one.

He didn't so much care about the other men treating her appropriately. He could have insisted that he be present for the questioning to make sure they did.

He made the decision mostly out of pure mistrust for Boxer and Butcher. They would be too concerned with keeping this search a secret if they weren't up to something—if they actually did plan to question her.

This was exactly the kind of underhanded maneuver that could make a man challenge Butcher as Kral. No Godless man could interfere with another man's wife—not for something like this—not without her husband's permission.

Hangman could hate Mora all he wanted. No one was going to step on his rights, not even his own Kral. He already didn't respect either Butcher or Boxer enough to put up with this.

Hangman might have bowed to his Kral's wishes if that Kral had been Shadow or Viking or just about anyone else.

A Kral would have to be pretty admirable for Hangman to go along with this. Neither Butcher nor Boxer was that man.

None of them noticed anything unusual about his silence. He barely heard the others talking until the other two scouting parties returned.

All the women greeted their husbands. Viking took the meat off the spit, divided it up, and put on another hunk.

"That Rigdebeak will be gone by tomorrow morning," Chaos remarked. "You'll have to go get us another one, little brother."

"Say the word," Hangman replied.

A few people laughed. Then they started telling stories about Hangman's exploits. He turned them out. He had heard it all before, especially since he was there at the time.

Katha took some of the roasted meat over to Mora and thrust it into her hands. "Eat it, Rabbit."

Mora looked down at the juicy slices in her hand. Katha sat down on the rock next to her—probably to look over her shoulder and make sure Mora really did eat it.

"Do you know what a rabbit is?" Katha went on. "It's a tiny, weak, helpless, terrified creature. It runs and hides instead of trying to fight. It's a prey creature for anything that wants it to hunt it. It can't protect itself, so it breeds a lot to make more of its own kind to replace so many of its kind getting killed. That's why they became extinct. They don't exist anymore. They all died out in ancient times."

The whole cave exploded with laughter. Hangman found himself starting to smirk. He looked away to stop himself.

Mora hung her head and the rest of the band laughed at her again. Then they all went back to eating and talking to each other. No one paid any attention to Mora after that—except for Katha.

Her attention unnerved Mora. Mora kept her head down and ate her food without looking up. She didn't make eye contact with anyone.

Chapter 32

M ora woke up sitting against the wall again. She had to sleep sitting up for the second night in a row. She couldn't keep this up. She had to lie down somewhere, so she would just have to get used to it.

All the men were gone again this morning. She didn't dare to ask what they were doing or why the Godless decided to camp in this area for so long. They were far out of their territory to the east.

Katha collared Mora the minute she got to her feet and tried to stretch her legs. "Take these water gourds down to the stream and refill them," Katha ordered. "Don't dilly-dally this time."

She shoved a bunch of empty gourds into Mora's hands. Each gourd had a cord attached to its mouth and base so a person could carry the gourd.

She looped all the cords over her arm before she remembered. "Where's the stream?" she asked.

Katha pointed out of the cave mouth. "Over there beyond those trees. Keep going in that direction. You can't miss it."

Katha went back to whatever she happened to be doing before. Mora set off toward the trees. She didn't see any of the men outside the cave, either. The women worked around the entrance. Rila glared at Mora. All the others ignored her.

She kept going and entered the trees. A wave of relief overwhelmed her as soon as she got away from the Godless. At least she was alone now.

She passed through a dense stand of jungle to a wide area without any trees in it. Grass grew around the outer edge. The center looked like bare dirt.

She spotted the stream beyond the trees ringing the opposite side of this open area. She picked up her pace to go down there.

She could enjoy a few blessed moments of solitude before she had to go back and face Katha again. No doubt Katha would find something to criticize just from Mora refilling these gourds.

Mora took a few paces into the open place, crossed the grass, and stepped onto the bare dirt. She took three more steps before the whole ground imploded under her.

All the dirt beneath her started to sink into a hole in the very center. She lost her footing and fell backward onto her seat.

She kicked out with both feet trying to climb backward out of the hole, but it kept funneling down, down, down into the hole.

The cone widened to encompass the whole open ground between the grass. The dirt at the bottom vanished into nothing. The sliding sides of the cone started to pull her down into the hole.

She panicked, flipped onto her stomach, and frantically clawed at the sides trying to scale her way back to solid ground. The earth crumbled beneath her. What she thought was dirt turned to sand that slipped through her fingers.

She fell farther and farther down and screamed in wild terror. She didn't know what was down there in that hole and she didn't want to find out. It would be something deadly and horrible. Everything in the jungle was.

She paddled her arms and legs a few more times, but she only wound up falling farther down. She screamed herself hoarse calling for help, but no one heard her.

She didn't dare to look behind her to see how close she was getting to the hole. She floundered her arms and legs as fast as she could, but all her efforts only made her fall faster.

At that moment, at the moment when she almost gave up hope and sank to her death, a tall tree nearby flexed sideways and bowed down under some weight.

She was too busy fighting for every inch of sandy wall she could climb. She didn't see the tree until it bowed down right on top of her.

She didn't even realize what was happening until she saw Hangman right in front of her. He hung onto the branches in the tree's topmost bushy canopy.

The treetop plunged into the hole, he grabbed her by the wrist, and the tree sprang back into position. She screamed again when he yanked her out of the hole and sailed through the air to the tree's highest height.

It wavered back and forth a dozen more times, bowed almost to the ground again, and he dropped her on the grass at the edge of the trees.

She crashed down on solid ground still crying out and practically suffocating from panic. She scrambled backward even farther away to get away from the hole even though she was already safe. This part of the ground was as solid as she could hope.

She collapsed at the base of a tree panting, gasping, and moaning as her terror subsided. She didn't snap out of it until the tree bowed again and Hangman jumped down to the ground.

He jumped from fifteen feet up, handed in a crouch, and walked toward her. His fierce eyes blazed out of his ruined face. "Haven't you ever heard of the Cursed Sand before? You walked right into it. What is the matter with you?"

"I thought...." She stumbled to her feet and tried to straighten herself out to face him. "I didn't....I didn't know....."

"A creature lives down there." He pointed to the hole. She couldn't see the bottom from here. "It traps its prey and they fall into its den. Didn't you know?"

She opened her mouth and closed it a few times before she got her brain working well enough to think straight. "I didn't know."

"Don't you have them in the south?" He scowled at her. "You must. We're in the south."

She tried to shrug it away. She was standing in front of the murderous psychopath Zyria warned her about.

This was the first time she and Hangman had ever spoken to each other. This might be the only conversation of their marriage. She certainly hoped so.

"Thank you," she exclaimed. "Thank you for saving me."

He curled his scarred lips at her and turned away. "You're as useless as they say. You're a danger to yourself and everyone around you. It's a misfortune on my Clan that I got stuck with you."

He turned his back on her and walked away. She probably should have let him, but she couldn't let it go at that.

She followed him. "I'm grateful.....I don't know how to tell you....."

"Then don't tell me," he snapped over his shoulder. "Just leave me alone. That's what you want, isn't it? You don't have to tell me anything. I already know."

"How did you....?" She glanced up at the tree. "How did you do that—with the tree? How did you get.....?" She stopped in her tracks and looked around at nothing. "Were you following me?"

"You can thank me for following you," he snapped. He actually stopped walking and turned around to glare at her. "You're too stupid to walk around loose. Look at you. You didn't even think to bring a weapon. What if you had met one of the Abnormits.....or a Coffincreep?"

Right at that moment, a huge insect landed on his arm. It was a Blitzword, a predatory hunting insect with four broad jointed wings sticking out from its long, tapered body.

He raised his arm to look at it. The creature covered his whole forearm from wrist to elbow. Its wings and body glistened with iridescent colors in the sunshine.

The creature widened its jaws to bite him and he struck his other hand down hard in a fist on top of it. He crushed its body, shattered its wings, and squashed the creature's head and part of its thorax right against his own skin.

Greenish goo splattered his arm. Pieces of broken exoskeleton and torn wings stuck in the goo.

Mora grimaced in disgust at the sight. "Ugh!" she exclaimed.

Hangman stared at the mess for a second and then glanced at her before he walked over to a nearby tree. He scraped the dead Blitzword off against the back and pulled handfuls of grass out of the ground to clean his hands.

She stood back wrinkling her nose at the whole operation. "Did you have to kill it?"

"And let it bite me?" Hangman snapped. "Their bite is poisonous. It could have killed me. Don't you even know that much?"

"Yes, but.....couldn't you......We swat them away at home."

He snorted at her. "You aren't at home anymore. You kill before the other thing kills you first. That's the way it works. If you don't learn that, you'll wind up some creature's meal and then I won't have to follow you around protecting you from things you should already know how to defeat. Your father is a coward and an idiot for not training you to protect yourself."

Her temper exploded. All her frustration from the last two days erupted in volcanic fury.

"Don't you dare say anything against my father!" she shrieked. "You filthy, rotten bastard! How dare you?! My father loves me! He protected me for years—which is more than I can say for you! He cares about me a hell of a lot better than you do!"

"He didn't protect you by leaving you incapable of taking care of yourself," Hangman snapped back. "You could have gotten killed just now because he didn't teach you to fight on your own. It could have been a much more dangerous creature like a Crusher or a

Gorlock. Then *I* could have gotten killed just now because you wouldn't have been able to help me. When are you going to wake up?"

"You bastard!" Her anger turned to frustrated, helpless desperation and she started crying again. She couldn't help it. "You don't care about me! You would just as soon kill me as look at me!"

He furrowed his brow. His facial muscles didn't quite work the same with all those scars disfiguring him. "What are you talking about? I never killed anyone other than the enemies of my Clan."

"Zyria told me all about you! You kill for fun—and she says you have an explosive temper—and you mistreat women! Don't think I don't know! Well, here I am! Do whatever you're going to do. I don't care! Just get it over with."

He stared at her with such intensity that she trembled. She couldn't tell if he was about to attack her or what.

He lowered his voice to a deadly snarl. "You should know better than to listen to Zyria. She has never seen me lose my temper—never."

"Don't you dare say anything against her! She has been nothing but kind to me! You won't even talk to me or look at me while all your relatives mistreat me! Zyria is the only friend I have!"

She couldn't stand the way he was looking at her, so she stormed off to the stream. She didn't dare to go back to the cave without the water.

She made sure to walk around the Cursed Sand. Whatever creature lived down there was in the process of tossing all the sand back up into the cone to make it look like level ground again.

Chapter 33

Mora threw herself down on the bank, buried her face in her hands, and burst into sobs again. She let herself pour out her disappointment, heartbreak, and desperation for the first time, now that she was finally alone.

She stayed a lot longer than she should have. She just needed to be alone for a little while—just until she got herself together.

Hangman was right. That was the real problem. She never learned to defend herself.

She, her parents, her grandparents and great-grandparents, and all her aunts and uncles—they all knew she would marry and leave her family band someday.

The odds of her marrying another Follower were tiny to non-existent. There were just too few people in the country now.

All the other Clans fought, hunted, and defended themselves in one way or another. Not many were as fierce and warlike as the Godless, but everyone always knew she would probably go to another Clan.

Her parents and all her other relatives—they let her down. They left her woefully unprepared for what she would face out here.

She saw herself from the Godless' point of view. No wonder they looked down on her. She embodied everything they hated—and for good reason.

All these Clans out here—the only Clans of the human race left over after the ancients passed away—all these Clans tried their hardest to keep the human race going. No one cared about anything else.

The Followers claimed to be doing that, too, but only the Godless and the other warlike Clans actually did it.

Having a bunch of children and raising them to adulthood wasn't enough. They actually had to be able to survive the dangers they would face—and the dangers their children would face.

Thinking that made Mora break down crying all over again. She wouldn't even be able to defend her own children—if she ever even had any.

She and her family band kept the children alive, fed, and cared for, but the Followers only accomplished that by having set rotating foraging territories and protected sheltering places to camp at night.

The Followers wouldn't have been able to survive if they really had to face any of the dangers in the jungle.

The Followers wouldn't have been able to raise children at all without that. Some creature would always come around hunting the children.

All the creatures of the jungle targeted the children. They were the weakest, the slowest, and the least able to defend themselves.

Mora wouldn't be able to rely on any of the skills she learned from the Followers. None of them meant anything out here.

That didn't matter because she would never have children. Hangman wouldn't go near her—and maybe he was right about that. What was she thinking leaving the cave without a weapon?

She wouldn't have been able to use one even if she did bring it. She would have fallen into the Cursed Sand. Something else would have come along to kill her if it wasn't that.

Except that it wouldn't. Hangman had been following her around to protect her. He must have figured out that she was too inept to take care of herself. Of course he did.

She glanced over her shoulder and immediately spun the other way when she saw him standing a few yards away from her.

He wasn't watching her. He stood with his back to her and cocked his head to one side. He kept angling his head from one direction to the other to catch every sound out in the jungle.

It couldn't be more obvious what he was doing. He was guarding her.

She bowed her head so he wouldn't see her looking and so she wouldn't see him. She didn't want to have anything to do with him, so she got busy filling the water gourds.

She held them under the water and had to pull her hands back when the long, arched ridge of some underwater monster broke the surface nearby. How was she supposed to collect water when that creature was lurking just beneath the surface waiting to grab her?

Hangman startled her by walking over to her. He stood right next to her. "Keep going," he snapped. "Don't stop."

She trained her eyes on her hands and pushed the gourd underwater. He stood way too close, but he didn't move.

Nothing happened for a minute. She sealed that gourd and pushed in the second one. The creature's arched back broke the surface and curved back down into the depths.

She sealed that gourd and picked up the third. Hangman's legs stuck up right next to her.

She tried not to notice that her head came up the level with his crotch. A thin piece of hide separated the two of them. Did he notice? Was he trying to send her a signal of some kind?

She distracted herself by pushing the gourd underwater. She held it there.

Nothing happened for a minute until the creature broke the surface and charged her. A long, snake-like body undulated back and forth behind a huge gaping mouth full of teeth.

The top jaw levered back. The whole head could have clamped on Mora all the way up to her elbows.

She started to rear back in horror to get away from the thing, but Hangman struck faster. He stepped behind her and stabbed the creature through the upper jaw.

She didn't see until that moment that he had attached one of his blades to a long, straight tree limb.

He lashed the handle of his blade to the end of the pole and used it as a spear to thrust his blade all the way into the creature's mouth, up through the farthest rear section of its upper palate, and impaled the creature through the brain.

She stared at the thing in shock as it went completely limp in the water. His attack killed it instantly.

He didn't act like he did anything out of the ordinary that time, either. He pretended not to notice her staring at him, the creature, the weapon, and everything else.

He used the weapon to haul the creature onto the bank. Its body stretched out to fifteen feet long.

He growled at her out of the side of his mouth. "You better fill those gourds before another one comes."

She sprang back to the edge of the stream and refilled all the rest of her gourds. A few more arched spines broke the surface farther away, but they didn't come near her.

Hangman used the time to wrench his weapon out of the creature's mouth. He stood up and untied the handle from the pole.

He didn't say another word to Mora. He went back to surveying the surrounding terrain and listening to every noise while she hooked all the gourd straps over her arm.

He left the creature's body on the bank and followed at a distance of several yards when she walked back to the cave. He didn't catch up with her or try to talk to her again.

She expected him to escort her all the way back to the cave, but he vanished as soon as she got to the tree line.

She turned around and searched the surrounding jungle. He was nowhere in sight. She even looked up at the canopy. He wasn't there, either.

His words came back to haunt her. *What are you talking about? I never killed anyone other than the enemies of my Clan.*

And then again, when he said, *You should know better than to listen to Zyria. She has never seen me lose my temper—never.*

Mora didn't notice his expression when he said it. She had been too upset by everything then.

She remembered it now. Talking to him gave her some better insight on the different shades of his facial expressions.

His scars made him harder to read than other people, but they didn't hide his eyes.

He wasn't offended by her statements about what Zyria said about him. He was confused. He really didn't know what she was talking about.

What if he was telling the truth? If Zyria lied about him, what else might she be lying about?

Chapter 34

"Hey—Rabbit!" Mora turned around and cringed when she saw Katha storming toward her from inside the cave. "I told you to bring that water hours ago! Where have you been? You better not have been hiding from work."

"I brought the water," Mora mumbled. "Here it is."

"Well, take it inside and then come straight back out here," Katha snapped. "You've wasted enough time already."

Mora took the gourds inside. No one else was in the cave at this time of the day.

She didn't see any men around at all. They must be all out in the jungle.

The women worked around the camp skinning and cleaning different animals and smoking the meat over fires.

Mora took a deep breath before she went out there. She would have to face whatever Katha had in store for her.

Mora cast a hasty glance around, but she still didn't see Hangman anywhere. He would probably just go back to ignoring her.

His words finally came back into her mind. She didn't let herself hear them when he said them, either. Now they ran in her head with a kind of finality she couldn't ignore.

Just leave me alone. That's what you want, isn't it? You don't have to tell me anything. I already know.

He would have seen how horrified she was to get stuck with a man like him. That must have been hard.

It must have been a nightmare for him to go to the gathering knowing no woman would choose him. No one would marry him at all unless she had no other option.

More understood much better now why he kept his distance from her. What man in his right mind would want a wife who thought he was disgusting and hideous?

He wouldn't go near Mora as long as he thought she hated him. He didn't want a woman who didn't want him back.

She couldn't change that now. She might never get a chance to tell him that she saw him differently now.

He saved her life twice in the space of a few minutes. He could have taken her and forced himself on her a dozen times since the gathering. He would have if Zyria had been telling the truth about him.

Instead, he saved Mora's life and walked away without doing anything. He guarded her and then vanished out of the picture. He would probably always keep doing that forever.

Her heart turned a somersault when she thought that. He would rather stay alone for the rest of his life than touch a woman who didn't want him.

That was the behavior of a very different man than the psychotic maniac Zyria led Mora to believe he was.

Why would Zyria lie about that? What possible reason could Zyria have to poison Mora's mind against her own husband—as if Mora's mind wasn't already poisoned enough.

His looks weren't the only thing that poisoned her against him. Decades of Follower prejudice against the Godless made it impossible for her to think of any of them in a positive light.

She would have hated any Godless man who took her as his wife. Chaos was one of the most attractive men in the whole band and she would have hated him, too.

She stacked her gourds in their usual place against one of the rocks and went back outside to meet up with Katha.

Katha glared at Mora more than ever, but Mora saw her mother-in-law in a different light now, too, especially when Katha told her to pick up the two rods Katha had been using to teach Mora to fight.

Katha pulled out her two axes. "Now defend yourself," she ordered. "Think that one of the Renegade Clan is coming to attack you and kill your family. Do you have that image in your mind?"

Mora nodded. She didn't think about her family band in the south—her Follower family.

She imagined her children—any children she ever had with Hangman. She would have to defend them.

She actually experienced a flood of gratitude that Katha of all people was taking the time and effort to teach Mora how to defend herself. Katha was the only one.

Her criticisms didn't sting so badly now. She was trying to help Mora.

Mora flexed her knees. Her arms and shoulders still hurt from yesterday, but she determined to do this or at least learn from her own failings.

Katha narrowed her eyes at Mora and struck out with her axes, but Katha didn't try to hit her.

Katha swung at Mora's head and missed on purpose. She fell short by several inches and gave Mora plenty of time to smack the axe with her rod.

Some of what Mora practiced yesterday came back to her. She tried to use the same combination of movements to parry Katha's attacks.

Katha kept them slow and far enough away not to put Mora in danger. Mora sensed Katha taking it easy on her.

Mora picked up her pace, swung faster, and finally took a step forward to drive Katha back.

Katha reacted instantly and doubled down on the speed. She advanced much more aggressively and forced Mora to retreat. Katha didn't check herself this time. She kept escalating until she knocked both rods out of Mora's hands.

Mora floundered to do something, but she couldn't defend herself with her bare hands.

Katha stood back and nodded. "That was better. Now go practice. Don't stop or slack off or give yourself any excuses this time. Get it done. The next time I look, I should see you still over there."

Mora didn't argue. She picked up her rods, went back to the same tree, and started tracing the same patterns.

She picked up speed sooner this time. The patterns became familiar. She didn't have to think about them as much. She stayed much longer and tried a lot harder. She pushed through her soreness to keep going.

She needed to get stronger, faster, and more capable—and she needed to do it quickly. Every day could be her last. She might face something dangerous the very next time Katha sent her to get water.

Mora was still out there practicing when a bunch of the men came back. Butcher, Shadow, Boxer, Magnet, Chaos, Viking, and Vulture all came in together.

All the rest of the men showed up a few minutes later. Their arrival turned the camp upside down. The women stopped what they were doing, came forward to greet their men, and everyone stood around talking outside the cave.

Mora watched from a distance. Hangman didn't come with them. Did he even go with them today or did he stay out alone all day?

The rest of the band was still talking when he showed up carrying the creature from the stream. It draped across his shoulder and its long body undulated in time to with footsteps.

He dropped it on the ground near one of the smoking fires. "Hangman—you're my hero!" Estia exclaimed. "I love Dushag meat!"

"I brought it just for you, Auntie," he replied and bent over the carcass. He pulled out his knife and started skinning it right there.

The others gathered around congratulating him on his kill and asking all the details about how he caught it.

He told them about attaching his weapon to a pole and spearing the Dushag through the roof of its mouth. He called his weapon a kukri. That must be the forward-bent blade he used.

He didn't tell anyone about Mora being there at the time. He said he put his own hands in the water to get himself a drink. He let his relatives believe that was what attracted the Dushag to attack.

He didn't look at Mora once. He concentrated on the task of skinning, gutting, and cutting up the Dushag. He actually smiled when he bestowed a hunk of the meat on his aunt to cook for the night.

That was the first time Mora had ever seen him smile. His crooked lips didn't function the same way as other people's when he smiled. The smile didn't change any part of his appearance—except for his eyes.

Smiling didn't make him look more appealing, but his eyes crinkled up and flickered with light. There really was more to him than Zyria let on.

Mora got a firsthand glimpse of the way he acted around his relatives. They all made a big deal about the things he did that no one else had the nerve to do.

He always brushed off these stories and even added details and circumstances to make his exploits seem more normal and less impressive than they were.

The group went inside to cook the meat for the night. She found herself watching both him and his relatives while they interacted with each other.

He wasn't a psychotic maniac at all. He was really a humble man who hated and deflected all recognition for how exceptional he was.

He didn't want anyone paying him this kind of attention. He just wanted to go about his business and do his job for his Clan.

Almost as if her thoughts made it happen, Zyria came up to Mora on the way into the cave. Zyria put her arm around Mora's shoulders and grinned extra broadly in Mora's face.

"Your practice was much better today!" Zyria breathed. "You did well against Katha. You might even be able to beat her in a few days."

"I doubt it," Mora mumbled. "You're all so much stronger and better trained than I am."

"No, you're good!" Zyria insisted. "You just need practice. You'll get it. I'm certain you will."

Mora's eyes darted around the cave. She noticed Hangman watching her with Zyria hanging onto Mora's shoulders. He immediately looked away and started doing something else to his weapon. She couldn't tell what it was.

Mora actually felt a palpable stab of relief when Zyria split away to go sit with Boxer. She put her arms around his shoulders next, kissed him, and the two cuddled in front of everyone.

Mora sat in her old place on the far edge of the group. She didn't want to talk to anyone, but the conversation turned to her in a few minutes anyway.

"You did better today," Katha told her again.

"Maybe she isn't completely useless after all," Rila added.

A few people laughed. Mora's eyes darted to Zyria. Both she and Boxer laughed, too.

Mora saw them in a new light now, too. Zyria laughed at Mora when Katha first humiliated her in front of everyone. Zyria didn't stick up for Mora then.

Zyria didn't mention to Katha and the others that it had been hard for Zyria when she first joined the Godless from another Clan. Zyria didn't tell Katha to take it easy on Mora.

Zyria also didn't speak up when Rila said Mora wasn't completely useless. Zyria didn't insist or even say a word about Mora doing well and only needing more practice.

Zyria didn't tell Katha that Mora was getting close to defeating Katha the next time the women confronted each other.

Mora wasn't getting close to defeating Katha—not by a million miles. Zyria still could have said an encouraging word about Mora to the rest of the band. Zyria didn't have to keep quiet.

Zyria wouldn't have kept quiet if she really believed those things. She would have said them out loud where everyone could hear her.

And then there were all the supposedly helpful things Zyria told Mora about Hangman. Zyria couched those comments as a word to the wise to tell Mora to be careful—but why?

Why would anyone in Hangman's own family band deliberately go out of her way to drive a wedge between Mora and Hangman?

They had been married for less than a day when Zyria stepped in. She isolated Mora by herself away from everyone else so she could tell Mora a bunch of lies about what a ruthless, murderous madman he was. Why?

Mora was beginning to see a pattern to all the stories his relatives told about him. All those stories involved him killing creatures or the band's enemies. No one ever mentioned him killing a person for fun.

The party even told the tale of a young Godless woman who had been on the road to the gathering with them. Her band met up with Butcher's band and they traveled together.

Boxer made some insulting comments about the young woman avoiding Hangman and immediately latching on to another young Godless man instead.

Then Hangman saved her life when a Demonex pounced on both of the two lovebirds. Hangman was the one who helped her and the woman ran straight back into the arms of another man. She didn't even have the manners to thank Hangman for saving her.

Mora flinched at the story. So that must have been the reason—another reason—why Hangman glared at Mora so badly when they first saw each other at the gathering.

He already knew no one would choose him. He expected her to reject him and she did.

Chapter 35

Katha approached Mora in the cave the next morning. Mora woke up sooner this time. She slept on the floor last night.

She didn't sleep well and had to constantly change her position from one aching side to the other and onto her back.

She determined to get used to this life if it was the last thing she did. The Godless all slept on the floor without complaining.

The men woke up and started moving around and going about their business as if they slept on the hard, cold ground every night—because they did.

They never complained or even showed any sign of stiffness or soreness. They all had a thousand things to talk about and think about other than the hardness of the floor.

Hangman was already gone by the time Mora woke up. He woke up while the others slept and went off alone.

None of his relatives even mentioned him being gone. Butcher and Shadow gathered the men together outside the cave to give instructions and directions about where the party would travel today and what they were doing.

They seemed to be making an extensive search of the area for some reason. No one ever mentioned why.

Neither Butcher, Shadow, nor any of the other men even seemed to notice that Hangman didn't stick around long enough to join them.

Maybe that was just his way of doing things. He didn't seem to enjoy the company of his band. He preferred to go alone—and for good reason.

He seemed to like doing things his own way. To hear the other men tell it, he traveled faster, struck harder when he attacked, and took more risks than anyone.

The company of his relatives might have felt like a tedious chore to him compared to the way he liked to do things.

The men left and Katha sent Mora down to the creek to fill up the water gourds again. "Come straight back and go on with your practicing," Mora told her. "We'll be leaving this area soon. You'll need all your skills and resources on the journey."

Mora glanced around at nothing.

"Did you hear me, Rabbit?!" Katha snapped. "I told you to go straight there and straight back without delaying anywhere. What's the matter with you?"

"Would you mind.....?" Mora stammered. "Would you mind....if I take a weapon? I don't feel right about going out there unarmed."

Katha narrowed her eyes at Mora for a second and then compressed her lips before she stormed off. She went into the cave and took out two long blades from one of the bundles in there.

Mora might have been mistaken, but she thought Katha took the blades from Hangman's possessions.

Katha came stalking back and held out the blades for Mora to take. "You can take these. They're about the same size as those rods you've been using, but they'll be heavier. They'll tire out your arms, but maybe that will help strengthen you. You can use the same techniques with these. That will be better than nothing."

Mora found herself smiling at her mother-in-law. "Thank you. I'm really grateful to you for teaching me. I know I'm not what you wanted in a daughter-in-law. I'll try hard and do my best."

Katha only scowled at her and humphed before she walked off to go help the other women butcher and smoke the men's kills.

Mora headed for the creek and made absolutely certain to avoid the Cursed Sand this time.

She kept a much closer watch on the surroundings, but she had to stop and figure out how to carry these weapons.

They were heavier than the rods, but not by much. The blades were also thicker—about two inches thick all the way down the ends of their rectangular blades.

They were made of metal—unlike every other Godless weapon Mora had seen so far.

The Godless used stone weapons. Hangman's kukris were not made of stone. They were made of some kind of dark brown glass chipped to a razor edge. They weren't metal.

She couldn't figure out why the Godless didn't use metal weapons. Hangman didn't trade his kukris for these blades even when he was carrying them around in his luggage. She would probably never find out.

She stopped at the edge of the Cursed Sand to try to figure out how to carry these weapons hands-free when she wasn't using them.

Leather thongs wrapped around each blade handle to give it a solid grip. Whoever wrapped the handles knotted the thongs and left a long tail hanging from the end.

She tied the thongs to the waistband of her loincloth at each hip. The blades hung down parallel to her legs.

She made sure to use slip knots she could undo with one tug. She would be able to stick her hands into the loops, grab the handles, pull the thongs loose, and there she would be fully armed when she needed to be.

She was just starting to feel pretty good about this when she spotted a juvenile Gurlg among the trees between her and the creek.

The creature must have either fallen from its nest or wandered away from its mother. The chick's head barely came up to her waist. Its mother was nowhere in sight.

Mora would have hidden from any creature before today, but she couldn't do that now—not with these weapons in her hands. She needed practice against real creatures, not just trees and helpful mothers-in-law.

The creature hopped around peering and pecking at insects in the leaves. The chick didn't even seem to realize it was lost or abandoned.

It spun around to glare at her and then charged her when it saw her coming. She held up both blades.

They did tire her arms out, but the adrenaline of actually fighting this creature blocked out all else. She needed to test herself. She needed to prove to herself that she wasn't as useless as everyone said.

The chick could have seriously injured her. It might even have been able to kill her if she didn't fight back at all.

She could have avoided the fight entirely because the chick didn't see her before she showed herself to it.

Those days were over. She slashed her blade from the top right down to the bottom left. Her weapon struck the chick across the beak and it lunged away squawking in protest.

It recovered right away and rushed her a second time. She swiped her other blade sideways from left to right and succeeded in cutting the chick across its chest.

It shrieked in rage, lunged for her again, and she brought down her weapon in another diagonal stroke. She wound up smashing the chick much harder on the beak and its beak actually cracked.

The chick screeched one last time, turned away, and bolted into the bushes.

Mora's shoulders slumped and her arms fell to her sides. Her shoulders felt much more exhausted after that little stunt. She couldn't keep it up for very long, but at least the creature didn't harm her.

She tied the two blades to her waistband, turned around—and froze in her tracks when she saw Hangman standing right behind her.

He stared at her and then his eyes dipped to the two weapons. He must have seen everything she just did with the Gurlg chick.

She found herself regarding him from a distance. What exactly was she supposed to say to him?

She would have liked to make up with him after yesterday, but nothing she thought of sounded appropriate enough.

His presence made it so obvious that he had been following her again. He stayed behind and avoided his uncle's orders so Hangman could keep an eye on her.

She waved at nothing. "I hope you don't mind. Your mother gave me these weapons."

"Anyone can use them," he snapped back. "They're extras."

She found her own eyes darting to his kukris. They were much smaller than these blades. They didn't bump into his legs and come close to cutting him when he moved around. His kukris didn't impede his movements at all.

He kept his kukris tucked into his waistband. He didn't have to tie them on. The weapons suited him so much better than these long, cumbersome blades. No wonder he used kukris instead.

Alien carried kukris, too—stone ones—but his were so much bigger than Hangman's. These small ones seemed to fit Hangman's lighter build.

"Thank you for following me," she blurted out. "I'm sorry I didn't say so yesterday. I should have. I know you didn't have to. You could have gone with them."

He snorted and turned away. Everything she said offended him. "I'm sure the Renegade Clan won't have a problem finding us and attacking us here, too. We don't have to go looking for them."

He took off walking through the jungle away from her. It sure looked like he was going to stop following her.

That had to be an illusion. He would probably double back and start following her again when she wasn't looking for him.

Her curiosity about him took over. She followed him. "Is that what Butcher and the others are looking for—the Renegade Clan? They're your enemies, aren't you? You said they might attack me."

"I just told you we don't have to go looking for them," he snapped over his shoulder. "We can find them by tripping over them—or practically."

"Can't you avoid them?" she asked. "Why do you have to attack them?"

He had been walking so fast and he spun around so fast she almost collided with him. "Don't ever say anything like that around my family."

"What?" she asked. "What did I say? I'm just wondering."

"You don't know what you're talking about," he snapped. "You're brainless. If we didn't attack and destroy every Renegade who trespasses on our territory, they would attack our camps, kill all the men, capture our women, and wipe us out of the country. They've already done it more than once. They're invading our territory and forcing us to retreat."

She frowned. "Oh. I didn't know that."

"You didn't know because you and your people are brainless morons who don't know anything about the country you live in. The Renegades will invade this country, too. They already are. I ambushed some of them the other day even farther south than this. They were lying in wait for the Whisperers who were leaving the gathering. How long do you think it will take for the Renegades to attack the Followers, too? Your people will be totally unprepared for their ferocity. Then the Renegades will wipe out the Followers and that will be the end of your idiotic peace experiment."

She furrowed her brow in thought. He certainly made a convincing case—if the Renegade Clan really was this far south.

He snorted again when he saw her reaction. "You really don't know anything, do you?" he sneered and turned away from her again.

She took a second to come back to her senses enough to go after him. "I'm...I'm sorry....for what I said yesterday....about my father....you were right....the Followers.....we don't know how to survive—not like the Godless do. I'm trying to learn. I'm trying to do right by your Clan. I hope you can see that."

He didn't answer at all. He kept his back to her and kept bushwhacking his way through the dense jungle.

She didn't see where he was going or why he was even out here by himself. "What are you doing?" she asked.

"Trying to get away from you," he snarled under his breath.

"Why do they call you Hangman?" she asked. "What's your real name?"

He wheeled around extra fast again. "Are you trying to insult me?! Hangman is my real name!"

"You mean....did your parents give you that name at birth?" She frowned again. "Why do the men all have names like that and women have real names?"

"The men are the ones with real names, you stupid fool!" he fumed. "We earn our names at initiation. Our parents give us the names of children at birth. At initiation, the other men take the old name away and give us the new name. No one uses the old name except as an insult."

"I'm....I'm sorry. How am I supposed to learn if I don't ask questions?"

He gave her a withering glare and turned his back on her. "Don't you ever even think of calling me anything but Hangman," he growled over his shoulder.

"Uh...okay. I won't. I just thought.....I didn't know if the others meant it as an insult to you......"

"It's a sign of respect," he snapped. "It's a mark of my status. They say it as a compliment and an indication of my place in this band."

"Oh. I didn't know."

He broke through a curtain of foliage just then. She didn't see where they were until she followed him through it.

She really did collide with him. He stood stock still on the other side of the thicket. He stood almost face to face against a Gorlock.

The creature glared at him in beady-eyed fury. Neither of them moved for a second.

Mora froze, too. She'd never gotten this close to any creature before—except the young warthogs she caught to bait her traps. She definitely never would have allowed herself to get this close to a fully grown Gorlock.

She found herself cowering behind Hangman. She sure hoped he knew how to handle one of these things.

That thought went straight out the window when the creature reared on its legs, straightened up to its full height, let out a deafening screech, and spread its wings to attack.

She staggered backward to get away from it, ran into the branches behind her, and tripped over. She sprawled on the ground.

Hangman didn't hesitate. He pulled his kukris and sprang straight upward just as the Gorlock swiped its wings at him.

He landed on the rock face of a nearby cliff. Mora didn't realize until that moment that they had walked right up next to the cliff. The bushes hid it until now.

He grasped the rough surface and clung there facing the Gorlock at the level of its head.

She didn't see how Hangman could hold onto the rock and his kukris at the same time, but he did somehow.

The Gorlock looked straight at him and then down at Mora lying sprawled on the ground.

She scrambled to get up. One of the long metal blades bumped her leg. She had completely forgotten about the weapons.

The instant the Gorlock took its eyes off Hangman, he launched himself off the wall, raised both his kukris to strike, and sailed through the air heading straight for the creature's head.

The Gorlock hopped back and batted its wing at him, caught him, and sent him flying across the open space in front of the wall. He landed in another patch of bushes and vanished out of sight behind the leaves.

Mora couldn't stand by and let the creature kill him—or her. She had these weapons. She might not be able to do much against this creature, but she had to at least try—at least to give Hangman time to recover—if he wasn't already dead.

She thrust her hands through the loops in her blades, pulled the thongs, and charged. She couldn't hit anything higher than the Gorlock's knee. That would have to be enough.

She rushed it and slashed one of her blades across the side of its ankle. Her blade cut through the skin and hit solid bone. She didn't damage the creature at all. She just made it mad.

It shrieked again, spun around to face her, and slashed its wing at her.

The wing hit her and she went flying straight into the granite cliff face. She slammed into it, hit the ground, and passed out.

Chapter 36

H angman fed a few more sticks into the fire and turned the Gorlock meat on the spit. A dribble of juice spilled onto the coals and made a hiss as it evaporated.

Mora stirred in her sleep across the fire from him. She lay on her side between the fire and the cliff.

Hangman might not need to keep her warm in the jungle heat, but he built the fire there just in case she did need it.

He found himself studying her more closely while she slept. She wasn't bad looking for a Follower girl. She had large black eyes that came to a point on the outer edges.

The skin sloped downward at the inner surface where her eyes met her nose. That little bit of skin gave her an exotic look. None of the Godless had that.

She looked much better with her hair down and all those clothes gone. She didn't look like a Godless woman, but that on its own somehow made her more appealing.

She was starting to grow on him. She still couldn't take care of herself, but she told the truth when she said she was trying.

She tried harder than he expected her to. He didn't expect her to try at all. He expected any Follower to curl up and die—or to fall to one of the creatures.

She engaged that Gurlg chick on purpose to challenge herself. He never expected that. She also deliberately engaged with the Gorlock. That counted for something.

He pulled out his knife, shaved off a piece of the cooked meat, and put it in his mouth. He should take her back to the cave as soon as she woke up, but he didn't want to.

He found himself getting curious about her. She interested him and elicited a kind of horrified fascination for her.

He felt himself starting to get curious to see how long she would last out here in the jungle. Which creature would be the one to kill her? How long could she possibly last with no skills, no strength, and no courage?

She had courage. That much was clear. She just needed to learn how to use it.

He opened one of his bags while he waited for her to wake up. It was already getting dark. He couldn't take her back to the cave now—not while she was unconscious.

He could have, but that would only humiliate her. He would have to explain how she got hit by a Gorlock. His family wouldn't understand how she got hit by a Gorlock.

He didn't want to explain it to them. This new understanding he was developing of her personality and her courage—he didn't want to share it with anyone—not until he found out more about her.

He pulled a bunch of pieces of twisted metal out of his bags. Wires and other pieces of useless junk hung from the fragments.

He started to dismantle them and break them into pieces when the meat sent another spurt of juice into the coals. He put the metal fragments down so he could bend over the fire to turn the meat again.

The noise roused Mora. She groaned, twisted onto her stomach, buried her face in the dirt, and then rolled onto her back.

Her clothes left more of her body exposed. She was too pale and bony to look like a Godless woman below the neck. She looked starved and fleshless—not like the toned, tanned, muscular women of Hangman's band.

That would change, though. She would put on weight, now that she was doing more physical activity.

He had been watching her practice the fighting moves his mother showed her. Mora tried hard at that, too—and it worked. She used them against that chick.

She didn't get a chance to use the techniques against the Gorlock, but everyone had to start somewhere.

He could only think of a handful of Godless women who would have been able to handle a fully grown Gorlock anyway.

The Gorlock hitting her and knocking her out didn't make her unique or pathetic. That could have happened to anyone. It could have happened to Hangman if the Gorlock had thrown him a few feet farther to the left.

She lay on her back with her eyes closed for a minute. He expected her to go back to sleep, but in a second, her eyes snapped open. She bolted upright to prop herself on her elbow while she looked around everywhere.

Her features turned white when she saw him sitting there. "Don't worry," he told her. "The Gorlock is gone. It won't threaten you again."

"What....?" She looked around everywhere and back at him. "Where are.....Are we...." She looked at the cliff. "We're in the same place."

"I didn't think it was wise to move you until you woke up on your own. Are you hungry?" He cut off a few more pieces of the meat. "I should tell you the Gorlock isn't gone—not completely. It's right here."

He held out a handful of the meat to her.

She stared at it trying to process what he was telling her. "That....that's the Gorlock...? But how? What happened after.....?" She looked back at the cliff in confusion.

"You attacked the Gorlock and slashed it across the foot. Don't you remember? It hit you and threw you against that wall. The impact knocked you out until right now."

"But what happened to the Gorlock? How did you....Did you kill it?"

"Of course I did. It would have pecked you to death and eaten you. Your attack gave me a chance to jump on it from behind and slash its neck."

She blinked at him, looked all around her again, and finally flopped down on her back again. Her hand flew to her temple. "My head hurts."

Hangman put his hand down. He'd been holding out the handful of meat through their whole conversation, but she didn't notice.

He put the dripping meat on top of his leather bag and went back to pulling his metal fragments and wires apart.

She lay on her back staring up at the sky. "I should have done more. I tried to help you, but I failed."

"You didn't fail at all. I wouldn't have been able to kill it if you didn't attack when you did. You did well—and you did well against the Gurlg chick, too. I was surprised that you took it on the way you did."

She didn't respond at first. She lapsed into silence for a minute and then shot up onto her elbow again. She moved too fast, grasped her head, and winced in pain. "Aarrgh!"

"Slow down," he told her. "You fell hard."

She looked around. "I'm sorry. I was confused for a minute. Do you still have some of that food? I'm hungry."

He stopped what he was doing, handed the meat over, and returned to his own work.

She sat all the way up, sat cross-legged by the fire, and started eating while she stared into the flames.

Neither of them spoke for a minute. "You stayed out here with me," she finally remarked.

"What did you think—that I would abandon you here to die? You're my wife. Do you think I've been following you around all this time for nothing?"

She didn't reply again for a second. "What are you working on?"

"I collect these things from the ancient cities. I take them apart and use the wire for certain purposes."

"Why do the Godless only use stone tools when you could use metal tools instead? You could fashion that metal into blades or arrowheads—or anything. Your women could use them for butchering and scraping hides."

"We use stone tools because stone is stronger and lasts longer. Metal breaks, bends, and weakens more quickly. Stone is better."

"Some people disagree," she returned.

He snorted again. "Look." He picked up one of his fragments and bent it easily between his power fingers. He bent it back and forth for a minute and then tore it along the seam he created by bending it.

He threw the fragment aside. "Metal is weak. It's far inferior to stone." He went back to work. "This wire can be useful, though."

He felt her studying him across the fire. She certainly changed her tone since their first encounter.

"Can I ask you a question?" she asked.

"Go ahead. You may not like the answer if it's something about how stupid the Followers are."

"It isn't that."

"Ask, then."

"How did you get your scars?"

His head shot up and he stared at her. He never expected her to ask that.

She cringed before that stare. At first he thought she either hated or feared him. Now he saw a different expression on her face.

She tried to look away and failed. "I'm....I'm sorry....I didn't mean to offend you. I was just curious. Forget I said it."

"You didn't offend me." He heard himself speaking to her too harshly. He stared at her so intently. He kept trying to figure her out, but looking at her like this obviously made her nervous.

He forced himself to go back to his work. "I got my scars at my initiation—if you really must know."

"Is the initiation dangerous? Do the other men put you through some kind of challenge?"

"The other men don't do anything," he mumbled. "The boy does it alone with no help or interference from the other men. Any involvement from the other men disqualifies the test."

"What is the test?"

"The boy has to fight a creature. He chooses which one."

"So which creature did you choose to fight?"

He stiffened before he said it. He already knew how she would react. "I fought a Crusher."

She gasped out loud and her hand flew to her mouth. That movement made him look up.

She had finished all the meat he gave her. Her hands were empty now.

He rolled up his salvaged wire, put it into his bag, and sat back to carve her another handful. He handed it to her, but she paid no attention.

"You fought a Crusher!!" she panted. "You...you got hurt.....but why.....? Your father....didn't he try to stop you?"

"He tried to talk me out of it, but he couldn't stop me. I just told you. The boy gets to choose which creature he fights. I was small and weak growing up. None of the men thought I would become anything. I had to prove myself."

She shut her mouth, looked at the flames, and noticed the food in her hand for the first time. She put a piece in her mouth still thinking over what he said.

He helped himself to another handful and sat back against a different rock. "Which creature a boy chooses is a tricky subject. The boy has to choose something small enough that he'll be able to defeat it. He can't choose something too big for him to handle, but he can't choose anything too small, either. The men would lose respect for him if the test wasn't difficult enough. The men would consider him weak and cowardly if he made it obvious that he was taking it easy on himself. Take Cross. He fought a Gorlock on his own. That's how he got his scars. He fought very well. I'm proud of him."

Her eyes darted up. "You fought a Crusher—by choice?!"

"I told you. I had to prove myself. I had to earn the respect of much older, more experienced, bigger men. Viking and Alien were both mature then—and so were Chaos, Magnet, and Vulture. I had to do something impressive."

"But....did you know you could defeat a Crusher?"

He shrugged and looked down at his food. He'd never told this story to someone before. Everyone he knew already knew the story.

The women of his family band heard the story from the men when Hangman came home from initiation. His mother almost died of grief when she saw his face. Shadow had to explain to her how Hangman got his scars.

"I decided I had to make a statement—to myself and the men of my Clan." He felt himself talking more to himself than to her. "I didn't want to live as a despised weakling all my life. I decided it would be better for me to die fighting a Crusher than to live with the disgrace of failing my initiation, so I chose the biggest, most dangerous monster I could think of—something that everyone would remember for a long time afterward. Then no one would be able to say I was weak."

"No one believes you're weak now," she pointed out.

"They think that because of what happened to me at my initiation. Things changed that day. That's how I became what I am. I decided to change and I did. I didn't get to be the biggest and the strongest, but I made up for it in other ways. I made up for it by becoming even deadlier than Viking, Alien, and all the others. I became someone they all look up to and respect."

She blinked her big eyes at him. "So what happened? How did you get scarred—and why did they call you Hangman?"

"The Crusher overpowered men when the fight started. It knocked me over and tore up my face with its claws. It even bit me in the face and picked me up by the face. That's how I got the scars."

"What happened?" she breathed. "How did you kill it?"

"It picked me up and threw me. I landed a little way away. I saw the Crusher coming back for me. I knew I couldn't let it hit me again, so the next time it gouged its horns at me, I grabbed one. It tossed its head up and flipped me onto its head. I grabbed it around the neck and slit its throat. Then I jumped clear." He looked up at her to see her staring at him. "I use that technique a lot now. It works well. It's one of the only ways to kill the large creatures. You have to get high enough onto their necks or heads. You can't hit them from the ground."

"That's amazing!" she whispered. "I understand now why they respect you so much."

He looked away. He didn't want her looking at him like that. "It wasn't just that. It's everything that happened after that. They wouldn't respect me at all for that if I didn't follow it up by staying that way." He stuffed the last piece of meat into his mouth and sat up to take the meat off the spit. "Are you still hungry? You can have some more if you are."

"I'm fine. Thank you for taking care of me."

He didn't respond except to put a few more sticks on the fire. He didn't like where this conversation was going.

"Your mother will be furious with me when I don't come back with the gourds," she went on.

"No, she won't. She'll realize that you're out here with me."

Mora tensed across the fire. He made sure not to look at her. Of course she would take it to mean that. Did she really expect him to initiate something now of all times?

He arranged the rest of his gear and stretched out on the ground. He used one of his bags as a pillow. "You should get some more sleep," he told her. "Your head will feel sore for a few days. Don't try to move too quickly."

He shut his eyes, but he still sensed her sitting there. Now she was the one watching him instead of the other way around.

He didn't open his eyes to look at her. He could have turned his back on her to make it even more obvious that he didn't plan to do anything with her, but she must be getting the message by now.

If she was half as smart as he suspected she was, she would understand that he never planned to do anything with her ever. Maybe then she would change her opinion about him.

Chapter 37

H angman strode through the jungle heading north. His family band was already on the move going in the same direction.

He woke up early, left Mora asleep, and went to check that the band got underway all right. He was traveling parallel to them, but he didn't want to join up with them—not yet.

Mora followed him in dutiful silence. She didn't bombard him with questions the way she did yesterday.

She stayed right behind him and walked in the pathway he forged through the undergrowth. She never deviated once in all the hours she traveled with him.

She certainly knew how to travel. She kept up with him as long as he kept walking. She didn't lag or complain or ask to stop to rest. She didn't shirk once.

He turned northwest and climbed a tall mountain slope. She didn't complain about that, either. She turned out to be much stronger than she looked.

He stopped at the top and flattened himself on his stomach on the grass. She stretched out next to him and they looked down the other side into a huge valley.

Two lines of mountains ringed the valley on either side. These weren't the mountains in Butcher's pictures. The Godless already knew about these mountains and this valley.

"Why are we here?" Mora murmured under her breath.

"Butcher's band stops by this valley every year when we come to the gathering—or we used to. I don't think he'll come this way again."

"Why do you stop by here? What's so special about this valley?"

"Them." Hangman pointed to a mob of hundreds of creatures grazing on the valley floor. "We come to see the Ashtaws."

The creatures were enormous herbivores with large, barrel-shaped bodies, long legs, long necks, and a long tail that came to a point at the end.

Thick, tough, ash-grey hide covered the Ashtaws' outer skin. The creatures didn't have any horns or spikes or fangs or poison. They were totally harmless except for their great size. They were even bigger than Crushers.

The tallest adults could stretch their necks to graze leaves from the highest trees. The juveniles milled around next to their parents' giant legs. The smallest newborn juveniles were about Alien's size.

"Shadow had the idea to domesticate these creatures," Hangman went on. "He thought we could use them in battle against our enemies, but none of us can figure out how to do it. I think Butcher may have given up on that by now. He didn't tell any of us to come over here. That's one of the reasons I didn't go back to rejoin the band just yet. I wanted to see them....I don't know why. There is no way to domesticate them."

Mora spun around fast. "But that should be easy! We handle and lead Ashtaws all the time."

Hangman gaped at her. "I don't believe you! These creatures are huge!"

"They're big, but they're sweet-tempered. We lure them into traps and snares all the time. They're the easiest to handle and the easiest to lead." She frowned at him. "Are you telling me you really don't know?"

"Know what? How could I know? I've never heard of anyone leading them anywhere."

She actually groaned and rolled her eyes to Heaven. "You might be strong and brave, but you really don't know anything. The leaves of the Fogpo tree—right down there! We passed a dozen of them on the way here. I saw them."

"So?" Hangman asked. "What about it?"

"The Ashtaws love Fogpo leaves! It's their favorite food. They can't resist it. They'll go anywhere if they think they can get some. It's the easiest way to lure one of them into a trap. Watch. I'll show you."

Hangman stared at her in horror as she got to her feet. She retreated down the hill, took off running into the jungle, and came back with a thin branch with a bunch of leaves rustling from the end.

She stopped next to him and his world came to a screeching halt when she actually set off down the other side of the hill toward the Ashtaws in the distance.

He grabbed her arm to hold her back. "I can't let you go down there, Mora. It's too dangerous."

"It isn't dangerous, Hangman," she fired back with a lot more venom than he had ever heard her use before. "I'm telling you we do this all the time. The creatures are placid and harmless. They love Fogpo leaves. Look. If it makes you feel better, I'll go for one of the juveniles. Okay?"

His eyes darted to the creatures. "I don't know about this...."

"You said you wanted to find out how to domesticate them. This is it. It's easy. Just let me show you." Her tone changed. "Just imagine the difference these creatures could make to your Clan if you did domesticate them."

His hand fell off her arm. Those words worked some kind of magic spell on him, but he absolutely could not bring himself to go with her when she turned away and headed off down the hill toward the creatures.

They were a long way off. It took her a while to go out there.

She got halfway there before she started rustling the leaves on the branch. They made a distinctive sound when they bumped into each other.

One young juvenile had wandered some distance away from its mother. She headed for that creature shaking the branch all the way.

The creature looked up and froze. The sound drifted across the open valley. The creature definitely heard it.

The Ashtaws must have learned to recognize that sound because the little one actually set off to meet up with her. She stopped where she was and kept shaking the branch until the creature halted right in front of her.

She let it munch the leaves for a minute. Then she turned around, held the branch sticking out to one side next to her, and started walking back up the long hill to where Hangman watched from his position.

He could not bring himself to believe what he was seeing. The creature followed her still munching away on the leaves.

It didn't tear the leaves off. It kept its head buried in the foliage so it could eat the leaves right off the branch.

Some of the adult Ashtaws heard the noise, too. They stopped grazing and came after her, too.

She showed no sign of alarm when she saw these massive creatures following her. Their long legs closed the gap, but she actually smiled up at them. Hangman had never seen her so relaxed and at ease.

He was the one who started to get worried when he saw the gigantic adults coming straight toward his hill. He would have to retreat into the jungle if Mora didn't stop them somehow.

He supposed she could always drop the branch on the ground, leave it for them to feast on, and walk or run away if she really had to.

They got within a dozen yards of her. One enormous adult lowered its head and buried its face in the leaves.

She stopped there and turned around to smile at the creature. At that moment, another airborne creature swooped down from directly overhead and dive-bombed the adult Ashtaw.

Hangman had been so consumed with watching Mora lure these creatures around like pets. He didn't see the fully grown Boultar until it collided with the Ashtaw's head.

The Boultars were enormous airborne monsters. They looked like birds except that they didn't have feathers.

Flakes of bony tissue covered the Boultars' leathery skin to take the place of feathers on its wings. The Boultars had nothing else on their bodies that even resembled feathers.

Their long beak and razor talons made them a menace to every other kind of creature no matter how big or small.

The Ashtaw swung its head up with a roar. The Boultar struck so fast that the Ashtaw forgot to let go of the branch.

The Ashtaw carried the branch with it and Mora, too. She completely forgot to let go before the Ashtaw flipped her into the air.

She let go at exactly the wrong time and fell from thirty feet in the air.

So many Ashtaws gathered around her to share the Fogpo leaves that she wound up falling straight onto the back of a much smaller adult. This one might have been an adolescent. It only stood fifteen feet at the shoulder.

She landed across its spine just as the Ashtaws wheeled away and stampeded away from the attacking Boultars.

Hangman launched to his feet and took off running down the hill to help Mora, but the Ashtaws kept running faster and faster with her on that one creature's back.

The Boultar banked around and went after the Ashtaws. Hangman had to check himself when he saw another dozen Boultars all swooping down to attack the Ashtaws.

They banked low, zoomed over the grasslands, and snatched young Ashtaws off the ground.

The little ones squalled for their mothers. Some of the adult Ashtaws turned back. One enormous mother swiped her head at the Boultar that took her baby, smashed the creature out of the sky, and knocked her baby loose.

The little one fell to his death on the valley floor below. Other Boultars grabbed young Ashtaws on the wing and tried to fly off with them.

Some of the young Ashtaws were too big for the Boultars to lift. The Boultars' talons killed the Ashtaws there and the Boultars landed to devour their prey right on the grass.

Hangman ran between them, but he couldn't even see Mora anymore. How far would the Ashtaws carry her before they slowed down enough for her to slide off onto the ground?

He would just have to keep following the stampeding herd until he found her. He couldn't go back to his band without her.

He found her sooner than he expected. He climbed a hill and spotted her floundering on the grass at the bottom. She must have either fallen off or gotten thrown off.

She sat up, fell over, and struggled to straighten herself out. Hangman hustled down the hill toward her. "Mora!" he yelled. "Mora!!"

She looked up and her expression cleared in relief when she saw him. He couldn't remember ever feeling this relieved. She was all right.

He got halfway there. She put her hands on the ground to push herself to her feet when a big Boultar dropped out of the sky and landed between her and Hangman.

He stopped in his tracks and his hands flew to his weapons. The Boultar landed facing Mora. The creature had its back to Hangman.

He could always take out creatures the best from this position. He had to kill this Boultar before it attacked Mora.

Then he noticed the look of stark terror on her face when she looked up at the giant creature. She still carried both of those weapons at her sides, but she didn't think to use them. She didn't even think to grab them.

No Godless woman would ever have hesitated to fight a creature no matter how big it was. A Godless woman would know to fight back, but she didn't. She didn't even think of it. Her fear wiped out everything else.

Hangman could have stepped in and killed the creature on his own, but she had to learn. She had to overcome this fear. He saw that now. He couldn't be the one always saving her.

"Get up, Mora!" he called out. "You can fight it! You can drive it off if you just fight back! Stand up and take your weapons!"

His words took way too long to penetrate her brain. She had to struggle to tear her attention away from the Boultar. The creature made it worse by taking a step toward her, flapping its wings, and narrowing its eyes to study her.

It towered over her. It must have looked bigger and more dangerous than it was when she was still down on her knees like that.

Hangman changed his tone and snapped in a much sterner voice of command. "Take your weapons, Mora! You can fight this thing! The first time it tries to attack you, roll underneath it and cut its feet the way you attacked the Gorlock. Cut the tendon behind its ankle and cripple it. Then you can face it standing up. You can do this! You can make it fly away if you only fight back!"

She understood this time. Her expression changed and her features hardened. She clamped her lips shut and narrowed her eyes right back at the Boultar.

She slid her hands into the loops of her weapons and pulled the strings to release them.

Hangman didn't see how she did it before. It really was an ingenious way of carrying her weapons so she could grab them easily when she needed them.

She tightened her hold on them and flexed her arms in readiness, but she didn't get off her knees. Her gaze darted to the space under the Boultar's body—where its legs met its belly.

"You can do it, Mora!" he called out again. "Wait until it tries to attack you! Wait until it overextends its neck to peck you with its beak. Then dive past the beak and roll under its body. You can do this! I'm right here to help you if anything goes wrong."

She didn't seem to hear him. All her attention locked on the Boultar—the way it should.

He shut his mouth and resolved not to say anything else. She had to fight her own fight. He would only step in if he thought she was in danger.

The Boultar attacked sooner than he expected. The creature took another step and stabbed its pointed beak at Mora.

She reacted at exactly the right second, dove past the beak, rolled under the creature's body, and pivoted onto her knees behind and underneath the creature.

Hangman couldn't have orchestrated her attack better if he planned it in advance. She slashed her blade at the creature's ankle tendon behind the foot.

The creature shrieked in pain—and then, beyond Hangman's wildest dreams, she actually slashed her second blade across the tendon of the Boultar's other foot.

She cut both tendons and crippled the creature completely. It tried to spring around to face her. She rolled ten feet away and landed on her knees at a distance from the creature with her blades raised to defend herself.

The Boultar shrieked again and again, especially when it tried to land on its broken feet. It couldn't stand.

She stumbled to her feet with both weapons raised, but the creature only took wing, flew off into the sky, and left her standing there alone.

Chapter 38

Mora slumped and lowered her blades as the Boultar soared higher and higher into the sky. It was gone.

Hangman sauntered over to her. "Well done," he told her. "You did it."

"I didn't kill it," she mumbled. "I wanted to."

"You defended yourself. That was the best you've done so far. I'm proud of you."

Her head shot up, but he only regarded her as though his words meant nothing.

He turned away to leave. "Let's get back to the band. The Ashtaws are gone. We can think about what to do about them later."

Mora glanced around at the valley where the Ashtaws had been grazing just now. The valley was completely deserted now except for the Boultars.

They surrounded the carcasses of young Ashtaws they killed. So many Boultars crowded each carcass that she couldn't see the bodies anymore.

The Boultars squawked, squabbled, and fought each other over the meat. They paid no attention to Hangman and Mora.

She had to think hard before she shook herself out of her trance. Everything that happened in the last few minutes caught up with her.

She still didn't fully grasp what happened when she got thrown onto that Ashtaw's back. Then she got into a fight against a fully grown Boultar.

She didn't exactly get into a fight against it, but at least she stopped it from killing her.

Hangman looked at her over his shoulder. He was waiting for her to follow him back to their band.

She blundered after him in between trying to tie her blades back onto her waistband. They were working out better than she hoped.

She did need to find a way to stop them from bumping into her legs. They would have been a lot more comfortable if not for that.

He climbed the same hill and down the other side. The two of them had a long way to walk before they returned to the spot where they first saw the Ashtaws.

She fell in behind him when they entered the jungle. She walked in his wake and didn't break the silence with questions or comments.

At least the situation had thawed between her and Hangman. They snap and yell at each other anymore. That was an improvement on the way things were when they started.

The sun started to go down long before they met up with the band. She didn't even know where to find them, but Hangman seemed to know where he was going. She didn't.

She let her thoughts drift back to her confrontation with the Boultar. She didn't even really understand how she found the courage to do what she did.

His encouragement definitely helped. He told her what to do. She never would have thought to cripple the creature. That was a pure genius move.

He understood these things so much better than she did. She started to envy the Godless. They lived a hard life—much harder than the Followers.

The Godless had it so much easier in a different way,. They grew up learning to fight from an early age. They learned with other children and their parents and older relatives.

All Godless children grew up with people encouraging them the way Hangman encouraged her just now.

The children probably got lots of practice fighting less dangerous targets like that Gurlg chick. The children could pick and choose what to fight until they overcome the larger creatures.

Hangman startled her out of her trance by stopping dead in his tracks. He jerked around to his right and glared off into the undergrowth.

Mora didn't see anything over there. The foliage grew too thick for her to see anything. "What is it?" she asked. "What's wrong?"

"Another Gorlock," he muttered. "Come on!"

He grabbed her by the wrist and pulled her into a run. They took off into the jungle.

He ran fast—a lot faster than she could keep up with. She stumbled but he never let her slow down. If anything, he pulled her faster.

Something crashed in the bushes to her right. She barely glanced in that direction and saw a Gorlock's head sticking up above the canopy.

Its head swam through the leaves on a parallel course with Hangman's. The creature must be following them.

He veered to the left to evade it—and burst through into a clearing between the trees.

Mora bumped into him when he stopped again. Her stomach plummeted into her shoes when she saw a large Demonex crouching across the clearing.

The creature lay on its stomach with its head up. It might have been resting when it heard the commotion nearby.

The Demonex bared its teeth and snarled at Hangman and Mora. No one moved for a second.

Some kind of ripple went down the creature's body as all its muscles tensed. Mora wouldn't have noticed it if Hangman hadn't reacted with lightning speed.

He let go of Mora's wrist and grabbed his kukris, but the Demonex reacted so much faster. It launched off the ground, soared across the clearing, and landed all its weight on him before he could even raise his weapons.

The impact knocked Hangman over. He hit Mora and she toppled the other way before he landed on his back with the Demonex right on top of him.

She hit the ground and sprang up grabbing for her blades, but Hangman and the Demonex already locked together in mortal combat.

The Demonex lunged its fangs for his face. He turned aside just in time and the creature's fang cut him down the side of his neck from his ear to his shoulder.

He struck out with his kukris, but the creature's body stopped him from hitting its head or neck.

He plunged his kukri into the creature's ribs right behind the forelimb. The Demonex bellowed and dug its claws into his body.

Mora launched to her feet and charged the creature from the side. She didn't hold out any hope of being able to kill the creature. She just had to help Hangman as much as possible even if she couldn't help him very much.

The Demonex bellowed again and turned its head downward to crack its fangs in his face. Mora raised her blades to strike, but at that moment, the Gorlock burst through the trees on the opposite side of the clearing.

Mora skidded to a halt with her blades raised. She couldn't fight a Gorlock, but she raised her weapons anyway. Maybe she would be able to damage it enough to stop it from attacking. She could only hope.

The Demonex looked up, locked eyes on the Gorlock, and snarled. That snarl drew the Gorlock's attention to the Demonex.

The Demonex sprang off Hangman, lunged for the Gorlock, and landed on the creature's neck. The Gorlock bellowed and the two creatures went at it with fangs, claws, and blows.

Mora charged forward a second time, grabbed Hangman, and pulled him to his feet. He looked a lot bloodier than he should have been.

It took her a second to realize that the Demonex didn't release its claws before it leapt off him. Its claws tore the flesh on his legs, sides, and chest.

He stumbled after her and they both raced away into the jungle. She didn't know where she was going. She didn't care.

He brought her back to reality by pulling her to the right. "This way!"

She followed him, but dusk settled over the jungle in a little while. It would get too dark to see as soon as night set in.

She looked around for somewhere to stop when they came to another stream. Hangman leapt over it, clambered up the opposite bank, and collapsed at the base of a tree.

"We can stop here," he panted. "We have to spend the night somewhere."

"You're bleeding." She bent over his legs, but the wounds on his chest and sides looked worse. "Stay here. I'll be right back and I'll build a fire."

She didn't wait for him to answer. Those wounds were much deeper than she realized.

She gathered leaves to make a healing paste and she also gathered Gooji sap. She didn't want to risk those wounds getting infected.

She had no way to carry the sap, so she cut an enormous leaf from the jungle and folded the sap crumbs into that.

She went back to find Hangman still covered in blood and sprawled at the base of the tree. He hadn't moved.

She put everything down near him and gathered a bunch of twigs and larger branches. "I can't start the fire by myself," she told him. "You'll have to do that. I'm sorry."

He groaned when he heaved himself off the tree. "You'll learn. It isn't hard."

He selected one of the sticks and spun it between his hands to create an ember the way Chaos did. She balled up a bunch of dry grass into a rat's nest and handed it to him.

She spent the rest of the time assembling her fire while he blew on the bundle and it ignited.

She stuffed the flaming bundle under her twigs and the fire caught. He opened his bag and handed her a wooden bowl. "You can make the paste in that."

She smiled at him, but he didn't return it. He sank back against the tree, rested his head against the trunk, and shut his eyes.

Turning his head like that gave her a perfect view of the gash down the side of his neck. Blood oozed from it and ran down his neck. It looked even worse like this.

She left, gathered some fuzzy soft down from a different plant, and hunted in his bags until she found another wooden bowl identical to the first.

She filled it with water from the stream, squatted down next to him, soaked the ball of down, and sponged the water onto his neck to wash the blood off.

He flinched and started to pull away before he realized what she was doing. He opened his eyes for a second before he closed them again.

"We need to get these clean," she told him. "I'll make you some Gooji juice. You should drink that tonight as soon as it's ready."

She remembered to add wood to the fire when she said that. It would take a long time to make the juice, but she was in no rush to leave here—not with him in this condition.

"How do you know all this?" he growled without opening his eyes.

"We have healing in the Followers. We don't have rules against healing injuries."

"I'm surprised," he grumbled. "I'm surprised you don't leave your wounded behind to die."

She made a face, but he didn't see. "I'm sorry I didn't get to the Demonex before it injured you."

"You couldn't have done anything. It landed on me before either of us could do anything." He winced again when she started cleaning the wounds on his chest. "At least we know about the Ashtaws now. We know because of you."

"What will you do about it? Will you tell your uncle that we can domesticate them after all?"

"I don't know if I'll tell him. It depends on how far north the band has traveled by the time we catch up with them. If we're too far north or too busy with everything else, it might not do any good to tell him. It won't make any difference until we travel south again."

"Don't you have Ashtaws up north? Can't you find a herd closer to your territory?"

"We don't have as many. The country is too rugged. They stick to the open valleys. We would have to travel farther to find another herd. Butcher might not think it's as important as other things."

He opened his eyes when she started dabbing the down onto his legs. He studied her while she worked over him to clean his wounds.

She put the water aside and hunted around until she found a rock she wanted to heat for the Gooji juice. Then she got busy grinding the leaves into a paste.

She tried not to notice Hangman staring at her the whole time. What was he thinking right now? She didn't want to think about it.

"At least you didn't get seriously hurt," she remarked.

"I've gotten more seriously hurt than this before."

She looked up and held out a finger loaded with a glob of the paste. He turned his head so she could smear the paste down the gash. She dabbed it in place to seal the cut.

"Did your scars get infected after your initiation? I bet you had to drink a lot of Gooji juice after that."

"I did—but as my family is always pointing out, this won't make me any uglier."

She found herself laughing. "At least you can see the positive side of it."

She put the paste on all his other wounds. He sat perfectly still through the whole procedure.

He stared at her without looking away when she touched his chest, sides, and legs. The tension became unbearable.

She couldn't look back at him. She couldn't let herself see all the hidden meanings in his eyes.

She put the paste bowl aside. "We should take this with us. You should keep putting it on."

"I know," he told her.

She busied herself making the Gooji juice after that. He pulled a piece of hide out of one of his bags, opened it, and shared some of the Gorlock meat from yesterday with her.

She used two sticks to lower the hot rock into the water to boil the Gooji juice. Then they both sat back to eat while they waited for the juice to cool.

She didn't know what to say to break the silence. Should she break the silence at all? At least she and Hangman could speak to each other and have a civil conversation now.

Chapter 39

Mora got up to go gather some more firewood. She occupied herself with a dozen little chores so she wouldn't have to either talk to Hangman or look at him.

His ugliness didn't bother her anymore. The way he looked at her racked her nerves. He wouldn't look at her at all for days. Now he wouldn't look away.

His eyes became torturously penetrating. His scars made his eyes stand out in unimaginable ways. He made her tremble just by looking at her.

She really hoped he didn't think she avoided eye contact because of his ugliness. Part of her no longer even considered him ugly.

Seeing him this close somehow erased her first impression. His ruined face just looked like Hangman now. It looked normal for him—almost as if he never could have possibly looked any different.

She found it impossible to believe he had only been like this for three years. He went from a skinny, undersized weakling to this in three years. No wonder his older male relatives respected him so much.

She couldn't imagine that undersized kid even being the same person as the Hangman sitting in front of her now.

She also couldn't imagine him looking any different. Seeing Shadow, Katha, Cross, and all their other relatives didn't give Mora any insight into what Hangman looked like before his initiation.

He really did become a completely different person. His old self died forever. His new self bore no resemblance to the person he was.

She understood so much better now why he considered any mention of his old self an insult. It was an insult. It was an insult to the outstanding man he'd worked hard to turn himself into.

She came back from gathering another load of firewood, put it down, and tested the juice. "It's ready," she told him. "You should drink it now."

He pretended not to notice when she handed him the bowl and his fingers brushed hers. He tipped up the bowl and downed the contents in a few gulps.

He put the bowl aside and swiveled over to lie down by the fire. He usually slept on his side, but he stretched out on his back this time and shut his eyes with a groan.

"Don't let me get into any more fights tomorrow," he muttered. "If we meet with any dangers, you can defend me and kill whatever it is. I'm taking tomorrow off."

She laughed, but he didn't open his eyes. He turned his head toward the flames to move the cut side of his neck away from the dirt.

She retreated to the other side of the fire and lay down on her side, but she found herself studying him in the firelight.

He would never start anything with her. She knew that for certain now. He would just keep on this way forever. He wouldn't be the one to take their marriage to the next level.

Her behavior toward him recently might be enough to convince him that she didn't hate him. He would never assume it meant she wanted him.

She would have to convince him of that another way.

She didn't want him—not that way. She didn't even know him. She couldn't even be certain that she liked him, but she did respect him.

She had to respect him for the help he'd given her. She would have respected him for that alone, but so many other things made her respect him, too.

She couldn't even count the ways she respected him—and he was her husband whether she wanted him to be or not.

She respected him for not ever touching her. She respected him for completely turning his back on her. She understood that so much better now.

She pushed herself into a sitting position, got to her feet, tiptoed around the fire, stretched out next to him, and put her arms around him.

He stiffened and his head swung up. "What are you doing?" he snarled.

"We're married," she murmured. "I don't want to dread it anymore."

He tensed, pulled away, and rolled onto his side facing the fire. He turned his back on her. "You don't want me. You've made that obvious a million times. Don't play games with me."

"It isn't a game, Hangman." She took a chance and laid her hand on his shoulder. "It's going to happen sooner or later. It has to. We can't be married without having children. I don't want to be afraid of it anymore."

He didn't answer. She probably should have walked away. She didn't want to do that.

This might be the only time when she and Hangman got to spend any time alone together. She didn't want to wake up tomorrow with this hanging over her head.

She ran her hand down his back. He shivered at her touch. Did he dread it as much as she did.....or did he secretly long for it?

Was that the reason he got so furious at the gathering—because he knew he could never have what the other young people so obviously enjoyed?

She scooted in behind him, wrapped her arms around him, and pressed her body into him from behind. His bare skin felt electric and made her shiver.

He tensed again when she held onto him. She tried to make sure to put her hands and arms in places where he wasn't wounded. She didn't feel any of the wounds.

He took a minute before he twisted over on his back. "Won't you ever leave me alone?" he growled.

She raised her hand to touch his face, but he jerked his head away.

"Do you really plan to avoid me for our entire marriage?" she asked. "You would bring shame on your Clan if any of the others found out."

"I've seen the way you look at me," he countered. "I know you don't really want me. You can't convince me that you do."

"And I've seen the way you look at me. You don't want to do it with a cowardly little rabbit, do you? I'm as disgusting to you as you are to me. We're going to be married for a long time. We might as well find a way to work it out."

"You don't even know how to do it, do you?" he countered. "Have you ever even seen it? Did you ever see it before the other night?"

She looked down and away from him, but she only wound up looking at his body.

"No, we keep it hidden in the Followers." She pushed herself up on her elbow and studied his body.

His body fascinated her. She let her fingertips trail over his chest, shoulders, and stomach.

"What's the matter?" he snapped. "Haven't you seen a man before?"

"Only my little brothers. I've never seen an adult man before—not like that."

She looked up to find him watching her again. They looked into each other's eyes for a second.

Now he really didn't look ugly to her. He just looked like a man—like himself. He didn't look like other men, but his ugliness somehow suited how unlike other men he was in every other way.

She leaned in and kissed him, but he jerked his head again a second time. "Stop it," he snapped.

She glanced back down at his body. The rest of him looked as normal as anyone could hope. "Does it bother you if I touch you?"

"Would you stop if I said yes?"

"Tell me if you want me to stop."

"Do what you want. I don't care what you do."

"How does it work?" she asked.

"How does what work?"

"When a man and a woman conceive a child. How do they do it?"

His head snapped around and his eyes widened. "You don't even know that?!"

"How could I if I've never seen it?"

He blinked at her for a second. "You really don't know?!"

"No. I didn't see what Boxer and Zyria and Chaos and Rila did the other night. I only saw them together, but I didn't see how they....did whatever they did."

He stared at her in silence for so long that she looked up at him again.

"What?" she asked. "You would have to show me how if we did that."

He didn't seem to hear her. She went back to studying his body. She made sure to avoid going near any of his wounds.

She couldn't explain to herself why she found his body so interesting except that she'd never seen a man this close up before.

She studied the line of dark hair running down from his navel. It vanished inside his waistband.

The hair on his chest and stomach felt soft and comforting—almost inviting like a pillow.

She ran her fingers through the hair below his navel. That was the moment when she noticed his loincloth bulging.

She put her hand on it and tried to flatten it out to make it go back to the shape it was before. Something hard jumped under there. It felt like something alive.

"What is it?" she asked.

He answered by pulling the strings on either side of his loincloth. He threw the piece of hide down between his legs to expose himself.

His thick, hard prick stood up straight once he freed it from the loincloth. It grew a few inches and pointed up at the canopy.

She stared at it for a second trying to understand it. It looked so different from the little boys she'd seen. This was much bigger and it pulsed with energy. Swollen veins surrounded the shaft. A roll of skin surrounded the head at the end.

She took hold of it and tried to tilt it so she could study it more closely. It spasmed and twitched again in her hand. It jumped and strained like a living creature—and yet it stayed attached to Hangman's body.

His breath strained when she handled it. He let out a broken gasp through his nose. She looked up at him and discovered him staring at her with a very different expression on his face.

She couldn't tell what he was experiencing right now, but he didn't stop her from touching him.

She turned back to studying his prick. The skin rolled up and down the shaft over those veins. His whole body shuddered when she did that.

His hand flew to her shoulder and tightened in a hard grip. What was wrong with him? He acted like her touch hurt him somehow.

She didn't want to hurt him, so she let go. She turned to look up at him again, but he acted first.

He reared off the ground, pushed her down onto her back, pushed her legs apart, and rose on his knees between her thighs.

He pulled the strings on either side of her waistband, threw down her loincloth, and leaned forward so his prick slid into her.

She froze when she felt the tight, almost painful fullness of his flesh filling her to the breaking point. She didn't understand—except that this must be it. This must be how it worked when men and women conceived.

He bent all the way over her and propped his arms on either side of her head. He stared down at her with the same strange expression on his face.

He couldn't have done this with anyone else, but he must have seen it plenty of times among his people. The Godless didn't hide that kind of thing from each other.

He eased his weight down on top of her to drive all the way into her, but once he got there, he stopped.

He stayed in that position without moving. Did he even know what to do next?

That moment—that moment when she felt him inside her—it exploded her apart with an unbearable surge of excitement and desire.

Her body took over and she thrust up against him. Her inner muscles clenched around him trying to feel all of him at once.

That one instant of tightness caused a responding reaction in him. He burst into a frenzy of short rapid thrusts pumping into her as fast and hard as he possibly could.

He grimaced in what looked like agony. He clamped his eyes shut and bared his teeth, but he only kept it up for a few seconds before he slammed in, groaned under his breath, and something hot flooded inside her from his prick.

His shaft convulsed and strained with pulsations as it ejected into her. All those sensations excited her beyond anything she'd ever felt, but she couldn't satisfy herself like this.

He immediately started to go soft, groaned again, and rolled off her onto the ground. He shut his eyes and turned his face away.

She lay sprawled on the ground with her legs still spread while her mind raced. What just happened? Was that it?

A million thoughts, feelings, and desires overwhelmed her. She didn't want it to be over just yet. Boxer and Zyria didn't do it that way. Neither did Chaos and Rila.

The night air tingled the wetness between her legs. It tickled, but she didn't need to be lying here exposed anymore.

She sat up and considered tying on her loincloth. Why shouldn't she if that was all there was to it?

She didn't understand. This whole experience confused her more than she was before. Finding out how it worked didn't tell her anything.

She looked around at nothing and noticed Hangman lying there naked. He didn't put his loincloth back on. He didn't need to. He was all alone in the jungle with his wife.

She sat up and stared at his body again. She took much more time to examine every detail of him, especially everything his loincloth covered up before.

She got extra fascinated by the crumpled sack of some kind of flesh between his legs. What could that possibly be good for? It looked bizarre.

She got so interested in it that she put out her hand without thinking, picked up his limp prick, and pulled it back so she could examine the sack.

He snapped alert in an instant. His head spun around and he stared at her. "What are you doing?!" he gasped.

"I just wanted to see. Does it hurt?"

"No, it doesn't hurt! What are you doing? You said you wanted to get it over."

"I want to understand." She bent over and fingered the sack. "What is this?"

His hand shot to her wrist, but he didn't take her hand away. "Be careful."

"What does it feel like?"

"It's sensitive. All of it is."

"Does it feel good?"

He hesitated. His tone changed when he said, "It feels good when you touch it."

She definitely heard that note of strain in his voice again. Was that why he gasped earlier—because it felt good?

He gasped because she rolled the skin of his prick up and down. She did it again and it started to grow and swell in her hand.

He moved his own hand away from her wrist and rested it on her shoulder again. The more she touched him, the more his fingers tightened.

His prick expanded more and became even stiffer and more strained than before. It jerked and fought against her hand the more she moved it.

She alternated between touching his sack, but she made sure to do it gently. The crinkled skin intrigued her.

The skin kept undulating as the wrinkles contracted in certain spots, relaxed in others, and the waves of wrinkles migrated around and around over the surface.

She pulled the skin up and noticed two oblong egg-shaped balls under the skin. Hangman groaned when she tried to finger them.

His prick became throbbing, pulsating hot in her hand. He didn't tell her to stop. "Does it still feel good?" she asked.

"Yes!" he whispered in a broken undertone. "Don't stop!"

She looked up and almost did stop when she saw his face contorting in all kinds of excruciating ways. Did she do that?

His tormented eyes locked on her with unimaginable power. He grabbed her wrist and moved her hand up and down his shaft in a steady rhythm.

His breath strained through his teeth. His ruined lips shivered with every stroke.

Seeing him like this sent a jet of fire through her. She wanted him. She wanted to feel for him what she saw the others experiencing in the cave that night.

She bent down and kissed him again—and this time, he kissed her back. His lips felt hard and not very responsive, but she kissed him anyway. She kissed sideways from his mouth to his cheek and all over his scarred face.

His scars turned her on beyond anything she ever thought possible. She wanted him more than she could stand.

She gave up the battle against herself, climbed on top of him the way she'd seen Zyria climb on top of Boxer, and steered his prick inside her.

She moaned in ecstasy when she sat down on it. It satisfied something she never knew she needed. This was the way she would get what she didn't get the first time.

His thickness filled her up beyond endurance. It spiraled her into such a sea of pleasure that she couldn't stand it.

She swayed as her mind reeled out of all rationality. That one movement lit her on fire and she rocked back to get more of that feeling.

Hangman grabbed hold of her hips. "Look at me," he whispered.

Her eyes floated open in a delirium of overpowering desire. She barely saw his scars at all. She only saw his eyes—his haunted eyes that saw all of what she was.

He pulled her by the hips to drive himself into her. She screamed as a brutal surge of power split her mind in half. She couldn't do this.

Her body switched gears again. She folded forward and planted her hands on his chest.

His body looked so perfect from up here. Everything about him looked perfect—and now he was giving her what she most desired.

She bucked her hips back. She would have tried that eventually because she saw Zyria doing it, but her body did it automatically without her even trying.

As soon as she started, the power exploded inside her. It blasted her apart beyond her ability to cope, but she couldn't stop.

Unimaginable pleasure flooded her from his prick driving into her. He crushed her hips in a death grip and slammed her down on him again and again.

She couldn't control her own movements or his. She teetered out of her mind into a world of bursting rapture that destroyed the whole world.

The cataclysm didn't stop until he rolled her off him, laid her down on her back, and clasped her in his arms still pumping into her endlessly.

He kept going on and on and on. He didn't stop at all. He pumped her full of so much pleasure she couldn't think. She could only scream as all that beautiful rapture took her over and wiped out everything else.

Chapter 40

H angman opened his eyes, blinked up at the canopy, and felt all the wounds on his neck and body.

He also felt a deep sense of calm he'd never felt before. Some kind of wild animal he'd never known was there now lay sleeping peacefully in his soul.

He didn't have to think too hard to know what the animal was. Mora. She satisfied something in him—something that had been eating away at him for years.

He shut his eyes and floated back into memories from last night. She gave herself to him. She even kissed him.

He never would have believed in a million years that any woman would do that.

She didn't just do it out of curiosity or because she wanted to get it over with. She wouldn't have done it a second time unless she wanted him.

She did it more than a second time. They did it a dozen times last night—or it might have been more. He lost count after the second one.

How had he been living without this for so many years? He couldn't even bring himself to sit up and look at her. He didn't want to shatter the illusion.

Now he was married to her. He had to take her back to the band and share her with everyone else.

He didn't want to. He wanted to stay out here alone in the jungle, but no one could live alone in this world.

She might have conceived last night. The two of them would need the whole band to help defend the children.

He would have to hunt. She wouldn't be able to protect the children on her own. Life didn't work that way out here.

He didn't want last night to end, but it already did end. The sun shone through the canopy overhead.

He didn't hear her moving around. She must still be asleep.

He would have liked to turn around and put his arms around her while she slept. He would have liked to express just a little bit of the gratitude he felt that she gave him last night.

He could almost live the rest of his life without ever experiencing that again. One night would have been enough. It would have been more than enough just to feel that way.

The look in her eyes when she looked down at him while she rode him.....or when he drove between her legs looking down at her from above......He would never forget that look.

She wanted him. She didn't have to say it. Her eyes and face and body told him.

She kept coming back and meeting him every time one phase ended and another started. She never pushed him away or stopped him. She kept going with him until they both passed out from exhaustion.

The energy between them had been unlike anything Hangman ever witnessed in any other couple—ever. How was this even possible?

Did anyone else in the world experience this? Some of the couples he'd seen just bumped into each other a few times and went on about their everyday business. Some didn't even look at each other.

She even let him turn her on her hands and knees and do it with her that way. She actually seemed to love it.

Her body felt absolutely sublime when he took her. He suffered an excruciating wave of painful longing when he remembered how she felt.

He also started to get hard just when he remembered how she felt. He couldn't go back to that or they would be here all day and probably another night.

He sat up and tied his loincloth back on. The fire had gone out while they slept.

Mora lay sprawled a few feet away. She fell with her thighs apart and all her juicy flesh spread out where he could see every delicious fold and petal.

He would have liked to explore her body the way she explored his. He would have liked to give her back some of that pleasure, but he didn't want to wake her up.

He had removed her top during the night. Her round, ripe breasts pointed up at him right now.

He tasted them, sucked on them, and even bit them last night. He was the only man who ever touched her. No one else ever would—not unless he died.

She stirred just then—almost as if his attention woke her up. She squirmed on the ground and then jolted. Her arms and hands closed around her body as though she suddenly realized she was naked.

He rested his hand on her shoulder. "Don't worry," he murmured. "No one is here. Here. Eat some food. We need to get on the road soon."

She looked all around her before she woke up enough to remember where she was. Then she looked up at him.

He got another tidal wave of memories of all her different shades last night. He would never forget any of it.

She sat up and pulled her arms and legs up to her chest to hide herself. He pretended not to notice her avoiding eye contact.

"We'll make it back to the band today," he told her. "Whatever you do, don't tell anyone about anything that happened out here. Do you understand? Don't tell them about the Ashtaws....."

"Why?" she asked. "You said your uncle wanted to domesticate them."

"He did want to, but I don't know if he still does. Either way, it will be for me to discuss it with my uncles and my father. They would be offended if you tried to tell them yourself."

She looked down at the food in her hand. "I don't understand how your Clan works."

"That's why I'm telling you. Don't tell them about any of it—not the creatures we fought—none of it."

She mumbled, "If you say so."

He took his water bowl down to the stream and brought her some water. She got dressed while he was away and thanked him when she took the bowl from him.

He remained standing while she pulled herself together. He wasn't sure how to deal with her after last night, so he kept his distance.

He felt much more protective of her now—which made him much more anxious to get her back to his band.

The thought that she might conceive—it changed everything for him.

He never thought he would do it with her. He thought he would hold her at a distance and she would hold him at a distance—possibly forever.

He never let himself even consider taking her—not when she so obviously hated him.

She completely changed her tune yesterday. He actually started to like and respect her—and then last night turned the tables on him again.

She could conceive. She could bear his children. He could become a father. He *would* become a father if he kept doing it with her. That much was inevitable.

The whole concept staggered his mind. He didn't recognize himself in the same thought as becoming a father. He'd spent so many years studiously avoiding even thinking about it.

He always kept himself under a strict rein. He never let himself expect that no woman would ever choose to marry him. He turned out to be right. She didn't choose him.

Now they were together and there was no going back. He couldn't undo last night and he didn't want to.

He *would* do it with her again. He would do it with her again a lot—as much as he could in the time they had together in between all his other responsibilities.

Father. He didn't know how to think about that, but she gave him that. She gave him a hell of a lot more than that.

She finally stood up and retied her weapons to her waistband. "I need to find a way to stop these from bumping around," she mumbled under her breath. "I'm going to cut myself one of these days."

"That's simple," he told her. "I'll make some sheaths for them."

Her head shot up. Her eyes stabbed him in the guts with all the painful memories of last night. "You will?!" she gasped. "You would do that—for me?"

"Of course. They're dangerous hanging there like that. All I have to do is create a pouch that ties to your thigh—right here." He pointed to her leg. "The blade can rest in there. It won't interfere with you drawing them and it won't interfere with your movements. You can move your leg around just the same."

She stared at him with huge eyes. "Really?"

"Of course. I've seen others use the same system. It won't be difficult."

She shut her mouth and gulped. "Thank you....so much....for everything."

"Don't mention it. Let's go. I want to get back to the band."

They set off heading north. She followed in his wake the way she did yesterday, but he spotted her looking around much more carefully now.

She didn't know enough to use her ears more than her eyes, but she would learn.

He made a mental note to tell her—maybe the next time he got her alone in the jungle. He would sit her somewhere and tell her to close her eyes.

Then he would point out and name all the creatures she was hearing. He would describe their movements and wake her up to the possibility that she could track and detect dangerous creatures in the jungle long before they got near enough for her to see.

She had a lot to learn, but at least now he knew she was willing. Her attitude impressed him—a lot.

He didn't talk to her about it. He didn't want to show his hand or make himself vulnerable to her—not until he knew he could trust her.

He made himself vulnerable enough last night. He let her kiss him and touch him in ways no one ever had—in ways he never dreamed anyone would.

She might go back to wrinkling her nose in disgust the minute they got back to the band. She might push him away and pretend it never happened.

He told himself he didn't care. He could wrinkle his nose at *her* in disgust and push her away and pretend it never happened as well as she could.

He kept walking for hours, veered northeast, and picked the band's trail. He wasn't far from catching up with them. He would catch up with them by nightfall at the latest.

He considered telling Mora that—just so she knew how much farther they had to travel.

She kept up with him so well. She could walk all day at a fast pace. She even kept up with him when they ran from the Gorlock. She was stronger than anyone in the band realized.

He stopped in his tracks when he heard a sound to his left. It was a person—no, it was two people.

He frowned at the undergrowth in front of him. He couldn't see them from here, but he detected them moving north.

They didn't belong to his band. Anyone who belonged to his band would be with the main party.

He couldn't think of anyone besides him and Mora who would be out here. The whole band had been together the last time he checked on them. This had to be someone else.

"What's wrong?" Mora whispered in his ear.

He listened for a second and heard the distinct clink of metal. They had to be Renegades.

"Climb on my back and hold on tight," he whispered back.

He bent down and she climbed on. He could carry her petite frame easily.

She wrapped her arms around his neck, but she didn't choke him. She positioned her arms across his collarbones to make it more comfortable for him.

He ignored her thighs wrapped around him from behind.

He couldn't hold onto her. He sprang into the trees, climbed up to the canopy, and balanced along branches making his way farther north.

He tracked the Renegades' movements, veered in front of them, and set Mora down in the crook of a tree.

Her eyes widened when he held his finger to his lips to keep her quiet. She hung onto the tree trunk so she wouldn't wobble.

He turned his back on her and trained his ears to the sound of the Renegades coming closer. He had to make sure they really were Renegades before he did anything. They could have been anyone.

Renegades would only be out here for one reason—to follow Butcher's band. Butcher and the others needed to know about this right away.

Did the Renegades follow Butcher's band away from the gathering, too? Did the Renegades plan to kill all the Godless men and capture the women?

It didn't matter what they were planning. He had to stop them right now.

He only heard two of them, so this must be some kind of scout patrol or advanced reconnaissance for the main attack party.

These two would follow the Godless, find out where they camped, and then bring in the attack party when the time came.

These two Renegades might even follow the Godless all the way back to their long camp. That would be disastrous.

Mora earned herself another credit in his book by keeping perfectly quiet the entire time. Her people taught her well how to hide and stay silent when it mattered.

She didn't make a sound, not even when the Renegades walked into view directly under Hangman's tree. He only had to catch the first glimpse of them to recognize that they *were* Renegades.

Nothing else mattered. He dropped out of the branches and landed in front of one of them. He could have dropped on top of the guy and killed both of them instantly, but that wasn't the Godless way.

He paused just long enough for both Renegades to grab for their weapons. Hangman struck without mercy, drove his kukri into the first man's eye socket, twisted hard to crack the skull, and let the body drop.

The other Renegade swung his long blade at Hangman. Hangman reared back out of range and then rushed the guy and snapped his neck.

Hangman stopped there and listened hard to make sure these were the only two scouts in the area. He didn't hear anything but creatures.

These wouldn't be the last—not by a mile. More Renegades would come this way. The attack party might even come this way.

He jumped into the branches, loaded Mora on his back, and carried her down to the ground. "Stay here," he told her. "I'll be right back."

She was too busy staring at the dead Renegades to hear. He climbed back up into the branches, collected a bunch of vines, and returned to the ground to braid them into a rope.

He wouldn't have bothered doing this on the ground, but he wanted to stay near her. He should have left her in the branches. She would have been safer there, but he didn't want to frighten her more than she already was.

He had to climb up to sling his ropes from the high branches. He made a length long enough to haul the dead bodies in the trees.

He strung the bodies up at a distance from each other, cut their faces across the mouth from ear to ear, gouged out their eyes, and disemboweled both of them so their entrails spilled out.

Their internal viscera held their organs together so their entrails didn't hit the ground. The creatures would have a much harder time devouring these corpses. They would last longer—long enough for the attack party to catch up and see them.

Then the Renegades would understand that a person killed these men and hung them in the trees as a warning.

He returned to the ground to find Mora staring at him in horror. She didn't ask if he really had to do that or why he did it. She didn't say anything.

He didn't explain it to her. She better understand the danger pretty quick if she expected to survive out here.

He set off through the jungle and she followed him without a word. If they had been planning to camp on their own tonight, he would have talked to her about it, but he didn't get a chance to before they returned to his band.

Chapter 41

Hangman stopped Mora just inside the tree line. They could both see the Godless moving around in their camp in a different clearing.

"Remember what I said, Mora," he murmured. "Don't say a word to anyone about what we've seen or what happened to us. Do you understand? Telling anyone could ruin everything."

She cast her eyes to the ground. "I understand," she murmured. "I won't say anything."

He led the way into the clearing and she followed behind him. She had been walking behind him for the last two days.

Everyone looked up and then a few people laughed when they saw Hangman and Mora together. He read it all in their faces. They knew he and Mora had been together all this time.

They would surmise that he and Mora did it with each other. They were married now. His relatives didn't need to know the details or what it meant.

Mora split away from him and headed for a group of women on the other side of the camp. Katha and Estia intercepted her and started talking to her.

Hangman turned his back on them. He didn't belong in the company of women.

He trusted Mora to keep her silence. The other women wouldn't ask enough questions to find out the truth about anything Hangman and Mora had been doing in their absence.

Hangman found his father, Butcher, Fang, and most of his older cousins sitting in a makeshift shelter. This one had four walls with a small door.

Butcher and his brothers sat against the back wall with the cousins sitting around. They were looking at and talking about the pictures again.

Butcher looked up. "Where have you been?!" he snapped. "We thought you were really gone this time."

"You should know better, Uncle," Hangman replied. "I wasn't gone."

"Where were you?!" Butcher demanded again. "What was so important—besides that new wife of yours?"

"Actually, I went to see the Ashtaws, Uncle."

Butcher's head shot up. So did everyone else's. "You what?" Butcher choked.

"I only went to look at them. I didn't think there was any way to domesticate them, but I found out there really is a way."

"There is no way!" Viking interrupted. "They're too big! We can't even get near them."

"That's what I thought, but you're wrong. There is a way—a very simple way. I can prove it to you."

"This better not be a trick," Butcher snapped. "You could have helped us look for these mountains, but instead, you were running around the countryside romancing your new wife. Don't spin me a tale now."

"When have I ever spun you a tale, Uncle?" Hangman asked. "I'm telling the truth. I just told you I can prove it to you."

"The Ashtaws are miles out of our way," Alien pointed out. "We're already halfway to the long camp."

Hangman shrugged. "That will be for Uncle to decide."

"Well?" Butcher barked. "What is this way you say you can prove you can domesticate them?"

"I was on my way out there to check on them—just to look at them—and I noticed Mora in danger again. I stopped to help her and then I didn't want to double back to return her to the camp. I took her to the Ashtaw valley. She says the Followers are in the habit of leading the Ashtaws around wherever the Followers please."

"That's impossible!" Boxer exclaimed.

"That's what I thought. She told me the Ashtaws can't get enough of Fogpo leaves. The Followers can lure the Ashtaws anywhere they want by using Fogpo leaves."

"I don't believe it!" Butcher snapped. "It can't be that simple."

"She showed me how they do it. She picked a branch of Fogpo leaves and walked right out into the herd. The creatures actually came toward her to eat the leaves. She walked away holding out the branch and they followed her. I think this might be the breakthrough we've been looking for."

Butcher glared at him. "You better be telling the truth about this."

"You can ask her yourself if you like—or we can go out to the valley and see for ourselves—but I would suggest you take her with you. She knows so much more about the creatures than we do. She's obviously handled them a lot. She's comfortable walking right out there among them. She even stood next to fully grown adults with no fear."

Viking gasped. "Her?! The cringing little rabbit....did *that?*"

Hangman nodded. "She's stronger and braver than you think."

Butcher humphed. "Bring her here. I want to question her."

"Of course, Uncle."

Hangman ducked out of the shelter and spotted Mora across the camp. She squatted by one of the fires where Katha, Rila, and the others were making soup with some of the leftover dried meat from previous kills.

Mora's eyes shot wide open when Hangman took her by the elbow. "Come with me," he murmured.

"What's wrong?" she whispered on their way across the camp.

"Nothing is wrong. I need you to confirm for my uncle what happened with the Ashtaws. He doesn't believe me. I don't think he'll believe you, either, but he might at least go out there and see you do it with his own eyes. Then maybe he'll decide to go ahead with his plan to domesticate them."

"You mean...." She tried to stop walking, but he propelled her forward. "What do you want me to say to him?"

"Just tell the truth. You don't have to do anything else."

"But if he already doesn't believe me......what if he thinks I'm lying?"

"Then we haven't lost anything."

He released his hold on her and entered the shelter first. She followed him inside.

Everyone present saw her shaking in front of Butcher and the other men. Most of them only stared at her in interested curiosity. Boxer leered at her like she really did make up the whole thing.

Butcher furrowed his brow in consternation. Viking did the same thing, but Hangman recognized that expression for what it was. That was just Viking's concentrating face.

"What's this about you taming the Ashtaws, girl?" Butcher snapped. "Tell us what you did."

"I....I didn't tame them.....Sir....." She faltered and looked around her in wild terror. "I just....I just offered them a Fogpo branch. They weren't tame."

"Hangman says your people tame them," Butcher countered. "He says you could train them to ride against our enemies."

"I....." She trailed off again and looked up at Hangman for help, but he couldn't help her. "My people....we don't tame them....Sir.....We only use Fogpo leaves to lure the Ashtaws into snares......That's all......"

"But you could tame them," Butcher insisted. "Is that what you're saying? Hangman thinks you can."

"I don't think......I only said.....I didn't think it would be hard to tame them.....Sir...."

"How would you tame them with only Fogpo leaves?" Shadow asked.

Mora squirmed out of her skin. She probably would have run away if she wasn't so petrified.

Hangman really would have liked to answer for her, but he couldn't. This was all on her.

"I don't know.....Sir....." she mumbled. "I would....I would.......I would......"

"Well?" Butcher barked. "You would what?"

"I would......I would capture some young ones.....and raise them by hand.....and get them used to being handled every day.....and give them all the Fogpo they wanted.....and then......."

Butcher waited for her to say something sel. "And then? What would you do then?"

"I would......I would get them used to carrying some kind of saddle....."

"What's a saddle?" Alien interrupted.

She flapped her hands in agitation. She started talking way too fast as the ideas spilled out of her unchecked. "It's a leather seat you strap to the creature's back. The rider sits in the seat and holds onto the reins—I mean the bridle—I mean the reins are leather straps attached to a bridle—which is a harness that goes around the creature's head to steer it.....The saddle strap goes around the creature's body......"

"A strap would have to be huge to go around an adult Ashtaw," Viking pointed out. "It could take us days to construct just one saddle."

Mora shut her mouth with difficulty. Hangman watched the confused tempest of emotions warring in her features. Would she be too terrified to say anything else?

"I don't believe it," Fang chimed in. "I don't believe anyone can train the Ashtaws to use against the Renegade Clan."

"We won't know unless we go out there to see for ourselves," Shadow pointed out. "Hangman is right. We have to find out for certain if we stand even the remotest chance of gaining such a decisive advantage."

Butcher nodded, but he wouldn't stop frowning. "We'll go take a look. If it turns out to be a dead end, we can always leave and follow a different course. We're too close to the valley as it is."

That made the decision. Hangman sent Mora back to the other women. She raced away without a backward glance.

He returned to the other men, but he didn't get involved with their discussion, not even their discussion about the Ashtaws. Mora would prove herself once she got there. Then they would all see that Hangman was right about her.

Butcher talked about other things. The men had been patrolling the terrain while the rest of the band traveled north. The men encountered plenty of Renegades, too, but always in pairs and triplets. No one saw any other larger attack parties.

None of these isolated patrols brought enough men to attack any Godless band, much less a fully defended camp.

Hangman broke his silence long enough to tell about the two Renegades he killed and hung from the trees. He didn't say anything else. His other fights against the Renegades and different creatures didn't change the Godless' position on anything.

The men left Butcher's shelter after the meeting. The men and women gathered around the fire for the evening.

Hangman sat down next to Mora, but he didn't kiss her or touch her in front of his relatives—not yet. That would come soon enough. He didn't want to flaunt it in front of everyone the way Boxer and Zyria did.

Butcher informed the women about the whole Ashtaw project. The women had plenty to say about the whole subject. Both Hangman and Mora remained silent during the discussion.

Mora did herself credit by offering no explanations to anyone about anything. She didn't defend herself or her people. She let the others insult her and the Followers.

She didn't even seem to get upset by their comments, not even when Estia and Rila called her a liar in front of everyone.

Mora just stared into the flames eating her food and drinking her soup out of the bowl Hangman gave her.

Hangman got another overwhelming feeling of pride in her. She didn't have to say a word. Their comments deflected right off her.

Butcher made the decision. None of these women's acid tongues could change it.

Nothing Mora said would have changed the women's opinion, either. How ironic that Mora should realize that now. She just had to show them. No one would believe her until she did.

Hangman wouldn't have believed it, either. He just didn't think she would handle herself this way in front of his relatives.

One person after another rolled over to go to sleep. Chaos and Rila wrapped their arms around each other. Boxer and Zyria started their usual nightly gyrations over there on their side of the fire.

Even Butcher and Estia curled up together. Shadow pulled Katha toward him, wrapped himself around her from behind, and fell asleep with his arms around her.

Hangman didn't want to wait any longer. He scooted closer to Mora and fixed his eyes on her so she would know what he planned to do.

She froze and a charge of tension went through her body when he pulled the ties on either side of her loincloth. She didn't look down and neither did he when it fell away.

She held his gaze when he pulled his loincloth off. He felt his relatives watching him—or maybe they weren't. This was nothing everyone didn't already expect.

Zyria's moans drowned out everything else. None of the other women made any noise. Zyria was the only one rude enough to act so ostentatious about it.

Mora never broke eye contact when Hangman pushed her down onto her back and climbed between her legs. She eased back on the ground and spread them for him. She bit back every sound, too. Of course she knew.

Her eyes slipped out of focus when he started doing it with her. He succumbed to all the overpowering feelings of last night. She was still there. What happened between them still held them together even now.

She grabbed his arms and then his hips when he picked up his pace. He kissed her once, but the look in her eyes wiped out his awareness of everything else. He just wanted to know she was still there. She was still the woman he connected with in the jungle.

She compressed her lips to silence herself and clamped her eyes shut when he drilled in and released. He sank down on top of her and rolled off onto his back, totally drained.

She curled over next to him, squirmed back into her loincloth, and crawled into the crook of his arm before they both fell the rest of the way asleep.

Chapter 42

Katha grabbed Mora's arm and pulled her to a stop in the middle of the jungle. The party had been traveling for most of the day on the way back to the Ashtaw valley.

"We'll stop here for the night," Katha announced. "You go hunt for food."

Mora's jaw dropped. "You want *me*....to hunt....for....."

"Make sure you bring back enough for the whole band. If anyone goes hungry tonight, it will be because of you."

Mora's eyes darted around the rest of the group. Some of the men watched the exchange between her and Katha.

Hangman pretended not to hear. He sat down under a tree, pulled a few lengths of hide out of his bag, and started puncturing a bone needle into one of the strips.

He stitched up one edge of the scabbard he was making for Mora's blades. He paid too much attention to his work and pretended not to notice his mother ordering Mora around again.

The other men either listened or collapsed on the ground. No one seemed to notice that Katha was making a decision on behalf of the whole group.

Mora gulped when she realized what Katha was saying. Mora had to hunt food for the party to eat tonight.

No one mentioned that the Godless were still carrying enough smoked, dried meat to keep them going for at least another couple of days.

Mora shut her mouth and forced herself to nod. "Of course. I understand. I won't let you down."

Katha furrowed her brow in a scowl, snapped, "You better not," and turned her back on Mora.

The others all sat down. Their behavior couldn't have been more obvious. They would sit here and wait for Mora to come back with her kill—whatever that turned out to be.

Mora couldn't resent Katha for being hard on her—not anymore. Katha only did these things to help Mora. Mora understood that now.

She actually admired Katha for that. Mora had to learn to hunt for herself, her family, and her new Clan. What better motivator than this?

She walked off in the opposite direction. She tried to use the information Hangman gave her about the creatures' sounds to locate one she would be able to subdue without getting herself killed.

She heard a lot of creatures nearby. She heard Gorlocks and Demonex in the distance. She even heard a Stalkion roaring many miles away.

She walked for half an hour before she heard a mother Gurlg chirping to her clutch of chicks.

If this had been any other day, she would have gone after one of the chicks. She wouldn't have any trouble killing one of them.

One chick wouldn't feed the whole band. The mother Gurlg would attack if Mora tried to kill more than one.

Hangman's story about his initiation echoed in her mind. He got his scars because he went completely over the top in his choice of creature to fight.

He wanted to make an impression on his fellow warriors. He could have gotten killed.

Instead, he proved himself and earned their respect for all time. Mora had to do the same thing now. She had to make these people understand that she wasn't a frightened, useless rabbit destined for extinction.

She pulled her weapon, but she decided only to use one blade this time. She snuck through the bushes until she spotted the mother Gurlg pecking with her chicks.

The mother scratched up the ground with her huge claws, made loud chirping sounds, and pecked at grubs and worms she uncovered.

Her chicks scratched around her feet and ate the stuff she overturned for them. None of the creatures saw Mora watching them.

All of Hangman's suggestions and instructions came together in a coherent picture of what she had to do. She couldn't fight a fully grown Gurlg—especially not a mother protecting her chicks.

Rolling under the mother and cutting its feet tendons wouldn't work, either—not with the chicks in the way. The chicks might attack if Mora approached from the ground.

The only solution was to take out the mother at her most vulnerable point—her neck.

Mora studied the nearby trees, retreated out of sight, and climbed up into them. Then she advanced from branch to branch the way Hangman did.

The Gurlgs kept their heads down and concentrated on their pecking. They didn't see Mora until she positioned herself in a tree right at the level the mother's head would be if she had been standing upright.

Mora decided how to get the mother's attention. Mora had to irritate the mother and anger her enough to make her attack.

The surrounding trees would stop the mother from coming at Mora full force. The mother would have to overextend her neck to try to peck Mora.

Mora chose her position with extra care, pulled some berries from a nearby cluster of foliage, and threw a handful of berries at the mother Gurlg.

The mother's head snapped up and she looked all around her to see what hit her. Mora threw a few more berries and hit the mother bird in the face.

The mother spun around fast and squawked in annoyance. Then she narrowed her beady black eyes when she saw Mora.

Mora couldn't stop herself from retreating a little further into the canopy. This better work. Mora had no other way to protect herself.

If the mother caught Mora in her beak, the mother would pull Mora down to the ground. Then nothing would stop the mother and the chicks from devouring Mora right here and now.

Then the Godless would know they were right about her. She couldn't survive out here. Mora couldn't let that happen.

She took a fresh grip on her blade with one hand and threw some more berries at the mother's face. One of the berries hit the mother right in the eye.

She shrieked in fury and lunged her sharp head between the branches to catch Mora. Mora slapped her blade against the mother's beak to drive her into a frenzy.

It worked. The mother kept letting out deafening screeches and darting her head further between the branches. Mora could just imagine what the Godless were thinking and saying about the mother Gurlg's noises.

Mora chose her moment, jabbed her blade at the mother one more time, and poked the mother bird in the side of the face hard enough to draw blood.

The mother gave a spine-chilling shriek that sounded more like a roar. She lunged deeper, farther, and harder to finally grab Mora.

Mora sidestepped only a few inches. She still lacked the strength to completely decapitate the bird. She didn't have to.

She grabbed her blade with both hands and chopped the weapon down into the spine right behind the creature's head.

The blade embedded in the spinal cord. She didn't have the power to cut any deeper than that, but it was enough.

The blade stuck in the bone, but the damage was done. The creature folded at the knees and thumped down in the dirt.

The creature's weight yanked the blade out of Mora's hands. She let it go and the creature fell away, dead.

The mother's fall scared the chicks into flying away. The impact of the Gurlg's weight hitting the ground knocked Mora's blade out. It landed in the dirt.

She stayed where she was for a minute and stared down at the dead creature. She didn't want to believe she actually did it.

This was by far the biggest creature she had ever killed. In fact, it was the only creature she had killed.

She never would have believed she could kill a creature this big. She expected to wake up any second and realize that she only dreamed it.

She didn't dream it. Now she had to take the meat back to the Godless.

She at first considered dragging the carcass there, but it was too big for her. She would just have to section the body and carry it back piece by piece.

She was still standing on the same branch when an Abnormit came out of the nearby undergrowth. The creature inspected the dead Gurlg and bit into the side of its neck.

Mora couldn't let the Abnormits take this creature—not after she just made her first kill.

She clambered down there, used her blade to stab the Abnormit, and then hacked off one of the Gurlg's legs.

She had to cut it at the knee joint. The whole leg was even too big for her.

She sheathed her blade, hefted the bloody section onto her shoulder, and hiked back to the Godless. They still slouched around in the same places.

Hangman's head shot up when she entered their camp. He stopped work and stared at her carrying her prize.

She didn't let herself make contact with anyone when she dropped the leg section in front of Katha.

Mora walked away without a word. She got covered in blood by the time she made a dozen trips to bring the rest of the meat back.

No one else said a word, either. The women built fires, cut up the meat to cook it for the night, and sliced the rest to smoke it.

She left them there with the meat, went down to a nearby creek, and washed the blood off her weapons and body. She also took off her clothes, rinsed them in the water, and wrung them out before she put them back on.

She didn't hurry back to the camp or the Godless. She didn't want to see anyone right now, not even Hangman.

She proved herself to herself more than any of the rest of them. She just wanted to sit here and think about what she just did.

She still wasn't strong enough or skilled enough to survive in the jungle, but she was learning. Today was the first step.

She didn't stay away to throw it in the women's faces that they insulted her. She didn't stay away to make a point to anyone.

She didn't even really care about their opinion anymore. She could have lived the rest of her life without ever proving herself.

This was all hers. Not even Hangman helped her this time—even though he did.

He showed her the way. He taught her how to overcome the creatures' superior size and strength. He coached her, built up her confidence, and showed her all the different steps of the process.

She would always be grateful to him for that. She sent up a silent prayer of gratitude and relief that she got him as her husband.

She thought at first that marrying him would be the greatest misfortune of her life. She thought he was hideous and hateful.

Now she couldn't think of any man she would rather be married to. What other man would take the time to help her the way he did?

He didn't have to do any of that—not after the way she rejected him and looked down on him at first.

She took a long time before she stood up, tied on her weapons, and returned to the camp.

Everyone was already eating. They were eating the meat she provided.

Katha squatted by the fire carving off slices of the cooked meat and serving it to everyone as they finished their first portions.

No one looked up or made eye contact with her when she sat down next to Hangman. A bowl of meat slices sat on the ground in front of him, but he was too busy working on her sheaths to eat the food.

He stopped what he was doing just long enough to move the bowl over in front of her. Then he went back to stitching.

She picked up the first slice and put it into her mouth. It tasted delicious—far better than any other food she'd eaten since she came to live with the Godless.

She killed this creature. She did it.

She ate in silence without drawing attention to herself. She didn't need recognition or praise. That one act of Hangman moving his bowl in front of her was all the acknowledgment she needed.

She finished the food. Katha took the bowl without acknowledging Mora, either.

Katha refilled the bowl and put it down in front of Hangman. He ignored that food, too. He straightened up and raised the hide strips he had been working on. "Stand up and see if this works for your blades."

Mora got to her feet. She had to untie one side of her loincloth, take off her blade, slide the ties through the sheath strap, and retie the loincloth.

The scabbard consisted of two long rectangles of hide sewn across one long edge and the lower short edge.

She had to tie the lower edge around her thigh. The blade rested inside the open pocket. The sewn lower edge supported the blade's weight so it didn't flap around.

She retied the blade handle to her waistband the way she usually did. She used the same knots as before. She could thrust her hands through the loops, pull the knots free, and draw her blades the same way.

The minute she did that, they would slide out through the open front edge of the pocket. The sheath didn't secure the weapon. The sheaths just supported them to stop them from bumping into Mora's legs.

"This is perfect!" she exclaimed. "Thank you!"

He scrutinized the stitching, tugged the sheaths and ties on her waist and leg, and adjusted a few things.

She tried not to notice him handling her body in front of everyone, but no one paid any attention—except for Katha.

She stopped work, turned all the way around, and watched Hangman make all the adjustments he wanted to the sheaths. Katha didn't comment, though.

Hangman sank back onto the ground and finally picked up his bowl to eat. Mora sat down next to him.

The scabbards angled down her thighs. The ties wrapped around her legs above the knee. Her blades didn't interfere with her movements anymore.

She would have liked to thank Hangman again for the effort he put into this for her sake. She would have liked to show him some affection to make him understand how much she appreciated it.

He wouldn't appreciate something like that—not now. She remained silent—and then Katha put another bowl of meat in front of Mora.

Katha made one moment of powerful, intense eye contact before Katha turned her back and went back to what she was doing.

Katha didn't criticize anything about Mora this time. Katha didn't say a single word about Mora or her successful kill or Hangman's workmanship or anything else.

Katha's silence secured Mora's victory more than anything else. None of the other women insulted Mora or even mentioned her. Their silence spoke volumes.

Mora was one of their band now. No one commented on her or even noticed her. They didn't comment or notice each other, either. She was just there the same way they were.

She was Hangman's wife the same way Rila was Chaos's wife and Zyria was Boxer's wife. Mora was just another feature of the landscape now.

Chapter 43

Hangman, Chaos, Viking, Alien, Vulture, Magnet, Boxer, Butcher, Shadow, and Fang flattened themselves behind the hill. The men gazed out over thousands of Ashtaws grazing across the valley.

"I forgot how big they are," Viking murmured. "You won't catch me riding one of them."

"Not even if you could get your mount to step on Renegades?" Magnet asked. "You wouldn't have to fight them. You could just steer your mount to trample them."

"None of that is going to happen if we can't train them." Butcher turned to Hangman. "Show us how she did it."

"I don't know how she did it," Hangman replied. "I've already told you everything I know. She took a Fogpo branch out there and the creatures came over to her to eat the leaves."

Butcher swiped his finger at Alien. "Get a Fogpo branch and go out there. I want to see how it works."

"No chance," Alien countered. "I'm not going out there—not with a hundred Fogpo branches."

"Me, neither," Vulture added. "The creatures could make one wrong step and squash whoever went out there. I'm staying here."

Butcher turned back to Hangman. Hangman saw his uncle about to send him out there to tempt the Ashtaws.

"I really think you should send Mora, Uncle," Hangman told him. "She knows the creatures the best. She's used to this. She isn't afraid of them. Anyone else might spook them into stampeding from us."

"Are you trying to get rid of your Follower wife?" Boxer teased.

Hangman ignored him and focused on the Ashtaw herd. It looked a lot bigger now, too—even bigger than when Hangman came here with Mora alone.

He really didn't want to go out there, either—not even for the chance to domesticate these creatures.

Mora was the only person in the whole band who didn't fear the Ashtaws' enormous size. Not even Butcher volunteered to go down there.

"Fine. Go get her," Butcher muttered. "Tell her to bring us some young ones if she can."

Hangman crawled backward down the hill and returned to the spot in the undergrowth where Cross, Feather, and Banjo stood guard over the women.

Hangman pulled Mora out of the group. "You need to show my uncle what you did with the Ashtaws."

"Does he believe you now?"

"He won't believe until you show him what you showed me. He says for you to lead some young ones away if you can."

Her expression cleared and she looked around the jungle until she found a Fogpo tree. She snapped off three good-sized branches and nodded. "I'm ready."

Hangman led her back up the hill. He lay back down with his male relatives. She didn't. She set off walking straight upright toward the herd in the distance.

She didn't have to cross as much of the open grassland. Several giant mothers grazed along the creek with a dozen juveniles playing around and occasionally eating.

The mothers saw Mora coming, raised their heads, and chewed while they watched her cross the stream and approach the young ones.

Mora rustled the branches of Fogpo leaves. The sound brought the little ones running. Four of them gathered around her. She held the leaves apart so the creatures wouldn't crush her in their eagerness to get to the food.

The mothers put their heads down and went back to grazing. None of them paid attention to their young butting Mora to get to the leaves. Then two young ones butted each other.

Mora transferred her branches to one hand and stroked the creatures all over their bodies. Each one stood as tall as her head, but they let her handle them with no problem.

She let them eat for a minute. Then she turned away and walked off for the hill where Hangman and the men watched in breathless silence.

All four young Ashtaws followed her. They kept diving for the leaves, butting each other out of the way, and snatching leaves to munch them on the way.

She made it as far as the stream before two of the mothers stopped grazing to come after her, too. She smiled up the hill toward where the men lay on their stomachs. Then she glanced behind her and noticed the mothers.

Their enormous tree-trunk legs thumped the earth every time they took a step. They overtook Mora in a few strides, but they didn't attack. They were too mild-natured.

The two mothers lowered their heads to nudge their young where the mothers wanted the young ones to go. Then the mothers smelled the leaves.

One of the mothers grabbed a mouthful of leaves and tried to tug the branch out of Mora's hand. She stopped to tighten her grip.

Her laughter floated across the fields when the mothers stuck their huge heads into the group. The mothers pushed their young ones out of the way so the mothers could take the leaves instead.

Mora petted the young ones and even patted one of the mothers while they ate. All the men could see her grinning like crazy.

Hangman got consumed with watching her. She shone with pleasure at what she was doing. She never looked like that any other time—except when he took her.

Alien snapped Hangman back to high alert. Alien stuck out his beefy arm and pointed across the valley. "Look!"

Hangman's stomach dropped when a long line of black figures swept down the opposite side of the valley.

They only looked black from this distance. They separated so the men could see individual people—people carrying metal weapons.

Hundreds of Renegades charged down the opposite side of the valley and onto the flat grassland. They ignored the Ashtaws and headed straight for the Godless hiding on the hilltop.

Hangman launched to his feet. "Mora—look out!"

Alien grabbed him to pull him down, but Hangman shook off his cousin. Hangman pulled his kukris and sprinted down the hill, but it was already too late.

Mora's smile evaporated when she saw the Renegades closing in on her. They came in overwhelming numbers and she stood the closest to them. They would overrun her in a matter of seconds.

Viking, Chaos, Magnet, and Vulture all raced down the hill behind Hangman. The Renegades were still far enough away for the men to get to Mora in time.

The Renegades' arrival spooked the Ashtaws on that side of the valley. They bellowed in alarm and an answering wave of pounding feet thundered away up the valley in another stampede.

The mother Ashtaw closest to Mora looked up, saw the rest of the herd galloping away, and the mother bellowed to her baby, too.

The two mothers and the four young ones wheeled to break away. The stampede spread down the valley. More adults and juveniles thundered all around Mora. All the Ashtaws broke away to flee in the same direction.

Mora dropped her Fogpo branches, dove for the nearest juvenile, and grabbed it by strapping both arms around its neck. It squalled in protest, but she hung on even as more adults plowed into her from behind.

She and the juvenile went down under dozens of running feet. Hangman lost sight of her in the mayhem—and then the Renegades broke through the stampede.

The Renegades charged across the valley heading straight for the outnumbered Godless. Hangman looked everywhere for Mora, but too many Ashtaws blocked his view.

He had to pay attention when the Renegades charged him. They no longer looked black. They were just men with short hair, the usual combination of clothes, and their metal blades that flashed in the sun.

Their weapons reminded him of Mora. He had to find her—wherever she was out here.

The Renegades surrounded the five men. Six Renegades came after Hangman. He fought his hardest just to hold them at bay as even more Renegades streamed past him up the hill.

His instincts told him to fall back there and defend his family. Cross was back there. Katha was back there. Shadow and all Hangman's uncles, cousins, and their wives were back there.

He couldn't move. The Renegades surrounded him. He slashed his kukris in all directions, but he couldn't stop the Renegades from stabbing him from whichever direction he wasn't facing.

One of their blades impaled him through the thigh. He roared in pain, wheeled backward to face his attacker, and a different Renegade stabbed him through the side.

He went into a frenzy, rushed two of them in front of him, and hacked his righthand kukri at someone's head.

In that moment, a different blade plunged into his upper chest right where his collarbone met his shoulder. His knees gave out and someone hit him over the back of the head. He blacked out.

Chapter 44

Hangman groaned when someone rolled him onto his back. Then he screamed when strong hands smeared leaf paste on his wounds. He lunged off the ground and his eyes flew open to attack the person who hurt him.

Alien planted his meaty hand on Hangman's chest and forced him down while Alien finished the procedure.

Hangman had no choice but to lie still until Alien released him. Alien put the paste bowl aside, grabbed Hangman by the shoulders including his injured shoulder, dragged him to his feet, and shook him upright.

"Can you stand, little brother?" Alien growled. "We need to fall back from here. The Renegades are taking the whole valley."

Hangman dragged his eyes into focus when he remembered what happened. "Mora ....."

Alien clamped his lips shut, cast his eyes to the ground, and shook his head. "She's gone. We don't even know where her body is."

"No! She can't be!" Hangman shoved Alien out of the way and staggered a few paces closer to the stream.

None of the Ashtaws were here anymore, but they would come back as soon as they realized it was safe.

Mora wasn't here. A bloody patch of grass marked the spot where she and the young Ashtaw went down under the stampeding herd. Her body wasn't there. The young Ashtaw's body wasn't there. Nothing was there except the blood on the grass.

Alien came over to him. "Let's go, little brother. No good can come of staying here. The Renegades are searching the valley. They'll kill anyone they find when they come back."

Alien didn't wait for Hangman to come. Alien took hold of Hangman's shoulders, turned him around, and marched him up the hill toward the spot where the men had been hiding.

Hangman limped on his injured leg. He had to hug his arm against his side. The pain of his wounds drove him mad. He needed Gooji juice tonight, but he wouldn't get it here.

He stumbled more than once on his way up the hill. Alien helped him.

They both stopped at the top when they saw Shadow on his knees next to Butcher. Butcher lay on his back with most of his chest caved in.

Hangman swallowed hard. The Renegades wouldn't have been able to do this kind of damage. They fought with blades.

Butcher's injuries looked more like one of the adult Ashtaws stepped on him. Hangman didn't think the Ashtaws stampeded up here, but he may have been wrong. He didn't see anything after the Renegades attacked him.

Shadow clasped one of Butcher's hands between both of his own. Butcher didn't see his brother. Butcher stared up at the sky not seeing anything.

Hangman and Alien inched a little closer, but Hangman didn't want to interrupt whatever might be passing between the two brothers.

Shadow served Butcher as his Kral for so long. Shadow could have become Kral whenever he wanted. Did Shadow know all along that this day would eventually come? Was that the reason he never challenged his brother's authority?

Butcher pulled his hand away and tried to fumble around on the ground next to his hip. He didn't turn his head or look at what he was doing. He kept staring straight up. He couldn't see.

Shadow grabbed the leather bag containing the pictures. He pushed the bag into Butcher's hands, but neither of them could free the bag from under Butcher's weight. He lay on the strap that crossed his chest and back.

He held out the bag to Shadow. Shadow grasped the bag with Butcher's hand still clenched around it. Shadow didn't try to take it from him. They both held the bag at the same time.

Shadow bowed his head and a tear streaked down his cheek. This was the first time Hangman had ever seen his father shed tears.

Did Shadow support Butcher out of love? Was that the real reason? Hangman never once considered that possibility. He always assumed Shadow was playing some complicated game of political maneuvering.

Butcher let go of the bag and laid his hand against his brother's cheek. Butcher actually smiled when he felt his brother's tears, but Butcher still didn't turn his head or take his eyes off the sky overhead.

Shadow slumped as if under a great weight. His hands holding the bag fell onto the grass. He didn't raise his head, not even when Butcher's arm flopped onto the ground and Butcher lay still at last.

He never closed his eyes. He never turned his head. He just stopped moving.

Shadow didn't rise. Hangman didn't dare to go over there, not even to offer his father comfort.

Alien was the one who did it in the end. He advanced, stopped next to Shadow, and gripped Shadow's shoulder in a death squeeze.

Hangman distinctly heard Alien say, "My Kral," in a broken undertone.

Shadow looked up and stared at his brother's dead body. Was Fang even still alive? Was Shadow completely alone now?

Alien didn't wait around for Shadow to acknowledge the succession of power. Shadow was Kral of this band now.

Alien strode around the other side of Butcher's body, squatted down, and wrapped his burly arms around Butcher's chest.

Alien used his great strength to sit Butcher up. Alien held him in one arm and took the bag strap off Butcher's chest.

Alien pushed the bag of pictures into Shadow's hands. Then Alien removed all the rest of Butcher's bags, weapons, and other personal items.

Shadow stayed there, bowed and broken, until Alien picked up Butcher's body, slung it over his shoulder, and gathered all of Butcher's personal effects in his other hand.

Alien nodded at Hangman. Hangman could finally come forward, but he still hesitated to get his father's attention.

"We must withdraw," Alien repeated. "The Renegades are too close."

Shadow nodded and pushed himself to his feet. He stared down at the bag in his hands. He really had to think about the fact that it was his now.

Shadow turned around to glance toward the Ashtaw valley. Shadow came face to face with Hangman standing right behind him.

Hangman gulped. His voice shook when he said, "My Kral."

Shadow lowered his eyes back to the bag in his hands and finally nodded. "Thank you, my son."

"We should go, Father," Hangman told him. "We should find out if any of the others survived."

Shadow nodded again. He still wasn't thinking clearly.

Hangman took a few steps past him toward the trees. Hangman and Alien went first. They had to wait for Shadow to catch up.

He came farther and farther out of his trance the longer the three of them walked. They entered the trees. Hangman scanned the surroundings for any sound of human beings.

The three men found Katha, Cross, Vulture, Rila, and the others hiding in the trees a few miles deeper in the jungle. The party overtook Fang, Boxer, Magnet, Feather, Banjo, and Viking coming from a different direction.

Hangman didn't even ask if any of them had seen Mora.

How did he become so attached to her so fast only for her to vanish out of his life so quickly? Why did she have to die just when he started to value her the most?

She died trying to help the Godless. She tried to carry out Butcher's order to bring back the juvenile Ashtaws.

She could have saved herself if she only ran when the stampede started. She didn't. She stayed just long enough to try to finish what he sent her there to do.

The party set off back toward the east—back toward their own territory. No one talked. Estia cried silently the whole way there. Alien carried Butcher's body until sundown.

The group slumped at the base of some trees. Katha and Rila started a fire on the bare ground.

Alien lowered Butcher's body into a sitting position against one of the nearby trunks. Then Alien climbed up into the branches.

Hangman went with him. They worked together to construct a platform in the high canopy. It wouldn't protect Butcher's body from hungry creatures, but anything was better than leaving him on the ground or burying him in the earth to rot.

The two men returned to the ground and worked for an hour to braid a length of rope out of vines. They wrapped it around Butcher's body and used it to haul the body up to the platform.

Everyone in the band climbed up there and perched in the branches while Alien and Hangman positioned Butcher on the platform. They closed his eyes and Magnet placed some of the trinkets from Butcher's bags around the body, in Butcher's hands, and on his chest.

No one said a word. They sat in silence and kept watch over Butcher's body.

He was a decent Kral. Hangman didn't agree with every decision Butcher made. Hangman would have been a very different Kral—and Shadow would be a very different Kral.

Butcher had been a decent man, though. No one could claim he didn't protect his Clan. He always did what he thought was best for his family, his band, and the Clan.

That was the best thing Hangman could say about any man, especially the Kral of a Godless band. It was the only job requirement and Butcher fulfilled it for decades.

Katha sat with her arm around Estia's shoulders. No one else showed any sign of distress.

Boxer and Magnet would take care of their mother from now on. She probably wouldn't leave the long camp again in this life. She would stay behind when the band took young people to the gathering. She didn't need to hunt, now that she had two grown sons to do it for her.

Chapter 45

The band retreated to the ground one after the other and left Butcher lying there on his platform in the branches. Shadow stayed behind until the last. He carried the leather bag over his shoulder now.

All the men acknowledged him as their Kral. No one challenged him. Of course not. Shadow would make an outstanding Kral.

His ascension overwhelmed Hangman in a profound sense of relief. Butcher's death and Shadow's ascension completed something that had been out of alignment for years.

That sense of relief almost wiped out the tragedy of losing Mora. Hangman hadn't been married to her long enough to truly feel any sense of loss, now that she was gone.

His life would go straight back to what it was before he met her. He would go back to being alone. He always expected to live this way, but now he knew what he was missing.

That feeling of peace and completion he felt after spending the night with her—he would never feel that with any woman ever again. He didn't want to.

He wanted to preserve that night in his mind forever. He wanted his body to become a temple to the gift she gave him.

She proved herself—to everyone. She didn't die a scared little rabbit cut down by the deadly jungle. She died in service to her Clan. No one could ask anything else of her.

He squatted next to the fire and took some dried food out of his bag to eat it. It was Gurlg meat from the creature she killed. She was a hunter, a fighter, and a Godless until the end. He honored her as much as he honored Butcher.

Katha opened a folded leaf full of Gooji sap. She used it to brew the juice to heal everyone's injuries.

Hangman clenched his teeth to stop himself from shaking in pain and exhaustion. He really needed to pass out again, but he had to stay conscious enough to drink the juice before he collapsed completely.

He took one bite of the meat before he heard a squalling noise coming from the trees to the north. It was the broken cry of a juvenile Ashtaw calling out for its mother.

The sound set Hangman's hair on end. Then he heard Mora's voice talking to the creature. She was trying to soothe it. She had to talk too loudly to make herself heard over the creature's noises.

All Hangman's pain evaporated. He shot off the ground and took off running in that direction. His relatives all came with him. No one stayed behind, not even Estia.

They found Mora in a small clearing. She held a Fogpo branch in one hand and kept her other arm wrapped around the creature's neck.

She had steered the little one between two trees and wedged its head between the tight trunks to hold it in place. The creature thrashed back and forth trying to get out. She had to use all her strength to hold it there.

Her voice shook with desperation as she pleaded with the creature to eat the leaves and calm down. She cast a panicked look around. Tears glistened in her eyes before she saw Hangman and the others.

He skidded to a halt when he saw blood running down her leg. What must she have gone through to get the creature out of the valley in the middle of both an Ashtaw stampede and a Renegade attack?

She must have dug deep and tapped all her ingenuity and internal resources to get the creature this far away from the valley and restrain it here for as long as she could.

Alien sprang forward. He still carried the rope he used to raise Butcher's body into the branches. Alien looped the rope around the creature's neck. Mora almost fell over when she staggered away from the creature.

Hangman caught her, held her up, and led her back to the camp.

The young Ashtaw responded by rearing, crashing its neck between the trunks, and backing out of its prison to freedom. It would have run off if Alien didn't hold it back.

The creature started to struggle and bellow again. It became more resistant the more Alien restrained it. Mora tore herself out of Hangman's grasp, retrieved the Fogpo branches, and returned to the creature's head.

The Ashtaw calmed down immediately, now that the trunks no longer held it captive. It took a mouthful of leaves and munched them.

"That's right," she murmured in a shaky undertone. "No one is going to hurt you."

She stroked her hand down its neck to soothe it. It didn't react to her touch at all.

She made eye contact with Alien and took the rope out of his hands. He passed it over willingly and she smiled at him.

"Are you sure you can walk?" Hangman's eyes darted down to her leg. "You're hurt."

"Not as hurt as you." She tried one last time to smile and failed. "I should be the one to handle him. He knows me. I can keep him calm. I'll take him to the camp and then....."

She trailed off and swayed on her heels again.

Katha stepped forward. "You better let Hangman help you. Come back to the camp. I'm making some Gooji juice for all of you."

Katha led the way. Hangman stayed near Mora, but she didn't lean on him for support. She kept a hold on the rope in one hand and the Fogpo branch in the other. She kept shooting sidelong glances at his injuries.

He barely felt them now. She made it—and she brought one of the Ashtaws with her. This was a massive windfall for his band.

The others surrounded Mora and Hangman on their way back to the camp. Katha gave Hangman the first dose of Gooji juice and Alien insisted on reapplying the leaf paste to Hangman's injuries.

Then Katha treated Mora. She tied the rope to a nearby tree, but Alien wouldn't let her go pick more branches for the creature. Alien did it himself while she rested.

Katha put leaf paste on a long gash running down Mora's leg. Black bruises surrounded it where one of the Ashtaws stepped on her.

"Did you hold onto the little one the whole time?" Zyria asked.

Mora nodded down at her cut. "I had to. I didn't want to let him run off. Then all our effort getting here would have been for nothing."

"How did you get the creature out of the valley without anyone seeing you?" Nagara asked.

"The men were all so busy fighting the Renegades. The Renegades who weren't fighting the men or going after you were too busy dealing with the stampede. The Renegades tried to search the valley for any other Godless. They didn't want to believe such a small band came out here to see the Ashtaws. The stampede kept interfering with their search. They didn't see me take the creature away."

Alien looked up at the young Ashtaw's face. "He seems to like you."

"He does," Mora murmured. "He was happy to go with me until I got him between those trees. He didn't like that."

"He didn't try to return to his mother?" Katha asked.

Mora shook her head. "He forgot all about her as long as I gave him enough Fogpo leaves to eat."

"You did very well, Mora," Shadow remarked. "You're more resourceful than any of us gave you credit for. You're an asset to the Godless."

She looked at him and started to smile. She froze just as fast and her smile evaporated when she realized who was speaking to her and why.

She gaped at Shadow in horror. Then her terrified eyes darted around the circle of faces. She saw right away who wasn't here anymore.

Her gaze snapped back to Shadow. He stared straight back at her as the puzzle pieces clicked in her mind.

She gulped and lowered her eyes to her hands. She had to fight to make herself heard when she said, "Yes, Sir. I'll do anything I can to help your band."

Those words closed the last door. She knew now. Butcher was gone. Shadow was Kral now.

Katha went back to brewing the next dose of Gooji juice. Hangman couldn't hold himself upright any long.

He would have liked to put his arms around Mora and get close to her. He never experienced relief like this before. He wasn't alone. He still had her.

He couldn't put his arms around her right now. His pain became unbearable.

He gasped a few times when he stretched out on the ground next to her. She watched him until he closed his eyes.

He concentrated on just holding himself together and not losing his mind before he passed out.

In that moment, she rested her hand on his shoulder—his uninjured shoulder. She left it there and didn't take it any further.

That one touch relaxed him enough. He could finally let it all go and drift off into a black slumber.

Chapter 46

Mora woke up when someone nudged her arm. She struggled to blink the sleep out of her eyes.

It took her a minute to realize what she was seeing when a young Ashtaw bumped its nose against her shoulder for the second time.

The creature grunted and then pawed its huge foot at the Fogpo branch on the ground. The creature had stripped all the leaves off it.

She scrambled to her feet. The other Godless were just waking up. Hangman wasn't here anymore. He must have woken up feeling better even after getting injured yesterday.

She found another Fogpo tree, broke off multiple branches, and took them back to the creature. She had to limp on her injured leg, but at least now she knew she would be okay. She was back with Hangman's family band—without Butcher.

He must have died in the Renegade attack—or maybe the stampede. No one talked about where Butcher was or what happened to him. She didn't ask.

She dumped the pile of branches in front of the Ashtaw and took one of the band's many water gourds to the nearby stream to bring the creature water.

She petted him while he ate. He was becoming progressively tamer the longer he spent with her.

She waited until the others woke up before she tried to talk to him. She wanted him to get used to her voice.

Pouring water into the wooden bowls didn't work to give him water. She used the branches to lead him to the stream where he could drink as much as he wanted.

"I should give you a name," she told him. "It should be a regular name—not a Godless name. You haven't gone through initiation yet."

She laughed at her own joke. No one was around to hear her or take offense to it.

"I know. I'll call you Igno," she decided. "What do you think?"

He grunted and slurped while he drank. He didn't react to the name, so the vote was carried by one.

She took him back to the camp, tied him to the same tree, and put the branches in front of him.

She hoped he would cooperate when she led him on their journey north. She hoped he would learn to follow her without her constantly having to bribe him with Fogpo leaves. That would get old.

The Godless didn't hurry to leave this camp. She didn't see anyone as injured as Hangman. Was he out there running through the jungle right now even after what he went through yesterday?

She didn't look forward to walking on her injured leg. It would be harder for him.

He didn't return until close to noon. Some of the men stood guard at certain times. Everyone else lounged in camp, ate their leftover food, and dozed.

Hangman dropped out of the trees from directly overhead. He didn't even flinch when he landed on his injured leg.

He didn't seem to have any trouble using his injured arm, either. He used it to swing off branches and vault to the ground.

Shadow looked up when Hangman returned. Hangman only gave Mora one look before he squatted down next to his father.

"What did you find out?" Viking asked.

"The Renegades are all over the valley," Hangman replied. "They're running patrols around the perimeter, especially on the eastern side. They obviously expect us to come back from that direction."

"How many of them are there?" Shadow asked.

Hangman shrugged. "I'd say three hundred at least—enough to surround and guard the whole valley."

"Do you see the Renegades doing anything with the Ashtaws?" Magnet asked.

"Not at all," Hangman replied. "The Renegades ignore them completely. If anything, the Renegades seem to regard the Ashtaws as a nuisance—but the Renegades don't dare to interfere with the creatures. The Renegades fear the Ashtaws' size as much as we do."

Shadow used a stick to poke the coals in front of him. "Then we can't go back to the valley—not now. We'll take this one with us to the long camp. Mora can work with him and figure out a way to tame him to carry a rider. We won't take any more Ashtaws until we figure out a way to take more than one—maybe even dozens."

Mora caught Hangman's eye. He'd been so insistent that she not speak up and voice her opinions in front of Butcher. What if Shadow felt differently about it? She had to try it.

"Um....excuse me....Sir....." she stammered. "Um.....your brother......he wanted me to bring as many young Ashtaws as I could.....to start taming them and training them....."

"Yes?" Shadow asked. "If you know something, tell me now. I need all the information you can give me about them."

"I was only thinking....it might be easier.....if we raised them from birth.....I mean......if you want to train dozens of Ashtaws to carry riders in war.....against your enemies....."

"How would we raise them from birth?" Magnet interjected. "We would need adult Ashtaws to use as breeding stock. Our territory doesn't have valleys big enough for Ashtaws. That's why we have to come down here."

"We couldn't tame fully grown adults anyway," Chaos added. "They're too big."

"But don't you see.....?" Mora stammered. "Igno here will grow up. He'll become an adult. All your mounts will be—and that's what you want. The adults will be more destructive to your enemies. It would work better if you had a population of tame Ashtaws. You could tame the young ones from birth and get them used to being handled by people. They would grow up seeing the adults ridden by people. It would become normal to them."

Shadow frowned. "I understand what you're saying, but all of that may be beyond the scope of what we're capable of. It will take great effort and resource to tame even one of these creatures. We aren't ready to start with many of them."

She lowered her eyes. "Yes, Sir. I understand."

Shadow went back to stirring the fire. "We'll stay here tonight and leave in the morning. We should make it back to long camp tomorrow.

No one said anything else. Mora spent the day dealing with Igno. He cooperated with everything she did. She didn't need to lure him with leaves to take him down to the stream for water.

He let some of the warriors come over and pet him. He made low rumbling noises in his big chest that sounded like contentment.

The Godless moved out the next day. Igno followed Mora everywhere. She only fed him when they stopped for rest. He behaved perfectly all day.

She hesitated to take him into the long camp once the party made it all the way home.

She halted at the edge of the camp and held onto Igno's rope while she studied the camp for the first time.

The long camp occupied a place in the mountains between a collection of higher peaks. She understood now why this territory would be no good for keeping Ashtaws, especially a large number of them.

The Godless built much sturdier houses here with four walls instead of three. Gaps between the branches let air flow through each house. The walls offered a degree of privacy she hadn't seen from the Godless before.

More women lived here along with children of all ages. The place echoed with voices coming from all sides.

All the relatives came out of their houses to greet the traveling party. A few people remarked on Hangman's new wife, but everyone put Mora out of their minds pretty soon.

The Godless were much more interested in Igno. The children couldn't get enough of him and touched him all over.

Their mothers tried to pull them away from him until everyone figured out that he was friendly and tame.

Hangman showed her where to tie Igno in the trees outside the long camp. She fed him Fogpo leaves and took him to the nearby stream to drink before she left him alone with his meal.

"Where are we going?" she asked on their way back into the camp.

"We'll stay at my house." Hangman steered her sideways. "It's over here."

"You have your own house? I didn't know."

"All the men take their own houses after initiation. It isn't appropriate for an initiated man to live with his parents. Here it is."

He pushed open the door to a small, one-room house constructed like all the others. The interior looked exactly the same as all the temporary shelters she'd seen on the party's travels.

A pile of animal hides lay along the back wall. That was the only furniture in the house except for a hollow in the center with a few blackened pieces of charcoal in it.

Hangman sat down on the pile of hides and pulled Mora down next to him. He opened his bag, took out some of the dried Gurlg meat, and tore it in half to share with her.

"What will you do with the creature now?" he asked.

"I suppose I'll have to start working out a way to construct a saddle and bridle. That's going to be difficult since I've never done it before."

"What do they look like?"

She traced her finger in the dust at her feet. "The saddle has a strap that goes around the creature's belly—like this. Then, at the top, it has a seat so your legs go down on either side of the animal's back. You rest your feet in stirrups—here."

Hangman frowned at the drawing. "It seems like you've seen these before."

"Only in pictures in books. I'll have to experiment.....which means I'll need to find materials....."

"I'll bring you some. You work on designing them. I'll supply whatever you need."

She looked up. "Thank you. I could start getting him used to the strap around his stomach. That would be simple enough. I can work out the seat part later."

He nodded, but right then, they heard a shriek from outside.

They both ran out there and discovered a child sobbing in his mother's arms. He pointed behind him toward Igno.

The young Ashtaw barely noticed the boy. Igno was more interested in his meal of Fogpo leaves.

Mora went over to him, but she didn't see anything wrong. It took a long time for the mother to calm the boy down to figure out what happened.

He apparently decided it would be funny to hold a Fogpo branch in front of Igno's face and then yank it away so Igno couldn't get the leaves.

The boy didn't react fast enough. Igno grabbed the branch and frightened the boy by tearing it out of his hands with brute force.

Mora stood next to Igno petting his shoulder while he ate. He acted perfectly placid and nonchalant about it now.

The mother took her hysterical child back to their house. Mora watched them go—and noticed all the rest of the band standing around watching, too.

Some people shot Igno sidelong glances. Some retreated from him even though he wasn't doing anything dangerous. He just stood there eating and blinking at everything in his usual calm way.

Shadow spoke up as soon as the boy's sobs died away. "From now on, no one will go near the creature unless Mora is with you. Leave the creature alone. She'll be responsible for taming it and attending to its needs. This is a large creature capable of killing one of us. This animal is nothing to trifle with. Stay away from it unless you have some particular reason to go near it."

The rest of the Godless wandered off, returned to their own houses, and eventually the hum of activity settled over the camp.

Hangman came over to Mora and Igno. Hangman stroked the creature's long neck.

"Maybe it would be better if people did spend time with him," she murmured once they were alone with the creature. "He needs to get used to people other than me."

"We can start with just you and me—and maybe some of the warriors who were with us in the traveling party. He's already used to them and they're used to him. That should be enough for now. Finish tending to him and come home with me. You've done enough for today."

Chapter 47

M ora untied Igno's neck rope and rubbed him down. Hangman and the other men had left the long camp early. Now she had to get down to the business of taming Igno and teaching him how to carry a rider.

She coiled the rope and kept it in her hand while she waited for Igno to finish drinking at the stream outside the camp. This moment would prove if he was ready to take the next step in his training.

He raised his head with water dribbling from his lips. He made another contented rumbling noise in his big chest. It was time.

"Come on, Igno," she told him. "Follow me back to the camp."

She turned away and headed up the bank. She climbed halfway up before she stopped and looked back.

"Come on, Igno," she called again. "This way. That's right. Come with me. You know me. Follow me. You know what to do."

She took a few more steps before he grumbled something, lowered his head, and ambled after her.

She climbed faster to stay in front of him. He scrambled up the bank and followed her across level ground to the trees where she usually kept him tied.

She stopped him there, but she didn't tie him. She petted him while she talked to him. "Good boy! That was perfect. You deserve a reward. Come on."

She set off through the jungle and he followed her to another stand of Fogpo trees. She left him untied so he could munch all he wanted.

Hangman still hadn't given her any hides or other materials to work on her saddle and bridle. She didn't want to wait to start getting Igno used to the sensation of carrying a rider.

She waited until he thrust his head into the high branches. She hoped he would distract himself and not notice when she threw her rope over his back.

He grunted under his breath, but he didn't stop eating. She left the rope lying there slack. Then she ducked underneath his belly, pulled the rope through, and tied it very loosely around his body.

She waited between each move so he could get used to it. He completely ignored the rope even when she tightened the knot. She didn't make it very tight. She just made it tight enough so he could feel it.

He tolerated it and gave his full attention to his food. He didn't care about anything else.

He didn't even seem to notice when she left the rope there after he finished eating. He followed her back to the camp.

She had to remove the rope so she could tie him again. She definitely needed to escalate her training if he cooperated this well.

She made up her mind to tie the rope around him tighter next time. She would put it on before she fed him and leave it on until she brought him back.

She would need to do even more than that if he developed this quickly.

Getting him used to some kind of bridle would be the really difficult part. The bridles she'd seen in pictures used a piece of metal inside the creature's mouth. She didn't see how she would be able to get Igno used to that.

She was still standing there staring at the creature and thinking about the whole project when Zyria came up to her. The woman stopped at her side and studied Igno, too.

"He's so sweet-tempered," Zyria remarked. "I never thought I would see any creature that enjoyed human company so much."

Mora lowered her eyes and started coiling up the rope again. "Yes, he's a nice one—but that could be because he's so young."

"How will you train him to carry a rider?" Zyria shot Mora a grin on the side. "You can be the first to ride him. He might not carry anyone else."

"Maybe. I wouldn't mind riding him." Mora opened her mouth to tell Zyria about the time when Mora got thrown onto an adult Ashtaw's back and carried a long way across the valley.

Hangman's warning came back to her. She didn't know if she should still be keeping that to herself, but he didn't outright tell her that she *could* talk about it.

Her previous experience with Zyria closed Mora's mouth. She didn't know if she should confide in Zyria or not, but in the end, Mora didn't tell her about that incident.

Mora didn't see what difference it would make if she did tell Zyria. All the Godless knew now that Mora could handle Ashtaws.

She didn't feel right about telling Zyria anything, not even something as innocent as that.

Mora was just making up her mind not to say anything when Alien came over to them. Mora didn't realize until right now that Alien had stayed behind when the other men left this morning.

"Hangman asked me to give you this." Alien handed over a large piece of hide.

It had been fleshed and cleaned of all hair, scale, and anything else Mora might have been able to use to identify which creature it came from.

"He also told me to give you another length of rope if you need it," Alien went on.

"Thank you!" Mora exclaimed. "This is perfect. It's exactly what I needed."

Alien squatted down nearby and squinted up at Igno. "What do you plan to do with him next?"

"I was just planning on how to get him accustomed to wearing a saddle and bridle—but I need to make them first. I just took him out to browse with the rope tied around him. He was very comfortable. I didn't think he would take to it so easily, so I really need to step it up and move on to the next thing."

"It's complicated, isn't it?" Zyria remarked. "I wonder who will be brave enough to ride him as soon as you finish getting bucked off."

Mora bit back the urge to defend Igno. She wouldn't ride him if she thought she was in any danger of getting bucked off.

"You're right about one thing," Mora replied instead. "I'll have to construct some kind of weighted human form and put it on Igno's back. He can carry around the dummy before we try it with a real person."

Zyria grinned at her again. "I can't wait to see it."

Alien stood up. "I better get back to work. Let me know and I'll give you the other rope."

"Thank you, Alien," Mora called after him.

She didn't want to stay alone with Zyria, so Mora followed Alien back to the camp. He split off to meet up with his brothers to patrol the camp perimeter.

Mora needed some way to occupy herself—some way that didn't involve Zyria. Mora decided to take the bull by the horns and went to find Katha instead.

Katha, Estia, Rila, and Nagara all sat together in front of Estia's house. She lived there alone now.

A young girl sat on the ground in front of Estia while she braided the girl's hair. Rila and Nagara scraped a different hide that they stretched out between them.

Katha was busy hammering one large rock against a bone tool to chip a different rock into a weapon.

Mora hesitated to interrupt the women, but she wouldn't get a better time to do this.

She took a deep breath, walked over to Estia's house, and squatted down next to Katha. The other women ignored Mora completely.

Mora waited for a break in their conversation. They were talking about some of their female relatives who were preparing to give birth soon.

"I was wondering...." Mora stammered as soon as she could do it without interrupting. "I was wondering if you could teach me some more—either how to fight, hunt, fish—whatever you think I need."

Katha's head shot up. "You *want* me to teach you?!"

Mora forced herself to nod. "I know I have a lot to learn. I was wondering....if you're willing....I would really appreciate it......I know you tried to help me before....I'm sorry I wasn't more grateful when I first came to the Godless....."

She trailed off. Katha's eyes sparked with so much fire that Mora couldn't look at her.

Mora wound up looking at the stones in front of Katha—the stones Katha was in the process of turning into weapons. Katha knew so much more about this life. She knew more than Mora could ever learn.

The other women didn't make a sound. The silence became oppressive. Mora was just making up her mind to walk away when Katha put down her hammering rock and bone tool.

"All right. I'll take you. Go put your things away and meet me back here."

Mora raced back to the tent she shared with Hangman, stashed the hide Alien, and charged back to Estia's house.

Katha put her stones and tools away inside the house she shared with Shadow. She met up with Mora, surveyed the younger woman up and down, and jerked her chin toward the trees. "Follow me."

Mora followed in silence, but her curiosity got the better of her in a few minutes. "What is it like to be married to the Kral?" Mora asked.

"Nothing is different for me," Katha replied. "Nothing changed for me when Butcher died. Things changed for Shadow, but not for me."

"I'm sure Shadow will make an excellent Kral," Mora remarked. "The men all admire him."

Katha didn't answer that at all. She stopped next to the stream. "Do you know how to hunt the Dushag?"

"No....." Mora squeaked. "But I've seen Hangman doing it."

"What did he do?" Katha demanded.

"He....he told me to put my hands in the water to fill the gourds for the traveling party. He used my movements to attract the Dushag—and then he speared it through the head."

Katha nodded. "That's the best way. You have to lure them into coming close enough and opening their mouth to strike. You can't stab them through the top of the head. Their bony skull protects them."

Mora gulped. "You want me to do that?! How would I lure one of them and spear it at the same time?"

"Not at the same time, you silly girl!" Katha snapped. "I'll lure it. You'll spear it." She waved at nothing. "Find a pole and tie up your blade to form a spear. When the Dushag comes close enough, you'll spear it."

"How would I do that if I didn't have you here to lure it into attacking?"

Katha shrugged. "You would think of something. Some men capture an Abnormit and tie it in the shallow water so it thrashes around and creates a commotion. Some use a Gurlg chick or any other creature they can find. The possibilities are endless. Now quit stalling. I have things to do."

Mora had to hike out into the jungle before she found a pole strong enough to serve as a spear shaft. Then she used vines to secure her blade to the shaft.

The pole had to be strong enough to support her blade. It was much longer and heavier than Hangman's kukris. She wished now that she had thought to bring a much smaller knife for this.

She got halfway through the binding process. Katha stood off to one side doing something or other.

Mora bent over her work when she heard a deafening screech from directly overhead. She and Katha both instinctively moved closer together.

Mora dropped the pole and the vine so she could hold her blade in her hand, but she didn't need it.

A Boultar and a Ridgebeak grappled, wrestled, and battled in midair above the canopy. They tumbled over and over each other, tore each other with their beaks and talons, and they both shrieked in fury.

Without warning, the Ridgebeak overcame the Boultar, slashed its talons across the Boultar's neck, and broke away before the Boultar could retaliate.

The Boultar tried to correct, but the Ridgebeak struck a second time, snatched a claw full of the Boultar's wing, and launched into the sky with one tremendous flap of its giant wings.

The force of that tug plus the Boultar's falling weight ripped the Ridgebeak's talons out of the Boultar's wing.

The Ridgebeak's claws shredded the wing. The Ridgebeak took off into the sky and left the Boultar floundering a thousand feet above the ground with only one wing to support it.

The Boultar tried everything to fly, but it kept screaming in pain every time it moved its wing. It couldn't stay aloft.

Gravity caught it and it plummeted through the canopy. It slammed into the ground a few hundred yards from where Katha and Mora watched.

Katha sprang forward. "Come on! We have to get there before anything else eats it."

She took off running through the jungle with Mora right on her heels. Mora didn't dare to put her blade away.

Katha pulled up short at a distance from the stricken Boultar. The fall must have injured it even more. It lay sprawled on its chest, tried to flap its one injured wing, and kept contorting from one direction to another trying to protect itself from invisible enemies.

Its injured wing lay in useless, tattered rags on the other side of its body. One of the creature's legs stuck out at the wrong angle, too.

"We have to kill it and take it back to the camp," Katha breathed.

"How can we?" Mora whispered back. The Boultar kept diving, stabbing, and slashing its pointed beak even though the two women were nowhere even close to it. "How can we even get near it?"

"We'll double-team it. We'll approach from opposite sides. It will go for one of us and the other can strike from the opposite side when the Boultar turns its head away. Ready?"

Mora wasn't ready, but her previous experience gave her the confidence she needed to face this.

Katha wouldn't send Mora against this Boultar unless Katha thought they could win. If Mora did wind up being the one to kill the Boultar, it wouldn't be facing her at the time.

It was injured. This wasn't the same as facing a fully grown, perfectly healthy Boultar. She did that before and lived to tell the tale. Maybe she could do the same thing now.

She couldn't let Katha down. If Mora backed out, Katha would never let her forget it. Katha was giving Mora a chance to prove herself—again. This was another chance for Mora to be Godless.

Katha inched sideways through a gap between the trees. Mora sidestepped the other way. The two women circled the creature until they flanked the Boultar from opposite sides.

Katha's plan worked immediately. The Boultar kept swinging its head from one direction to the other trying to hit the women. The creature couldn't face both ways at the same time.

Katha darted in and jabbed her blade in the Boultar's face. The creature spun around, shrieked at her, and dove to peck her.

Mora rushed the creature from behind, but the Boultar reacted too fast. Mora had to spring away before it impaled her.

Katha attacked again, but the same thing happened. "This isn't working!" Mora called over. "I'm going to try something different."

"Don't do anything stupid!" Katha snapped.

"I won't! Just attack it the minute it turns its head. I'll do the rest."

Katha muttered something under her breath about Mora being crazy, but Mora already knew what she had to do. She sheathed her blade. She wouldn't need it.

She braced herself, rushed the Boultar, and it spun around to attack her again. It dove its neck forward to stab its pointed beak.

She reacted without thinking, lunged for the beak, wrapped her arms around it, and dove sideways to plaster herself against the creature's body.

She held onto the beak with all her might. Her weight pinned the Boultar's head all the way backward so its neck arched in Katha's direction.

The Boultar struggled. Its strength would have overcome Mora's efforts to hold it there. She only held on for a few seconds.

Katha attacked just as fast, rushed in, and chopped her blade into the creature's neck right behind the skull.

The Boultar went limp in Mora's hands and her knees folded under her. She buckled onto the ground breathing hard and sweating all over. Her arms and hands shook from the effort.

Katha studied the dead Boultar for a second and then circled it to stand next to Mora. Katha's hand fell on Mora's shoulder.

"Well done," Katha murmured. "That was very brave—and it worked. I'm impressed. Now come on and help me butcher it. We have to take it back to the camp."

Chapter 48

Hangman and his cousins entered the long camp and smelled the succulent aroma of roasting Boultar meat.

Mora sat cross-legged on the ground in front of Estia's house with Estia, Katha, Rila, and Nagana. Mora had cut Alien's hide into strips. She was busy sewing it with sinew and a bone needle.

She looked up and met Hangman's gaze when he returned, but she didn't greet him nor did she stop working. She immediately looked away and refused to look at him again. Did something go wrong?

The other women talked and joked with each other. They didn't tease or insult her. He even spotted her biting back a smile at the things they said.

He didn't sense any tension in the camp. Mora sat with the other women doing the same household tasks the other women did. They appeared to accept her as one of their own now.

A bunch of other mothers tended the cooking fires, cut up roasted meat, and passed it out to the children. None of the women in front of Estia's house joined in the meal.

Hangman crossed the camp and squatted down next to Alien. Alien was busy shaving the bark off a long, straight tree branch.

"What's happening around here?" Hangman asked. "Did you kill that Boultar? Shadow won't be happy to hear that you left the women and children unguarded."

Alien didn't stop working. "I didn't leave the camp. Katha and Mora killed that Boultar. They went out together and came back with it a few hours ago."

Hangman froze, but he didn't show any outward sign of surprise.

He thought Mora would stop trying to hunt and fight once she made it to the safety of the long camp. Did Katha make her go out to hunt? Was that why she didn't greet him—because she was embarrassed?

He glanced in her direction just in time to see her stand up. She held up the hide project she had been working on. It looked like a thick, wide strap connected by some kind of loop that held it in a circle.

Rila said something and all the women burst out laughing. Mora laughed with them and squatted down to do something else to the strap.

Hangman wanted to find out what happened between her and Katha. Should he intervene to stop Katha from being so hard on Mora?

He never would have considered making things easier for her. Now he didn't want anyone messing with her, not even his own mother.

He got to his feet, crossed the camp, got a portion of the Boultar meat from one of the mothers, and returned to Estia's house. "Come here, Mora," he told her. "I want to talk to you."

She collected all her hide pieces and all her tools. She gathered everything in her arms and followed him without question.

He pushed open the door to his house, held the door open for her, and followed her inside. He sat down in his usual place and laid out the meat in a bowl for both of them to share.

She arranged her hides, tools, and pieces in another corner before she sat down in front of him and helped herself to the meat.

She didn't ask permission if she could share it. She didn't have to. It was hers. She helped kill this Boultar if she didn't kill it herself.

She didn't wait for him to question her about it. "I've been thinking about the Ashtaws," she told him.

He frowned at her. "What about them? Shadow already decided to leave them where they are."

"We could go back there—just the two of us. We could take some more young ones and raise them away from the herd. Igno is so easygoing. Taming him is so much easier than I thought it would be. We should get some more of them."

He shook his head. "Shadow already decided against it—and he's right. We have nowhere to keep more Ashtaws and going back to the valley is too dangerous."

Her face fell. "This is the quickest way to domesticate them. Isn't that the point—to use them to defend the band?"

"You didn't see the Renegade Clan patrolling the valley—and don't say we could get there and back without being seen. The whole country is crawling with Renegades.

Traveling with one Ashtaw was already dangerous enough. Traveling with several would draw too much attention to ourselves. Then the Renegades would know what we were doing. Our advantage would be ruined."

She looked down at the bowl, took another piece of meat, and ate it. Hangman studied her. She didn't act embarrassed or humiliated or even subdued about something Katha might have done.

Mora didn't even think about killing the Boultar. He had to know the truth.

"Did you kill this Boultar?" he asked.

"No, I just held it down while Katha killed it."

His eyes flew open. "You what?"

"I asked her to teach me....you know.....more....about how to hunt and everything. I didn't want to stop learning once we made it back here, so I asked her. She was going to teach me how to spear a Dushag......"

Now it was Hangman's turn to lower his eyes. He wished now that he hadn't asked.

"Then we saw a Ridgebeak and a Boultar fighting in midair. The Ridgebeak injured the Boultar and it crashed in the jungle. We tried to kill it, but in the end, I had to hold its beak down while she killed it. Then we brought it back here. That's what happened."

He stopped listening before she finished. He really shouldn't have asked. Why did he even question her anymore?

Holding a fully grown Boultar down while someone else killed it—that was such a Godless thing to do. It was the perfect solution to the problem of the Boultar's size, strength, and its sharp beak.

She kept eating the meat. She didn't ask him if he brought the meat for her. It was her meat.

He watched her eat for a while. He didn't help himself to any of the food. Part of him felt like he should get her permission to share her kill.

That would have been rude and she sure acted hungry. He waited until she finished almost all of it. Then he took the bowl outside and got a second helping.

He took it back and found her working on her hides again. He ate while he watched her work. She kept holding up the strap and then the much smaller harness she said she planned to turn into a bridle.

She kept rotating them from one direction to another and readjusting everything the way she wanted it.

He asked her one question about how she planned to use these straps. After that, she talked endlessly about everything she did with Igno today and everything she planned to do with him from now on.

She explained in elaborate detail how she would construct a weighted model of a person, lower it from the tree branches onto the saddle, and somehow secure it to Igno's back so he could feel himself carrying a person.

Then she would try the same thing when she got onto his back from high branches. That was how she planned to ride him for the first time. Only then would she work out a way to mount him from the ground.

"My uncle read me a book once when I was younger about how the ancients trained their pack animals to kneel down on the ground," she rambled. "Then the rider would climb on and give a command to make the creature stand up. That sounds too complicated for the Ashtaws, but they're so big that I don't see any other way to mount them. They're too big to live under the trees. We would need some other way to mouth them. We would even need another way to saddle them. We wouldn't be able to reach them when a fully grown adult is standing up at its full height."

Hangman listened in silence. He didn't understand half of what she said, but he had to marvel at the way her mind worked.

She put all her attention and effort into this exactly the way Butcher and Shadow told her to. If this worked and turned the tide in the Godless' favor, the Clan would have her to thank for it.

Chapter 49

Hangman scrambled down a tree and landed in the group with his father, Fang, Cross, and all the cousins.

"Did you see anything up there?" Shadow asked.

Hangman shook his head. "The Renegades are all hanging off to the west. They aren't coming this far east—not yet. They're probably waiting to consolidate their new territory before they make another push."

"We've already searched the west country anyway." Shadow pointed in a few different directions. "We haven't searched as far north as we might. We'll search that area next."

"What about the south?" Boxer asked. "We haven't penetrated as far as we might there, either. We've always held back so we don't venture into other Clans' territory."

"We already know enough about the mountains to the south," Shadow replied. "We would be able to see if any of the mountains match the pictures. We'll head north. The Black Seam Mountains block our view of the country. If the mountains we're looking for aren't in the Black Seam, they may be in another range farther north. Let's go."

The party set off. Shadow traveled a lot faster than Butcher. Shadow ran most of the way. Even his nephews had to work hard to keep up with him.

Fang didn't keep up at all. He fell farther and farther behind until the party left him and he vanished into the jungle.

Shadow didn't keep track of his one surviving brother. Fang would return to the long camp. Maybe he would pretend that Shadow assigned him to help defend the place.

Shadow was too polite and too politically astute to criticize his brother in public. Shadow would let Fang take whatever position he wanted—whichever position Fang most wanted to hold.

If that meant guarding the long camp, then Shadow would leave him there. At least Fang wouldn't slow the search parties down.

Even some of the cousins had to gasp for breath just to hold Shadow's pace. They dripped with sweat by the time he called a stop at the base of one of the Black Seam Mountains.

Shadow's practiced eye skimmed his nephews one at a time, but he didn't linger over them. He never revealed by even a flicker of his eyelash whether he approved or disapproved of their physical fitness.

Hangman copied his father and didn't draw attention to the fact that he was one of the only men here not sweating and struggling to breathe. Cross held up pretty well, too. No one could complain about him.

Shadow only stopped for a few minutes before he set off again. He never cut his driving pace. He ran up the mountains, raced along narrow pathways, and didn't stop again until he got to the top of the mountain.

Boxer, Feather, and Vulture all collapsed on their backs as soon as Shadow stopped.

He pretended not to see them or hear them groaning. He squatted on the highest peak, opened his bag of pictures, and held them up to compare them with every mountain in view.

"None of them matches," he muttered.

"Father...." Hangman interrupted. "There may be another possibility we haven't thought of. These mountains may look different from different angles. They might look completely different from the south than they do from the north. We wouldn't recognize them."

"Then what hope do we have of finding these weapons?" Chaos asked. "We would have to scour the whole countryside."

Boxer interrupted from behind them. "Maybe Mora knows something about the country to the south. She might even know where these mountains are."

Goosebumps erupted on Hangman's arms. This was the second time Boxer mentioned asking Mora about the country to the south. Why?

Too many disconnected examples of these hints kept popping up at the most unexpected times. Mora. Was she the missing link in all of this? Boxer seemed to think so.....and Zyria sure went out of her way to befriend Mora.

Shadow put his pictures away. "We can't see the mountains from here anyway."

"My father didn't search the south country very well," Boxer repeated. "He didn't travel as fast or as far as you. We could have covered more territory if we ran instead of walked—and we could have spread out. We didn't need to travel in one party or even three parties. We could each have gone in a different direction."

Hangman cringed. He had been thinking the same thing about Butcher's search. Hangman didn't disagree with anything Boxer said. Hangman just wasn't rude enough to say those words out loud.

Boxer even had the nerve to criticize Butcher after the man died in battle. Shadow wouldn't appreciate anyone speaking about his brother and his former Kral like that.

Shadow himself was far too polite to challenge Boxer in front of the whole search party. Shadow said nothing while he put his pictures away.

"We'll return to the long camp, spend one night there, and then head south. We'll avoid the Renegades and stick to the gathering route. Then we'll split up and search as much of the territory as we can before we return. I don't want to spend too much time away from the long camp."

No one replied or raised any objections. Hangman's stomach turned again when he caught Boxer grinning to himself. His plan worked. He convinced Shadow to go south.

Shadow set off at another fast run down the mountain. The others followed in a single-file line.

Cross ran right behind his father. Hangman brought up the rear. He didn't have to. He did it so he could think.

He looked forward to seeing Mora when he got home. He didn't like to admit how much she was growing on him, but she was.

He found himself getting overly interested in her whole Ashtaw project. He really hoped it worked—not just for the Clan, but for her, too.

Chapter 50

Mora came out of the house she shared with Hangman and heard a note of excitement running through the long camp.

She stopped Nagana. "What's going on?"

"The men are coming back early." Nagana tore away. "I have to go! I have to get ready!"

Mora's heart skipped a beat. She didn't expect Hangman to return so soon. He made it sound like he and the other men would be gone for days. Now they were returning after less than one.

She completed some chores around the camp, but she didn't have much to do. The camp had enough food and other supplies. The house looked neat enough.

The strap she used to train Igno to carry a saddle hung from one of the roofbeams. He wore it perfectly today while he grazed. He didn't mind her cinching it tight.

She hung the bridle from the same beam, but she hadn't worked up the courage to put it on him yet.

She decided to cut him some Fogpo branches now and lead him to the stream for water. She didn't want to interrupt her evening with Hangman to do it later.

She headed for the trees where she usually kept Igno tied up. She didn't get halfway there before one of the young adolescent girls stumbled out of the trees in front of her.

The girl's wild eyes darted everywhere and locked on Mora. "You killed him! He's dead!" The girl's voice started to rise. She stumbled into the camp pointing at Mora and yelling out for everyone to hear. "She killed him! He's dead! The creature is dead!"

Mora gaped at the girl in disbelief. Igno couldn't be dead. She certainly didn't kill him. He had been alive and well just a few hours ago.

She burst through the undergrowth and stared at his body lying on the ground. Someone had tied a rope around his neck.

They used some kind of constricting knot to make the rope cut into the flesh. A rim of dried blood surrounded the rope and soaked into it.

His head and the whole top of his neck had turned black from the blood trapped there. He wasn't breathing.

Word spread like wildfire. People gathered from all over the camp to stare at Igno's body. He really was dead.

"She killed him!" someone else shrieked.

"I did not!" Mora exclaimed. "I was the one who took care of him!"

"You killed him to stop the Godless from using him against the Renegade Clan!" another woman interjected. "You're a spy sent by the Renegade Clan to weaken us!"

"I don't belong to the Renegade Clan!" she insisted. "I came from the Followers! We never kill anything except for food."

"You're a liar!" one of the young boys snapped. "You always hated Igno!"

"I never hated him!" Mora felt her emotions getting the better of her. "I took care of him!"

Just then, Fang showed up with Banjo and Magnet. Banjo and Magnet had been standing guard over the camp. Mora didn't know where Fang came from.

"What's going on?" Fang demanded. "What's the big problem?"

"Mora killed the creature!" the same boy replied.

"I did not!" Mora practically screamed. "I came over here to take care of him before the other men came back. I would never hurt him!"

Fang glared at her and took hold of her elbow. "You better come back to the camp while we figure this out."

"I didn't kill him! I would never hurt him!"

"You were the last one seen with him," Zyria pointed out. "No one else was over here."

Mora got so confused that she didn't remember the girl who originally found Igno's body. Mora wouldn't have been able to identify the girl right now anyway.

Fang marched her into the very center of the camp and parked her in front of everyone. They all glared at her—or most of them did.

Katha, Estia, Rila, and Nagana stood in a line off to one side. The four of them took up a position in front of Estia's house.

"I don't believe Mora killed the creature," Katha declared. "She just spent four days making that strap to train the creature to carry a rider. Mora didn't harm the creature. Someone else did it."

Fang raised his voice. "Did anyone see Mora near the creature today?"

Half a dozen hands shot up. "I'm always near the creature!" Mora choked. "I take care of him every day. I have to go near him."

"I want to know who else was near the creature today," Rila interjected. "Who else went over into those trees?"

A few more people raised their hands. "I went over there just now," the same girl replied. "I found the creature dead."

"You accused Mora of killing him when you had no reason to think she did," Estia countered. "That was wrong of you. Now everyone in the whole band thinks she did it when none of us has any proof."

A few people muttered under their breath. Mora looked around her in all directions. Four women. Four women stood up for her. Everyone else glared at her in outright hatred.

What did the Godless do to punish wrongdoers? What would they do to her if they decided that she did kill Igno?

Fang turned around to confront her. "Have you ever had any contact with the Renegade Clan? Did your people mix with them before the gathering?"

"Of course not!" She couldn't hold back tears. "I loved Igno! You all know I did! I couldn't be a spy or an infiltrator! I never wanted to come to the Godless in the first place! I only came because I had to! I never asked to come here!"

She was in the middle of blurting all of this out when the other men entered the camp. Shadow led the way followed by his sons and nephews.

They slowed down when they saw Fang holding Mora by the elbow and everyone else in the whole band gathered around in a circle.

"Is anything wrong?" Shadow asked in his most diplomatic tone.

Katha spilled out the whole story including all the accusations against Mora. Then Katha repeated what Mora just said in her own defense.

Mora couldn't hold herself together anymore. She took one look at Hangman staring at her with his hard dark eyes.

She broke down in tears. The accusation sounded so much worse when Katha told it like that. Katha had been one of the women defending Mora, but the whole story sounded awfully incriminating.

Shadow turned to Mora. "When was the last time you saw the creature alive?"

She struggled to gulp down her tears so she could answer. "It was.....this morning....I took him to graze.....and I used the strap around his body......"

She crumbled in tears again when she thought about how hopeful she had been for Igno's training.

"Mora is telling the truth, Father," Hangman interjected. "She never knew she would come to our band at the gathering. No one could have planted her to help the Renegade Clan defeat us—and no one here saw her do any harm to the creature. Everyone here has seen her taking care of him and treating him as kindly as her own child. I challenge anyone here to recall any time when she ever did anything else."

Mora's head shot up and she stared at him through her tears. She expected him to remain silent and let her face the band on her own.

He stood up for her. He defended her.

No one answered him—no one except Shadow. "You are right, my son. No one could have cared for the creature better than you have, Mora. No one here believes you killed him."

"If she didn't kill him, who did?" Estia asked. "If we believe her, then the real killer is here among us. Someone here really did help the Renegade Clan against us."

The assembled relatives exchanged glances. Mora couldn't look at any of them.

Hangman didn't wait for the others to come up with any answers. He strode around his father, pulled Fang away from her, took hold of her elbow, and steered her back to his house.

He pushed her inside, shut the door, and sat her down on the pile of hides across the room.

She fell apart completely, now that she finally got behind walls. "It's all for nothing! All that work! All that time and effort! I could have gotten killed capturing Igno—and Butcher *did* get killed so we could capture him! It's all for nothing! All that time and effort wasted—for what?"

She buried her face in her hands and let out all her fear and anguish. Now what was she going to do?

She couldn't even show her face outside this house without people looking at her sideways. Everyone would always question if she was a Renegade Clan infiltrator—or worse.

Katha and the others defended her. Mora would never forget that. They were the ones who insulted her the most when she first joined this band. Katha treated her so ruthlessly then. Now they were the ones who stood up for her—them and Hangman.

He sat down next to her, but he didn't touch her and he didn't speak. He just sat there. His presence made her cry even harder. How did this even happen?

Estia was right. Mora didn't kill Igno, so who did? The killer was out there in the camp right now. The killer pretended to be innocent and stood in silence while the others accused Mora.

Hangman sat in silence until she finished crying. She cried more for Igno than for herself. He never hurt anyone. He didn't deserve to die like that.

The Godless would butcher his carcass and pass around the meat for food. That was the Godless way. They would be stupid to waste such a large windfall.

She didn't resent them for that. She didn't even balk at eating the meat herself. Eating Igno didn't dishonor his memory. It was the greatest compliment the Godless could pay him.

She couldn't imagine who killed him. Why would they?

She couldn't picture any member of this band actively helping the Renegade Clan—but what did she really know about these people anyway?

Hangman didn't move or speak until she had been sitting there staring at her hands for a long time. He pulled open one of his bags and handed her a piece of dried meat from another kill. It wasn't Ashtaw meat.

She mumbled, "Thank you," and started eating it.

She wished she could thank him properly for defending her. She really needed to find a way to repay the women who stuck up for her. She owed them an even bigger debt. Katha and the others probably saved her life tonight. They protected her until the men showed up.

Hangman snapped her back to reality real quick. "We're leaving in the morning."

She spun around to stare at him. "What?"

"We're going back south. We're leaving in the morning. We only came back for tonight. We went north today, so we'll go south tomorrow. I don't know how long we'll be gone. It could be a while."

She blinked. She barely got to spend any time with him. Now he was leaving again.

He nodded at the meat in her hand. "Eat your food."

She bit into it and chewed, but she didn't taste it anymore. She didn't want him to leave. She didn't want to face the camp on her own, but she would have to.

Would she ever be able to stop looking over her shoulder? Would she ever be able to trust anyone in this band after today?

She would constantly question if the person in front of her was the real killer. She would constantly question if the person in front of her set her up to take the blame.

Why would anyone do that? Why would anyone in this band hate her that much?

She might once have believed that Katha and Rila hated her that much. They didn't anymore. She knew that now. They actually respected her.

They let her sit with them as one of them. They treated her the same way they treated every other woman in the band. They treated her and talked to her as if she had always been Godless. That was the greatest compliment they could give her.

They ate the food she killed. They gave it to their children. They laughed and joked around her. They laughed and joked about something other than how useless and weak she was.

Hangman waited a while before he took out some more dried meat for himself, stretched out on the pile of hides that served as their bed, and pulled Mora down next to him. He put his arm around her shoulders while they both ate in silence.

She didn't have to wonder how tonight would go. He told her to prepare her and get her head back in the game. He wouldn't want to leave indefinitely without taking her tonight. She expected nothing less.

She wanted to spend one last night with him. She wanted to enjoy his company before he vanished into the jungle. When would she ever see him again?

Every trip—every time he left the camp—even the briefest trip down to the stream could be the last. She had to appreciate the time with him while it lasted.

Chapter 51

Hangman squatted on the branch of a tall tree and surveyed the ruined city in the distance. It wasn't the same city the Godless bypassed on their way south to the gathering.

This one sat along the same highway even farther south. The search party had penetrated deep into the Followers' territory in search of the mountains in the pictures.

Shadow used his speed to cover much more ground than Butcher ever had. The party traveled farther in the same amount of time.

Crushers stomped through the city hunting for people and anything else the Crushers could catch. Their giant bodies bumped against buildings and knocked blocks and rubble loose. The debris rained into the streets.

"I don't see any people in there," Viking remarked. "I wonder if the Crushers ever catch anyone anymore."

"They're losing interest," Hangman pointed out. "Look. The Crushers are leaving."

The party watched four enormous Crushers stomp out of the city. They headed west toward the Jagged Points.

Boxer pointed to some tall buildings on the east side of the city. "We should climb those buildings. We would be able to see more of the countryside from up there. We would be able to see if any mountains farther south look promising enough to keep going."

"Good idea," Shadow replied. "The Crushers won't see us in there. We'll be safe if they come back."

"We won't be safe if they knock the buildings down," Chaos pointed out.

"If they come back, we can climb down," Shadow decided. "Boxer is right. Those buildings are taller than any mountain we've seen yet. We can use them to survey the landscape. Let's go before more Crushers come."

The party scaled down the trees to the ground. Shadow hesitated at the edge of the trees. He didn't want to go out into the open. Hangman didn't want to, either.

He saw no advantage to going into the city just to climb those buildings, but he wasn't Kral of this band.

Shadow had avoided Butcher's worst mistakes. All the men saw Shadow changing the way the hunting and search parties did things. Shadow didn't wait to ease into the new adjustments. He just changed it.

Everyone knew Shadow's way was better. No one argued, not even Boxer and Magnet. Magnet was too smart not to see that Shadow was the better Kral.

If Boxer felt any resentment about someone taking his father's place and leaving Boxer out of the line of succession, he didn't show it. He obeyed everything Shadow told him to do.

Hangman still couldn't stop his hackles from rising whenever Boxer made one of his supposedly helpful suggestions. The party came south because of his suggestion. Now the party was going to climb that building because of Boxer's suggestion.

Shadow had no reason to question Boxer's motives. Hangman himself had no reason to question Boxer's motives.

Too many tiny details kept popping up between Boxer, Zyria, and Mora. Mora's name ended up in Boxer's mouth a few too many times.

Then Igno turned up dead. Estia asked the obvious question. If Mora didn't kill Igno, who did?

Hangman had no reason to suspect Zyria of doing it. Zyria had no reason to frame Mora for killing Igno—except that Boxer kept mentioning Mora in connection with the weapons—and Boxer was Zyria's husband.

Zyria had been inside the camp when Igno died. Boxer had not been inside the camp when Igno died.

Boxer had been outside the camp dropping Mora's name in Shadow's ear to suggest that the search party come south to look for the weapons.

Why was Hangman the only person who made all these connections? He already knew the answer.

He was the only person who heard Boxer make all these references. Hangman was the only person who knew about Zyria lying to Mora about Hangman being violent.

Hangman was the only person who knew about Zyria befriending Mora when no one else would even look at her.

The whole sequence of events left a bad taste in his mouth. He couldn't ignore all these connections. They didn't paint a very nice picture.

He had no reason to think Boxer meant anything by suggesting the search party climb that building. Hangman still pulled out his kukris on the way there. He kept a close eye on the surroundings for any danger.

There was no danger here. The Crushers didn't come back. The party didn't see any people. The whole city appeared deserted. It sounded quiet—too quiet. Something was wrong.

He should have raised the alarm, but he couldn't exactly order his own Kral to change his plans.

Hangman wasn't the only person who sensed something wrong. Viking took his huge axe off his back and carried it in his hands.

Cross, Chaos, and Vulture all noticed Viking and Hangman acting skittish. The others drew their weapons, too. Boxer didn't. He strolled along as calmly as ever.

His behavior set Hangman's teeth on edge more than anything else. Any Godless warrior would have taken a cue from his relatives and drawn his weapon even if he didn't sense danger.

Any of their members sensing danger of any kind would be reason enough to draw his weapon, even if only as a precaution.

Boxer actually smiled at the surroundings. He acted like he was perfectly safe here—as if he couldn't conceive of anything threatening him.

That on its own was a sign of danger. Every place and everything in this world threatened Boxer. He never should have let his guard down—ever.

None of the others noticed anything wrong with Boxer. None of the others put the pieces together the way Hangman did.

Shadow halted at the building entrance. He turned all the way around and all the men searched the surroundings for any danger. There was none.

Hangman and Alien guarded the doorway while Shadow entered. The rest followed him. Hangman, Viking, and Alien brought up the rear.

Hangman's agitation spiked off the charts once he got inside the walls. He couldn't see anything outside. He couldn't see anything coming at him or about to attack.

The party climbed up and up and up. The stairs angled around and around each other to the very top level. Shadow led the way out onto the roof. The men could definitely see more from up here.

Vast stretches of jungle carpeted the landscape as far as the eye could see. The Jagged Points looked small from up here. A rim of blue ocean gleamed on the western horizon beyond the mountains.

The party could see multiple mountain ranges on all sides. None of them looked like the mountains in the pictures. None of the mountains were close enough for the party to travel to in their search of the weapons.

Shadow sighed. "At least we checked. Let's go. If we travel fast, we can get home in a few days."

He led the way back downstairs. He jogged it this time and sprang down two stairs at a time to shorten the process.

Hangman, Alien, and Viking brought up the rear again. Cross followed right behind Shadow at the front with Chaos, Magnet, and Vulture behind them.

Boxer wound up near the rear of the party in front of Banjo who walked in front of Viking.

Hangman couldn't see Boxer's expression from here. What did he think—that his suggestion proved to be a useless waste of time?

Hangman would make sure to check on the way back out of the city. Boxer better not be smiling about this—not after he cost the party all this time for nothing.

Shadow opened the door to leave the building. Cross and the cousins exited behind him.

Chaos and Magnet got out of the building before a deafening crash echoed through the city outside. Hangman couldn't see enough to know what caused it.

The men charged the door and rushed out into a full-scale Renegade assault on the search party. The Renegades surrounded the entrance. There could be no question. Boxer had led the party into a trap.

Cross and Shadow got trapped on one side of the circle. They closed together to fight back six Renegades closing on that side.

The Renegades overwhelmed Chaos and Magnet first before any of their relatives could get out of the building to help them.

Hangman, Viking, and Alien got pinned against the building. Ten or twelve Renegades came after them and surrounded them so none of the men could get away.

Hangman swiped his kukris back and forth, but he couldn't fight this many enemies. Not even Viking's and Alien's great size and powerful weapons could stop the Renegades from moving in.

A scream echoed across the street from somewhere. Hangman couldn't even see his relatives anymore—no one besides Viking and Alien.

The Renegades pushed in so close they could hit the three men anytime from any direction. Viking spun to his left to defend himself from Renegades on that side.

Another Renegade dove in from his right and impaled Viking through the shoulder. He bellowed in pain, swung his axe at the attacker, and got hit again by another attacker on his left.

All three cousins had exactly the same problem. One of the Renegades slashed his blade across Hangman's chest and laid him open to the bone.

Hangman flinched and staggered back against the wall. He and his cousins couldn't get away no matter what they did or where they went.

Bellows, groans, and shrieks echoed from all directions. Who was dying out there? Hangman didn't even have to ask. He and his relatives didn't stand a chance.

Viking and Alien backed up, too. The three cousins flattened themselves against the building, but that only gave the Renegades the space they needed to close in for the kill.

At that moment, as if in answer to Hangman's prayers, a deep thump shook the ground—and then another.

The Renegades all spun backward when five massive Crushers stomped into the city streets. The noise must have attracted them. Crushers always picked up the sound of human activity—especially in cities. It was their favorite hunting ground.

The Renegades raised their weapons and backed away. They didn't stand their ground to face the creatures.

The Crushers swiveled around the nearest building—the building the Renegades used to ambush the Godless band.

The Crushers tilted their heads sideways and eyed the people in front of them. All the combatants from both Clans stood exposed and defenseless right in front of the creatures.

"Run for it!" Shadow ordered. "Fall back to the north!"

Hangman, Viking, and Alien stepped away from the wall. Hangman glanced up at the Crushers. He still had enough distance between them so he could get away without them catching him.

That was the moment when he saw Magnet and Vulture lying on the ground. Neither of them got up.

Chaos knelt next to his brother and didn't rise. Chaos hunched over hugging his arm across his stomach. Blood drenched his face and dripped from his hair. He didn't even look up at the Crushers moving in on him.

Viking reacted without thinking. He charged Chaos, grabbed his younger brother in his burly arms, and picked up Chaos off the ground.

Chaos went ballistic. He kicked and struggled to get away. "NO!!" he roared. "NO!! Don't leave him behind!!"

"He's gone!" Viking roared.

"NO!!" Chaos bellowed, but Viking didn't let him go.

The others all backed away and then wheeled and ran for it.

The Crushers gave chase, but they got distracted by the Renegades. There were a lot more Renegades than Godless. The Renegades ran off in a different direction.

Three of the four Crushers went after them. That left one coming after the Godless.

Shadow, Hangman, Boxer, Banjo, and Alien dodged around different buildings, doubled back, and evaded the Crusher until all the men retreated into the jungle outside the city.

The Crusher followed them for a few miles before it gave up and went back to the city to join its friends.

Shadow kept running for another mile before he collapsed under the trees. Viking put Chaos down on the ground. He wouldn't stop roaring and shrieking in broken fury.

"We have to get him off the ground!" Hangman yelled over the noise. "The blood will attract too many creatures. Pick him up, Viking! Take him into the trees!"

No one argued. Hangman tried not to notice that everyone in their party was bleeding, including him. He was bleeding at least as much as Chaos.

Chaos flew into another frenzy of struggling when Viking picked him up for the second time. Hangman saw the truth now. Chaos was more in pain from his injuries than he was distraught over his younger brother's death.

Hangman cast one glance toward Boxer. He sat slumped to one side and stared at the ground. Did it ever cross his mind that his own brother might die in this ambush?

Hangman couldn't think about that right now. He made sure Cross and Shadow both got into the branches. Both of them had suffered injuries, but they could still move around well enough.

Hangman traveled through the canopy, collected a bunch of leaves to make the healing paste, and then scraped up a bunch of Gooji sap. He wouldn't be able to make the juice—not without going down to the ground.

He refused to do that now—not when he and his relatives were in such bad shape.

He delivered the leaves to Cross and Shadow, told them to make the paste for everyone, and then found a stream to bring back water to everyone.

It took a long, long time to clean up all the blood and apply the paste to all their wounds. No one spoke through the whole procedure.

Cross applied the past to Hangman's wounds. Hangman pretended to look off in the other direction, but he used the time to study Boxer instead.

He also sustained injuries, but they were superficial at best. Did he arrange for the Renegades to injure him only lightly to make it look like he wasn't involved?

Why would he do that if he planned for any of the men to survive the ambush at all? Why did Boxer sell out the Godless in the first place? What could he possibly hope to gain by it?

Cross's soft voice brought Hangman back to reality. "You should take care of Chaos, Hangman."

Hangman looked up. Chaos sat off to one side by himself. No one had applied leaf paste to his injuries yet.

Viking didn't go near his brother. Viking sat huddled in the crook of a tree looking away into the jungle. The reality was setting in for him, too.

He looked southward—toward the city where the party left Magnet and Vulture. The Godless could never go back there to retrieve the bodies of their dead cousins. The Crushers might have eaten the bodies by now.

Hangman took the bowl of paste from Cross. Cross retreated and sat down next to Shadow. No one else went near Chaos. That left it up to Hangman.

Chapter 52

Hangman took the bowl of leaf paste, a bowl of water, a ball of fluff, and perched on the branch in front of Chaos's face.

Chaos's mouth and cheeks wrenched and twisted in all directions. He fought hard to contain all the anguish tearing him apart, but it didn't work.

"He didn't deserve to die like that, Hangman," Chaos choked. "He didn't deserve to die like that."

"I know, brother." Hangman raised the soaked ball and started wiping the blood off Chaos's face and neck. "No one deserves to die like that. He was a brave man of the Godless Clan. He never disgraced his Clan—not once."

Chaos lowered his eyes and gulped down buried sobs. "How did they find us? How did they know we would go into that building?"

"We'll never know," Shadow murmured from his place behind them. "They must have followed us here. They must have seen us go into the building."

"If they followed us here, they must have known we were searching for something," Alien interjected. "They might have found out what we're looking for. Maybe they wanted to steal the pictures so the Renegades can find the weapons for themselves."

"I don't see how they could find out about the pictures," Shadow pointed out. "We've never told anyone, not even our own wives. That was Butcher's rule."

"Maybe the Renegades didn't know what we were searching for," Cross suggested. "Maybe they just saw us in the area, followed us, and ambushed us. They might not know we were searching for anything."

"What difference does it make why they ambushed us?!" Chaos practically shrieked. "Vulture is just as dead either way!"

Hangman couldn't keep silent a second longer. "I know how they found us. They didn't follow us. They knew where we would be and why. They know everything—which means other Renegades know about the weapons, too. They came to this city long before us. They came here specifically to ambush us."

Shadow's head shot up. "How do you know?"

"Boxer has been dropping hints about us coming here for a long time. He's been suggesting that Mora knew something about the weapons, and if we came south, we could find out what the Followers know. Zyria befriended Mora when no one else would help her. Zyria questioned Mora about the cities to the south to find out what Mora knew and if she knew what we were searching for. You made the decision to come south a second time because of Boxer's suggestion, Father. You decided to climb that building because of his suggestion. That's how the Renegades found us. He told them he would lead us here so they could attack us."

Shadow glared at him and then all eyes turned to Boxer. "Is that true, Boxer?" Shadow hissed. "Did you lead us to that building? Did you lead us into a Renegade trap?"

"You don't know what you're talking about!" Boxer fired back. "I never did anything!"

"You were the one who convinced Shadow to come south," Alien pointed out. "You were the one who said we should use that building to survey the countryside."

"And you were the one who suggested that we find out if Mora knew about the weapons," Hangman added. "You and Zyria must have talked about that."

Shadow's voice dropped deeper into his chest. "Did you tell your wife about the weapons, Boxer?"

"And before you answer that, remember that your brother is dead because of you," Viking snarled. "How does it feel to know you killed your own brother?"

Boxer's terrified eyes darted around the circle of faces. Chaos narrowed his eyes in fury as the men all saw the truth written on Boxer's face.

He opened and closed his mouth a few different times. "Why, Boxer?" Shadow murmured. "Why would you sell out your own Clan?"

"You bastard!" Chaos croaked. "I'll kill you for this!"

Shadow held up his hand. "Not so fast, little brother. We have our own way of doing this." He waved at the others. "Take him."

"NO!!" Boxer shrieked. He jumped to his feet and lunged off the branch.

Hangman leapt up so fast he dropped the leaf paste and the bowl of water. He could move faster than anyone else in the group, but Boxer still got the jump on them.

Cross darted sideways, cut Boxer off, and tackled him. The men were still so high in the branches that Cross and Boxer wound up crashing down through layers of canopy before they bounced onto more branches.

That fall gave Hangman, Feather, and Alien enough time to catch up with them. Alien seized Boxer by the hair to restrain him and then picked him up bodily in his beefy arms.

Boxer yelled and screamed himself hoarse. He thrashed and fought, but Alien overpowered him easily.

All the men descended to the ground—all except Cross. He took off through the canopy at a fast run and vanished into the undergrowth.

Hangman followed Alien. Hangman wasn't strong enough to restrain a man as big as Boxer.

Chaos hobbled after them when the men returned to the ground. Viking, Shadow, and Banjo helped Alien yank Boxer's arms and legs out in four directions.

They held him down on the ground while Feather and Hangman cut stakes from the branches and tied Boxer down on the ground.

"NO!!" he bellowed. "NO!! You can't do this to me!!"

Shadow straightened up, now that he didn't have to hold onto his nephew anymore. "Tell the truth, Boxer," Shadow ordered. "You set up that ambush to help the Renegade Clan, didn't you?"

"YES!!" Boxer shrieked. "Yes, I did it—but I didn't know Magnet would die! The Renegades were only supposed to steal your bag—not kill anyone."

"You stupid idiot!" Chaos roared. "Someone was always going to die! They would have killed us all—including you!"

"Why did you do it, Boxer?" Shadow asked. "Your father was Kral. Now your brother is dead. Why? Why would you turn against your own family like this?"

"I did it for Zyria! She begged me to help her and I couldn't refuse. She wanted to find out what Mora knew about the south country—about the weapons....."

"So Zyria knows about the weapons. Did you tell the Renegade Clan?"

"NO!!" Boxer roared. "I never told them anything!"

"Except where to ambush us," Chaos snarled. "Isn't that enough?"

"Why would Zyria help the Renegade Clan?" Hangman asked. "She comes from the Whisperers."

"Not originally!" Boxer countered. "She was born in the Renegade Clan. She married—and they cast her out for infidelity. She pretended that her family got killed so the

Whisperers would take her in. They kept her and married her to one of their warriors until he died in battle. They didn't have anyone else of marriageable age, so they brought her to the gathering. That's how she wound up with me."

A scratching sound distracted everyone. Hangman looked over his shoulder just as Cross came out of the jungle trees.

He walked backward and scattered a carpet of pollen on the ground. A mass of giant ants followed him. They gobbled up the pollen. They had to pause each time to pick up the grains. That slowed them down enough for him to stay out of their range.

He looked over his shoulder to make sure he was heading in the right direction. He backed up, scattered some more pollen, and repeated the process.

Boxer raised his head enough to see the ants coming. Cross led them straight toward the spot where Boxer lay staked out on the ground.

"NO!!" Boxer shrieked. "No.....please....Shadow.....no.....don't do this.....I'll do anyt hing.....don't let me die like this......give me a weapon.....please......

"Tell me the truth once and for all," Shadow growled. "Did Zyria tell the Renegades about the weapons?"

"I don't know!!" Boxer stole another terrified look at the ants. "I didn't tell them! I swear it! I would never do that!"

"But you would do everything else," Chaos snapped. "You betrayed your own people—for a woman."

Boxer whimpered in terror again and spun around to face Shadow. "Shadow...I'm your nephew......your brother's son.....don't do this.....let me stand up.....No!"

He didn't get a chance to finish before Cross made it as far as Boxer's position. Hangman and the other men scrambled into the trees to keep out of the ants' way.

Cross tossed the last handfuls of pollen around Boxer and on top of his helpless body. Then Cross raced away, clambered up a tree, and took refuge in the branches with Hangman and the others.

Boxer's screams echoed louder as the ants moved in. He kept begging for his life right up until the moment when they crawled on top of him.

One of them bit him in the leg. His screams spiked off the charts and then burst into wordless howls as the ants started to devour him alive.

He screeched in terror and agony right up until the moment when they started eating his face and neck. Their bodies muffled his screams and then his screams died away completely.

They left the sound of clicking mandibles and the squelching sound of bloody flesh being torn apart.

The Godless men sat in silence and watched the ants eat Boxer down to the bare skeleton. Then they crunched into his bones.

They ate him all the way down to the bare dirt and left nothing. They even extended their tiny, slithering proboscises and licked up all the blood off the ground.

Then they devoured the ropes, the wooden stakes, and every single crumb of pollen all over the ground before they marched off into the jungle heading somewhere else. They left absolutely nothing behind.

The men sat in silence long after the ants departed. Hangman had to force himself to climb down, collect his bowl of leaf paste, and gather another bowl of water before he returned to perch in front of Chaos.

Chaos's features kept spasming everywhere while Hangman cleaned his wounds. No one spoke. Chaos kept his eyes averted and never looked at Hangman once, not even when Hangman told him to lean back so Hangman could look at the wound in Chaos's stomach.

It penetrated the abdomen. Chaos definitely needed Gooji juice tonight.

Hangman left his relatives sitting in the branches while he went down to the ground alone, built a fire, and gathered everything he needed to brew the juice. The others joined him one after the other, starting with Cross and then Shadow.

"Thank you for telling us about Boxer, my son," Shadow murmured. "I'm sorry your bride got caught in the middle of this."

Hangman didn't look up from what he was doing. "She might still be in the middle of this. We have to question her as soon as we get back to the long camp."

Shadow lowered his voice even further so the others wouldn't hear him. "How bad is Chaos's condition? Will he make it?"

Hangman only shrugged down at the flames. "It's bad. He may not be able to travel. He may not even survive, but I'm sure Viking will carry him either way."

Shadow nodded into the embers. "We should keep traveling. We shouldn't wait. The Renegade Clan could come back anytime."

They had to stop talking when the other men climbed down one after the other. Alien, Feather, and Banjo came first. Viking and Chaos stayed in the trees for a long time.

The whole group heard Viking talking in a low murmur and Chaos answering him in a choked undertone. The group didn't feel right with so few men. Vulture was gone and Fang wasn't here.

Butcher and both his sons were gone. It almost felt like Butcher never existed at all. Hangman could convince himself that Shadow, Fang, and Midnight never had another brother.

Viking climbed down from the trees first. "How is he?" Alien asked.

Viking didn't look up from the flames. "He isn't good. I'll have to carry him tomorrow."

"Do what you have to do to take care of your brother," Shadow told him. "We'll travel as slowly as you need to get him back to the long camp."

Viking only nodded. No one else mentioned Chaos before he climbed down, too.

He made a lot more noise. He fell a few times before he dropped onto the ground and took his place with his cousins.

Hangman drank a dose of Gooji juice, served more of it to everyone who needed it, and handed the bowl to Chaos last. "Drink it, brother. We can't lose you, too. We need you too much."

Chaos looked away, but he downed the juice without a word and put the bowl aside. Then he stretched out on the ground and shut his eyes.

The others stayed awake in silence for a long time before Cross spoke up. "What will we do if the Renegades do know about the weapons?"

"They don't have the weapons," Alien muttered. "The Renegades would be using the weapons against us now if the Renegades knew where to find them. The Renegades are as much in the dark about the weapons' location as we are."

"We'll just have to keep searching," Shadow replied. "It will be difficult with them encroaching on so much of our territory, but we've already searched the areas they're taking. The Renegades won't find the weapons there. Now you all better get some sleep. We won't solve anything tonight."

He leaned back against a tree trunk, but he didn't go to sleep. No one else moved.

Hangman didn't want to sleep. Too many ideas battled in his mind. Mora was involved in this one way or the other. Boxer and Zyria involved her in it even if Mora was totally innocent.

Hangman had to find out just how involved she was. He had to find out right now if she was one of the traitors or if Boxer and Zyria just decided to use her for their own ends.

He couldn't let himself think about a future with her if she was a traitor. He had to shut his feelings down right now—before he saw her again. He wouldn't let himself feel anything for her again until he found out the truth.

If she was a traitor, he would be the first to stake her to the ground for the ants to devour. That was the least she deserved if she betrayed his Clan and him.

Chapter 53

Mora came out of the house she shared with Hangman. She had it to herself now that he and the men were out on another search party.

She understood much better now what Zyria said about the men searching for something, but none of the women knew what it was. The men who stayed behind to guard the long camp never said a word about why their band was searching for something.

She turned the corner of the house and lifted down the hide strap she used to train Igno. Now what was she supposed to do with it?

She would have to repurpose it into something else the band could use. She would probably never use it on another Ashtaw. She might never even see one if she stayed in Godless territory for the rest of her life.

She turned it this way and that, but it didn't give her any answers. She hung it back up and gathered her water gourds to go down to the stream.

She was just coming out of her house for the second time when she collided with Jerun, Hangman's youngest brother. He was barely nine years old—nowhere near old enough for initiation.

"They're coming!" he called loud enough for everyone to hear him.

"Who's coming?" Katha asked from a dozen feet away.

"The men are coming back! The search party is coming back!" Jerun raced away through the camp delivering the news to everyone.

The word spread from mouth to mouth. Mora put her gourds down. She would have to get water later.

The excitement became infectious as wives, children, and relatives gathered in the middle of the camp. The younger boys kept running out into the jungle and coming back to say that the men were nearly here.

Women murmured to each other. The children's energy escalated to a frenzy.

Dead silence fell over the camp when Shadow strode out of the trees followed by Hangman. Alien, Feather, and Banjo came next.

Viking came last. He carried Chaos slung over his shoulder. Chaos was unconscious. Cross wasn't with the men at all.

"Chaos!!" Rila charged out of line, rushed Viking, and tried to take Chaos down.

Viking pushed her away hard enough to make her stumble back toward the crowd of women.

Mora's blood ran cold when she saw Hangman's face—and all the men's faces. They clamped their mouths shut and glared at all the women staring back at them.

Hangman's hard, cold, dark eyes locked on Mora. He didn't look away. His scarred features closed up into a wall of solid rock. He leveled her with a fierce, brutal glare the way he did when they first met at the gathering.

She wanted to run from that look, but she couldn't.

Zyria's voice startled everyone to high alert. "Boxer!" she screamed and ran from one man to another looking everywhere. "Boxer! Where's Boxer?! Where is my husband?" She rushed to Shadow and grabbed his arm. "Tell me where my husband is!!"

He reacted so fast that he took the whole assembly by surprise. He didn't push her away. He grabbed her by the arm and yanked her into the group of men.

Hangman, Alien, Feather, and Banjo seized her. The four of them dragged her screaming and struggling to the center of the camp.

Shadow pulled four stakes out of one of his bags. He must have prepared the stakes ahead of time.

The four men grappled Zyria down on the ground and held her arms and legs out to the four directions. They pinned her there as hard as they could while Shadow went around her driving the stakes into the ground.

He pulled out a length of rope next. She burst into a fresh bout of screaming and thrashing while he tied her to the stakes.

She kept yelling for Boxer and demanding to know where her husband was. She never asked where Magnet was.

Viking stood off to one side with his brother draped over his shoulder. Viking didn't help out nor did he put Chaos down while the men exacted judgment against Zyria.

Shadow strode around her and stopped next to her feet. "You know why you're here. You gave information to the Renegade Clan so they could ambush us and kill us. Two of our men are dead because of you."

"You rotten bastards!" she shrieked. "Let me go!"

"Answer my questions," Shadow insisted. "This is your last chance to tell the truth. Boxer is dead and he told us all about you. You didn't come from the Whisperers. You belong to the Renegade Clan. You've been helping them against us all this time."

"Did you kill the young Ashtaw?" Hangman interrupted. "Did you tie a rope around his neck and stand here while all our people accused Mora of killing him?"

"YES!!" she shrieked. "YES, I KILLED HIM—AND I'LL KILL ALL OF YOU, TOO! I'LL KILL ALL YOU STINKING, ROTTEN GODLESS! YOU'LL NEVER WIN! THE RENEGADE CLAN WILL DESTROY YOU UNTIL THEY WIPE YOUR FOUL CLAN OFF THE MAP!!"

Almost as if her words made it happen, Cross stepped out of the trees right then. He walked backwards and sprinkled handfuls of pollen on the ground behind him.

He kept glancing over his shoulder to see where he was going. The men parted to let him through and a massive army of ants marched into the camp behind him.

They came slowly so they could pick up all the pollen. He led them straight toward Zyria.

Mothers gathered their children in their arms. Everyone retreated to get out of the ants' way. The Godless left a clear path for the ants to advance on Zyria.

"YOU'LL ALL DIE FOR THIS!!" she roared. "YOU'LL ALL BECOME FOOD FOR THE JUNGLE!! THE RENEGADE CLAN WILL DEFEAT YOU!! YOU'LL DISAPPEAR AND THE RENEGADE CLAN WILL TAKE THIS TERRITORY!! YOU'LL SEE......"

Her threats turned to full-throated screams as the ants climbed on top of her. One of them bit into her arm.

The hair stood up on the back of Mora's neck when Zyria started shrieking and screeching in agony as the ants devoured her.

She choked on her own blood and then fell silent as they gnawed her down to the bone.

No one moved or spoke while the ants consumed her whole skeleton and every drop of blood on the bare ground. They ate the stakes and the rope.

They would have started on the village itself next, but Cross came forward and lured them out of the camp with another trail of pollen.

Mora stared at the spot where Zyria had just been lying. Mora always sensed that Zyria wasn't as friendly as she claimed to be.

Mora never dreamed Zyria could have been up to something like this. Mora actually believed in Zyria at first.

Mora cringed when she remembered telling Hangman that Zyria was her only friend. Mora must have been truly desperate then if she let Zyria take her in so easily.

Mora startled back to her senses when someone took hold of her arm. She spun around in surprise, but Hangman only tightened his grip. His fingers actually hurt her.

His stony expression didn't soften in the slightest. He marched her out of the crowd and held onto her arm in a crushing hold when he turned her around to face the whole band.

"Boxer and Zyria questioned you about the cities to the south," he snapped. "Didn't they?"

"Yes!" She squirmed and tried to pull her arm out of his grasp, but he only held her tighter. He clamped his hand down hard enough to make her cry out in pain. "I told you they did! Ow, Hangman! Leave me alone!"

"What did they tell you?" he demanded. "Did he tell you anything about the Renegade Clan—or what my people were looking for in the south?"

"NO!!" she yelped. "I told you that! I told you Zyria only wanted to know what it was like! That's all she said!"

"Have you ever spoken to anyone in the Renegade Clan—ever? Have you ever spoken to one of them? Tell the truth."

"No!" Her eyes darted all around. Were the men about to stake her to the ground next?

"You said you traveled through the cities to the south on your way to the gathering." He had to shake her to make pay attention to him. "You knew their names. Tell us where you went."

"Ow! Stop it! I told you where we went! We traveled through Portland and Seattle! My people's territory is south of Portland! I never did anything with the Renegade Clan, Hangman! I swear it!"

"Where did you travel in those cities?! How did you get to the gathering? What parts did you travel through?"

"We didn't travel through any of them!" she shrieked. "We traveled up the highway from one side to the other. We searched a few stores on either side of the road to find supplies, but we didn't find anything. We ran from Crushers a few times and we went straight through. That's all!"

"Where did you run? Which direction?"

She yelled out in pain again when he twisted her arm. "We ran north, okay?! We ran to the north! What more do you want to know?"

"You never told the Renegade Clan what we were looking for? You better not be lying."

"I never talked to the Renegade Clan at all! How could I tell them what you were looking for? You never told me. I never found out you were looking for something until Zyria said so."

"Did she tell you what we were looking for?" he demanded.

"NO!!" she screamed. "I don't know!!"

He glared at her once before he let go of her arm. He let his hand drop.

She shrank to get away from him, but she had nowhere to go to get away from him.

Everyone else in the whole band stood around listening to their conversation. All the men glared at her.

That was the moment when she realized Shadow was holding four more stakes in his hand. Everyone present stood ready to stake her out for the ants.

No one moved for a second. No one came forward to grab her, wrestle her down on the ground, and tie her to those stakes.

A few people turned away at the back of the crowd. Estia covered her mouth to choke back sobs before she ran for the shelter of her own house. Her husband was dead. Now both her sons were dead, too.

Rila rushed forward, grabbed Chaos, and this time, Viking helped lower Chaos off his shoulder. Viking carried Chaos to the house Chaos shared with Rila. The three of them disappeared inside.

Shadow turned away with a disgusted grimace, threw the stakes down on the ground near one of the fires, and stormed off to his own house.

He didn't look at anyone before he went inside. Katha shot Mora one look. Mora couldn't read it before Katha followed Shadow inside. Mora lost sight of both of them.

The rest of the band milled around for a second. Hangman startled Mora out of her skin when he touched her elbow. "Come with me, Mora," he murmured. "Don't stand around out here anymore."

He took a few steps toward their house. She stood frozen to the spot. She couldn't stop staring around at everyone.

The last few minutes took a long time to sink into her brain. The men didn't explain exactly what happened on their trip to the south.

Everyone had to put it together from pieces of what they didn't say. Magnet didn't come back from that trip. Neither did Vulture and neither did Boxer.

The Renegade Clan ambushed the men—somewhere in one of the cities to the south. Hangman didn't say which one—like it mattered.

The men fed Zyria to the ants. The men would have done the same thing to Mora if she answered any of Hangman's questions wrong.

She couldn't shake her agitation. She squirmed in her skin trying to think straight enough to decide what to do.

Hangman turned back to look at her. He waited, and when she still didn't move, he took hold of her elbow again.

He didn't hurt her this time. He steered her toward their house, opened the door, and pushed her inside.

She buckled next to the pile of hides and stared at the floor, too dazed to move. Hangman rummaged around the house doing something or other. She didn't even have the energy to look up to see what he was doing.

He finally sat down and then stretched out on the pile of hides. He folded his arm behind his head in perfect relaxation until he remembered to take his kukris out and set them aside.

He waited another long time for her to pull her head out of the clouds. He waited a long time and let his hand fall on her arm. "Don't worry about it," he murmured. "It's over."

She looked around at nothing. She should make him something to eat, but her hands shook too badly when she tried to do anything. She had to knit her fingers together.

She couldn't steady herself. All the horror came rushing back of watching the ants devour Zyria.

Mora shouldn't have been horrified by that—not after finding out what Zyria did. Mora should have been glad that the men removed such a snake from Mora's life.

Who knew what Zyria would have tried to do with Mora? Zyria might have been trying to get Mora involved in selling out the Godless exactly the way Hangman accused Mora of doing.

He sat up, rummaged in his bags, brought out some dried meat he carried for traveling, and handed her a piece before he stretched out in the same place.

She took it, but she couldn't eat it—not with her hands shaking so badly. She choked when she stammered out a hasty, "Thank you." She couldn't do more than that. She felt ice cold all over.

That cold came from the inside. Did anyone in the band still believe she helped Zyria and Boxer sell out the Godless? Would everyone keep suspecting her of that, too, even after Zyria admitted to killing Igno?

"Has anything happened here while I've been gone?" he asked.

Her head shot up. She barely saw him. "Huh?"

"I said has anything happened here while I've been gone," he repeated. "Talk to me. Don't think about it."

"I can't stop thinking about it." She looked away and immediately saw the ants all over Zyria's body again. They ate all of her, even the bones.

He waited for her to say something else. When she didn't, he took hold of her arm—gently again this time—and pulled her down on top of him.

He put his arm around her shoulders and kissed her on the hair. "Don't think about it. It's over. No one suspects you anymore."

She had to summon all her will to speak. "Do you do that to all traitors?"

"Of course. It's the least they deserve. We did it to Boxer as soon as we realized he was the one who led us into the ambush. Chaos and Viking would have killed the bastard themselves. We had to give them justice—them and Magnet."

She shut her eyes tight. She couldn't imagine a worse fate than getting devoured by the ants. That must be why the Godless did it. It was the worst punishment they could come up with for the worst crimes.

"I didn't know...." she stammered. "I didn't know about.....about her......"

"I know," he murmured. "You don't have to worry about it. She deceived the whole band—not just you. Everyone believes you. You cleared yourself."

"How?" she choked. "What did I say that you didn't already know? Did you really think I told the Renegade Clan anything?"

"You said you went straight through the city on the main highway. You said you and your people ran away to the north to escape the Crushers. The ambush happened on the east side. You wouldn't have gone there—but it doesn't matter because the Followers don't deal with the Renegade Clan."

"I spent all my life around my family," she blurted out. "I never had to deal with someone lying to me like that—pretending to be my friend and then doing the opposite as soon as it suited her. I stopped talking to her as soon as I realized." She shut her eyes again. "The Godless know so much more about the world than the Followers do. You were right about them doing wrong not teaching us to defend ourselves."

"You don't have to explain yourself anymore." He bent his head like he was trying to see her face. "I know you didn't do anything."

She didn't know what to say. Would she ever get over seeing those ants? She'd seen them countless times in the Followers' territory, but never like that. She never dreamed anyone could be so cruel to another human being.

The Godless just stood around watching and listening to Zyria scream until she didn't scream anymore. Everyone watched while the ants finished off every piece of her and every drop of blood.

Hangman got her attention by rubbing her back. "We have to leave again in the morning. We only came back to deal with this."

She winced. "Do you really have to leave?"

"Yes. We have to take revenge on the Renegades for this ambush. We can't go back to the south, now that they know what we're looking for."

She didn't ask what they were looking for. She obviously wasn't supposed to know.

"Boxer and Zyria told the Renegade Clan our secret, so we have to make sure they don't use the information against us. Now we have to change all our plans to something the Renegades won't expect."

"Why don't you use the Ashtaws? The Renegades won't expect that."

"We don't have time to raise and train the young ones. Now the Renegade Clan controls the valley. We would have to wage war on them anyway and we probably still wouldn't win."

"There has to be a way." She tried to shake that out of her head. "We might be able to use them without training them."

He stiffened under her. "How do you mean?"

"We could use some kind of blinder system to steer the adults. We wouldn't have to train them. We would just have to mount them and attach the blinders to their heads."

"How would we do either without training them?" He frowned at her. "What's a blinder system?"

She pulled herself out of his arms and sat up. She still felt herself trembling, but talking to him about something else took her mind off the ants.

She drew a sketch in the dust at her feet and outlined the head of an Ashtaw. "These flaps cover the eyes. You pull the reins—here and here. Each rein pulls back one of the blinders so the Ashtaw can see out of that eye. The creature goes off in that direction. That's how you steer the creature where you want it to go."

He scowled at the drawing. "This is incredible. How did you find out about this?"

"I read about it in a book."

He shrugged that away. He never wanted to talk about the Followers' learning.

He put his arm behind her back again. "Come here. I want you."

He pulled her down on top of him again. She couldn't face that—not yet—but she would have to. He'd been gone so much recently. Now he was leaving again. He might be gone even longer this time.

She wanted to do it with him. She just didn't know how with all this agitation burning her up inside—or freezing her inside. She couldn't tell which it was.

He rubbed her back some more and kissed her hair again. She really needed to sit up and deal with him. She couldn't keep ignoring him, but she found it impossible to break out of this frozen state.

At least he was being warm and patient about it. She wished she could express her gratitude for that.

She *could* express it. She could express it by giving him what he wanted. She wanted to.

She forced herself to sit up and smile down at him. As soon as she saw his eyes, she actually meant that smile. She really was happy to see him.

She was more than happy that he was taking it easy on her after what just happened. She would never stop being grateful to him for that.

He raised both hands, cupped her cheeks, and pulled her down on him to kiss her. Their lips came within a few inches of meeting before she tore herself away and puked on the floor right next to the bed.

"I'm sorry!" she croaked. "I don't know what's wrong with me."

He snorted and pushed himself up. "And here I thought you were happy to see me."

"I'm so sorry!" she stammered. "I'll clean it up. I don't know what happened." She panicked when he stood up. "I *am* happy to see you! Please don't leave!"

"Stay here," he muttered and pushed her down on the bed. "Lie down. Don't move."

He left her there and walked out of the house. She would have liked to clean up the mess she just made, but the sick feeling of cold drained all her strength. She wasn't even sure anymore if she *could* get up.

He came back in a minute. She started to sit up and immediately sank back on the bed. "What's happening?" she asked.

"Stay where you are. Don't get up." He picked up one of his kukris and used it to dig under the puddle of puke.

He pried up a section of dirt and carried it outside with the puke still on it. He came back a minute later, sat down next to the bed, popped the lid off one of his water gourds, took a drink, and handed it to her.

She used the water to rinse her mouth out. She would have preferred to spit the water out, but she had to swallow it instead.

Mora opened her mouth to apologize again, but just then, the door opened and Katha entered. Hangman got to his feet, walked back out of the house, and left the two women alone.

Mora tried to sit up again. "What's wrong?" She glanced toward the door. Did she offend Hangman by puking right in front of him when he was trying to get close to her?

"Nothing is wrong," Katha replied. "Lie down."

Mora sank back on the bed. She almost struggled to fight back when Katha started pressing Mora's abdomen and inched her fingers down, down, down toward her pubic bone.

Mora really did fight back and slapped Katha's hands away when the older woman grabbed Mora's breasts. "What are you doing?!" Mora exclaimed. "Get your hands off me!"

Katha made a face. "Don't worry, little rabbit. I'll leave you alone. There's nothing wrong with you—and don't worry about the sickness. It will pass. You aren't in any danger."

"I'm not?" Mora frowned. "What's wrong with me then?"

"Nothing's wrong with you. You're pregnant."

End of Book 1.

Keep Reading

Rise of the Giants Series: Book 2: Clan of Heroes

With the ruthless Renegade Clan closing on all sides and time running out, the fearless warriors of the Godless Clan must tap hidden resources of courage and ingenuity to stay one step ahead of their enemies.

No one knows how to deal with theRenegades' terrible and unknown weapons that the Godless have never seen before. Disaster befalls the Godless when the Renegades invade the Godless' hidden sanctuary, decimate the Clan, destroy the camp, and carry off

Mora and the other women. Hangman must become an even more formidable force of vengeance to free Mora from captivity and save her from certain death.

Separated from everyone and everything he knows, thrown on his own skills and cunning, he'll discover a new Clan he never knew existed and find out what it really means to become the leader of his people.

You can find it at your favorite book retailer.

Sign Up Once--Get all Theo Mann's free books including brand new releases

S ign Up Once--Get all Theo Mann's free books including brand new releases

In a world where everything is out to kill you, humans must fight for survival every day against huge dangerous creatures and enemy Clans. The Godless Clan has enough to worry about already. They don't need to fight their own.

Sixteen-year-old Shadow knows exactly what to do when he discovers a girl from an enemy band hiding in the jungle. He takes her captive as a prisoner of war, but the Godless have a strict code of honor when dealing with women—even enemy women.

He and Katha will have to fight for their very survival and overcome generations of mistrust before they make it back to their people—who just might be the most dangerous enemies either of them has ever faced.

Sign up at www.theomann.com to read it for free

About Theo Mann

I write 70 books per year—and yes, before you ask, all these books are my original creative work. Nothing written under my name is AI-generated or ghostwritten because I write better than AI and any ghostwriter out there.

People don't read fiction for entertainment or to escape from reality. People read fiction to see their humanity reflected in another person's character and story.

This is my promise to you. When you read my books, you'll see your own humanity reflected in the characters and stories. I take this commitment to my readers very seriously. My books are an intimate form of communication between us. I would never disrespect my readers by turning that over to a machine or another writer. This is my bond between me and you as my reader.

I write 20,000 words per day as my daily work output. If anyone with a public platform would like to challenge me to prove this in a controlled environment, feel free to contact me on this website's contact page.

I worked as a professional ghostwriter for fifteen years. Now I'm on a mission to set a Guinness World Record by writing 700 books over the next ten years and 1400 books over the next twenty years, all originally written by me. See my website for the full book list.

I'm also the author of *Proof for the Existence of God* and the *Crimes Against Fiction* blog. You can find all my nonfiction work at www.crimes-against-fiction.com.

If you have a story idea, or if you would like me to explore a series in more depth, or if you'd like me to explore a character by writing a spinoff series about that character or world, leave me a message on my website's contact page. I answer all reader emails, so ask me anything, tell me what you liked and didn't like, and let me know where you'd like your favorite series to go. I would love to hear your ideas and find out what you'd like to read next.

Find out more at www.theomann.com.

Also by Theo Mann (so far)

www.ingramcontent.com/pod-product-compliance
Lightning Source LLC
Chambersburg PA
CBHW071051250626
47159CB00002B/434